...fall in love with the man she longed to seduce...

"You don't look the way I expected," Sophia informed him.

Ross arched a brow in sardonic inquiry. "Oh?"

"I thought you would be a portly old gentleman with a wig and a pipe."

That drew a brief laugh from him, low and scratchy, and he realized that it been a long time since he had made such a sound. For some reason he could not help asking, "Are you disappointed to find otherwise?"

"No," she said, sounding a bit breathless. "No, I am not disappointed."

The temperature in the office rose to a blistering degree.

LISA KLEYPAS

LADY SOPHIA'S LOVER

AVON BOOKS
An Imprint of HarperCollinsPublishers

This is a work of fiction. Names, characters, places, and incidents are products of the author's imagination or are used fictitiously and are not to be construed as real. Any resemblance to actual events, locales, organizations, or persons, living or dead, is entirely coincidental.

AVON BOOKS
An Imprint of HarperCollins*Publishers*
10 East 53rd Street
New York, New York 10022-5299

First Avon Books paperback printing: June 2002

Avon Trademark Reg. U.S. Pat. Off. and in Other Countries, Marca Registrada, Hecho en U.S.A.
HarperCollins ® is a registered trademark of HarperCollins Publishers Inc.

Printed in the U.S.A.

10 9 8 7 6 5 4 3 2 1

To my editor, Lucia Macro

Thank you for your guidance, friendship,
and the wonderful enthusiasm
for our work together
that I have never taken for granted.

Sometimes in life we are blessed with the appearance
of the right person at the right time . . .
and at a difficult crossroads in my career,
that was you.
Only an editor with your talent
could have helped me to find my direction,
and what's more,
you've even kept me on track.
How lucky I am to have you.

With thanks and love always,

L.K.

Chapter 1

*I*t had been too long since he had bedded a woman.

Sir Ross Cannon could think of no other explanation for his reaction to Sophia Sydney . . . a response so powerful that he was forced to sit behind his desk to conceal a sudden, uncontrollable erection. Perplexed, he stared intently at the woman, wondering why her mere presence was enough to ignite such raging heat inside him. No one ever caught him off guard this way.

She was undeniably lovely, with her honey-shaded hair and blue eyes, but she possessed a quality that surpassed physical beauty: a hint of passion contained beneath the frail gravity of her facade. Like any man, Ross was aroused more by what was concealed than by what was revealed. And clearly, Sophia Sydney was a woman of many secrets.

Silently he strove to control his sexual awareness of her, focusing on the scarred mahogany surface of his desk until the flare of heat subsided. When he was finally able to meet her unfathomable gaze, he remained quiet, having learned long ago that silence was a powerful instrument. People were uncomfortable with silence—they usually sought to fill it, revealing much in the process.

However, Sophia did not erupt into nervous chatter as so many women did. She stared at him warily and did not speak. Obviously she was prepared to outwait him.

"Miss Sydney," he finally said, "my clerk informs me that you would not disclose the reason for your visit."

"If I had told him why, I would not have been allowed past the threshold. You see, I have come about the position you advertised."

Ross was seldom surprised by anything, having seen and experienced far too much in the course of his work. However, the notion that she would want to work *here*, for him, was no less than astonishing. Apparently she had no idea of what the job entailed. "I require an assistant, Miss Sydney. Someone who will act as a part-time clerk and records-keeper. Bow Street is not the place for a woman."

"The advertisement did not specify that your assistant had to be male," she pointed out. "I can read, write, manage household expenditures, and keep account books. Why shouldn't I be considered for the job?"

A hint of challenge had colored her deferential tone. Fascinated and vaguely unsettled, Ross wondered if they had ever met before. No—he would have remembered her. And yet there was something oddly familiar about her.

"What is your age?" he asked abruptly. "Twenty-two? Twenty-three?"

"I am eight-and-twenty, sir."

"Really." He did not believe her. She appeared far too young to have reached an age that was considered to be advanced spinsterhood.

"Yes, really." Seeming amused, she moved to lean over his desk, placing her hands before him. "You see? One can always tell a woman's age by her hands."

Ross studied the small hands that had been proffered without vanity. They were not the hands of a girl, but of a capable woman—one who had known hard work. Although her nails were scrupulously clean, they were filed almost to the quick. Her fingers were marked with thin white scars that had come from accidental cuts and scrapes, and with a crescent-shaped burn that must have come from a bake-pan or pot.

Sophia resumed her seat, the light sliding gently over her rich brown hair. "You don't look the way I expected, either," she informed him.

Ross arched a brow in sardonic inquiry. "Oh?"

"I thought you would be a portly old gentleman with a wig and a pipe."

That drew a brief laugh from him, low and scratchy, and he realized that it had been a long time since he had made such a sound. For some reason he could not help asking, "Are you disappointed to find otherwise?"

"No," she said, sounding a bit breathless. "No, I am not disappointed."

The temperature in the office rose to a blistering degree. Ross could not help wondering if she found him attractive. He would soon be forty, and he looked his age. Threads of silver had begun to appear in his black hair. Years of relentless work and little sleep had left their mark, and the reckless pace of his life had left him almost rawboned. He did not have the settled, pampered look that many married men his age possessed. Of course, they did not prowl the streets at night as he did, investigating murders and robberies, visiting prisons, and putting down riots.

He saw the assessing way Sophia glanced around his office, which had been furnished in a Spartan style. One wall was covered with maps, the other fitted with bookshelves. Only one picture adorned the room, a landscape of rocks and forest and stream, with gray hills rising in the distance. Ross had often stared at the landscape during times of calamity or tension, finding that the cool, quiet darkness of the painting never failed to soothe him.

Brusquely he resumed the interview. "Have you brought references, Miss Sydney?"

She shook her head. "I am afraid that my former employer will not recommend me."

"Why not?"

Finally her composure was disrupted, a wash of color spreading over her face. "For many years I have worked for a distant cousin. She allowed me to reside in her household after my parents died, despite the fact that she was not a woman of great means. In return for her charity, I was required to serve as a maid-of-all-work. I believe that Cousin Ernestine was pleased with my efforts, until . . ." Words seemed to clot in her throat, and sudden perspiration lent her skin a pearly shimmer.

Ross had heard every possible tale of disaster, evil, and human misery during his ten years as Chief Magistrate at Bow Street. Although he was not callous by any means, he had learned to put a certain emotional distance between himself and those who came to plea before him. But the sight of Sophia's anxiety filled him with the insane urge to comfort her, to pick her up and soothe her. *Holy hell*, he thought in grim surprise, struggling to master the unwanted surge of protectiveness.

"Go on, Miss Sydney," he said curtly.

She nodded and took a deep breath. "I did something very wrong. I-I took a lover. I never had before . . . but he was a guest at a great estate near the village . . . I met him while walking. I had never been courted by anyone like him. I fell in love with him, and we—" She stopped and averted her gaze, apparently unable to look at Ross any longer. "He promised to marry me, and I was foolish enough to believe him. When he tired of me, he abandoned me without a second thought. Of course, I realize now that it was ridiculous to think that a man of his station might have taken me to wife."

"He was an aristocrat?" Cannon asked.

She studied the shapes of her knees through the drape of her skirts. "Not precisely. He was—is—the youngest son of a noble family."

"His name?"

"I would prefer not to reveal it, sir. It is all in the past now. Suffice it to say that my cousin learned of the affair from the lady of the manor, who also revealed that my lover was married. Needless to say, there was a scandal, and Cousin Ernestine told me to leave." Sophia smoothed her gown in a nervous gesture, her palms running over the fabric that covered her lap. "I know that this is evidence of an immoral character. But I promise you that I am not easily given to . . . to dalliances. If you could manage to overlook my past—"

"Miss Sydney." Cannon waited until she could bring herself to look at him once more. "I would be a hypocrite if I condemned you for the affair. We have all made mistakes."

"Not you, surely."

That elicited a wry smile from him. "Especially me."

Her blue eyes were alert. "What kind of mistakes?"

The question amused him. He liked her fearlessness, as well as the layer of vulnerability beneath. "None that you need know about, Miss Sydney."

She smiled slowly. "Then I remain skeptical as to your having made any."

It was the kind of smile a woman might wear in the sultry aftermath of lovemaking. Very few women possessed such effortless sensuality, a natural warmth that made a man feel like a prize stallion on a stud farm. Dumbfounded, Ross concentrated on the surface of his desk. Unfortunately, that did nothing to dispel the lurid images that had flooded his brain. He wanted to reach across the desk and pull her on top of the slick mahogany and strip her naked. He wanted to kiss her breasts, stomach, thighs . . . to part the curls between her legs and bury his face in the tender salt-scented folds, and lick and suckle until she screamed in ecstasy. When he had made her ready for him again, he would unfasten his trousers and drive himself deep inside her, to thrust until his raging desire was satisfied. And then . . .

Infuriated by his lack of self-control, Ross drummed his fingers on the desk. He struggled to remember the thread of conversation. "Before we discuss my past," he said, "we had better attend to yours. Tell me, did a child result from this liaison?"

"No, sir."

"That is fortunate," he said.

"Yes, sir."

"Is Shropshire your birthplace?"

"No, sir. I was born, along with my younger brother, in a little town on the Severn. We . . ." Sophia paused, a shadow passing over her expression, and Ross sensed that the past held many painful memories for her. "We were orphaned when our parents drowned in a boating accident. I was not yet thirteen. My father was a viscount, but we had little land, and no funds to support it. There were no relatives able or willing to care for two virtually impoverished children. A few people in the village took turns looking after my brother and me, but I'm afraid . . ." She hesitated and spoke more cautiously. "My brother, John, and I were quite wild. We ran about the village committing acts of mischief until

we were caught in a bit of thievery at the local
bakeshop. It was then that I went to live with Cousin
Ernestine."

"What became of your brother?"

She responded with a distant stare, her manner
turning wooden. "He is dead now. The title is extinct,
and the family lands are being held in abeyance, as
there is no eligible male to inherit."

Being no stranger to grief, Ross was sensitive to it in
others. He understood at once that whatever had happened to her brother, it had left a deep scar on her soul.
"I'm sorry," he said softly.

She was rigid, seeming not to hear him.

After a long moment, Ross spoke gruffly. "If your father was a viscount, then you should be addressed as
'Lady Sophia.' "

His remark earned a faint, bitter smile. "I suppose
so. However, it would be rather pretentious for me to
insist on a courtesy title, wouldn't it? My days as 'Lady
Sophia' are over. All I desire is to find suitable employment, and perhaps to make a new beginning."

Ross considered her closely. "Miss Sydney, I could
not in good conscience hire a woman as my assistant.
Among other things, you would be required to list the
occupants of the prisoners' van bearing criminals to
and from Newgate, compile reports of the Bow Street
runners, and take depositions from the assortment of
foul characters who parade daily through this building.
Such tasks would be offensive to a woman's sensibilities."

"I wouldn't mind," she said with equanimity. "As I have already explained, I am neither sheltered nor innocent. I am not young, nor do I have a reputation or social standing to preserve. Many women work in hospitals, prisons, and charity wards, and they encounter all kinds of desperate and lawless people. I will survive just as they have."

"You cannot be my assistant," Ross said firmly. He raised a hand in a silencing gesture as she tried to interrupt. "However, my former housekeeper has just retired, and I would be willing to hire you as her replacement. That would be a far more suitable employment for you."

"I could take a hand in certain household matters," she conceded. "In addition to working as your assistant."

"You propose to do both?" In a gently sardonic tone, he asked, "Don't you think that might be too much work for one person to handle?"

"People say that you do the work of six men," she shot back. "If that is true, I could certainly manage to do the work of two."

"I am not offering you two positions. I am offering only one—that of housekeeper."

Strangely, his authoritative statement made her smile. There was no mistaking the challenge in her eyes, but it was a friendly provocation, as if she knew somehow that he was not about to let her walk away. "No, thank you," she said. "I'll have what I want or nothing at all."

Ross's face hardened into the expression that cowed even the most seasoned Bow Street runners. "Miss Sydney, it is clear that you don't understand the dangers you would be exposed to. An attractive woman has no business mingling with criminals whose behavior ranges from mischief-making to depravities I could not begin to describe."

She seemed unruffled at the prospect. "I would be surrounded by more than a hundred law enforcement officers, including constables, horse patrols, and a half-dozen or so Bow Street runners. I daresay I would be safer working here than I would be shopping at Regent Street."

"Miss Sydney—"

"Sir Ross," she interrupted, standing and bracing her hands on his desk. Her high-necked dress revealed nothing as she leaned toward him. However, if she had been wearing a low décolletage, her breasts would have been presented to him like two succulent apples on a tray. Stimulated unbearably by the thought, Ross forced himself to focus on her face. Her lips curled in a faint smile. "You have nothing to lose by letting me try," she pointed out. "Give me a month to prove my worth."

Ross stared at her intently. There was something manufactured about her display of charm. She was trying to manipulate him into giving her something she wanted—and she was succeeding. But why in God's name did she want to work for him? He realized suddenly that he could not let her go without discovering her motives.

"If I fail to please you," she added, "you can always hire someone else."

Ross was known for being a supremely rational man. It would be impractical for him to hire this woman. Stupid, even. He knew exactly what the others at Bow Street would make of it. They would assume that he had hired her because of her sexual appeal. The uncomfortable truth was, they would be right. It had been a long time since he had been so strongly attracted to a woman. He wanted to keep her here, to enjoy her beauty and intelligence, and to discover if she returned his interest. His mind weighed the scruples of such a decision, but his thoughts were eclipsed by male urges that refused to be quelled.

And for the first time in his magisterial career, he ignored reason in favor of desire.

Scowling, he picked up a haphazard pile of papers and handed them to her. "Are you familiar with the *Hue and Cry*?"

Cautiously she accepted the ungainly stack. "I believe it is a weekly publication of police news?"

He nodded. "It contains descriptions of offenders at large and details of their crimes. It is one of Bow Street's most effective tools in apprehending criminals, particularly the ones who come from counties outside my jurisdiction. That stack you're holding has notices from mayors and magistrates all across England."

Sophia scanned the top few notes and read aloud.
" 'Arthur Clewen, by trade a blacksmith, about five feet ten inches high, with dark curled hair, effeminate voice,

large nose, charged with fraud in Chichester . . . Mary Thompson, alias Hobbes, alias Chiswit, a tall girl thin of frame, with light straight hair, charged with stabbing murder in Wolverhampton . . .' "

"Those notes must be compiled and copied every week," Ross said tersely. "It's tedious, and I have far more pressing matters to attend to. From now on, that will be one of your responsibilities." He pointed to a small table in the corner, every available inch of its scarred surface covered with books, files, and correspondence. "You may work there. You'll have to share my office, as there is no room for you elsewhere. As things stand, I'm away on investigations much of the time."

"You will hire me, then," she said, her voice rich with satisfaction. "Thank you, Sir Ross."

He slanted her an ironic glance. "If I find that you are not suited for the position, you will accept my decision without protest."

"Yes, sir."

"One more thing. You will not be required to go to the prisoners' van each morning. Vickery will do it."

"But you said that it was part of your assistant's responsibility, and I—"

"Are you arguing with me, Miss Sydney?"

She closed her mouth abruptly. "No, Sir Ross."

He gave her a brief nod. "The *Hue and Cry* must be finished by two o'clock. After you're done, go to Bow Street number four and find a dark-haired lad named Ernest. Tell him where your possessions are—he will fetch them after he delivers the *Hue and Cry* to the printer."

"There is no need to make him gather my things," Sophia protested. "I will go to the lodging house by myself at a more convenient time."

"You are not to walk anywhere in London alone. From now on, you are under my protection. If you wish to go somewhere, you will be accompanied by Ernest or one of the runners."

She didn't like that—he saw the resentful flicker in her eyes. But she did not argue. Ross continued in a businesslike manner. "You'll have the rest of the day to make yourself familiar with the public office and private residence. Later I will introduce you to my colleagues as they appear for their court sessions."

"Will I also be introduced to the Bow Street runners?"

"I doubt you will be able to avoid them for long," Ross said dryly. The thought of the runners' reaction to his female assistant caused his mouth to tighten. He wondered if that was Sophia's motive for working here. Women all over England had made the runners objects of romantic fantasy. Their imaginings were fueled by the ha'penny novels that portrayed the runners as heroic men of action. It was possible that Sophia wished to attract one of them. If so, she would not have to try hard. The runners were a randy lot, and all but one of them were unmarried.

"By the way, I do not condone any romantic involvements at Bow Street," Ross said. "The runners, the constables, and the clerks are all unavailable to you. Naturally I will offer no objections if you wish to carry on with someone *outside* the public office."

"What about you?" she startled him by asking softly. "Are you unavailable as well?"

Perplexed, hungering, Ross wondered what kind of game she was trying to play. He kept his expression blank as he replied, "Naturally."

She smiled slightly as she went to the small, overladen table.

In less than an hour, Sophia had efficiently arranged and copied the notes in a neat hand that would delight the printer to no end. She was so quiet and economical in her movements that Ross would have forgotten she was there, except that her scent filtered through the air. It was a tantalizing distraction that he could not dismiss. Breathing deeply, he tried to identify the fragrance. He detected tea and vanilla, blended with the elixir of warm female skin. Stealing glances at her delicate profile, he was fascinated by the way the light moved over her hair. She had small ears, a sharply defined chin, a soft snippet of a nose, and eyelashes that cast spiky shadows on her cheeks.

Absorbed in her task, Sophia bent over a page and wrote carefully. Ross could not help but imagine how those adept hands might feel on his body, if they would be warm or cool. Would she touch a man with hesitancy or boldness? Her exterior was delicate, subdued, but there were hints of something provocative beneath . . . an intimation that she could be unmoored by sexuality, if only a man could reach deep enough inside her.

The conjecture caused Ross's blood to stir faster. He damned himself for being so drawn to her. The force of his unspent passion seemed to fill the room. How strange that the past months, years, of celibacy had been so tolerable until now. Suddenly it had become unbearable, his accumulated hunger for a woman's soft flesh, his need for a tender sheath clamped around his cock, a sweet, responsive mouth returning his kisses . . .

Just as his desire reached an excruciating pitch, Sophia approached his desk with the copies. "Is this how you like it to be done?" she asked.

He scanned them quickly, hardly seeing the neat lines of script. With a cursory nod, he handed them back to her.

"I'll give them to Ernest, then," she said, her gown rustling softly as she left. The door closed with a quiet click, affording him some much-needed privacy. Releasing an explosive breath, Ross went to the chair where Sophia had sat, his fingers coasting over its back and arms. Driven by primal urges, he hunted for any trace of warmth her hands might have left on the wood. He breathed deeply, seeking to absorb a lingering hint of her fragrance.

Yes, he thought with purely masculine agitation, he had been celibate for too long.

Although he was often tormented by his physical needs, Ross had too much respect for women to hire a prostitute. He had become well acquainted with the profession from the perspective of the magisterial bench, and he would not take advantage of such a woman. Moreover, the transaction would be a mockery of what he had shared with his wife.

He had considered the idea of marrying again, but he had not yet found a woman who seemed remotely suitable. The wife of a police magistrate would have to be strong and independent. And she would have to fit easily into the social circles his family frequented, as well as the dark world of Bow Street. Most of all, she would have to be satisfied with his friendship, not his love. He would not allow himself to fall in love again, not as he had with Eleanor. The pain of losing her had been too great, and his heart had been ripped in half when she died.

He only wished that the need for sex could be dismissed as easily as the need for love.

For decades, Bow Street No. 4 had served as a private residence, public office, and court. However, when Sir Ross Cannon had been appointed Chief Magistrate ten years earlier, he had expanded his powers and jurisdictions until it had been necessary to purchase the adjacent building. Now No. 4 served primarily as Sir Ross's private home, while No. 3 contained offices, courtrooms, records rooms, and an underground strong room where prisoners were held and interrogated.

Sophia quickly made herself familiar with the layout of No. 4 as she searched for the errand boy. She located Ernest in the belowstairs kitchen as he ate a lunch of bread and cheese at a large wooden table. The dark-haired, gangly-limbed boy was afflicted with wild blushes as Sophia introduced herself. After she gave him the *Hue and Cry*, and asked him to retrieve her belongings from a nearby lodging house, the boy scampered away like a terrier after a rat.

Relieved to find herself alone, Sophia wandered into the dry larder. It was fitted with slate shelves that held, among other things, a round of cheese, a pot of butter, a jug of milk, and cuts of meat. The little room was shadowy and dark, silent except for the steady drip of water in the adjoining wet larder. Suddenly overcome with the tension that had accumulated inside her all afternoon, Sophia felt herself begin to tremble and shiver until her teeth chattered violently. Hot tears gushed from her eyes, and she pressed the length of her sleeve hard against the aching sockets.

Dear God, how she hated him.

It had taken all her strength and will to sit in that cluttered office with Sir Ross, appearing serene while her blood boiled with loathing. She had hidden her antipathy well; she thought she had even made him want her. His eyes had flickered with a reluctant attraction that he couldn't quite hide. That was good; it was what she had hoped for. Because she wanted to do something worse than kill Sir Ross Cannon. She intended to ruin him in every way, to make him suffer until death would be preferable. And somehow fate seemed to be accommodating her plan.

From the moment Sophia had seen the advertisement in the *Times*, that an assistant was wanted at the Bow Street public office, a plan had sprung fully formed into her mind. She would obtain the job at Bow Street and thereby gain access to records and files. Eventually she would find what she needed to destroy Sir Ross's reputation and force him to resign.

There were rumors of corruption surrounding the runners and their activities—reports of illegal raids, brutality, and intimidation, not to mention acting outside their described jurisdictions. Everyone knew that Sir Ross and his "people," as he termed them, were a law unto themselves. Once an already suspicious public was given solid proof of their misconduct, the paragon known as Sir Ross Cannon would be ruined beyond redemption. Sophia would uncover whatever information was necessary to bring about his downfall.

But that wasn't enough. She wanted the betrayal to be deeper, more painful than that. She was going to seduce the so-called Monk of Bow Street and make him fall in love with her. And then she would bring his world down around his ears.

The scalding tears abated, and Sophia turned to rest her forehead against a cool edge of slate, sighing shakily. One thought sustained her: Sir Ross was going to pay for taking away the last person on earth who had loved her. Her brother, John, whose remains were buried in a mass grave, mingling with the rotting skeletons of thieves and murderers.

Regaining her self-control, Sophia contemplated what she had learned of Sir Ross so far. He was not at all what she had expected. She had thought he would be a pompous, heavyset man, jowly and vain and corrupt. She had not wanted him to be attractive.

But Sir Ross *was* handsome, much as she hated to admit it. He was a man in his prime, tall and big-framed and a bit too lean. His features were strong and austere, with straight black brows shadowing the most extraordinary pair of eyes she had ever seen. They were light gray, so bright that it seemed as if the white-hot energy of lightning had been trapped inside the black-rimmed irises. He possessed a quality that had unnerved her, a tremendous volatility burning beneath his remote surface. And he wore his authority comfortably, a man who could make decisions and live with them no matter what the outcome.

Hearing the sounds of someone entering the kitchen from the door that led to the street above, Sophia ventured from the larder. She saw a woman not much older than she, skinny and dark-haired, with bad teeth. But the woman's smile was genuine, and she was tidy and well kept, her apron washed and pressed. The cook-maid, Sophia surmised, giving her a friendly smile.

"Hullo," the woman said shyly, bobbing in a curtsy. "May I help you, miss?"

"I am Miss Sydney, Sir Ross's new assistant."

"Assistant," the woman repeated in confusion. "But you're not a man."

"No, indeed," Sophia said evenly, surveying the kitchen.

"I'm the cook-maid, Eliza," the woman offered, staring at her with wide eyes. "There's another maid, Lucie, and an errand boy . . ."

"Ernest? Yes, I've already met him."

Daylight shone through the casement windows, revealing the kitchen to be a small but well-fitted room with a stone-flagged floor. A brick-built stove with a cast-iron top and stone supports was mounted against one wall. Four or five pots could be heated at different temperatures at the same time on such a stove. An iron cylindrical roaster was set horizontally in the wall, the door flush with the brickwork. The design was so clever and modern that Sophia could not help exclaiming in admiration.

"Oh, it must be wonderful to cook in here!"

Eliza made a face. "I can manage plain cooking, as my ma taught me. And I don't mind going to market or tidying up. But I don't like standing at the stove over pots and pans—it never seems to come out right."

"Perhaps I could help," Sophia said. "I like to cook."

Eliza brightened at the information. "That would be lovely, miss!"

Sophia surveyed the kitchen dresser with its assortment of pots, pans, jugs, and utensils. A row of tarnished copper molds hung from hooks on the side—they clearly needed a good scrubbing. There were other items that needed attention as well. The pudding-cloths and jelly bags stacked on a dresser shelf were stained and required soaking. The sieves appeared to be dirty, and an unpleasant smell emanated from the drain-holes in the sink, which had to be scrubbed with large handfuls of soda.

"We all eat in the kitchen—master, servants, and constables alike," Eliza said, indicating the wooden table that dwarfed much of the room. "There is no proper dining hall. Sir Ross takes his meals here or in his office."

Sophia gazed at a dresser shelf that contained spices, tea, and a sack of coffee berries. She strove to sound detached as she asked, "Is Sir Ross a good master?"

"Oh, yes, miss!" the cook-maid said at once. "Though he can be a bit odd at times."

"In what way?"

"Sir Ross will work for days without a proper meal. Sometimes he will even sleep at his desk, rather than go to his own bed for a decent night's rest."

"Why does he work so hard?"

"No one knows the answer to that, p'rhaps not even Sir Ross himself. They say he was different before his wife passed on. She died in childbirth, and since then Sir Ross has been . . ." Eliza paused to search for an appropriate word.

"Distant?" Sophia suggested.

"Aye, distant and cold-natured. He tolerates no weakness in himself, and takes no interest in anything other than his duties."

"Perhaps he will marry again someday."

Eliza shrugged and smiled. "Gor, there are many fine ladies who would have him! They come to his office to ask him to help with their charities, or to complain about pickpockets and such. But it's plain they hope to catch his eye. And the less interest he shows, the more they pursue him."

"Sir Ross is sometimes called the Monk of Bow Street," Sophia murmured. "Does that mean he never . . ." She paused as a blush climbed her cheeks.

"Only he knows for certain," Eliza said thoughtfully. " 'Twould be a pity, wouldn't it? A waste of a good, healthy man." Her crooked teeth flashed in a grin, and she winked at Sophia. "But I think someday the right woman will know how to tempt him, don't you?"

Yes, Sophia thought with a swirl of satisfaction. She would be the one to end Sir Ross's monkish ways. She would win his trust, perhaps even his love . . . and she would use it to destroy him.

As news traveled fast on Bow Street, Ross was unsurprised when a knock came on the door not a quarter hour after Sophia had left. One of the assistant magistrates, Sir Grant Morgan, entered the office. "Good morning, Cannon," Grant Morgan said, his green eyes alight with good humor. No one could doubt that Morgan was enjoying his life as a newlywed. The other runners were both envious and entertained by the fact that the formerly stoic Morgan was so openly in love with his small, red-haired wife.

At a height of nearly six and a half feet, Grant Morgan was the only man Ross had to physically look up to. An orphan who had once worked at a Covent Garden fishmonger's stall, Morgan had enlisted in the foot patrol at age eighteen and been rapidly promoted through the ranks until Ross had selected him to join the elite force of a half-dozen runners. Recently he had been appointed to serve as assistant magistrate. Morgan was a good man, steady and intelligent, and one of the few people in the world whom Ross trusted.

Pulling the visitor's chair up to the desk, Morgan lowered his gigantic frame onto the leather seat. He gave Ross a speculative stare. "I caught a glimpse of Miss Sydney," he remarked. "Vickery told me that she is your new assistant. Naturally I replied that he must have been mistaken."

"Why?"

"Because hiring a woman for such a position would be impractical. Furthermore, enlisting a woman as comely as Miss Sydney to work at Bow Street would be damned foolish. And since I have never known you to be impractical or foolish, I told Vickery that he was wrong."

"He's right," Ross muttered.

Leaning to the side, Morgan rested his chin in the bracket of his thumb and forefinger and contemplated the Chief Magistrate speculatively. "She's going to be a clerk and file-keeper? And take depositions from foot-pads and highwaymen and buttock-and-file whores and—"

"Yes," Ross snapped.

Morgan's thick brows climbed halfway up his forehead. "To point out the obvious, every man who passes through this place—runners not excepted—is going to be on her like flies on a honeypot. She won't be able to get a damned thing done. Miss Sydney is trouble, and you know it." He paused and remarked idly, "What interests me is why you chose to hire her anyway."

"It's none of your business. Miss Sydney is *my* employee. I'll hire anyone I damn well want to, and the men had better leave her alone or answer to me."

Morgan stared at him in an assessing way that Ross didn't like. "My pardon," he said softly. "You seem to be rather touchy on the subject."

"I'm not touchy, dammit!"

Morgan responded with a supremely annoying grin. "I believe this is the first time I've ever heard you swear, Cannon."

Too late, Ross understood the source of Morgan's amusement. Somehow his normally emotionless facade had cracked. He fought to mask his irritation, drumming his fingers on the desk in an impatient staccato.

Morgan watched his struggle with a lingering grin. Apparently he could not resist making one more comment. "Well, there is one point that no one will dispute—she makes a prettier clerk than Vickery."

Ross pinned him with a forbidding stare. "Morgan, the next time I advertise for an employee, I will make certain to hire some long-toothed old crone in the hopes of pleasing you. Now, may we turn the discussion to some other matter . . . perhaps even something relating to work?"

"By all means," Morgan said agreeably. "Actually, I came to give you the latest report on Nick Gentry."

Ross's eyes narrowed at the news. Of all the criminals he desired to be caught, tried, and hanged, Gentry was easily the first on the list. He was the opposite of everything Ross sought to uphold.

Taking advantage of the law that gave rewards to any citizen who apprehended a highwayman, burglar, or deserter, Nick Gentry and his men had established an office in London and set themselves up as professional thief-takers. When Gentry caught a highwayman, he received not only a commission upon conviction, but also the highwayman's horse, arms, and money. If he recovered stolen goods, he not only charged a fee, he also took a percentage of the property's value. When Gentry and his men could not gather enough evidence against a particular felon, they planted or manufactured some. They also seduced young boys into crime, purely for the purpose of arresting them later and collecting the bounties.

Gentry was regarded with both admiration and fear in the underworld, where he was the undisputed king. His office had become the rendezvous for every criminal of note in England. Gentry was guilty of all kinds of corruption, including fraud, bribery, thievery, and even murder. Most maddening of all, the man was regarded by much of London as some sort of public benefactor. He cut a dashing figure in his fine clothes, riding his big black horse through the alleys and thoroughfares of London. Small boys dreamed of growing up to be like him. Women of high or low birth were excited by his intriguing appearance.

"I'd like to see that bastard dance in the wind," Ross muttered. "Tell me what you have."

"We have witness accounts that Gentry arranged for the escape of three of his men from Newgate. The clerk has already taken two depositions."

Ross went very still, in the manner of a predator catching scent of its most desired prey. "Bring him in for questioning," he said. "And do it quickly, before he goes to ground."

Morgan nodded, knowing that if Gentry caught wind of danger and decided to go into hiding, he would be impossible to locate. "I assume you'll want to question him yourself?"

Ross nodded. Ordinarily he would have left such matters in Morgan's capable hands, but not when Nick Gentry was involved. Gentry was his personal adversary, and Ross had devoted a great deal of effort to bringing the wily thief-taker down.

"Very well, sir." Morgan unfolded his long frame from the chair and stood. "I'll have Gentry taken into custody as soon as he is located. I'll dispatch Sayer and Gee immediately." He paused, and a wry smile softened the hard angles of his face. "That is, if they are not too busy ogling your assistant."

Ross suppressed a biting reply with great difficulty, his normally controlled temper igniting at the idea of Sophia Sydney being harassed by his own men. "Do something for me, Morgan," he said through tight lips. "Make it known that if any of my runners or any member of the foot or horse patrol bothers Miss Sydney, they will regret it."

"Yes, sir." Morgan turned to leave, but not before Ross saw the hint of a smile on his lips.

"What is so bloody amusing?"

Morgan replied in a bland tone. "I was merely reflecting, sir, that you may come to regret not hiring a long-toothed old crone."

After partaking of an evening meal of warmed-over mutton stew, Sophia unpacked her belongings in the upstairs room that had been given to her. The room was tiny, and it had been furnished simply. However, it was clean, and the bed seemed comfortable, and there was another advantage that Sophia liked. Her window faced the west side of Bow Street No. 3, allowing her to see directly into Cannon's office. The lamplight outlined the shape of his dark head and highlighted the hard edge of his profile as he turned toward his bookshelves. It was late, and he should have retired for the evening. At the very least, he should be enjoying a good supper instead of the unappetizing dish of mutton stew that Eliza had sent over.

Sophia changed into her night rail and returned to the window, watching as Cannon rubbed his face and bent diligently over his desk. She thought of all the things Eliza and Lucie had told her about the Chief Magistrate. With the typical servants' love of gossip, they had provided a great deal of information.

It seemed that Sir Ross's supporters, of which there were many, revered him for his compassion, whereas an equal number of critics denounced him for his sternness. He was the most powerful magistrate in England, even acting as an unofficial adviser to the government. He trained his runners with progressive new methods, applying scientific principles to law enforcement in a way that earned both admiration and mistrust from the public. Sophia had been entertained as Eliza and Lucie attempted to explain how the runners sometimes solved crimes by examining teeth, hair, bullets, and wounds. None of it made sense to her, but apparently Sir Ross's techniques had untangled mysteries as intricate as the Gordian knot.

The servants held Sir Ross in high regard, as did everyone else who worked at Bow Street. Sophia came to the unsettling realization that the magistrate was not the entirely evil person she had considered him to be. It did not change her resolve to avenge John's death, however. In fact, strict adherence to principle was probably what had led to the tragedy that had claimed her brother's life. No doubt Sir Ross lived by the letter of the law, putting principle above compassion, and legislation above mercy.

The thought caused Sophia's anger to flare violently. Who was Sir Ross, that he should decide who lived or died? Why was he fit to sit in judgment upon others? Was he so infallible, so wise and perfect? He probably thought he was, the arrogant bastard.

But she was perplexed by the memory of his easy

forgiveness that morning, when she had confessed the story of her short-lived affair. Most people would have condemned her as a harlot and said that her dismissal was well deserved. She had expected Sir Ross to censure her. Instead he seemed understanding and kind, and had even admitted that he himself had made mistakes.

Troubled, she nudged the frayed muslin curtain aside to gain a better view of his office window.

As if he could somehow feel Sophia's gaze, Sir Ross turned and glanced directly at her. Although there was no lamp or candle burning in her room, the moonlight was sufficient to illuminate her. He could see that she was dressed only in the fragile night rail.

Being a gentleman, Sir Ross should have turned away immediately. But he stared at her intently, as if he were a hungry wolf and she were a rabbit that had ventured too far from the warren. Though Sophia's entire body burned with embarrassment, she lingered to give him a good look. Silently she counted the seconds: one . . . two . . . three. Then she moved aside slowly, drew the curtain shut, and raised her palms to her flaming face. She should be pleased that he had shown an interest in what she looked like in her nightclothes. Instead she was profoundly uneasy, almost frightened— as if her plan to seduce and destroy him might somehow end in her own downfall.

Chapter 2

$\mathcal{R}$oss began the day as usual, performing his morning ablutions with economic speed and dressing in his usual attire of a dark coat and gray trousers. He tied his black silk cravat in a simple knot, and brushed his hair until it settled neatly into place. Giving a cursory glance in the looking glass beside the washstand, he saw that the smudges beneath his eyes were more pronounced than usual. He had not slept well the previous night. He had been occupied with thoughts of Sophia, his body teeming with the awareness that she was sleeping only a few rooms away.

It had been impossible to stop thinking about the moment when he had seen her at the window, her long hair streaming in ripples, her nightgown ghostly in the moonlight. Ross had been utterly seduced by the image, his blood coursing as he imagined what the female body beneath the gown might look like.

Scowling, Ross vowed that there would be no more nightly reveries concerning Sophia. No more fantasies, and certainly no more gazing at her window. From now on it would be work as usual.

Grimly determined, he went down to the kitchen, where he intended to fetch his first jug of coffee and carry it to his office. When that was done, he would take his daily walk through Covent Garden and the surrounding streets, much in the manner of a physician taking the pulse of a favorite patient. No matter how detailed the reports of the Bow Street runners were, there was nothing quite like seeing and hearing things for himself.

Ross took pleasure in the orderly progression of activities at Bow Street each day. Just after dawn, the bells of St. Paul's rang through Covent Garden and along the tranquil shop fronts and residences of Bow Street. The sounds of market carts caused shutters to snap open and curtains to be drawn, as did the cries of muffin sellers and newspaper boys. At seven o'clock, smells of hot bread and rolls floated from the baker's, and at eight, patrons would begin to drift through the opening doors of the coffeehouses. When nine o'clock arrived, people would gather at the Bow Street office, waiting for the clerks and officers to open the doors. At ten, the sitting magistrate—who happened to be Morgan today—would assume his place at court.

Everything as it should be, Ross thought with satisfaction.

As Ross entered the kitchen, he saw Ernest sitting at the scrubbed wooden table. The boy wolfed down a plate of breakfast as if it were the first decent meal he'd had in months. Sophia stood at the range with the scrawny cook-maid, apparently showing her how to prepare the morning's fare. "Turn them like this," Sophia was saying, expertly flipping a row of little cakes on a griddle pan. The kitchen atmosphere was especially fragrant today, spiced with frying bacon, coffee, and sizzling batter.

Sophia looked fresh and wholesome, the trim curves of her figure outlined by a white apron that covered her charcoal-gray dress. Her gleaming hair was pinned in a coil at the top of her head and tied with a blue ribbon. As she saw him standing in the doorway, a smile lit her sapphire eyes, and she was so dazzlingly pretty that Ross felt a painful jab low in his stomach.

"Good morning, Sir Ross," she said. "Will you have some breakfast?"

"No, thank you," he replied automatically. "Only a jug of coffee. I never . . ." He paused as the cook set a platter on the table. It was piled with steaming batter cakes sitting in a pool of blackberry sauce. He had a special fondness for blackberries.

"Just one or two?" Sophia coaxed.

Abruptly it became less important that he adhere to his usual habits. Perhaps he could make time for a little breakfast, Ross reasoned. A five-minute delay would make no difference in his schedule.

He found himself seated at the table facing a plate

heaped with cakes, crisp bacon, and coddled eggs. Sophia filled a mug with steaming black coffee, and smiled at him once more before resuming her place at the range with Eliza. Ross picked up his fork and stared at it as if he didn't quite know what to do with it.

"They're good, sir," Ernest ventured, stuffing his mouth so greedily that it seemed likely he would choke.

Ross took a bite of the fruit-soaked cake and washed it down with a swallow of hot coffee. As he continued to eat, he felt an unfamiliar sense of well-being. Good God, it had been a long time since he'd had anything other than Eliza's wretched concoctions.

For the next few minutes Ross ate until the platter of cakes was demolished. Sophia came now and then to refill his cup or offer more bacon. The cozy warmth of the kitchen and the sight of Sophia as she moved about the room caused a tide of unwilling pleasure inside him. Setting down his fork, Ross stood and regarded her without smiling. "I must go now. Thank you for the breakfast, Miss Sydney."

One last mug of coffee was pressed into his hands, and Sophia's dark blue eyes stared into his. "Will you spend the day in the office, sir?"

Ross shook his head, fascinated by the little wisps of hair that had stuck to her forehead. The heat of the stove had made her cheeks pink and glistening. He wanted to kiss, lick, taste her. "I will be out for most of the morning," he said, his voice raspy. "I am conducting an investigation—there was a murder in Russell Square last evening."

"Be careful."

It had been a long time since anyone had said that to him. Ross damned himself for feeling so easily unsettled . . . but there it was, that velvety tickle of pleasure he could not seem to elude. He nodded shortly, giving her a wary glance before leaving.

Sophia spent the first half of the day attending to a waist-high pile of papers, briefs, and correspondence that had been shoved into a corner of Sir Ross's office. As she filed the mass of information, she welcomed the opportunity to become familiar with the criminal records room, which was dusty and unkempt. It would take days, perhaps weeks, to organize the drawers of materials properly. While Sophia worked, she reflected on what she had learned of Sir Ross so far, including the stray comments she had heard from servants and clerks and runners. It seemed that the Chief Magistrate was an inhumanly self-controlled man who never swore or shouted or drank to excess. A few soft-voiced directions from him would make the fearsome runners hasten to obey. Sir Ross was admired by all who worked for him, but at the same time they delighted in jesting about his cold and methodical nature.

Sophia did not believe that he was cold. She perceived something beneath his austere facade, a powerfully contained sexuality that would be all-consuming if it were ever set free. Given the intensity of his nature,

Sir Ross would not approach lovemaking in a casual way. It was too important, too rare for him; he would have to care deeply for his partner before he slept with her. If Sophia were to succeed in seducing him, she would have to earn his affection. But how did one go about making such a man fall in love? She suspected that he would respond to a woman who supplied the softness that was clearly missing in his life. After all, he was not some godlike being with limitless strength. He was a man, one who pushed himself too hard. For a man who carried so many burdens on his shoulders, it would be a relief to have someone take care of *his* needs.

Returning to Sir Ross's private office, Sophia used a rag to wipe the dust from the windowsill. She happened to see the object of her thoughts on the street below, as Sir Ross paused at the iron fence that fronted the building. He appeared to be speaking to a woman who had been waiting at the gate. The woman wore a brown shawl that covered her hair and shoulders, and Sophia remembered that Mr. Vickery had turned her away earlier in the day. The woman had wanted to see Sir Ross, and the clerk had told her to return tomorrow, since the Chief Magistrate was occupied with pressing matters.

However, Sir Ross opened the gate for the woman and walked with her to the entrance of Bow Street No. 3. Sophia was touched by his consideration for someone who was surely of a much lower class. She was ill-dressed and haggard, yet the Chief Magistrate gave her his arm as courteously as if she were a duchess.

When Sir Ross brought the woman into his office, Sophia noticed the hitch of a frown between his black brows. "Good afternoon, Miss Sydney," he said evenly, guiding his visitor to a chair. The woman was thin, middle-aged, and haggard in appearance, her eyes red from crying. "This is Miss Trimmer, who I understand was turned away by Vickery this morning."

"I believe Mr. Vickery was concerned that your schedule was already quite full," Sophia murmured.

"I can always make time when it is necessary." Sir Ross half sat, half leaned against his desk, his arms folded across his chest. He spoke in a gently encouraging tone that Sophia had not heard from him before. "You said that you fear for your sister's safety, Miss Trimmer. Pray tell me what has caused such concern."

The trembling spinster clutched the ends of her shawl and spoke in a choked voice. "My younger sister, Martha, is married to Mr. Jeremy Fowler." She paused, evidently overcome by emotion.

"Mr. Fowler's employment is . . . ?" Sir Ross prompted inquiringly.

"He is an apothecary. They live above the shop at St. James's market. There is trouble between Mr. Fowler and Martha, and—" She stopped and twisted the knitted shawl in tight, frantic fists. "She did something a month ago that put him in a rage. And I haven't seen her since."

"She is missing from her home?"

"No, sir . . . Mr. Fowler keeps Martha locked in a room and won't let her out. She's been there almost four weeks. No one can go inside to see her . . . I think she has taken ill, and I've begged Mr. Fowler to let her go, but he won't, as he's still of a mind to punish her."

"Punish her for what?" Sir Ross asked quietly.

Red flags of shame crossed the woman's narrow cheeks. "I think Martha took up with another man. It was very bad of her, I know. But Martha is good at heart, and I'm certain she is sorry for what she did and wants Mr. Fowler's forgiveness." Miss Trimmer's eyes watered, and she blotted them with her shawl. "No one will help me free my poor sister, as they all say it's a matter between husband and wife. Mr. Fowler says he's only done this because he loves Martha so, and she hurt him so awfully. No one, not even the rest of the Trimmers, blames him for locking her away."

Sir Ross's eyes were hard and icy. "I am always puzzled by this so-called love that causes men to brutalize their wives. In my opinion, a man who truly loves a woman would never intentionally harm her, no matter how great the betrayal." His gaze softened as he regarded the desperate woman before him. "I will send a runner to the Fowler residence immediately, Miss Trimmer."

"Oh, sir," she faltered, weeping in patent relief. "Thank you, and bless you a thousand times."

Sir Ross glanced at Sophia. "Do you know which men are available today, Miss Sydney?"

"Mr. Sayer and Mr. Ruthven," Sophia murmured, relieved that he intended to free the captive Martha. She would not have been surprised if he had declined to help, as it was commonly thought that husbands had the right to do whatever they liked with their wives.

"Tell Ruthven to come."

Sophia hastened to obey. She soon returned with Mr. Ruthven, a large, dark-haired runner with a rugged countenance and an aggressive disposition. His appetite for physical combat was well known, and few men were willing to provoke him. Unfortunately, his mind was not suited for the subtleties of investigative work, and therefore Sir Ross used him for tasks that were more physical than cerebral in nature.

"Go with Miss Trimmer to St. James's market," Sir Ross told the runner calmly. "She will show you to the rooms above Fowler's Apothecary Shop, where her sister has been imprisoned for well nigh a month. Do whatever is necessary to free her, and be mindful of the possibility that you will meet with some resistance from her husband."

Realizing that he was being called upon to intervene in a marital dispute, the runner scowled slightly. "Sir, I was just on my way to the Tothill Bank—there was a robbery there, and I—"

"You'll have time to earn your private commissions later," Sir Ross said. "This is more important."

"Yes, sir." Clearly annoyed, Ruthven turned to leave.

"Ruthven," Sir Ross murmured, "what if it were *your* sister who had been locked in a room for a month?"

The runner considered his words, becoming a bit shamefaced. "I will take care of it immediately, Sir Ross."

"Good," the magistrate said brusquely. "And, Ruthven, after you free Mrs. Fowler, I want to question her husband."

"Shall I bring him directly to the strong room, sir?"

"No, take him to Newgate. He can wait there and contemplate his actions for a while before I talk to him."

As the runner escorted Miss Trimmer from the office, Sophia approached Sir Ross and regarded him thoughtfully. He remained in his half-seated position on the desk, which brought their faces nearly level. His expression was brooding, deep brackets carved on either side of his lips. Although Sophia had heard of the Chief Magistrate's well-known compassion for women and children, she was surprised by his willingness to interfere in a conflict between husband and wife. A wife was legally considered to be a man's property, and he could do as he pleased with her, short of actual murder. "That was very kind of you," she said.

The frown remained on Sir Ross's face. "I'd like to make Fowler suffer in the same way his wife has. I can only keep him in Newgate for three days—not nearly long enough."

Sophia was in complete agreement, but she could not resist playing the devil's advocate. "Some would say that Mrs. Fowler deserved such punishment for sleeping with another man," she pointed out.

"Regardless of her behavior, her husband had no right to retaliate in such a manner."

"What would *your* response be if your wife betrayed you with someone else?"

It was apparent that the question surprised the magistrate. In one abrupt moment Sophia had turned the conversation into something personal. Sir Ross stared at her steadily, sudden tension causing his shoulder muscles to strain tightly against his coat. "I don't know," he admitted. "My wife was not the kind of woman who would have succumbed to that particular temptation. The issue was never a concern for me."

"What if you married again?" Sophia asked, held prisoner by his vivid silver gaze. "Wouldn't you worry about your wife's fidelity?"

"No."

"Why not?"

"Because I would keep her so busy in my bed that she would have neither the time nor the inclination to seek another man's company."

The words caused an odd quiver to shoot through Sophia's belly. It was an admission of nothing less than an all-consuming sexual appetite. It confirmed everything she had learned about him so far. Sir Ross was not a man to do anything by half measures. Before she could stop herself, Sophia imagined what it might be like to lie tangled with him in intimacy, his mouth at her breasts, his hands moving gently over her body. Her face flamed with a mixture of embarrassment and awareness.

"Forgive me," he said softly. "I should not have spoken so frankly."

Another surprise—Sophia had never encountered a man from any walk of life who would lower himself to apologize to an employee, much less to a female one. "It was my fault," she managed to say. "I should not have asked such personal questions. I don't know why I did."

"Don't you?" His gaze snared hers again, and the hot flicker in his eyes made it difficult for her to breathe.

Sophia had been trying to discover more about his character and the workings of his heart. It was all for the purpose of manipulation, of course. All part of her quest to make him fall in love with her. Unfortunately, she was finding it difficult to ignore a growing attraction to the man she planned to hurt. She wanted to remain cool and uninvolved when they finally shared a bed. However, there were so many seductive qualities about him: his intelligence, his compassion for vulnerable creatures, the raw need beneath his self-controlled facade.

Just as she felt a reluctant softening in her heart toward him, she thought of her dead brother, and her determination burned with new vigor. John must be avenged, or else his life would be robbed of any meaning at all. To let go of the past meant that she had failed John, and that was something she could not do.

After a moment of calculation, she admitted carefully, "I suppose I am curious about you. You rarely talk about yourself, or of your past."

"There is little in my past that would interest you," he assured her. "I am an ordinary man from an equally ordinary family."

The statement should have reeked of false humility.

After all, Sir Ross was a man of remarkable accomplishments and abilities. Surely he was aware of his own achievements, his keen mind, his good looks, his sterling reputation. However, Sophia realized that he did not consider himself superior to any other man. He demanded so much of himself that he could never live up to his own impossible standards.

"You are not ordinary," she half whispered. "You are fascinating."

There was no doubt that Sir Ross was often approached by women who had a personal interest in him. As a handsome widower with deep pockets and considerable social and political influence, he was probably the most eligible man in London. Yet Sophia's bold statement had clearly caught him off guard. He gave her a baffled stare, seeming unable to form a reply.

Silence weighted the air. Finally Sophia spoke, trying to sound brisk. "I will see about supper. Will you eat in the kitchen or here?"

Sir Ross focused on his desk with inordinate attention. "Send a tray up here. I have more to do tonight."

"You should sleep," she said. "You work far too much."

He picked up a letter and broke the seal. "Good night, Miss Sydney," he murmured, his gaze falling on the page.

Sophia left the office and wandered through the hallway with a frown. Why should she care if he refused to get the rest he needed? Let him work himself into an early grave, she thought. It hardly mattered to her if he ruined his health, the stubborn ox! But the irritation stayed with her as she recalled the weary smudges beneath his eyes. She reasoned that her concern stemmed from her desire for revenge. After all, one could hardly seduce a man when he was exhausted and half starved.

On the days that Ross served as sitting magistrate, Sophia brought his lunch plate to the office after early court sessions were finished. While he ate at his desk, she would straighten his papers and dust his shelves and carry reports to the criminal records room. However, he was not one to take regular meals, often regarding food as an unwelcome interruption to his work.

The first time that Ross had refused lunch, informing Sophia that he was too busy to eat, she had offered the plate to Vickery, who was copying a runner's report.

"Vickery is busy also," Ross said shortly. "You may take the plate away."

"Yes, sir," Sophia replied, seeming not at all perturbed. "Perhaps later—"

"I *am* a bit hungry," the clerk interrupted, staring at the covered plate with stark longing. A stocky man with a hearty appetite, Vickery did not like to miss a meal. "That smells delicious, Miss Sydney . . . may I ask what it is?"

"Marjoram sausage and potatoes. And green peas in cream."

Ross's appetite kindled at the savory fragrance that wafted from the plate. Lately Sophia had taken a strong hand in the kitchen, showing the inept cook-maid how to prepare edible meals. She paid close attention to his likes and dislikes, observing that he preferred well-seasoned food and had an incurable sweet tooth. In the past several days Ross had succumbed to the temptation of crisp-crusted charlotte pudding mounded high with orange filling . . . plum cake rich with molasses and currants . . . sugared apples wedged between thick layers of dough. Not surprisingly, he had begun to put on weight. The hollows of his cheeks had filled out, and his clothes no longer hung in loose folds—all of which would doubtless please his mother, who had often worried over his leanness.

Vickery closed his eyes and inhaled deeply. "Green peas in cream . . . my mother used to make them that way. Tell me, Miss Sydney, did you add a pinch of nutmeg as she did?"

"Why, yes—" Sophia began.

"Give him the tray," Ross growled. "It's obvious that I won't have a moment's peace otherwise."

Sophia sent him a vaguely apologetic smile as she obeyed.

Vickery accepted the lunch tray and unfolded the cloth napkin with obvious delight. Beaming, he called after her when she left, "Thank you, Miss Sydney!"

While Ross signed warrants, he was irritably aware of Vickery's lip-smacking and moans of enjoyment as he devoured the lunch. "Do you have to make so much noise?" Ross finally asked, looking up from his desk with a scowl.

Vickery stuffed his mouth with another large spoonful of peas. "Forgive me, sir. But this is a meal fit for a king. The next time you wish to forgo your lunch, sir, I will gladly take it in your stead."

There would not be a next time, Ross had vowed silently, annoyed beyond bearing to see someone else enjoying *his* meal. From then on, lunch in his office became a sacred ritual, and no one dared to interfere.

Sophia's influence soon extended to more personal details of his life. She made certain that the ewer of water for his morning shave was always steaming hot, and she added glycerine to his shaving soap to soften his obstinate beard. Observing that his boots and shoes needed attention, she mixed her own recipe for blacking and frequently nagged Ernest to keep Ross's footwear polished.

One morning, having discovered that most of his cravats had disappeared from the top drawer of his gentleman's chest, Ross went to the kitchen in his shirtsleeves. He found Sophia at the table, making notes in a little stitched-together book. Noticing that he was not wearing his coat or waistcoat, she gave him a swift but thorough glance that went from head to toe. At this sign of discreet feminine interest, Ross suddenly had trouble remembering why he had come downstairs in the first place.

"Miss Sydney—" he began gruffly.

"Your cravats," she said with a snap of her slender

fingers, evidently recalling that she had removed them from his chest. "I washed and pressed them yesterday, but I forgot to have them returned to your room. I will send Lucie up with them shortly."

"Thank you," Ross said, distracted by a silky lock of golden hair that had slid loose from her topknot. He was almost overcome by the temptation to reach out and wind the soft strands around his finger.

"Before you return to your room, sir, you should be aware that some of your cravats are gone."

"Gone?" he repeated with an inquiring frown.

"I sold them to the ragman." An impudent smile danced on her lips as she continued, silently daring him to protest. "Several of them were frayed and worn. A man in your position couldn't possibly be seen in them. So you will have to purchase new ones."

"I see." Thoroughly engaged by her impertinence, Ross leaned over her and placed one hand on the top of the chair where she sat. Although he did not touch her, she was completely trapped. "Well, Miss Sydney, since you have taken it upon yourself to dispose of my cravats, I think you should be the one to replace them. Ernest will accompany you to Bond Street this afternoon, and you can purchase the new ones on my credit. I will leave the selection to your taste."

Her head tilted back so she could meet his gaze, and her eyes sparkled with anticipation at the thought of a shopping expedition. "With pleasure, sir."

As Ross stared into Sophia's upturned face, he was

greatly puzzled. It had been a long time since anyone had paid such close attention to such trivial matters as his cravats and the temperature of his shaving water. But part of him relished it . . . the almost wifely attentiveness on which he was becoming far too dependent. As with all things he did not understand, Ross examined Sophia's possible motives. He could not come up with a single reason that she would wish to pamper him.

Sophia's thick lashes lowered as she glanced once more to where his shirt revealed his bare throat. Her breath quickened slightly, betraying her awareness of him. He thought of sliding his hand behind her neck, holding her steady as he bent to capture her mouth. But it had been a long time since he had made such an advance to a woman, and he was not completely certain that she would welcome his attentions.

"Miss Sydney," he murmured, staring into the soft sapphire depths of her eyes, "the next time you dispose of my clothing, you had better give me advance warning." A roguish smile tugged at his lips as he leaned a fraction closer and added, "I would hate to come down here without my trousers."

To Ross's chagrin, he was not the only man at Bow Street to appreciate Sophia's considerable charms. As Morgan had predicted, the runners were after her like a pack of frolicsome wolves, sniffing and nipping at her heels. Before reporting to him at nine each morning, they would wait at the kitchen door for leftover scraps from breakfast. They would tease and flirt with her, and spin exaggerated tales of their own accomplishments.

Discovering that Sophia was willing to treat minor wounds, the men began to invent aches and pains that required her attention. After learning that she had bound at least three hairy sprained ankles and administered two poultices and wrapped a sore throat in the course of a single week, Ross lost his temper.

"You tell the runners," he snapped at Vickery, "that if they are becoming so damned clumsy and sickly of late, they can see a bloody sawbones! I am forbidding Miss Sydney to treat any more injuries, do you understand?"

"Yes, sir." Vickery stared at him with obvious amazement. "I've never seen you in a temper before, Sir Ross."

"I'm not in a temper!"

"You are shouting and cursing," Vickery pointed out reasonably. "If that isn't a temper, what is?"

Ross struggled to emerge from the red haze that had surrounded him. With great effort, he modulated his tone. "I raised my voice merely for the purpose of being emphatic," he said through his teeth. "My point is, the runners are not going to fake injuries and illness as an excuse to have Miss Sydney doctor them. She has enough responsibility as it is—I won't have her plagued by the pack of rutting idiots who work for me."

"Yes, sir," Vickery replied, averting his face, but not before Ross saw the twitch of a perceptive smile at his lips.

As word of Bow Street's pretty new employee spread among the patrols, Sophia was besieged by eager constables. She treated them all with the same friendly politeness. Ross sensed that she was guarding herself and her heart very carefully. After the wretched way she had been treated by her lover, any man would have an uphill battle to gain her trust.

Ross was increasingly curious about the man who had betrayed Sophia—what he had looked like, and what it was about him that had attracted her. Unable to help himself, Ross finally asked Eliza if Sophia had confided anything about her erstwhile lover. It was Sophia's day off, and she had taken Ernest on an outing to Bond Street. Bow Street seemed strangely empty without her, and though the day was only half over, Ross found himself watching the clock impatiently.

A knowing smile crossed the cook-maid's face at his question.

"If Sophia did say anything about him, Sir Ross, it was told in confidence. Besides, you lectured me just last month about my gossiping ways, and now I've made a pledge to reform myself."

Ross gave her a hard, level stare. "Eliza, why is it that now, when I'm finally interested in something you have to gossip about, you've decided to reform?"

She laughed, her crooked teeth displayed like a basket of gaming chips. "I'll tell you what she has said about him—if you will tell me why you want to know."

Ross kept his face expressionless. "I was merely asking out of a polite concern for her well-being."

Eliza snorted with skeptical amusement. "I'll tell

you, sir, but you mustn't let on, or Miss Sophia will have me done to a turn. His name was Anthony. She said he was young and handsome, with fair hair. She likes fair-haired men, you see."

Ross received the information with a slight frown. "Go on."

"They met while Miss Sophia was out on a walk and he was riding through the woods. He charmed her . . . quoting poetry and such."

Ross grunted in displeasure. The image of Sophia in another man's arms—a fair-haired, poetry-quoting one—chafed like new leather against a blister. "Unfortunately, he forgot to mention that he had a wife."

"Yes. The coward simply left her after he'd taken his pleasure—he never bothered to tell her about his wife. Miss Sophia says she will never love again."

"She'll marry someday," Ross replied cynically. "It is only a matter of time."

"Yes, Miss Sophia will probably marry," Eliza said pragmatically. "What I said was, she will never *love* again."

He shrugged casually. "If one is to marry, it is best to do it for reasons other than love."

"That is exactly what Miss Sophia says." Eliza took her leave, pausing at the door to add with a bit too much sincerity, "How sensible you both are!" She departed with a chuckle while Ross scowled after her.

After a fortnight of diligent work, the runners Sayer and Gee finally managed to locate Nick Gentry, the

popular figure of the London underworld. Every parlor and tavern was instantly ablaze with the news that
he had been taken to Bow Street and held for questioning. The minute that Gentry was brought to the
premises, he was imprisoned in the strong room, an
area that Sophia had never been allowed to see. Naturally her curiosity about the forbidden cellar-level
room was rampant, but Sir Ross had ordered her to
stay away from it.

As word of Nick Gentry's detainment spread
through the slums and rookeries of London, a large
crowd gathered outside Bow Street No. 3, blocking the
entire thoroughfare so that no vehicles could pass.
Gentry's influence permeated every corner of the city.
Although he called himself a thief-taker, he had in real-
ity done much to organize crime in London. He di-
rected gangs in their illegal activities, telling them how
and when to commit crimes they might not have attempted without his guidance. Pickpockets, burglars,
whores, and murderers all reported to him, receiving
his assistance in matters ranging from disposing of
stolen goods to helping felons avoid arrest.

Sophia had hoped for a glimpse of the notorious
criminal, but he had been brought to Bow Street under
cover of night. Sir Ross had been with him in the
strong room every minute, settling in for a long period
of questioning. "Sir Ross can only 'old Gentry for three
days," Ernest informed Sophia breathlessly. " 'E'll try his
hardest to make Gentry admit to helping those men escape Newgate, but Gentry will never crack."

"You sound as if you admire Mr. Gentry," Sophia remarked.

The boy considered the question thoughtfully, blushing under her attention. "Well . . . Nick Gentry is not all bad. 'E does 'elp people sometimes . . . gives them jobs and money . . ."

"What kind of jobs?" Sophia asked dryly. "Surely not legitimate ones."

Ernest shrugged uncomfortably. "And he does arrest thieves and highwaymen, just as the runners do."

"From what Sir Ross says," Sophia murmured, "Mr. Gentry encourages people to commit crimes, and then he arrests them for it. Rather like creating criminals for his own profit, isn't it?"

Ernest shot her a defensive glance, then smiled. "Oh, Gentry 'as 'is faults, Miss Sydney, but 'e's a rum one, jus' the same. I can't explain in a way ye would understand."

Sophia did understand, however. Sometimes a man proved to be so charismatic that the public was willing to overlook his sins. It seemed that Nick Gentry had captured the imaginations of aristocrat, merchant, and pickpocket alike . . . everyone in London was fascinated by him. His rivalry with Sir Ross only made him that much more intriguing.

Sir Ross did not come up from the strong room for the entire day, only sent Ernest back and forth with requests for water, or for a particular file from the criminal records room. Sayer and Gee, the two runners who had apprehended Gentry, also remained present for the questioning, although they sometimes emerged for a few moments of respite and fresh air.

Consumed by curiosity, Sophia approached Eddie Sayer as he stood outside in the stone-flagged courtyard behind Bow Street No. 4. The calls and cries from the crowd in front of the building were annoyingly persistent in demanding the release of Nick Gentry. Sophia was grateful for the iron fence that kept the protesters away from the buildings, but she feared that soon someone might decide to scale the partition.

Sayer had lifted his broad face to the cool spring breeze and was breathing deeply. Although the wind was tainted with the familiar scents of the London streets, manure and coal dust being prevalent, it seemed preferable to the atmosphere of the strong room. Hearing Sophia's footsteps on the stone, Sayer turned and grinned, his brown eyes twinkling. He was a large, dashing young man who flirted with every woman he encountered, no matter her age, appearance, or marital status.

"Ah, Miss Sydney ... just the companion I was hoping for. No doubt you've come out here for a passionate tryst. Finally going to admit your feelings for me, eh?"

"Yes," Sophia said dryly, having learned that the best way to deal with the runners was to match their irreverence. "I have finally been swept up in the romantic atmosphere of Bow Street. Where shall we tryst, Mr. Sayer?"

The tall young man grinned. "I'm afraid I shall have to disappoint you, my fair one. Cannon only gave me five minutes' leave—not nearly enough time. Besides, I'm not one for trysting on hard stone. Please contain your disappointment."

Sophia folded her arms and regarded him with a slight smile. "How is it in the strong room, Mr. Sayer?"

The runner sighed, suddenly looking weary. "Cannon hasn't gotten much out of Gentry so far. It's like trying to fell an oak with a butter knife. Cannon keeps chipping away at him, though." He rubbed his face and groaned. "I suppose it is time for me to go back down there."

"Good luck," she said sympathetically, and watched him cross the courtyard back to the strong-room door.

The afternoon passed, and as evening approached, the mood of the crowd at Bow Street became more violent. Peering through the windows, Sophia saw that some of the protesters were carrying clubs, and there were small fires in the street where furniture had been brought and set alight. Bottles of liquor had been procured from The Brown Bear, the tavern opposite the public office, and the crowd was drinking freely. To Sophia's horror, the homes on either side of the public office were being assaulted; windows were broken, and clubs and fists beat angrily on the barricaded doors.

When evening fell the mob had lost all reason. Ernest appeared at No. 4, telling Sophia and the servants to stay inside. The available runners were attempting to disperse the crowd. If they proved unsuccessful, they would summon help from the military.

"No need to worry," Eliza said breathlessly, her face pale. "The runners will put down the riot. They're good, brave men—they'll keep us safe."

"Where is Sir Ross?" Sophia asked Ernest, trying to remain calm, although the constant screaming of the mob was shredding her nerves.

"Still in the strong room with Gentry," Ernest replied. "'E says he'll shoot Gentry himself before letting the crowd have 'im."

As the boy dashed back to the adjoining building, Sophia returned to the window. She flinched as rocks and bottles were thrown, striking the house. "This is madness," she exclaimed. "Does Sir Ross know how bad it is getting? Before long they'll reduce the place to matchsticks!"

All three women jumped as a rock shattered the window, sending a shower of splintered glass to the floor.

"My God!" Eliza exclaimed.

"Heaven save us," Lucie squealed, her eyes like saucers. "What should we do?"

"Stay away from the windows," Sophia said shortly. "I'm going to the strong room."

The noise outside was deafening, the air acrid with smoke. Although no one had yet managed to scale the iron fence, Sophia could see a ladder being passed over the top of the writhing mob. Lifting her skirts, she ran through the courtyard and wrenched open the door that led to the strong room.

Stairs descended to a dark void. She climbed down carefully, since the stone beneath her feet was slick. The walls were green with mold, and the air was permeated with a sour stench that reminded her of urine. Sophia heard the sound of masculine voices, Sir Ross's among them. Following a dull glow at the bottom of the stairs, she found a narrow corridor that opened into a cellar-space. Lamplight flickered across the bars of three holding cells and cast a grid of shadows across the dirt floor. At the far end of the strong room, a table and chairs were positioned near a barred vent that gave onto the street level. The mob's ceaseless roar filtered through the opening.

Sophia saw two runners, Sir Ross, and a tall, well-dressed man who lounged insolently near the vent. One shoulder was braced casually against the wall, while his hands were buried deep in the pockets of his coat. He must be Nick Gentry, Sophia thought. Before she had a glimpse of his face, however, Sir Ross turned and approached her in a few swift strides.

"*What are you doing here?*" His voice was edged with a savagery that made her flinch.

Despite the coolness of the room, Cannon was in his shirtsleeves, the broad shape of his shoulders and the heavy muscles of his arms visible through the clinging white linen. The neck of the shirt was unbuttoned, revealing the edge of a thick pelt of hair on his chest. Sophia's startled gaze lifted to his face, which was hard and fierce, the gray eyes burning with wrath.

"I told you not to come down here," he snapped. Although he was not precisely shouting, his voice was resonant with fury.

"I'm sorry, but there is something you must know—"

"When I tell you not to do something, *you obey me,* no matter what happens. Do you understand?"

"Yes, O lord and master," Sophia said sarcastically, her tension and worry sparking into anger. "However, I thought you should be informed that the mob is about to overtake number four. The constables can't hold them back much longer. They're breaking the windows. If you don't send for the military soon, they'll burn both buildings to the ground."

"Sayer." Sir Ross turned to the runner. "Go have a look outside. If the situation warrants, send for a troop of horse guards." He glanced back at Sophia. "And *you*—go upstairs and stay inside until I tell you otherwise."

Stung by the sharp way he spoke to her, she nodded and left the strong room as fast as her feet could take her.

As the housekeeper left the strong room, Nick Gentry, who had been contemplating the barred window-vent, turned back around.

"Nice little piece," he commented, obviously referring to Sophia. "Got 'er working the brass for you, Cannon? I think I'll take 'er when you're done."

Being familiar with street cant, Ross knew exactly what "working the brass" meant. It referred to a style of iron bed with brass knobs, and the activities that might take place on it. Usually the taunts of a prisoner had no effect on Ross. However, this seemed to be the one occasion when he couldn't control himself. The reference to Sophia as if she were a common prostitute was all it took to sent his fury skyrocketing.

"Either close that hole in the middle of your face," he snarled to Gentry, "or I'll do it for you."

Gentry grinned, clearly pleased with the success of his jab. "You've been trying to make me talk all day, and now you want me to shut my gob?"

Nick Gentry was well dressed and surprisingly young. He was also handsome, with dark hair and blue eyes and an easy smile. His accent, though not that of a gentleman, was far more refined than that of the average Cockney. One could almost mistake him for one of the aristocratic young bucks who spent their time gambling and chasing a light-skirt while they waited for their inheritances. But something about his face betrayed that he was a creature of the streets . . . a coldness that showed in the eyes and robbed the smile of all meaning. Somewhere in his past, Nick Gentry had learned that life was a bitter contest for dominance. He intended to win, and he played by no recognizable set of rules. Loyalty, fairness, mercy—these were qualities that he did not recognize. Ross found it amazing that a brutish bastard like Gentry had garnered so much support among the masses.

Gentry sent him a sly grin, as if he could read Ross's thoughts. "You'll have trouble on your hands tonight, Cannon. Listen to that crowd . . . they'll smash this place to the ground if you don't let me go."

"You're not going anywhere for the next two days," Ross said. "You're going to molder in the strong room for as long as I can legally keep you here. You may as well make yourself comfortable."

"In this slosh-pot?" Gentry returned sourly. "Not bloody likely."

Chapter 3

As Sophia emerged from the strong room, she was alarmed to discover that the mob had finally raged out of control. Men were climbing the fence and dropping to the ground, scurrying like rodents toward the building. A group of constables and horse patrols worked to disperse the rioters, but their efforts seemed to have little effect.

She rushed inside No. 3 in search of safety, but unfortunately, it was no better there. It seemed that every room and hallway was filled, the walls reverberating with the sounds of angry shouting. Runners had arrested the most violent protesters and were taking them in handcuffed groups to the holding rooms.

One of the court clerks, Mr. Vickery, milled about with the night-charge book, trying frantically to record the names of those who had been arrested. Catching sight of Sophia, he called out something to her, but the noise in the hall was deafening. *Go back,* he seemed to be saying, waving with his hand for her to leave.

Sophia turned to obey, but more of the mob

swarmed through the doors. She was jostled and shoved to the side, fighting to keep from being pushed beneath trampling feet. It was hot and deafening in the hall, and the smells of alcohol and unwashed bodies filled the air with a nasty stench. Sophia was crushed against the wall and jabbed by elbows and shoulders, her head bumping hard against the hard paneling.

Trying not to panic, Sophia looked for the court clerk, but he was no longer visible. "Mr. Vickery!" she cried, her voice lost amid the uproar. "Mr. Vickery!"

Some of the rioters began to paw at her bodice, rough hands seeking the shape of her breasts. The shoulder of her dress ripped, and the gleam of a white shoulder seemed to inflame them. Sophia shoved at the coarse hands, but she was jammed against the wall until the breath was driven from her lungs. Someone pulled at her hair, and her scalp smarted while tears of pain sprang to her eyes.

"Here, now," a runner shouted indignantly, struggling to reach her. "Get your hands off her, you sodding bastards!"

Sophia turned away from the encroaching bodies, pressing the side of her face to the wall. She struggled for air as she was suffocated and mauled at the same time. Her ribs squeezed until it seemed they would crack. Her mind swam dizzily, and it became difficult for her to think. "Get away from me," she gasped. "Stop it, stop, *stop*—"

Suddenly the pressure eased, and she heard the men around her grunting in pain. Stunned, Sophia turned to see a huge, dark shape plowing through the sea of tightly packed bodies. It was Sir Ross, his gray eyes focused on Sophia. There was a strange expression on his face, at once blank and violent. He was brutally efficient as he shoved and struck his way through the crowd, not seeming to care that he left a path of bruises and bloody noses in his wake.

Reaching Sophia, Sir Ross pulled her into his arms, making a protective cage of his own body and the wall. She attached herself to him with a sigh of relief, blindly accepting his protection. He was still in his shirtsleeves, the thin white linen imbued with the heat and scent of his skin. Huddling against his broad chest, Sophia heard the deep thunder of his voice as he shouted to the agitators that Nick Gentry would remain in custody, and that all those who had ventured inside the public office were going to be arrested and sent to Newgate. His words had an immediate effect. The intruders nearest the doors began to file outside rapidly, having no wish to be imprisoned at the stone jug, as the infamous prison was called.

"Jensen, Walker, Gee," Sir Ross commanded the runners, "take your charges to the public house across the street and lock them in the cellar. Flagstad, send for more horse patrols to clear the crowd. Vickery, take names later. Right now, go outside and recite the Riot Act as loudly as you can."

"Sir, I don't remember the exact words of the Riot Act," the court clerk said anxiously.

"Then make up something," Sir Ross growled.

That remark seemed to amuse many of the protestors, and snorts of laughter burst through the hallway. As the runners began to move the men outside, the crush of bodies began to ease.

Sophia flinched as she felt someone fumbling at her skirts. She pressed closer to Sir Ross, her arms clutching around his lean midriff. Before she could say a word, he realized the problem.

"You!" Sir Ross snarled at the man behind her. "Lay a hand on this woman again, and you will lose it—along with other portions of your anatomy."

Another rumble of laughter erupted all around.

Clasped safely in the circle of Sir Ross's arms, Sophia marveled at the way he was able to dominate a crowd with his mere presence. Everything had been chaos, and he had restored order in less than a minute. The muscles of his back flexed as he pulled her between his thighs, holding her in the shelter of his body.

Sophia kept her cheek pressed to his chest, against the steady but rapid rhythm of his heart. Her nostrils were filled with the crisp scent of his shaving soap, the hint of coffee, and the salty tang of sweat. The thick dark curls of his chest tickled her cheek. Anthony had been smooth-chested. What would it be like to be held against this masculine wealth of hair? Swallowing hard, Sophia glanced at the shadow of day-old bristle that covered his jaw and upper throat. His huge hand rested on the center of her back, and she thought of how it might feel against her breast, his long fingers cupping her tender flesh, his thumb stroking her nipple . . .

My God—the frantic words swept through her brain—*don't think about it, don't.* But her body was filled with a strange, warm ache, and she could only breathe in shallow gasps. It was all she could do to keep from thrusting herself at him shamelessly, crushing her mouth against his.

"It's all right." His low whisper brushed against her ear. "Don't be afraid."

He had mistaken her trembling for fear. Good; it was far better that he think she was a silly coward, rather than suspect the truth. Mortified, Sophia tried to calm herself. She moistened her dry lips and spoke against his shirtfront. "I'm glad you finally decided to do something," she said, trying to sound impudent. "You waited long enough."

Ross made a soft sound that could be taken for either irritation or amusement. "I was busy with Gentry."

"I thought I would be crushed," she said shakily.

She was astonished as he cuddled her closer. "You're safe," he murmured. "No one is going to harm you."

Realizing that he was more than ready to comfort her, Sophia decided that this was a golden opportunity to appeal to his protective streak. She knew Sir Ross well enough by now to be certain that he could not resist the lure of a damsel in distress. Although part of her cringed in embarrassment, she continued to cling to him as if she were overcome by fear.

"I called to Mr. Vickery, but he couldn't hear me," she said, letting a plaintive note enter her voice.

He murmured softly and rubbed her spine with a comforting stroke. Although Sophia tried to ignore the pleasure of his touch, it spread through her body in an insidious tide. Closing her eyes, she wondered how long she could endure the slow caress of his hand. Her breasts fell full and heavy against his chest, her nipples turning hard.

Gently Sir Ross tucked a loose lock of hair behind her ear. The brush of his fingertips on her skin sent a ripple of warm sensation through her. "Were you hurt in the crush, Sophia?"

"I . . . I'm a bit bruised." Pretending to be overwrought, she put her arms around his neck and held on tightly. The closeness of his large body made her feel safe, supported, protected. She wanted to stand like this forever. He was her enemy, she reminded herself . . . but for the moment, that did not matter nearly as much as it should have.

Sir Ross gave a cursory glance around them as the hall began to clear. She gasped as he bent to pick her up. "Oh, sir, there is no need. I can walk, I'm—"

He ignored her protests as he carried her through the hall. For a woman who was used to taking care of herself, it was acutely embarrassing to play the helpless maiden. However, it was necessary to further her goal. Turning pink, Sophia clung to the hard breadth of his shoulders. Fortunately, the constables and handcuffed agitators were far too busy to pay any attention as Sir Ross carried her through the hall and up a flight of stairs.

When they reached his office, Sir Ross set her carefully on her feet. "Are you all right?"

She nodded, her heartbeat hurtling in a reckless cadence.

"I want to talk about something," he said quietly. "When you came to the strong room earlier, you happened to interrupt during a rather tense moment of the questioning, and I—"

"I'm sorry."

"Let me finish." A sudden smile curved his lips. "I've never known anyone with such a propensity for interrupting me."

Sophia managed to keep her mouth closed, and his smile deepened.

"Questioning Gentry is hardly a pleasant occupation. I've been in a foul mood all afternoon, and seeing you down there was the last straw. I rarely lose my temper, and I regret doing so in front of you."

Sophia found it amazing that a man of his position would apologize to her for such a slight offense. Somewhat unnerved, she moistened her lips and asked, "Why is it so important that I stay away from there?"

Carefully he took hold of the loose lock of blonde hair that had fallen to her shoulder. His long fingers rubbed the silken strands as if he were releasing the perfume of a flower petal. "I promised myself when I hired you that I would try to protect you. There are some things that a woman should never be exposed to. That strong room has contained some of the most vile people on earth."

"Like Nick Gentry?"

Sir Ross frowned. "Yes. It is bad enough that you are exposed to the rabble who cross through the Bow Street office daily. But I won't allow you in the vicinity of men like Gentry."

"I am hardly a child who needs to be sheltered. I am a woman of twenty-eight."

For some reason the remark caused his eyes to gleam with amusement. "Well, despite your vast number of years, I would like to preserve as much of your innocence as possible."

"But I am not innocent. You know that, after what I've told you of my past."

He released the lock of her hair and framed the sides of her face with the tips of his fingers. "You *are* an innocent, Sophia. As I've said from the beginning, you should not be working here. You should be married to a man who will take care of you."

"I don't want to marry, ever."

"No?" To her surprise, he did not jeer or laugh. "Why not? Because of your disappointment in love? That will fade in time."

"Will it?" she asked, not believing him. It wasn't what she had learned about Anthony that had made her a skeptic about love. It was what she had learned about herself.

"There are many men worth trusting," he told her

seriously. "Men who will give you the honesty and respect you deserve. You'll find one of them someday, and marry him."

Sophia sent him a flirtatious glance from beneath her lashes. "But if I left Bow Street, who would take care of you?"

A gruff laugh escaped him, and his hands dropped from her face. But his searching gaze held hers, and Sophia felt her insides tighten in response.

"You can't spend the rest of your life working for a surly old magistrate at the Bow Street public office," he said.

Sophia smiled at the way Sir Ross described himself. Rather than argue the point, however, she stepped away and viewed his office critically. "I will tidy up in here."

Sir Ross shook his head. "It is late. You need to rest. Your work will wait until the morrow."

"Very well. I shall retire for the evening . . . if you will also."

He seemed vaguely annoyed by the suggestion. "No, I still have much to do. Good night, Miss Sydney."

Sophia knew that she should obey without further comment. But the shadows beneath his eyes and the deep brackets on the sides of his lips were proof that he was exhausted. Good heavens, why must he push himself so hard?

"I don't require any more sleep than you do, sir. If you stay up late, I am capable of doing the same. I also have work to do."

His brows lowered in a forbidding scowl. "Go to bed, Miss Sydney."

Sophia did not flinch. "Not until you do."

"My bedtime has nothing to do with yours," he said curtly, "unless you are suggesting that we go to bed together."

Clearly, the remark was meant to intimidate her into silence.

A reckless reply came to mind, one so bold that she bit her tongue to keep from speaking. And then she thought, *Why not?* It was time to declare her sexual interest in him . . . time to advance her plan of seduction one more step.

"All right," she said quickly. "If that is what it takes to make you get the rest you require—so be it."

His dark face went blank. The lengthy silence that ensued was evidence of how greatly she had surprised him. *My God,* she thought in a flutter of panic. *Now I've done it.* She could not predict how Sir Ross would respond. Being a gentleman—a notoriously celibate one—he might refuse her proposition. However, there was something in his expression—a flicker in his gray eyes—that made her wonder if he might not accept the impulsive invitation. And if he did, she would have to carry it out and sleep with him. The thought jarred her very soul. This was what she had planned, what she had wanted to achieve, but she was suddenly terrified.

Terrified by the realization of how much she wanted him.

Slowly Sir Ross approached, following as she backed away one step, then another, until her spine was flattened against the door. His alert gaze did not move from her flushed face as he braced his hands on the door, placing them on either side of her head.

"My bedroom or yours?" he asked softly.

Perhaps he expected her to back down, stammer, run away.

Her hands curled into balls of tension. "Which would you prefer?" she parried.

His head tilted as he studied her, his eyes oddly caressing. "My bed is bigger."

"Oh," was all she could manage to whisper. Her heart crashed repeatedly against the wall of her chest, pounding the breath from her lungs.

He looked at her as if he could read her every thought and emotion. "However," he murmured, relenting, "if we retire together, I doubt that either of us would get much rest."

"P-probably not," she agreed unsteadily.

"Therefore, I suppose it would be for the best if we adhered to our usual arrangement."

"Our usual . . ."

"You go to your bed, and I'll go to mine."

Relief flooded her, leaving her weak, but at the same time she was aware of a subtle wash of disappointment. "You won't stay up late, then?" she asked.

He grinned at her perseverance. "Good God, you're tenacious. No, I won't cross you. I fear the consequences if I do." Standing back, he opened the door for her. "Miss Sydney, there is just one more thing."

Sophia paused before leaving. "Yes, sir?"

He reached for her, his hand sliding around the back of her neck. Sophia was too startled to move or breathe, her entire body stiffening as his head lowered to hers. He touched her only with his lips and with his hand at her nape, but she was as helpless as if she had been bound to him with iron chains.

There had been no time to prepare herself . . . she was defenseless and stunned, unable to withhold her response. At first his lips were gentle, exquisitely careful, as if he feared bruising her. Then he coaxed her to give him more, his mouth settling more firmly on hers. The taste of him, his intimate flavor laced with the hint of coffee, affected her like a drug. The tip of his tongue slid past her teeth in silken exploration. He tasted the interior of her mouth, stroked the slick insides of her cheeks. Anthony had never kissed her like this, feeding her rising passion as if he were layering kindling on a blaze. Devastated by his skill, Sophia swayed dizzily and clutched his hard neck.

Oh, if only he would hold her tightly and lock her full length against his . . . but he still touched her only with that one hand, and consumed her mouth with patient hunger. Sensing the force of his passion, held so securely in check, Sophia instinctively sought a way to release it. Her hands fluttered to the sides of his face, stroking the bristle of his cheeks and jaw.

Ross made a quiet sound in his throat. Suddenly he took hold of her shoulders and eased her away from his body, ignoring her whimpering protest. Sophia's gaze locked with his in a moment of searing wonder. The stillness was broken only by their panting breaths. No man had ever looked at Sophia that way, as if he could eat her with his gaze, as if he wanted to possess every inch of her body and every flicker of her soul. She was frightened by the power of her response to him, the unmentionable desires that shocked her.

Sir Ross regarded her without smiling. "Good night, Sophia."

She mumbled in reply and fled, moving as fast as possible without actually breaking into a run. Her mind swam with confusion as she returned to Bow Street No. 4. Dimly she noted that the mob was dissipating and that the street was orderly once again. Horse patrols crossed in front of the building, briskly dispersing the crowd.

As she entered the private residence, she saw that Eliza and Lucie had swept away the broken glass and were busy covering the gaping window with oilcloth. "Miss Sophia!" Eliza gasped as she saw her torn gown and disheveled hair. "What happened? Did one of those filthy rioters get hold of you?"

"No," Sophia replied distractedly. "There was a bit of a crush inside number three, but Sir Ross had it cleared away in no time." Spying the broom standing in the corner, she reached for it automatically, but the two women ushered her away, insisting that she get some rest. Reluctantly she complied, lighting a candle stub to take to her room.

Her legs were leaden as she trudged up the stairs. Upon reaching her room, she closed the door with great care and set the brass candleholder on the small bedside table.

Recollections filled her mind . . . Sir Ross's light, smiling gray eyes, the way his chest moved as he breathed, the heat of his mouth, the searing liquid pleasure of his kiss . . .

Anthony had crowed about his experience with women, his skills as a lover, but Sophia now understood that it had been only empty boasting. In the space of a few short minutes, Sir Ross had aroused her far beyond anything she had felt with Anthony . . . and he had left her with the unspoken promise of more. It was frightening, the realization that she would not be able to stay unaffected when she finally shared a bed with him. Half angry, half despairing, Sophia wondered why Sir Ross couldn't have been the portly, pompous fool she had expected him to be. He was going to make it horribly difficult for her to betray him; she would not escape the experience unscathed.

Disheartened, she changed into her night rail, brushed her hair, and washed her face in cool water. Her body was still sensitive, all her nerves clamoring for the sweet stimulation of Sir Ross's hands and lips. Sighing, she carried a candle to her window, pushing the little curtain aside. Most of Bow Street No. 3 was dark now, but lamplight shone from Sir Ross's office.

She could see the dark outline of his head as he sat at his desk.

Still working, she told herself in sudden annoyance. Was he going to renege on his promise to get some rest?

As if he sensed that she was watching, Sir Ross rose and stretched, then glanced out his window. His face was partially shadowed as he stared at her across the way. A moment later, with a mockingly deferential bow, he turned and extinguished the lamp on his desk, leaving his office in darkness.

Chapter 4

Ross questioned Nick Gentry for three days in the ruthlessly persistent style that usually wrung confessions from the most hardened characters. However, Gentry was in a different category from any other man Ross had ever encountered. He was steely and yet oddly relaxed, in the manner of a man who had nothing to fear and nothing to lose. Ross tried in vain to discern what mattered to him, what weaknesses he might have, but no information appeared to be forthcoming. For hours on end Ross engaged Gentry regarding his so-called thief-taking activities, his past, his associations with various crime gangs in London, with maddeningly little results.

Since all of London was aware of Gentry's detainment at Bow Street, and because all eyes were upon them, Ross did not dare hold the young crime lord for one minute longer than the allotted three days. On the third morning, Ross ordered Gentry's release to be effected just before dawn, at a time so early that it would prevent victorious demonstrations from the supporters who assembled every day in defense of the young perpetrator.

Containing his foul mood behind an expressionless mask, Ross went to his office without stopping for breakfast. He did not want to eat, or sit in the comforting warmth of the kitchen, or enjoy Sophia's small attentions. He wanted to sit at his desk and immerse himself in the pile of work that awaited him.

Today Sir Grant Morgan was the sitting magistrate at Bow Street, a fact for which Ross was profoundly grateful. He was in no humor to hear cases and sort through testimony and ask questions of the innocent and the guilty. He wanted to brood alone in his office.

As was his habit, Morgan came to Ross's office to talk for a few minutes before going to court. Ross welcomed his company, for Morgan was one of the few men who understood and shared Ross's determination to bring Nick Gentry down. Over the past six months, since Morgan had been promoted from the runners to serve as an assistant magistrate, he had more than justified Ross's faith in him. As a runner, Morgan had been known for his quick temper and impulsiveness, along with his intelligence and courage. Some critics had warned that he did not have a suitable temperament to become a Bow Street magistrate. "Your weakness," Ross had told him more than once, "is your habit of making up your mind too quickly, before taking all the evidence into account."

"I go with my instincts," Morgan had parried.

"Instinct is a fine thing," Ross had said dryly, "but you must stay open to all possibilities. No one's instincts are infallible."

"Not even yours?" came the pointed question.

"Not even mine."

Morgan was quickly maturing into a far more thoughtful and flexible man. As a magistrate, he was perhaps a bit more stern in his judgments than Ross, but he was careful to be excruciatingly fair. Someday when Ross retired, he would hand over the Bow Street office—and the leadership of the runners—to Morgan without a single regret. But that would be a long time from now. Ross was in no hurry to step down.

As the two men talked, there was a light knock at the door.

"Come in," Ross said curtly.

Sophia entered the room with a jug of steaming coffee. Ross tried to quell an instant surge of pleasure at the sight of her. Her slender figure was clad in a gray dress with a long-sleeved pelisse buttoned neatly over the bodice. The dark blue color of the pelisse made her eyes glow like sapphires. Her shining golden hair was mostly concealed by her bonnet—he wanted to pull the offending thing off at once.

After he had kissed her the night before last, Ross and Sophia had tacitly agreed to avoid each other. For one thing, Ross had needed to keep his focus on the necessary work of questioning Gentry. For another, it was obvious that Sophia had been unnerved by the episode. She had not been able to meet his gaze ever since, and he had seen the way her hands trembled when she served him breakfast the following morning.

Yet she had not seemed to dislike kissing him. Rather the opposite, in fact. She had responded to him with a sweetness that had been most . . . pleasing. Arousing. Ross had been surprised at first by how tentative and unschooled she had seemed. Perhaps her lover had not liked kissing, or had not been proficient at it, for there was much that Sophia had not been taught. All the same, she was the most desirable woman he had ever known.

"Good morning," Sophia said, her wary gaze going first to Morgan, then settling on Ross. She filled the empty mug on his desk. "I thought you might enjoy some freshly brewed coffee before I go out."

"Where are you going?" Ross asked, disgruntled at the realization that it was her day off.

"I am going to market, as Eliza is not able. She tripped on the stairs this morning and injured her knee. I believe it will heal quickly, but in the meantime, she must not exert herself."

"Who is going to market with you?"

"No one, sir."

"Not Lucie?"

"She has gone to visit her family in the country," Sophia reminded him. "She left yesterday morning."

Ross was entirely familiar with the Covent Garden market and the assortment of pickpockets, thieves, loose-living theater folk, and randy bucks who mingled in the arcaded square. It was not safe for a woman like Sophia to go there alone, especially when she was still so new to the city. She could be approached, raped, or robbed so damned easily that it made his heart skip a beat to think of it.

"You are not going by yourself," he informed Sophia curtly. "Every randy lout and rake in the vicinity will come to bother you."

"Eliza often goes by herself, and never has any problem."

"As I cannot reply without making an unflattering remark about Eliza, I will hold my silence on that point. However, *you* are not going to Covent Garden alone. You will take one of the runners with you."

"They're all gone," Morgan interceded, glancing from Sophia to Ross with an alert look in his eyes.

"*All* of them?" Ross asked in flaring annoyance.

"Yes. You assigned Flagstad to the Bank of England— it's time for quarterly dividends—and Ruthven is investigating a burglary, and Gee is—"

"What about Ernest?"

Morgan spread his hands in a gesture of futility. "Ernest is delivering the latest edition of the *Hue and Cry* to the printer."

Ross returned his attention to Sophia. "You will wait until Ernest returns, and he will accompany you to market."

"That won't be until midmorning," she said indignantly. "I can't wait that long—all the best goods will be gone by then. In fact, the stalls are being picked over right now."

"That is a pity," Ross said without a shred of remorse. "Because you are not going alone. That is my final word on the subject."

Sophia leaned over his desk. For the first time in two days, she met his gaze directly. Ross was conscious of a deep delight curling through him as he saw the sparks of challenge in her blue eyes. "Sir Ross, when we first met, I wondered if you had any flaws. Now I have discovered that you do."

"Oh?" He arched one brow. "What are my flaws?"

"You are overbearing, and you are unreasonably stubborn."

Morgan interrupted with a snicker. "It has taken you a full *month* of working here to reach that conclusion, Miss Sydney?"

"I am not overbearing," Ross countered evenly. "I merely happen to know what is best for everyone."

Sophia laughed and considered him thoughtfully in the silence that followed. Ross waited for her next move, fascinated by the little pucker that appeared between her fine brows. Then her forehead cleared as she appeared to reach a satisfying conclusion. "Very well, Sir Ross, I will not go to market alone. I will take the only available escort—which appears to be you. You may meet me at the front door in ten minutes."

Robbed of any reply, Ross watched as Sophia left the office. He was being managed, he thought with a twinge of annoyance, and damned adroitly, too. On the other hand, it had been a long time since any woman had tried to manage him, much less had succeeded, and for some reason he was enjoying it immensely.

As the door closed smartly behind Sophia, Morgan turned to look at Ross. His shrewd eyes were filled with speculation.

"Why are you staring like that?" Ross muttered.

"I've never seen you bicker like that before."

"I wasn't bickering. I was having a discussion."

"You were bickering," Morgan insisted, "in a way that could be construed as flirtation."

Ross scowled. "I was discussing an issue of safety, Morgan, which is vastly different from flirtation."

Morgan smiled wryly. "Whatever you say, sir."

Deliberately Ross lifted his mug of coffee and drained half of it in one swallow. Rising from his chair, he picked up his coat and put it on.

Morgan viewed him with surprise. "Where are you going, Cannon?"

Ross pushed a pile of documents across the desk to him. "To market, of course. Look over these warrants for me, will you?"

"But . . . but . . ." For the first time in Ross's memory, Morgan seemed bereft of speech. "I have to prepare for court!"

"It won't start for a quarter hour," Ross pointed out. "For God's sake, how much time do you need?" He suppressed a grin as he left the office, feeling strangely light-hearted.

* * *

Having accompanied Eliza to the Covent Garden market on a few occasions, Sophia was familiar with the famous square, two sides of which were lined with arcades called piazzas. The best flower, fruit, and vegetable stalls were located beneath these piazzas, where nobility, thieves, theater folk, writers, and strumpets mingled freely. All class distinctions seemed to vanish at Covent Garden, creating a jovial carnivallike atmosphere as business of various kinds was conducted.

Today a troupe of street entertainers wandered about the square—a pair of jugglers, a clown-faced tumbler, even a sword-swallower. Sophia watched aghast as the man slid a sword down his throat and extracted it skillfully. She flinched, expecting him to expire on the spot of internal wounds. Instead he grinned and bowed to her, deftly using his hat to catch the coin that Sir Ross tossed to him.

"How does he do it?" Sophia asked the Chief Magistrate.

He smiled into her wide eyes. "Most of the time they have previously swallowed a length of tubing that acts as a scabbard once the sword is inserted."

"Ugh." She shuddered and took his arm, tugging him toward the fruit stalls. "Let's hurry—I will be surprised if any apples are left by now."

As Sophia moved from one stall to another, Sir Ross accompanied her obligingly. He did not interfere with her transactions, only waited patiently as she bargained for the best prices and quality. He hefted the considerable weight of the market basket with ease, while she filled it with an ever-growing assortment of fruit and vegetables, a round of cheese, and a fine turbot wrapped in brown paper.

The moment the market crowd realized that the celebrated Chief Magistrate of Bow Street was present, chattering Cockney voices rose in a cheerful cacophony. The stall-holders and marketgoers held Sir Ross in high esteem, calling to him, reaching out to touch the sleeve of his coat. They all seemed to know him personally, or at least pretended to, and Sophia found many small gifts being pushed at her—an extra apple, a bundle of kippers, a sprig of sage.

"Sir Ross . . . 'ere's a relish fer ye!" was an oft-repeated phrase, and Sophia finally asked him what the cant words meant.

"A relish is a small gift, usually considered to be a luxury, as a return for a favor."

"You have done favors for all of these people?" she asked.

"Many of them," he admitted.

"Such as?"

His broad shoulders lifted in a shrug. "A few of them have sons or nephews who have run afoul of the law— thievery, vandalism, and the like. The usual punishment for such offenses is to flog a boy, hang him, or send him to a prison where he will be even further corrupted. But I had the notion to send some of these boys to the navy or merchant service, to train as officers' servants."

"And thereby give them a chance at a new kind of life," Sophia said. "What a splendid plan."

"It has worked well so far," he said offhandedly, and sought to change the subject. "Look at that table of smoked fish—do you know how to make kedgeree?"

"Certainly I do," Sophia replied. "But you haven't finished telling me about your good deeds."

"I've done nothing all that praiseworthy. I've just used a bit of common sense. It is obvious that putting a mischief-making boy in prison with hardened criminals will result in his corruption. And that even if the law makes no distinction between the crimes of adults and juveniles, some consideration must be given to those of tender age."

Sophia turned away, pretending to look over the row of stalls while blind rage consumed her. She felt almost sick with it, choking on suppressed fury and tears. So he had found a way to avoid sending young boys to prison—he no longer condemned them to the torture of the prison hulks. *Too damned late*, she thought with freshly spiking hatred. Had Sir Ross come to this realization earlier, her brother would still be alive. She wanted to scream and rail at him, at the unfairness of it. She wanted John back; she wanted to erase every excruciating moment on the prison ship that had led to his death. Instead he was gone. And she was alone. And Sir Ross was responsible.

Averting her anger-hardened face, Sophia went to a flower cart filled with a variety of blooms, including pink primroses, purple lilies, blue spired delphiniums, and fragile white camellias. She breathed in the perfumed air and forced herself to relax. Someday, she comforted herself silently, Sir Ross would have his comeuppance—and she would deliver it personally.

"Tell me," she said, bending over the fragrant blossoms, "how did a man who was born into a distinguished family come to serve as a chief magistrate?"

Sir Ross's gaze touched her profile as he replied. "My father insisted that I train for a profession, rather than lead a life of indolence. To please him, I studied the law. In the midst of my education, my father died in a hunting accident, and I left my studies to act as the head of the family. My interest in the law did not fade, however. It had become clear to me that there was much to be done in the areas of policing and judicial methods. Eventually I accepted an appointment at the Great Marlboro Street office, and soon thereafter I was asked to transfer to the Bow Street office and take over the leadership of the runners."

The old woman who stood at the head of the flower cart regarded Sophia with a smile partitioning the leathery terrain of her face.

"Good morning, dearie." She extended a little bunch of violets to Sophia and spoke to Sir Ross. "A pretty tart, she. Ye should make 'er yer trouble 'n' strife."

Sophia tucked the tiny bunch of violets in the side of her bonnet and fumbled at the little purse tied to her waist, intending to pay the wizened little woman.

Sir Ross stopped Sophia with a light touch on her

arm and gave the flower seller some coins from his own pocket. "I want a perfect rose," he told her. "Pink."

"Aye, Sir Ross." Grinning to reveal a row of broken brown teeth, the flower seller handed him a lovely, half-blooming pink rose, its petals still sparkling with morning dew.

Woodenly Sophia accepted the rose from Sir Ross and lifted it to her nose. The rich, powdery fragrance filled her nostrils. "It's lovely," she said stiffly. "Thank you."

As they walked away from the flower cart, Sophia picked her way carefully across a patch of broken pavement. She felt Sir Ross's steadying hand on her upper arm, and it took all her will to keep from shaking him off.

"Did that woman call me a tart?" she asked, wondering if she should have taken offense.

Sir Ross smiled slightly. "In street cant, that is considered a compliment. They attach no negative meaning to the word."

"I see. There was something else she said . . . what does 'trouble and strife' mean?"

"It's the Cockney term for 'wife.' "

"Oh." Uncomfortably she focused on the ground before them as they walked. "The Cockney way of speaking is quite fascinating, isn't it?" she babbled, trying to fill the silence. "Almost like a foreign language, really. I must confess, I don't understand half the things I hear at market."

"That," came his dry rejoinder, "is probably a good thing."

When they returned to the kitchen of Bow Street No. 4, Eliza was waiting, a sheepish smile on her face. "Thank you, Miss Sophia. I am sorry that I couldn't go to market."

"That's perfectly all right," Sophia said evenly. "You must take care of your knee so that it will heal properly."

Eliza's eyes widened when she saw that Sir Ross had accompanied Sophia. "Oh, sir . . . how very kind of you! I am very sorry to make so much trouble!"

"No trouble at all," he said.

Eliza's gaze locked onto the pink rose in Sophia's hand with keen attention. Although the cook-maid forbore to comment, the speculation in her eyes was obvious. Carefully Eliza lifted a few objects from the market basket and hobbled toward the dry larder. Her voice floated behind her. "Did they have all the ingredients for the seed cake, Miss Sophia? The caraway and rye, and the currants for the top?"

"Yes," Sophia replied as the cook-maid disappeared into the larder. "But we could find no red currants, and—"

Suddenly her words were smothered into silence as Sir Ross pulled her into his arms. His lips descended to hers in a kiss so tender and carnal that she could not help responding. Stunned, she struggled to retain her hatred of him, to remember the wrongs of the past, but his lips were utterly warm and compelling, and her thoughts scattered crazily. The pink rose dropped from her nerveless fingers. Sophia swayed against him, groping for his hard shoulders in a futile bid for balance. His tongue searched her mouth . . . delicious . . . sweetly intimate. Sophia inhaled sharply and tilted her head back in utter surrender, her entire existence distilled to this one burning moment.

Through the pounding heartbeat in her ears she dimly heard Eliza's concerned voice echoing from the larder. "No red currants? But what will we top the seed cake with?"

Sir Ross released Sophia's mouth, leaving her lips moist and kiss-softened. His face remained close to hers, and Sophia felt as if she were drowning in the silver pools of his eyes. His hand came to the side of her face, his fingers curving over her cheek, his thumb brushing the corner of her mouth. Somehow Sophia managed to answer Eliza. "We f-found golden currants instead—"

As soon as the words left her mouth, Sir Ross kissed her again, his tongue exploring, teasing. Her groping fingers touched the back of his neck, where the thick black hair curled against his nape. Sensation rustled through her, spurring her pulse to an intemperate pace. Taking advantage of her surrender, he kissed her more aggressively, hunting for the deepest, sweetest taste of her. As her knees weakened, his arms wrapped securely around her, supporting her body as he continued to ravish her mouth.

"Golden currants?" came Eliza's dissatisfied voice. "Well, the flavor won't be quite the same, but they will be better than nothing."

Sir Ross released Sophia and steadied her with his hands at her waist. While she stared at him blankly, he gave her a brief smile and left the kitchen just as Eliza reemerged from the larder.

"Miss Sophia, where is the sack of caster sugar? I thought I had carried it into the larder, but . . ." Eliza paused and glanced around the kitchen. "Where is Sir Ross?"

"He . . ." Sophia bent to retrieve the fallen rose. "He left."

Her pulse throbbed in all the vulnerable places of her body. She felt feverish, hungering for the kisses and caresses of a man she hated. She was a hypocrite, a wanton.

A fool.

"Miss Sydney," Ernest said, bringing a paper-wrapped package to the kitchen, "a man brought this for you not ten minutes back."

Sophia, who was sitting at the table for a midmorning cup of tea, received the large package with an exclamation of surprise. She had not made any purchases, nor had she ordered anything for the household. And the distant cousin who had taken her in sometime after her parents' death was not the kind who would send unexpected gifts. "I wonder what it could be," she murmured aloud, studying the package. Her name and the Bow Street address were written on the brown-paper surface, but there was no indication as to the sender.

"Was there a note attached?" Sophia asked Ernest. She picked up a knife and sawed at the rough twine that had been knotted around the parcel.

He shook his head. "P'rhaps there is one inside. May I open it for ye, miss? That string looks awful tough. The knife could slip, and ye might slice yer finger off. I'll 'elp ye."

Sophia smiled into his eager face. "Thank you, Ernest, that is very kind. But if I am not mistaken, didn't Sir Grant ask you to fetch the bottles of ink he ordered at the chemist's shop?"

"Yes, 'e did." Ernest heaved a world-weary sigh, as if he had been greatly put upon that day. "I'd best 'ave it 'ere when Sir Grant comes back from court."

Sophia's smile deepened as she bade him farewell. Returning her attention to the mysterious package, she expertly severed the rest of the twine and unwrapped the parcel. Layers of thin white tissue enveloped something soft and rustling. Curious, Sophia folded them back.

Her breath caught in her throat as she beheld a gown—not a plain, serviceable one like the others she owned, but made of silk and lace. It was suitable for a ball. But why would someone send such a garment to her? Her hands shook with a sudden tremor as she clawed past the gown for a note. The sender had either forgotten to include one or deliberately had not done so. She shook out the gown and stared at it in confusion. There was something familiar and disturbing about it, something that reached into the farthest corners of her memory . . .

Why, it reminded her of a gown of her mother's! As a little girl, Sophia had loved to try on her mother's dresses and shoes and jewelry, and had played princess for hours. Her favorite dress had been made of an unusual color, a gleaming silk that looked lavender in some lights, shimmering silver in others. This gown was the same rare shade, with the same low, scooped neckline and puffed sleeves trimmed with delicate white lace. However, this was not her mother's gown; it was a copy, made over in a modern style with a slightly lower waist and fuller skirts.

Profoundly troubled, Sophia folded the garment in the brown paper and rewrapped it. Who could have sent such a gift to her, and why, and was it merely a strange coincidence that the dress resembled her mother's?

Instinctively she left the kitchen and took the parcel with her, heading for the one person she trusted most. Later she would come to wonder why she had turned to Sir Ross without even thinking, when she had relied only on herself for so many years. It was a sign of some significant change in her, one that made her too uncomfortable to dwell on for long.

Sir Ross's door was closed, and the sound of voices indicated that he was in the midst of a meeting. Crestfallen, Sophia hesitated outside the door.

Just then Mr. Vickery happened to walk by. "Good morning, Miss Sydney," the court clerk said. "I don't think Sir Ross is ready to start depositions yet."

"I—I wished to speak with him on a personal matter." Sophia clutched the package tightly to her chest. "But I see that he is occupied, and I certainly do not wish to disturb him."

Vickery frowned and gave her a reflective glance. "Miss Sydney, Sir Ross has made it clear that if you ever have any concerns, he wishes to know immediately."

"It can wait," she said firmly. "It is a trivial matter. I will return later when Sir Ross is available. No, *no*, Mr. Vickery, *please* do not knock at that door." She groaned with distress as the clerk ignored her protests and rapped decisively at the portal.

To Sophia's consternation, the door opened to reveal Sir Ross accompanying a visitor to the threshold. The gray-haired gentleman was small of stature but imposing nonetheless, dressed in fine clothes with an elaborate white cravat tied over a lace-bedecked shirt. His sharp dark eyes focused on Sophia, and he turned to smile wryly at Sir Ross.

"Now I see, Cannon, why you are so eager to conclude our meeting. The company of this fetching creature is doubtless preferable to mine."

Ross's mouth quirked, and he did not deny the statement. "Good day, Lord Lyttleton. I will examine the draft of your bill most carefully. However, do not expect that my views will change."

"I want your support, Cannon," the gentleman said

in a soft, meaningful tone. "And if I receive it, you will find me a most useful friend."

"Of that I have no doubt."

They exchanged bows, and Lyttleton departed, the soles of his leather shoes making an expensive tapping sound on the worn wood floor.

Sir Ross's eyes gleamed as he stared at Sophia. "Come," he said softly, and guided her into his office. The pressure of his hand on her back was warm and light. Sophia sat in the chair he indicated, her spine straight, while he resumed his place behind the huge mahogany desk.

"Lyttleton." She repeated the name of the gentleman who had just left. "Surely that was not the same Lyttleton who is the Secretary of State for War?"

"None other."

"Oh, no," Sophia said, thoroughly flustered. "I hope I did not interrupt your meeting. Oh, I will cheerfully murder Mr. Vickery!"

Sir Ross responded with a deep chuckle. "You didn't interrupt anything. I was ready for Lyttleton to leave a half hour ago, thus your appearance was quite timely. Now, tell me why you are here. I suspect it has something to do with that parcel in your lap."

"First let me apologize for bothering you. I—"

"Sophia." He stared at her steadily. "I am always available to you. Always."

She could not seem to take her gaze from his. The air around them felt alive and sultry, like the stillness before a midsummer storm. Clumsily she leaned forward and placed the parcel on his desk. "I received this from Ernest just a little while ago. He said that a man delivered it to Bow Street and left no word as to the sender."

Sir Ross surveyed the address on the front of the package. As he pushed the brown paper aside, the lavender gown glimmered and rustled in the Spartan surroundings of the office. Sir Ross's face remained impassive, but one dark brow arched as he examined the beautiful garment.

"I don't know who could have sent it," Sophia said anxiously. "And there is something peculiar about it." She explained the resemblance between the lavender-silver gown and the one that had belonged to her mother.

When Sophia finished speaking, Sir Ross, who had listened intently, leaned back in his chair and considered her in a meditative way that she didn't quite like. "Miss Sydney . . . is it possible that the gown is a gift from your former lover?"

The thought gave Sophia a start of surprise as well as a flash of bitter amusement. "Oh, no. He has no idea that I am working here. Besides, there is no reason for him to send me a gift."

Sir Ross made a noncommittal sound and picked up a handful of the shining lavender fabric. The sight of his long fingers rubbing the delicate silk caused a peculiar flutter inside her. His thick black lashes lowered as he examined the gown; the stitching, the seams, the lace. "It is a costly garment," he said. "Well made, and of high-quality goods. But there is no dressmaker's label inside, which is unusual. I venture to guess that whoever sent the gown did not want it traced back to the modiste, who might reveal his—or her—identity."

"Then there is no way to find out who sent it?"

He looked up from the gown. "I am going to have one of the runners talk to Ernest about the messenger, as well as investigate the dressmakers who are most likely to have made this gown. The fabric is unusual—that will help to narrow the list."

"Thank you." Her hesitant smile vanished at his next question.

"Sophia, have you recently encountered any men who might have taken an interest in you? Anyone you shared a flirtation with, or spoke to at market, or—"

"No!" Sophia was not certain why the question agitated her so, but she felt her cheeks flood with heat. "I assure you, Sir Ross, I would not encourage any gentlemen that way . . . that is—" She broke off in confusion as she realized that she *had* encouraged a particular man that way—Sir Ross himself.

"It's all right, Sophia," he said quietly. "I would not blame you if you had. You are free to do as you wish."

Rattled, she spoke without thinking. "Well, I do not have a follower, and I have not behaved in a manner that might attract one. My last experience was certainly nothing I wish to repeat."

His gaze took on a wolflike alertness. "Because of the way he left you? Or is it that you found no pleasure in his arms?"

Sophia was startled that he would ask such an intimate question, and her face flamed. "I don't see that it has any bearing on the question of who sent this gown."

"It does not," he admitted. "But I am curious."

"Well, you will have to remain curious!" She struggled to restore her splintered composure. "May I leave now, sir? I have much to do, especially with Eliza being injured. Lucie has worked her fingers to the bone."

"Yes," he said brusquely. "I will have Sayer investigate the matter of the gown, and keep you informed of the developments."

"Thank you." Sophia stood and went to the door, while he followed close at her heels. He reached for the knob, but paused as Sophia spoke without looking at him. "I . . . I found no pleasure in his arms." She concentrated on the heavy oak paneling of the door. "But that was perhaps my fault more than his."

Sophia felt the hot touch of his breath against her hair, his lips hovering close to the top of her head. His nearness filled her with an ache of longing. Blindly she seized the doorknob and let herself out of the office, refusing to glance back at him.

Ross closed the door and went back to his desk, bracing his hands on the cluttered surface. He let out a tense sigh. The desire that he had kept under iron control for so long had raged in a tremendous inferno. All the force of his will, his physical needs, his obsessive nature, were now focused in one direction. Sophia. He could barely stand to be in the same room without touching her.

Closing his eyes, Ross absorbed the familiar atmosphere of the office. He had spent most of the past five years within these walls, surrounded by maps and books and documents. He had ventured out for investigations or other official business, but he always returned here, to the room that was the center of law enforcement in London. Suddenly it amazed him that he had devoted himself so completely to his work for so long.

The lavender ballgown glimmered richly on the desk. Ross imagined how Sophia would look in it . . . the color would suit her blue eyes and dark blonde hair beautifully. Who had sent it to her? He was suffused with a jealousy and violent possessiveness that astonished him. He wanted the exclusive rights to provide whatever she required, whatever would delight her.

Ross sighed heavily, trying to understand the mixture of joy and strong unwillingness that seethed inside him. He had vowed never to fall in love again. He had not forgotten how terrible it was to care so deeply for someone, to fear for her safety, to want her happiness more than his own. Somehow he would have to find a way to stop it from happening, to satisfy his boundless need for Sophia and yet keep from entrusting his heart to her.

Chapter 5

Early in the evening, when Sophia was certain that Sir Ross was away on an investigation, she solicited Lucie to help her turn the mattress on his bed and change the linens.

"Yes, miss," Lucie said, her cheeks bunching with an apologetic smile. "But it's like this, y'see. I can't stop me mitts from bleedin' ever since I scrubbed the coppers this afternoon."

"Your what? Your hands? Let me see them." Sophia inhaled sharply as she saw the poor maid's hands, so chapped from the sand-and-acid paste used to scrub pots that they were scabbed and bleeding. "Oh, Lucie, why didn't you tell me before now?" Scolding affectionately, she sat the girl at the kitchen table and went to the larder. Bringing out an assortment of bottles, she poured glycerine, elder-flower water, and oil into a bowl, then whisked the mixture briskly with a fork. "You must soak your hands in this for the next half hour, and tonight you must sleep with gloves on."

"I got none, miss."

"No gloves?" Sophia thought of her own gloves, the only pair she possessed, and she winced at the thought of sacrificing them. Immediately she felt a touch of shame as she glanced once more at the housemaid's raw hands. "Go to my room, then," she said, "and get mine from the basket beneath the night table."

Lucie stared at her in concern. "But I can't ruin yer gloves, miss."

"Oh, your hands are far more important than a silly pair of gloves."

"What about Sir Ross's mattress?"

"Never you mind about that. I'll take care of it by myself."

"But it's 'ard to turn without 'elp—"

"You sit and soak your hands," Sophia said, trying to sound stern. "Take care of them, or you'll be of no use to anyone tomorrow."

Lucie smiled at her gratefully. "No disrespect, Miss Sydney, but . . . ye're a love. A real love."

Sophia waved the words away and hurried to clean Sir Ross's bedroom before he returned. She set an armful of fresh bed linens on a chair and surveyed the room appraisingly. It had been dusted and swept, but the mattress needed turning, and Sir Ross's clothes from the previous day had still not been gathered for laundering.

The room suited Sir Ross quite well. Rich mahogany furniture was enhanced with dark green brocade upholstery and window draperies. One wall was adorned with an ancient, faded tapestry panel. A series of three framed engravings were hung on another wall, carica-tures portraying Sir Ross as a massive Olympian figure, dandling politicians and government officials on his knee as if they were children. One hand clutched the strings for a few Bow Street runner puppets, their pockets bulging with money. It was apparent that the caricatures were meant to criticize the tremendous power that Sir Ross and his runners had amassed.

Sophia well understood the source of the artist's grievance. Most Englishmen abhorred the notion of having a strong, organized police force, declaring such an arrangement to be unconstitutional and dangerous. They felt far more comfortable with the ancient parish-constable system, which called for average but un-trained citizens to serve as constables, each for the period of a year. However, the parish constables had been unable to deal with the proliferation of robbery, rape, murder, and fraud that plagued the populous city of London. Parliament had refused to authorize a true police force, so the Bow Street runners had become a law unto themselves, their powers mostly self-assumed. The only man they answered to was Sir Ross, who had made his own position far more powerful than had ever been intended.

Upon first seeing the censorious caricatures, Sophia had wondered why Sir Ross chose to hang them in his room. Now she realized that this was his way of re-minding himself that his every decision and action would come under the public scrutiny, and therefore his behavior must be above reproach.

Pushing these thoughts from her mind, Sophia stripped the linens from the huge bed. It was difficult work to turn the heavy mattress by herself, but after a great deal of huffing and puffing, she managed to settle it into place. She took pride in her ability to make a bed, stretching the sheets so tautly that one could bounce a coin off them. After smoothing the counterpane and fluffing the pillows, Sophia turned her attention to the pile of clothes on the chair. She draped the black silk cravat over one arm and picked up the discarded white linen shirt.

A pleasant, faintly earthy scent floated to her nostrils, the smell of Sir Ross's skin permeating the thin fabric. Curious, Sophia held the shirt up to her face, breathing in the fragrance of sweat and shaving soap along with the essence of a virile, healthy male. She had never found a man's scent so alluring. Despite her supposed love for Anthony, she had never really noticed such details about him. Disgusted with herself, Sophia decided that it must have been the *idea* of Anthony, the fantasy of him, that she had fallen in love with, rather than the actual man. She had wanted a fairy-tale prince to sweep her off her feet, and Anthony had obligingly played the role until it no longer suited him.

The door opened.

Startled, Sophia dropped the shirt and blanched guiltily. She was appalled to see Sir Ross enter the room, his large body clad in a black coat and trousers. Humiliation flooded her. Oh, that he should have caught her sniffing and fondling his shirt!

But Sir Ross's usual alertness seemed to have deserted him. In fact, his gaze was slightly unfocused, and Sophia realized that he hadn't noticed what she was doing. Confounded, she wondered if he had been drinking. That was not like him at all, but it was the only possible reason for the unsteadiness of his gait.

"You are back early from your investigation in Long Acre," she said. "I—I was just straightening your room."

He shook his head as if to clear it and approached her.

Sophia backed up against the dresser, staring at him in growing concern. "Are you ill, sir?"

Sir Ross reached her and clutched the dresser on either side of her. His face was bone-white, throwing the blackness of his hair and brows and lashes into startling relief. "We found the man we sought, hiding in a house on Rose Street," he said. A thick forelock fell over his pale, sweating forehead. "He climbed onto the roof . . . and jumped to the next house before Sayer could catch him. I joined in the chase . . . couldn't let him get away."

"You were chasing a man on the rooftops?" Sophia was horrified. "But that is dangerous! You could have been hurt."

"Actually . . ." Sir Ross looked sheepish, his balance wavering. "When I reached him, he pulled a pistol from his coat."

"You were shot at?" Sophia scanned his black coat

frantically. "Did he hit you? Dear God—" She ran her hands down the front of the tailored wool panels of the coat and found that the left side was cool and slippery. A stifled cry burst from her lips as her palm came away smeared with blood.

"It's just a scratch."

"Did you tell anyone?" Sophia demanded, frantically pulling him toward the bed. "Have you sent for a doctor?"

"I can tend it myself," he said testily. "A mere scratch, as I said—" He grunted with pain when Sophia tugged the coat from his shoulders and down his arms.

"Lie down!" She was horrified by the amount of blood that had stained his shirt, leaving his entire left side soaked in scarlet. Unbuttoning the garment, she lifted the fabric from his shoulder and gasped at the sight of an oozing bullet wound. "It is not a scratch, it is a *hole*. Don't you dare move. Why in God's name didn't you tell someone?"

"It is only a minor injury," he said grumpily.

Sophia snatched up the shirt from the previous day and pressed it firmly against the welling blood. Sir Ross's breath hissed between his clenched teeth.

"You obstinate man," Sophia said, stroking back the lock of hair that had adhered to his damp forehead. "You are not invulnerable, despite what you and everyone else at Bow Street seem to think! Hold this in place while I send for a doctor."

"Get Jacob Linley," he muttered. "At this time of evening he is usually across the street at Tom's."

"Tom's coffeehouse?"

Sir Ross nodded, his eyes closing. "Ernest will find him."

Sophia dashed outside the room, shouting for help. The servants appeared in less than a minute, all of them appearing thunderstruck by the information that Sir Ross had been wounded.

As the servants at Bow Street No. 4 were accustomed to emergencies of one kind or another, they were quick to respond. Ernest scampered away to locate the doctor, Eliza went in search of clean rags and linens, and Lucie ran next door to inform Sir Grant of the situation.

Sophia returned to Sir Ross, her heart pounding in fear when she saw him lying so still on the bed. Gently she took his hand away from the wad of bloodstained cloth and applied more pressure to the wound. He made a rough sound, his eyes slitting open.

"It's been years since the last time I was shot," he muttered. "Forgot how damn much it hurts."

Sophia was overwhelmed with worry. "I hope it hurts," she said vehemently. "Perhaps that will teach you not to be running about on rooftops! What possessed you to do such a thing?"

Sir Ross gave her a narrow-eyed glance. "For some reason the suspect didn't want to come down to the ground so that I could catch him more easily."

"It was my impression that the *runners* are supposed

to give chase," she replied tartly. "Whereas *you* are supposed to stay safe and tell them what to do."

"It doesn't always work that way."

Sophia bit back another sharp reply and leaned over to unfasten his cuffs. "I'm going to remove your shirt. Do you think you can manage to pull your arm from the sleeve, or shall I fetch the scissors?"

Sir Ross extended his arm in answer, and Sophia drew carefully on the cuff. She tugged the shirt away from his good side, revealing his thickly furred chest. He was more muscular than she had expected, his shoulders and chest well developed, his midriff furrowed with rows of tightly knit flesh. Sophia had never seen such an imposing masculine body. She felt her cheeks prickling with a flush as she leaned over him. Gently she slid her arm behind his neck. "I'll lift you up enough to pull the shirt away from your back," she said.

"I can do it myself." His pain-hazed silver eyes stared into hers, while his neck tightened against her arm.

"Let me do the work," she insisted, "or you will make the bleeding worse."

Slowly she lifted the weight of his head and tugged the shirt out from under him. Sir Ross's breath puffed against her chin. "When I pictured being in bed with you," he muttered, "this was not how I had envisioned it."

A surprised laugh caught in her throat. "I will overlook that remark, as you are no doubt delirious from loss of blood."

Sophia was grateful for the appearance of Eliza, who came bearing a ewer of hot water and a pile of clean, folded cloths. Sir Ross grumbled but did not move as the two women washed the bloodstains from his chest and throat.

"It appears the bullet is still in his shoulder," Eliza said pragmatically, easing away the wadded-up pad and replacing it with a fresh one. "A pity, as Dr. Linley will have to remove it. But the wound is not close to the heart."

Sophia leaned over Sir Ross and adjusted the pillow behind his head. The bullet could easily have pierced his heart, had the suspect's aim been any better. She was amazed by her reaction to the thought, the mixture of fear and anguish that engulfed her.

"I am fine," Sir Ross said gruffly, somehow reading her unspoken thoughts. "I will be up and about in a day or two."

"Oh, no, you will not," she replied. "You will stay in this bed until you are completely well again—no matter what I must do to keep you here."

Sophia was not aware that any sexual connotation could be attached to her promise until she saw the sudden glint of mockery in Sir Ross's eyes. She glared at him in silent warning, and he kept obligingly quiet, though his lips twitched in amusement. Nearby, Eliza developed a sudden interest in folding all the clean rags and cloths into tidy squares.

The tension in the room was broken by the welcome appearance of the doctor, Jacob Linley. He was lean and handsome, with gleaming blond hair and a ready smile. Sophia had heard of him before, since he was often summoned to Bow Street when medical attentions or opinions were required. However, this was the first time she had actually seen Dr. Linley.

"Cannon," he said easily, hefting a weighty brown leather bag and setting it on the bedside chair. "It seems that you had a bit of an adventure this evening." He went immediately to Sir Ross, his attention focused on the wound. "Hmm. A percussion cap shot at fairly close range, judging from the peppering around the wound. How did it happen?"

Sir Ross frowned slightly. "I joined in the pursuit of a murder suspect."

"He chased him across a rooftop," Sophia added, unable to hold her silence.

The doctor turned toward her. His hazel eyes contained a friendly twinkle. "A rooftop, you say? Well, I think that Sir Ross had better stay on the ground from now on, don't you?"

Sophia responded with a vigorous nod.

Still smiling, Dr. Linley made a brief but elegant bow. "I presume you are Miss Sydney, the assistant I have heard so much of? I admit that I thought the runners' rapturous descriptions of you were exaggerated. Now I see that they were in fact understating the case."

Before Sophia could reply, Sir Ross's sour voice came from the bed. "Are you going to prattle all evening, Linley, or are you going to remove this bullet?"

The doctor winked at Sophia and then turned businesslike. "I'll need a large ewer of scalding-hot water, some good, strong soap, a pot of honey, and a glass of brandy. And I will require more light in here."

Sophia hurried to fetch the required articles, and Eliza brought lanterns and candles.

By the time Sophia had returned from the kitchen, the room was ablaze as if it were midday. She arranged the ewer, soap, honey, and brandy neatly on the washstand. Going to the bedside, she saw the doctor carefully wiping a few silver instruments with a felt cloth.

Linley smiled at her obvious interest. "A wound is not as likely to turn putrid and malodorous if it is kept clean, although no one can explain why this is so. Therefore I keep my instruments and my hands as immaculate as possible."

"What is the honey for?"

"It makes an excellent wound dressing and seems to promote healing. It also keeps the tissue from sticking to the cloth when the dressing is changed."

"And the brandy?"

"I asked for that because I'm thirsty," Linley replied cheerfully, and took an appreciative swallow of the vintage. "Now, Miss Sydney, after I wash my hands, I am going to probe for the bullet—an unpleasant procedure which will make Sir Ross swear like a sailor. I advise that you wait in another room if you possess a weak stomach."

"I do not," Sophia said at once. "I wish to stay."

"Very well." Linley picked up a long, slender probe

and sat at the bedside. "Try to hold still," he warned Sir Ross quietly. "If it becomes too uncomfortable, I can send for Sir Grant to help hold you down—"

"I won't move," Ross assured him testily.

At the doctor's bidding, Sophia held a lamp over his shoulder. She kept her gaze on Sir Ross's taut face rather than on Dr. Linley's diligent handiwork. The only sign of the pain he must have felt was an occasional twitch of a muscle in his cheek, or a slight catch of his breath as the probe dug deeper. Finally the implement clicked against the bullet, which had lodged against a bone.

"There it is," Linley said calmly, a mist of perspiration causing his face to gleam. "It's a pity you have such a strong constitution, Cannon. You'd have done better to faint before I extract this thing."

"I never faint," Ross muttered. His gaze hunted for Sophia's face, and she smiled reassuringly into his pain-darkened eyes.

"Miss Sydney," Linley murmured, "hold this probe exactly as it is positioned, and do not alter the angle."

"Yes, sir." She complied instantly, and he reached for a delicate two-pronged instrument that looked like a pair of pincers.

"Steady hands," he remarked admiringly, resuming possession of the probe. Deftly he began to extract the bullet. "And a pretty countenance to boot. If you ever tire of working at Bow Street, Miss Sydney, I am going to hire you as *my* assistant."

Before Sophia could reply, Sir Ross interceded. "No," he growled. "She's mine." And with that he promptly fainted, the inky sweep of his lashes fanning his pale cheeks.

Chapter 6

*W*ith the removal of the lead slug from Sir Ross's shoulder, an alarming gush of bright red blood came forth. Sophia bit her lip as she watched Dr. Linley press a clean pad to the wound. The low growl of Sir Ross's words *She's mine* seemed to hang in the air. Lamely Sophia sought to explain away the phrase. "H-how kind of Sir Ross to express his appreciation of my work."

"That was not what he meant, Miss Sydney," Dr. Linley replied dryly, still focusing on his work. "Believe me, I understood quite well what he was expressing."

When the doctor finished applying a dressing to Sir Ross's shoulder, he glanced first at Sophia, then at Eliza, who was gathering a pile of soiled rags to be washed. "Who will be looking after Sir Ross?"

The question was greeted with silence as the two women glanced at each other. Sophia bit her lip, desperately wanting to take care of him. At the same time, she was alarmed by the awful tenderness that welled inside her. The revulsion she had once felt toward Sir

Ross was crumbling steadily. It seemed impossible to fortify her hatred, and that realization filled her with despair. *I'm sorry, John,* she thought bleakly. *I am failing you. You deserve better than this.* But for now, she was going to set aside her plans for vengeance. She had no choice. Later she would think about it all, and decide what to do.

"I will look after him," Sophia said. "Give me your instructions, Dr. Linley."

He answered readily. "The dressing must be changed twice a day. Apply it to the wound bed just as you saw me do tonight. If you notice a purulent drainage or foul odor, or if the shoulder turns red and swollen, send for me. Also, if the area right around the wound becomes hot to the touch compared to the surrounding skin, I will wish to know immediately." He paused to smile at Sir Ross, who was beginning to stir and blink. "Serve him the usual sickroom pap—beef tea, milk toast, mulled eggs—and for God's sake, limit his coffee so that he will rest." Still smiling, Linley bent to place a hand on Sir Ross's good shoulder. "I'm done with you tonight, my friend, though I will return in a day or two to torment you further. Now I will go tell Sir Grant that he is allowed to see you. I suspect he is waiting most impatiently downstairs."

The doctor left the room, his footsteps quiet for such a tall man. "What a pleasant gentleman," Sophia remarked.

"Yes," Eliza agreed with a chuckle, "and Dr. Linley is unmarried as well. Many fine ladies in London want his services, both professional and personal. Whoever brings him to scratch will be a lucky woman."

"What do you mean by personal services?" Sophia asked, perplexed. "Surely you are not referring to—"

"Oh, yes," the cook-maid said slyly. "They say Dr. Linley is skilled in the bedroom arts as well as—"

"Eliza," Sir Ross interrupted grumpily, "if you must engage in prurient gossip, please do it in a room where I am not forced to listen." He scowled at both women, his gaze settling on Sophia. "Surely there is something better for the two of you to discuss than 'bedroom arts.'"

Sophia's laughing gaze met Eliza's. "He is quite right," she said. "We should not lower ourselves to gossip in front of Sir Ross." She paused before adding mischievously, "You can tell me the rest about Dr. Linley when we're in the kitchen."

As the ache in his shoulder subsided to a continuous pain, Ross accepted Sophia's help in undressing. He did as much as possible by himself, but the effort soon exhausted him. By the time she had settled a white linen nightshirt over his head and helped to guide his injured arm through the sleeve, he was sore and depleted. "Thank you," he muttered, settling back against the pillows with a grunt of pain.

Sophia straightened the covers and brought them to his midriff. Her gaze searched his, her eyes dark with concern and some other, unfathomable emotion. "Sir Grant is waiting just outside the door. Will you see him now, or shall I tell him to return later?"

"I'll see him." A sigh escaped Ross. He did not want to talk with Morgan or anyone else. He wanted silence, peace, and Sophia's gentle presence beside him.

Instinctively she began to reach for him, then hesitated. Not for the first time, Ross sensed her inner struggle, a conflict between intimacy and repulsion, as if she were determined to deny herself something she wanted badly. She extended her hand to stroke his forehead and smooth back his hair with cool fingertips. "Don't talk with him for long," she murmured. "You need to rest. I will return soon with a supper tray."

"I'm not hungry."

She ignored his words as she left, and Ross grinned ruefully at the sure knowledge that she was not going to desist until he ate something.

Sir Grant Morgan entered the bedroom, ducking his head beneath the doorframe. His gaze flickered over Ross, lingering at the bulky shape of the wound dressing at his shoulder. "How are you?" he asked quietly, lowering himself to the bedside chair.

"Never better," Ross said. "The injury is trifling. I'll be back at work by tomorrow, or the next day at the latest."

For some reason Morgan laughed gruffly. "Damn you, Cannon. I'd like to know what *you* would say to *me*, had I taken the foolish risk that you did this evening."

"If I hadn't joined in the pursuit, Butler would have gotten away."

"Oh, yes," Morgan said sardonically. "Sayer said you

were a hell of an impressive sight. According to him, you climbed up to the roof like a damned cat and followed Butler right over to the next building. A five-foot jump between parapets, with certain death awaiting if you lost your footing. And after Butler fired, no one knew you'd been hit, because you kept going until you caught him. Sayer claims you're a bloody hero." Morgan's tone made it clear that he did not agree with the assessment.

"I did not fall," Ross pointed out, "and all has ended well. Let it rest at that."

"Let it rest?" Although Morgan was still controlling his temper fairly well, his face was covered with a betraying flush. "What right have you to risk your life in such a manner? Do you know what would become of Bow Street if you had died tonight? I need not remind you of all the people who would be only too happy to use your demise as an excuse to dismantle the runners and turn the whole of London over to private thief-takers and crime lords such as Nick Gentry."

"You wouldn't let that happen."

"I couldn't stop it," Morgan countered. "I haven't your skills, your knowledge, or your political influence— not yet, at any rate. Your death would jeopardize everything we've worked for—and that you should risk so much because of a *woman*, for God's sake—"

"What did you say?" Ross demanded. "You think I went on that rooftop because of a woman?"

"Because of Miss Sydney." Morgan's unwavering green eyes focused on him. "You've changed since she's come here, and tonight is a prime example of that. Although I won't pretend to understand what you're thinking—"

"Thank you," Ross muttered darkly.

"—it is clear that you are struggling with some problem. My guess is that it stems from your interest in Miss Sydney." The hard planes of Morgan's face relaxed as he viewed Ross with a perceptive gaze. "If you want her, take her," he said quietly. "God knows she would have you. That fact is obvious to everyone."

Ross brooded and made no reply. He was not the most self-aware of men, preferring to examine other people's motives and emotions in lieu of his own. To his uncomfortable surprise, Ross realized that Morgan was correct. He had indeed acted recklessly, out of frustration and yearning and perhaps even a strain of guilt. It seemed so long ago that his wife had died, and the pain he had carried for five years had faded. Lately there had been days at a time when he didn't even think about her, yet he had sincerely loved Eleanor. However, the memories had become distant and pale ever since Sophia had entered his life. Ross could not remember if he had felt this passionately about his wife. Surely it was indecent to compare them, but he couldn't help it. Eleanor, so willowy, pale, fragile. . . . and Sophia, with her golden beauty and feminine vitality.

He turned an expressionless face to Grant Morgan. "My interest in Miss Sydney is my own concern," he said flatly. "And as for my somewhat precipitous actions this evening, from now on I will try to limit my activities to those of a more cerebral nature."

"And leave the thief-taking to the runners—as *I* have learned to do," Morgan said sternly.

"Yes. However, I wish to correct you on one point—I am not irreplaceable. The time is not long in coming when you will easily be able to fill my shoes."

Morgan grinned suddenly, glancing down at his own gigantic feet. "Perhaps you're right. It's the fellow who has to fill *my* shoes who will have the most difficulty."

A light tap came at the door, and Sophia entered cautiously. She looked tousled and tempting, her hair coming loose from its pins. She carried a small tray with a covered dish, and a glass of what appeared to be barley water. Despite Ross's weariness, he felt his spirits surge in her presence.

Sophia smiled pleasantly at Morgan. "Good evening, Sir Grant. If you would like some supper, it would be no trouble to bring up another tray."

"No, thank you," Morgan replied pleasantly. "I will return home to my wife, as she is expecting me." Bidding them both good-bye, Morgan made to depart. He paused at the door, his gaze meeting Ross's over Sophia's head. "Consider what I said," he remarked meaningfully.

The pain in Ross's shoulder made rest difficult. He woke frequently and considered taking a spoonful of the opiate syrup that had been left on his night table.

But he rejected the idea, for he disliked being muddle-headed. He thought of Sophia sleeping a few rooms away, then conjured up a number of excuses he might use to summon her to his bedside. He was bored and uncomfortable, and he wanted her. The only thing that kept him from calling for her was his understanding that she needed to rest.

When dawn crept timidly over the city and sent its weak gray light through the half-open curtains, Ross was relieved to hear sounds of people stirring in the house. Sophia's light tread as she went to Ernest's tiny attic room to awaken him . . . the housemaids carrying coal pails and lighting the grates . . . Eliza's broken footsteps as she headed toward the kitchen.

Finally Sophia entered the bedroom, her face scrubbed and glowing, her hair pulled back in a thick plait that had been coiled and pinned at the nape of her neck. She carried a tray of supplies, set them on the night table, and came to the bedside.

"Good morning." Gently she laid her hand on his forehead, then pressed it against the beard-roughened space beneath his jawbone. "You're a bit feverish," she observed. "I will change the wound dressing, then have the maids fill a tepid bath. Dr. Linley said that a bath was acceptable as long as you don't get the bandages wet."

"Are you going to help me bathe?" Ross asked, enjoying the sudden tide of color that washed over her face.

"My nursing duties do not extend that far," Sophia replied primly, although amusement tugged at the corners of her lips. "If you require assistance with your bath, Ernest will provide it." She stared at him closely, apparently fascinated by the sight of his dark-stubbled face. "I've never seen you unshaven before."

Ross rubbed a hand over his scratchy jaw. "In the mornings I'm as prickly as a hedgehog."

She considered him appraisingly. "You look rather dashing, actually. Like a pirate."

He watched as Sophia busied herself, drawing the curtains aside to admit fresh daylight, pouring hot water into a washbasin, and carefully washing her hands. Although she tried to appear matter-of-fact about the situation, it was evident that she was not accustomed to being alone with a man in his bedroom. She did not quite meet his eyes when she returned to the bedside and laid out the materials for the new dressing.

"Sophia," he murmured, "if you are uncomfortable . . ."

"No," she said earnestly, her gaze flying to his. "I want to help you."

Ross could not suppress a mocking smile. "Your face is red."

The blush remained, but a dimple appeared in her cheek while she uncovered the pot of honey and drizzled the amber liquid onto a square of felt. "If I were you, Sir Ross, I would not tease someone who is about to doctor you."

Ross fell obligingly silent as she reached for the buttons on his nightshirt and began to unfasten them. With every inch of hair-matted chest that was revealed, the telltale color bloomed brighter in Sophia's face. She worked carefully, fumbling a little with the buttons. Ross became absurdly aware of the sound of his breathing. He fought to keep the movement of his lungs slow and regular, although his pulse had shot into a hard-driven rhythm. He could not remember the last time a woman had undressed him. It seemed the most erotic experience he'd ever had, Sophia leaning over him in the silent room, her brow puckered with concentration. The scent of honey hung in the air, mingling with Sophia's fresh, feminine smell.

She freed the last carved bone button of his night-shirt and tugged it to the side, exposing his bandaged shoulder. Sophia glanced at the expanse of his bare chest, but her face did not reveal her reaction. Ross wondered if she preferred a man to be smooth-chested. Her lover had been fair-haired and quoted poetry . . . well, *he* was as dark as a satyr, and he was damned if he could remember a single line of verse. He stirred uncomfortably, the atmosphere becoming heated and tense. The weight of the covers concealed his lower half, but even so, his rising erection made a distinct hill that Sophia would easily notice if she happened to glance in the right direction.

Ross heard the sudden unsteadiness of her breathing as she began on the bandage, reaching beneath his shoulder to discover the tucked-in end of the cloth. All at once it became too much for him—the soft, fragrant woman, the bed, his own half-naked condition. His intellect was vanquished by primitive male urges. He was filled with the need to take, to claim, to master. He made a gruff sound and caught Sophia around the waist and tugged her onto the bed with him.

She gasped as he half rolled and pinned her beneath him. "*Oh* . . . Sir Ross, what . . ." Her hands came up to his chest, fluttering like a panicked bird's wings. She wanted to push him away, but she did not want to injure his shoulder further. "I-I don't want to hurt you—"

"Then don't move," he said huskily, and lowered his head.

He caught her lips with his, searching for the deepest taste of her. At first Sophia seemed paralyzed. He savored the delicate fire of her mouth, angling his lips, the kiss turning wet and supple. She moaned and surrendered almost magically, kissing him as if she wanted to consume him.

Her voluminous skirts mounded between them, and he tugged at them impatiently, then slid his leg between hers. Her felt her fingers on his chest, stroking through the black curls, finding the bed of muscle beneath.

That touch, simple as it was, gave him a pleasure akin to agony. Hungrily Ross took his mouth from hers and kissed the side of her throat, moving from the hollow beneath her ear to the juncture of her neck and shoulder. She arched against him, her eyes closed, her face flushed. "S-someone will come—"

"No one is coming," he said, distracting her with kisses while his fingers moved urgently along the buttons of her gown. "If someone approaches, I'll hear the floor creak."

While she lay gasping beneath him, he parted her gown and pulled at the ribbon of her chemise. His large hand slid between the gaping muslin seams and found incredibly soft skin, the tender curve of her breast. He circled his thumb over the fragile peak until it hardened into a rosy point.

Sophia turned her face into his throat, her frantic breaths striking his skin. "Ross . . ."

The sound of his name on her lips was wildly exciting. Ross bent his head over her chest. Using the tip of his tongue, he traced a damp circle around the fragile edge where the pink of her nipple met the paleness of surrounding skin. The little bud turned darker, harder, and Sophia's entire body stiffened. Slowly he licked the crest in luxurious strokes that caused her to lift higher against him.

"Please . . ." Her hands clasped the back of his head, urging him downward. "Please, Ross."

"Do you want more?"

"Yes. Do it again, *oh, yes*—"

She whimpered as he bent and took her nipple into his mouth. He sucked steadily, nibbled with his teeth, while his fingers toyed with the hardening peak of her other breast. Sophia's fingers tangled in his hair, and she brought his head back to hers. She kissed him with an almost shocking intensity, as if nothing existed except the two of them on this bed. Her hands wandered over his back, exploring every plane and rise of muscle.

"Sophia," Ross said raggedly. "How many lonely years I've waited for you."

Her dazed blue eyes stared into his, her pupils dilating as she felt him pulling up the mass of her skirts. He found the shape of her knee, the tight band of the garter holding up her stockings, the frayed edge of her muslin drawers. His palm swept upward, locating the springy cushion at the top of her thighs. The hair prickled softly against the muslin, and Ross cupped her tenderly before moving to the curve of her belly. He found the tapes of her drawers, pulled them loose, and eased his hand beneath the layer of fabric. He pressed words of reassurance against her skin, his fingertips trailing into the damp triangle between her thighs. "So beautiful, Sophia, so sweet . . . how soft you are. Open for me. Yes."

Carefully he parted the swollen folds and stroked a gentle fingertip between them. Sophia jolted against him, and his hand stilled inside her drawers. "No, no," he whispered, "I won't hurt you. Let me."

He kissed her for a long time until she relaxed once more, and his fingers slid back between her legs. This time she did not resist. He brushed kisses across her parted lips, then moved to her ear and caught the delicate lobe in his teeth. "I want to make love to you," he murmured.

She hid her face against his neck while his hand continued to play softly. "Yes," she said, and burst into tears.

The sudden outbreak of emotion stunned him. Deducing that she was afraid, that she thought this experience would end as the last one had, he cradled her in his arms and kissed the salty wet curve of her cheek. His voice was rough with remorse. "Don't cry. Do you want to wait? It's all right, Sophia."

She held onto him with surprising strength, recklessly pressing her body against his. "I don't want to wait. Do it now. *Now.*"

The blonde curls pushed impatiently against his hand, inflaming him, and he responded with a groan of need. He inserted his finger into the opening of her body and thrust deep, while her saturated flesh clasped his knuckle. Sophia sobbed and squirmed, her mouth pressing against his neck in hot, open kisses. His finger withdrew from the tender folds between her thighs, and she jerked against him with a protesting cry. "Easy," he whispered. "Be patient, sweetheart."

"Please," she whimpered. "I need you. Please."

The shaft of his cock bobbed heavily as he settled himself atop her. He pushed the taut crest against her lush curls, his heart pounding fiercely as he began to enter her. "Put your arms around me," he said hoarsely.

Suddenly he heard a quiet sound . . . the betraying creak of the hallway floor, indicating that someone was walking toward his bedroom.

Savagely Ross considered killing whoever it was. After years of waiting, he had finally found his woman, his mate, and she was in his bed. He was in no mood to be interrupted. He rolled onto his side, and vicious pain knifed through his shoulder. He welcomed the excruciating ache, since it helped to distract him from the tormenting throb of his loins.

Sophia clung to him desperately. "Don't stop, don't, don't—"

Ross pulled her close and crushed his lips against her forehead. When he could manage to speak, his voice was raw with frustration. "Sophia, someone is coming. The door is unlocked. If you don't want to be seen with me like this, you have to get out of bed."

It took several seconds for her to comprehend his words. Abruptly the blood drained from her face. She clambered out of bed in a panicked flurry of sheets, covers, and rumpled skirts.

Jerking the sheets up to his waist, Ross rolled onto his stomach. He smothered a grunt of fury against the mattress. As he willed his tremendous erection to subside—without success—he heard the sounds of Sophia adjusting her clothing. She rushed to the washstand and began to make a great show of washing her hands, as if she had been busy preparing to change the wound dressing.

A quick knock came at the door, and Ernest's cheerful face appeared. The boy was oblivious to the thick tension in the room. "Good morning, Sir Ross! Eliza sent me to tell ye that yer mother will arrive soon. A footman just brought word o' it."

"Wonderful," Ross said through his clenched teeth. "*Thank you*, Ernest."

"Ye're welcome, sir!"

The errand boy scampered away, the door yawning wide open in his wake.

Ross lifted his head to stare at Sophia, who refused

to turn and face him. The splashing of her hands ceased, and she spoke while staring into the turbulent water. "I-I've just realized that it would make more sense for me to change your bandage after you bathe. I will send Ernest up with some breakfast, and Lucie will fill the hip bath."

"Sophia," he said softly. "Come here."

She ignored the command and fled, her high-pitched voice floating behind her. "I'll return soon . . ."

Despite his acute frustration, Ross could not prevent a rumble of moody laughter in his chest. "Go, then," he said, dropping his head back on the pillow. "You can't avoid me forever."

Sophia raced to her room and shut the door, her heart pounding so violently that her chest ached. "Oh, God," she whispered. She wandered dreamlike to the small, rectangular looking glass on her dresser. Her hair was disheveled, her lips swollen. There was a scrape on the side of her throat. Touching it with curiosity, Sophia realized that the abrasion had been made by the bristle of Sir Ross's night-beard. How strange it was that her skin had been marked by a man's kisses, a physical sign of how utterly he had claimed her.

Laying her forearms on the dresser-top, Sophia closed her eyes and groaned. She had never felt so tortured, her body feverish with unfulfilled desire, her heart aching with the knowledge that she was a weak-willed traitor. Once Ross had started kissing her, she had yielded without another thought. She had intended to become his lover, but her wish for revenge had undergone a devastating reversal. She no longer wanted to punish him, no matter how much he deserved it. She wanted to love him, to give him every part of herself . . . and that would result not in his destruction, but in her own.

When Ross was finished with breakfast and his bath, Sophia ventured upstairs once more. He was back in bed, looking impatient, his fingers delving into the newly changed bed linens. She was transfixed by the sight of him shaved and damp, his hair brushed back, his skin tan against the snowy white pillows. The blue-gray velvet of his dressing robe made his eyes look like distilled moonlight.

He met her gaze without smiling. "I don't know how much more of this I can stand," he muttered.

At first Sophia thought he was referring to the intimacy between them, and she colored deeply. Then she realized that he was chafing at his bedridden condition. "The extra rest will benefit you," she said. "You do not spend enough time in bed."

"You could remedy that."

"I meant *sleeping*." A nervous laugh escaped her. "Sir Ross, if you insist on embarrassing me, I will have to ask Eliza to change your dressing."

"No, don't." His lips twitched with a faint smile. "I'll be good."

He kept his promise, remaining still while she applied a new dressing. Sophia frowned as she finished her handiwork, having noticed that the wound looked red and swollen, although there was no sign of foul drainage. She touched Ross's forehead, which felt dry and hot. "Your fever is a bit higher than before. How do you feel?"

"I want to get out of bed and do something."

Sophia shook her head. "You'll stay there until Dr. Linley advises otherwise. In the meanwhile, I think that you should not allow your visitors to tire you."

"Good," he said wryly. "That will be a convenient excuse to get rid of my family, or they'll sit here and gabble all day."

"Shall I prepare some refreshments?" she asked.

"God, no. That will keep them here longer."

"Yes, sir." Although Sophia did not look at Ross, she felt his intent gaze on her.

"Sophia," he asked quietly, "what is the matter?"

She forced her lips into a bright, stiff smile. "Nothing!"

"About what happened earlier—"

To Sophia's intense relief, he was interrupted by the sound of footsteps and the hum of animated voices in the hall. Suddenly Eliza appeared in the doorway. "Sir Ross," she said, "Mrs. Cannon and Master Matthew have arrived—"

"Darling!" A tall, gray-haired woman swished past Eliza and went to the bedside. Her slim body was clad in a gown of sea-green silk; a hint of exotic perfume drifted in her wake. As her long hand caressed the side of Ross's face, the jeweled rings on her fingers glittered richly. Withdrawing to a corner of the room, Sophia viewed Mrs. Catherine Cannon with discreet interest. Ross's mother was not precisely a beauty, but she was so stylish and self-possessed that the overall effect was dazzling.

Ross murmured something to his mother, and she laughed as she sat on the edge of the bed. "Darling boy, I expected to find you gaunt and pale," she exclaimed. "Instead you look as well as I've ever seen you. Why, you've gained weight—almost a stone! It becomes you."

"You may thank Miss Sydney for that," Ross commented, his gaze finding Sophia. "Come forward—I want to introduce you to my mother."

Sophia remained in the corner but curtsied deferentially, giving Catherine a shy smile. "How do you do, Mrs. Cannon?"

The woman sent her a look of friendly scrutiny. "What a charming young woman," she remarked, glancing at Ross with an arched brow. "Rather too pretty to work at a place such as Bow Street."

"Indeed," came a sardonic voice from the doorway. "One wonders at my saintly brother's motives in hiring such a comely wench."

Ross's younger brother, Matthew, stood there in a practiced pose, his weight resting on one leg, his shoulder lodged against the frame. One could easily see the physical resemblance between the two men, who shared the same dark coloring and long, powerful forms. However, Matthew's features were less angular than Ross's, his nose smaller, his chin less defined. Per-

haps some women would call Matthew the more handsome of the two, for he retained a boyishness that gave
him a certain engaging quality. However, Sophia
thought that he looked like a half-baked version of his
older brother. Ross was utterly a man, elegant and seasoned and hard. Matthew was a callow imitation.

Glancing at the insolent pup in the doorway, Sophia
inclined her head in the slightest of nods. "Mr. Cannon," she murmured.

Ross viewed his brother with a frown. "Stop gaping,
Matthew, and come into the room. Where is your wife?"

His mother answered. "Poor Iona has a head cold,
and she was afraid of making you ill. She sends her
wishes for your swift recovery."

Skirting the edge of the room, Sophia curtsied once
more. "I will afford you some privacy," she murmured.
"Please ring if you need anything, Sir Ross."

As Sophia left the room, Ross glanced speculatively at
his brother. He didn't like the way Matthew had referred to her, or the way he had looked at her. Exasperated, he wondered when Matthew would stop viewing
every woman he met as a potential conquest.

Although Matthew's wife, Iona, was a lovely girl, it
was clear that he had not abandoned his interest in
other women. Whether he had ever slept with someone
outside his marriage was still open to speculation. But
if there was one thing that might possibly have kept
him in line, it was the sure knowledge that Ross would
not treat his infidelity lightly. Ross managed the finan-

cial affairs for the entire Cannon family, and he kept his younger brother on an allowance. If Ross ever had proof of Matthew's infidelity, he would not hesitate to discipline him with all the means at his disposal, including the swift tightening of the purse strings.

"How long has *she* worked here?" Matthew asked.

"Approximately two months."

"Rather inappropriate, is it not, for you to hire a woman like that? You know what people will say—that she is servicing you in more ways than one."

"Matthew," their mother protested in bewilderment, "such insinuations are not necessary."

Matthew responded with a smirk. "Mother, there are certain things a man knows just by looking at a woman. It is obvious that underneath Miss Sydney's exterior, she is a common slut."

Ross found it difficult to contain a flare of fury. His hand clenched around a wad of the bed linens. "You've always been a poor judge of character, Matthew. I'd advise you to keep your mouth shut—and remember that you are a married man."

Matthew stared at him warily. "What the bloody hell do you mean by that?"

"I mean that you seem to have taken an undue interest in my assistant."

"I have *not*," came Matthew's indignant reply. "I merely said—"

"Both of you, cease, I beg you," Catherine intervened with a startled laugh. "It distresses me to no end to hear you argue."

Ross shot an iron-cold glance at his brother. "I will not allow Matthew to insult the members of my household."

Matthew responded with a glare. "Tell me, what *is* your relationship with Miss Sydney, that you come to her defense so readily?"

Before Ross could reply, Catherine made an irritated sound. "Matthew, I am convinced that you are deliberately trying to annoy Ross! His relationship with Miss Sydney is his own concern, not ours. Now, wait outside the room, please, and let us have a few moments of peace."

"Gladly," Matthew replied in a surly tone. "I have never been much for the sickroom anyway."

As soon as he exited the room, Catherine leaned forward intently. "Now, Ross, what *is* your relationship with Miss Sydney?"

Ross could not restrain a burst of laughter. "You just said that was my own concern!"

"Well, yes, but I am your mother, and I have a right to know if you have taken an interest in someone."

He grinned at her avid curiosity. "I admit to nothing."

"*Ross,*" she protested. She rolled her eyes and smiled. "Well, it has been a long time since I have heard you laugh. I was beginning to think you had forgotten how. But really, dear . . . a servant? When you could have your pick of all the well-bred heiresses in England?"

Ross met her gaze directly, aware that the very idea of marrying a member of one's household staff was considered an appalling social transgression. Sexual liaisons with servants were acceptable, but a gentleman would never marry one. Ross did not give a damn. Years of interacting with everyone from royalty to the poverty-stricken had shown him that the class consciousness of his own society was sheer hypocrisy. He had seen that noblemen were capable of committing foul crimes, and that even the lowest street scavengers sometimes behaved with honor.

"Miss Sydney is a viscount's daughter," he told his mother. "Though I wouldn't care if her father had been a rag seller."

His mother made a face. "I fear that working so long at Bow Street has given you some rather democratic sensibilities." Clearly, the remark was not intended as a compliment. "However . . . a viscount's daughter? One could do worse, I suppose."

"You're making assumptions, Mother," Ross said dryly. "I haven't said that I have any intentions toward her."

"But you do," she returned smugly. "A mother knows these things. Now, tell me how a young woman of supposedly good blood has come to work at Bow Street."

His eyebrows arched into sardonic crescents. "Aren't you going to ask about my wound?"

"I vow to give you *another* wound if you do not tell me more about Miss Sydney!"

Chapter 7

Sophia did not come to Ross's room for several hours after his mother and brother had left. He fretted impatiently, wondering what menial tasks took precedence over him. She sent Lucie upstairs with his supper tray and medicine, as well as some reading materials to divert him. However, he had no appetite, and his head had begun to hurt. As the sun set and the walls darkened, Ross tossed and turned in the stuffy room. He was dry and hot and he ached everywhere, especially in his shoulder. Most maddening of all, he felt isolated. The rest of the world was carrying on without him, while he was confined to a sickbed. Awkwardly he stripped off his nightshirt and lay with the sheets pulled up to his waist, stewing in annoyance.

By the time Sophia appeared at the hour of eight, Ross was surly and exhausted, lying facedown on the mattress despite the pain it caused him.

"Sir Ross?" She turned up the lamp a bit. "Are you asleep? I've come to change your bandage."

"No, I'm not asleep," he grumbled. "I'm hot and my shoulder aches, and I'm tired of lying in this accursed bed."

She leaned over and felt his forehead. "Still feverish. Here, let me turn you over. No wonder your shoulder hurts, when you are resting on it like that." Her slender but strong arms helped him to lift up. Ross flopped over with a disgruntled sound, the sheets slipping down to his hips. Keeping an arm behind his neck, Sophia brought a glass to his lips, and he drank the cold, sweetened barley water in gulps. Her fresh scent seemed to cut through the stale atmosphere of the room.

"Who closed the windows?" she asked.

"My mother did. She says the outside air is bad for a fever."

"I don't think the night air will do you any harm." She went to open the windows and admit a refreshing breeze.

Ross leaned back against the pillows, relishing the relief from the stifling sickroom climate. "You've been gone all day," he said testily. He pulled the bed linens back up to his chest, wondering if she realized that he was naked beneath. "What have you been doing?"

"The girls and I cleaned the kitchen range and flues, and blackened the ironwork, and then we did some laundering and mending. Then I spent the rest of the afternoon making currant jam with Eliza."

"Let Eliza take care of those things tomorrow. You stay with me."

"Yes, sir," Sophia murmured, smiling at his autocratic tone. "If you wanted my company, you had only to ask."

Ross scowled and remained silent as she changed the dressing on his shoulder. His aggravation was soothed by the sight of Sophia's serene face, the dark lashes screening her blue eyes as she concentrated on her task. Remembering the sweet fire of her response, Ross felt a glow of triumph. Despite her fears, she had been willing to let him make love to her. He would not press the issue now, not until he was well again. But then . . . oh, then . . .

Sophia finished tying the ends of the bandage and dipped a cloth into a bowl of water. "No signs of festering," she said, wringing out the cloth. "I think the wound is healing. Perhaps your fever will break soon, and then you will be more comfortable."

The cool cloth moved over his hot face and forehead. A breeze from the window fanned across his damp skin, making him shiver in enjoyment. "Are you cold?" came Sophia's gentle voice.

Ross shook his head, his eyes closed. "No," he whispered. "Don't stop. That feels good."

She moistened the cloth again. He let out a slow breath while the coolness glided over his throat and chest. How long had it been since anyone had taken care of him? He couldn't remember. Steeped in gratitude, he listened to Sophia's lilting voice as she hummed a tune. "Do you know the words to that?" he asked drowsily.

"Some of them."

"Sing them to me."

"My voice is not distinguished," she said. "You will be sadly disappointed if you expect anything beyond the mediocre."

He caught at the slim fingers on his chest. "You could never disappoint me."

Sophia was silent for a long time, her fingers unmoving beneath his. Eventually she sang in a kind of melodic, tranquilizing whisper.

When I have found out my true love and delight
I'll welcome him kindly by day or by night;
For the bells shall be a-ringing,
*   and the drums make a noise*
To welcome my true love with ten thousand joys

When Sophia fell silent, Ross opened his eyes and saw that she wore a bittersweet expression, as if she were thinking of past heartbreak. Equal parts of jealousy and concern coiled inside him, and he searched for a way to jolt her from the mournful memories. "You're right," he said. "Your voice is not distinguished." He smiled as she adopted a threatening scowl. "But I like it very much," he added.

Sophia laid the damp cloth on his forehead. "Now it is *your* turn to entertain *me*," she said impishly. "You may begin at any time."

"I can't sing."

"Ah, well. I didn't expect you could, with a voice like yours."

"What is wrong with my voice?"

"It's gravelly. No one would expect you to possess a golden baritone." She laughed gently as she saw his disgruntlement. She slipped her hand beneath his neck and brought the glass of barley water to his lips. "Here, drink some more."

He drank the sickroom distillation with a grimace. "I haven't had barley water in years," he said.

"Eliza says you are never ill." Sophia set the glass aside. "In fact, most of the runners are amazed that you were wounded. They seem to think that mere bullets should have bounced off you like raindrops."

Ross smiled ruefully. "I've never claimed to be superhuman."

"Nevertheless, they all believe you to be so." She watched him closely as she continued. "Above human needs and weaknesses. Invulnerable."

They were both still, their gazes intricately locked, and Ross understood suddenly that she was asking some kind of question. "I'm not," he finally said. "I do have needs. And weaknesses."

Sophia's gaze lowered to the counterpane, and she smoothed away a wrinkle of fabric with great care. "But you don't give in to them."

He caught her fingers in his, drawing his thumb over the velvety surface of her short nails. "What do you want to know, Sophia?"

Her lashes swept upward. "Why have you not married since your wife passed away? It has been a long time. And you are still relatively young."

"Relatively?" he repeated with a scowl.

She smiled. "Tell me why you are called the Monk of Bow Street when you could so readily find someone to marry."

"I didn't want to marry again. I've managed well enough on my own."

"Did you love your wife?" she asked.

"Eleanor was easy to love." Ross tried to summon the image of his wife, her delicate, pale face, her silken blond hair. But it seemed that he had known her in another lifetime. With surprise, he realized that Eleanor was not quite real to him anymore. "She was refined . . . intelligent . . . very kind. She never spoke harshly of anyone." A reminiscent smile touched his lips. "Eleanor hated to hear anyone curse. She worked diligently to cure me of the habit."

"She must have been a special woman."

"Yes," he agreed. "But Eleanor was physically fragile— unusually so. In fact, her family did not want her to marry at all."

"Not ever? Why?"

"Eleanor became ill very easily. After I took her driving through the park one autumn afternoon, she caught a chill and had to rest in bed for a week. Her constitution was frail. Her parents were concerned that she would be overtaxed by the demands of marriage, not to mention my husbandly attentions. They feared that pregnancy might kill her." Guilt thickened his voice as he continued. "I managed to persuade them that I would protect Eleanor, and that no harm would ever befall her." Ross did not look at Sophia as she turned the cloth on his forehead. "We were happy for almost four years. We thought that she was infertile, because she never conceived. I was actually relieved by the idea."

"You did not want to have a child?"

"It did not matter to me. All I wanted was for Eleanor to be healthy and safe. But one day she told me that she was expecting. She was overjoyed at the news. She said that she had never felt so well. And so I convinced myself that she and the baby would be fine."

Ross stopped speaking, too troubled to continue. Any mention of Eleanor was unbearably difficult and private. Yet he did not want to withhold any part of his past from Sophia.

"What happened?" she whispered.

Ross felt something unlocking in his head. All his rigid self-control seemed to have dissolved. He began to tell her the things he had never confessed to anyone— he found it impossible to hold anything back from her.

"The day her labor pains began, I knew that something was wrong. Eleanor didn't bear the pain well. She became too weak to push. The labor lasted twenty-four hours, and as the second day began . . . God, it was a hellish nightmare. I sent for more doctors, and all four of them argued about what should be done for my wife. She was in hideous pain—she begged me to help her. I would have done anything. Anything." He wasn't aware that his fists were clenched until he felt Sophia's hands rub softly over the backs of them, soothing the knotted muscles and cords. "The only thing the doctors could agree on was that the baby was too large. I had to make a choice . . . Of course I told them to save Eleanor . . . but that meant they had to—" He broke off, his breath catching. It was impossible for him to tell her what they had done next. There were no words. "There was so much blood. Eleanor screamed and begged me to stop them. She wanted to die, give the baby a chance to live, but I couldn't let her go. And so they both . . ." Ross paused and fought to control his choppy breathing.

There was no movement or sound from Sophia. He thought that he had disgusted her, had said too much. She must be horrified.

"I made the wrong choice," he muttered. "They both died because of it." The coolness of the room, so enjoyable before, now made him shiver. He was numb, sick, frozen.

The cloth was removed from his forehead, and Sophia stroked his face. "It wasn't your fault," she said. "Surely you know that."

Clearly, she didn't understand the whole of the story. Ross tried to make her see the depth of his selfishness. "I shouldn't have married Eleanor. She would still be alive if I had left her alone."

"You don't know that for certain. But if that is true, and you had never married her, what would her life have been like? Cocooned, kept away from the world, unfulfilled, unloved." Sophia drew the covers higher around him and went to fetch a blanket from the bottom drawer of the dresser. She laid the weight of the quilted fabric over him and resumed her seat by the bed. "You did not force Eleanor to marry you. I am certain that she understood the chance she was taking. But the risk was worth it to Eleanor, because for the time that you were married, she was happy and loved. She lived as she wished to. Surely she would not wish you to blame yourself for what happened."

"It does not matter that she wouldn't have blamed me," he said gruffly. "I know where the fault lies— directly with me."

"Naturally you would think so," came Sophia's wry response. "You seem to believe that you are omnipotent, and that everything good and bad should be attributed to you. How difficult it must be for you to accept that some things are simply beyond your influence."

Her tender mockery was curiously comforting. As Ross stared into her eyes, he was conscious of an encroaching sense of relief. Although he didn't want to accept the feeling, he couldn't quite dismiss it.

"You are just a man, after all," she added. "Not some godlike being."

Just a man.

Of course he knew that. However, it wasn't until this moment that Ross acknowledged the burden he had felt to convince the entire world otherwise. He had done everything humanly possible to prove that he was invulnerable, and for the most part, he had succeeded. It was nearly a requirement of his position. People wanted to believe that the Chief Magistrate of Bow Street was all-powerful; they wanted to know that while they rested in their beds at night, he was working ceaselessly to protect them. And for years Ross had lived in isolation as a result. No one truly knew or understood him. But for the first time in his adult life, he had found someone who did not regard him with awe. She treated him as if he were an ordinary man.

Sophia left the bedside and moved about the room, quietly straightening articles on the washstand, folding discarded cloths and towels. Ross watched her with predatory intensity, thinking of what he would do to her, with her, when he had recovered his strength. Surely she had no idea about the turn of his thoughts, or she would not be quite so calm.

Chapter 8

"*You* are a *terrible* patient," Sophia exclaimed when she saw that Ross was dressed and out of bed. "Dr. Linley said that you should stay abed at least another day."

"He doesn't know everything," Ross replied, working his feet into his shoes.

"Neither do you!" Exasperated and worried, she followed his movements as he went to his dresser and searched in the top drawer for a fresh cravat. "What are you planning to do?"

"I'm going to my office for an hour or so."

"No doubt you'll spend the entire day working!"

In the past four days since Ross had been shot, it had been increasingly difficult for Sophia to make him rest. As his strength returned and his shoulder mended, he wanted to resume his usual breakneck pace. To keep him still, Sophia had brought piles of paperwork from his office, and had taken reams of notes while he dictated in bed, or in a chair by the hearth. She had served his meals and spent hours reading to him. Often she watched over him while he dozed, her gaze taking in every detail of his sleep-softened face, the way his hair tumbled onto his forehead, the relaxed lines of his mouth.

Sophia had become familiar with his scent, how his throat moved when he drank his coffee, the dense texture of his muscles beneath her fingers as she changed his wound dressing. The bristle of his jaw before he shaved. The rusty catch of his laughter, as if he were not used to making the sound. The way his black hair sprang in unruly waves before he brushed them smooth each morning. The way he surprised her with kisses when she collected his tray or straightened the pillows behind him . . . kisses like dark, sweet conspiracies, his hands gripping her with gentle insistence.

And instead of denying him, she responded with abandon.

To Sophia's shame, she had begun to have lurid fantasies about him. One night she had dreamed that she climbed into Ross's bed and laid her naked body full-length against his. She had awakened to discover that her sheets were damp with perspiration, her heart was thumping, and the place between her legs was alive with sensation. For the first time in her life, she had put her fingers to that throbbing peak and stroked gently. Delight shot through her loins as she imagined that Ross was touching her again, his mouth tugging at her breast, his fingers working skillfully between her thighs. Steeped in shame and guilt, she continued to stimulate herself, discovering that the more she rubbed, the sharper the pleasure became, until it ended in a wash of heat that drew a shaken moan from her lips.

Rolling onto her stomach, Sophia lay there dazed and puzzled. The feeling ebbed and her body became pleasantly heavy, and she wondered how she could face Ross the next day. She had never known such a feeling, a physical need that was alarming in its urgency.

In addition to her sexual attraction to Ross, Sophia felt an inescapable liking for him. She was fascinated by the quirks of his character. When confronted with an unpleasant duty, he did not try to avoid it, but instead threw himself into it with singular determination. Duty meant everything to him. If called on to wear a hair shirt for the sake of his dependents, he would have donned one without question.

She was amused by the fact that although Ross never lied, he shaded the truth to suit his purposes. If he ever raised his voice, for example, he asserted that he was not shouting but being "emphatic." He denied being stubborn and instead described himself as "firm." Neither was he dominating, only "decisive." Sophia laughed outright at his claims and discovered, to her delight, that he was not certain how to react. He was not a man whom anyone dared to tease, and Sophia sensed his cautious enjoyment of her baiting.

As they talked in the quiet evening hours, Sophia had shared the few memories she had of her own childhood: the feel of her father's whiskers when he had kissed her good night . . . a family picnic . . . the stories her mother had read to her. And the time when she and her little brother had mixed water into her mother's face powder and played with the paste, and how they had been sent to bed without supper.

Ross was able to draw more confessions from her despite her effort to hold them back. Before she quite realized it, she had found herself telling him about the months after her parents' death, when she and John had run wild in the village. "We were horrible little fiends," she had said, sitting in the bedside chair with her knees curled up and her arms locked around them. "We played nasty tricks, and vandalized shops and homes, and stole . . ." She paused and rubbed her forehead to ease a sudden pinching ache.

"What did you steal?"

"Food, mostly. We were always hungry. The families that tried to look after us did not have much to spare. When our behavior became too wicked to tolerate, they washed their hands of us." She hugged her knees more tightly. "It was my fault. John was too young to know better, but there was no excuse for my behavior. I should have guided him, taken care of him . . ."

"You were a child." Ross spoke with apparent carefulness, as if he understood the weight of the guilt that threatened to crush her. "It wasn't your fault."

She smiled without humor, not accepting the consolation.

"Sophia," he asked quietly, "how did John die?"

She stiffened as she fought the temptation to tell

him. That deep, soft voice was asking for the key to her soul. And if she gave it to him, he would scorn and punish her, and she would shrivel into nothing.

Rather than answer him, she had laughed unsteadily and invented some excuse to leave the room.

Now, as Ross extracted a dark silk cravat from the dresser, Sophia's thoughts were forced back to the present. The fact that Ross had taken it upon himself to leave his sickbed provided her with a welcome distraction, and she pounced on it eagerly.

"You will overtax yourself and collapse," she predicted. "And you will get no sympathy from me. You should heed the doctor's advice and rest!"

Standing before the looking glass, Ross tied the cravat with a slight wince of discomfort. "I'm not going to collapse," he said evenly. "But I have to leave this room, or I will go mad." His silvery gaze met hers in the reflective glass. "There is only one way you will get me back into that bed—and I don't think you are ready for that yet."

Sophia looked away from him immediately, turning hot with embarrassment. It was a sign of how familiar they had become, that he would acknowledge his desire for her so openly. "You must at least have some breakfast," she said. "I will go to the kitchen and make certain that Eliza has boiled the coffee."

"Thank you." The corners of his lips tilted in a wry smile, and he finished knotting his cravat with a deft tug.

Later that morning Sophia filed reports and depositions in the criminal records room while Ross conducted meetings in his office. Straightening the piles of paper before her, Sophia sighed despondently. During the first month of her employment, she had begun to copy information that she believed would be damaging to the Bow Street office and all who worked there. Most of it concerned mistakes that a few runners and constables had made, from procedural errors to mishandling of evidence. Ross had chosen to discipline the men privately, as the last thing the public office needed was a potentially ruinous scandal.

Sophia knew she had to gather much more information if she wanted sufficient ammunition to destroy Ross and his runners. For the past three weeks, however, she had done nothing to further her goal. To her self-disgust, she did not have the heart for it. She no longer wanted to hurt Ross. She despised herself for her own weakness, but she could not bring herself to betray him. She had come to care deeply about him despite her efforts to avoid it. Which meant that her poor brother's death would never be answered with justice, and his short life would therefore have no meaning at all.

Gloomily Sophia sorted through files until Ernest appeared suddenly and interrupted her labors. "Miss Sydney, Sir Ross wants ye."

She stared at the errand boy with immediate worry. "Why?"

"I don't know, miss."

"Where is Sir Ross? Is he all right?"

" 'E's in 'is office, miss." The boy left in his customary haste, off to perform more errands.

Sophia's stomach flipped with anxiety as she wondered if Ross had pushed himself too hard. It was possible that he had somehow ruptured his wound, or succumbed to fever once more, or exhausted himself with too much activity. She went to the office in a headlong rush, ignoring the startled faces of barristers and clerks she pushed by in the narrow hallway.

The door to the Chief Magistrate's office was open. Sophia crossed the threshold with swift strides. Ross was sitting at his desk, looking pale and a bit tired, his gaze lifting as he saw her. "Sophia, what—"

"I knew it was too soon for you to go back to work!" she exclaimed as she reached him. Impulsively she put her hands on him, feeling his forehead, the sides of his face. "Do you have fever? What is the matter? Has your shoulder started to bleed again, or is it—"

"Sophia," he interrupted. His large hands wrapped around hers, his thumbs nestling in her soft palms. A reassuring smile touched his lips. "I'm fine. There is no need for concern."

She stared at him closely, ascertaining for herself that he was all right. "Then why did you send for me?" she asked, bewildered.

Ross's gaze moved to a point beyond her shoulder. To Sophia's sudden consternation, she realized that they were not alone. Twisting, she glanced behind her and saw that Sir Grant was seated in the large leather visitor's chair. The giant was watching the pair of them with startled interest. Sophia snatched her hands away from Ross's and closed her eyes in humiliation.

"I'm sorry," she muttered, wishing she could somehow disappear. "I—I overstepped my bounds, Sir Ross. Forgive me."

He grinned at her embarrassment and spoke to Sir Grant. "Morgan, I have something to discuss with Miss Sydney."

"Apparently so," came Morgan's dry rejoinder. He bowed briefly, his green eyes twinkling as he glanced at Sophia. The door closed behind him.

Sophia covered her reddened face with her hands. Her voice filtered between her stiff fingers. "Oh, what must he think of me?"

Ross came from behind the desk and stood before her. "No doubt he thinks that you are a kind and caring woman."

"I am sorry," she said again. "I did not realize that Sir Grant was here. I should not have come to you so impetuously, nor should I have . . . It's just that I am in the habit of . . ."

"Of touching me?"

She squirmed in discomfort. "I have become too familiar with you. Now that you are well again, things must return to the way they were before."

"I hope not," he replied quietly. "I enjoy our familiarity, Sophia." He reached for her, but Sophia stepped back hastily.

Averting her eyes, she asked in a subdued tone, "Why *did* you send for me?"

A long moment passed before he replied. "I've just received word from my mother of what she assures me is a great crisis in her household."

"No one is ill, I hope?"

"I'm afraid it is far more serious than that," he said sardonically. "It pertains to an upcoming birthday party she is giving for my grandfather."

Perplexed, Sophia looked up into his dark face as he continued.

"Apparently my mother's housekeeper, Mrs. Bridgewell, has suddenly gotten married. She had been seeing an army sergeant, who proposed to her when he learned that the regiment was soon to be moved to Ireland. Naturally Mrs. Bridgewell wished to accompany her new husband to his new post. The family wishes her well, but unfortunately, her absence occurs in the midst of preparations for my grandfather's ninetieth birthday celebration."

"Oh, dear. When will the event take place?"

"In precisely a week."

"Oh, dear," Sophia said again, remembering from the great household she had worked at in Shropshire that such large festivities required meticulous planning and near-flawless execution. Food, flowers, guest accommodations . . . there would be an overwhelming mass of work involved. Sophia pitied the underservants who would be required to step in to manage things.

"Who will arrange things for your mother, then?"

"You," Ross muttered with a scowl. "She wants you.

The family carriage is waiting outside. If you are willing, you are to leave for Berkshire at once."

"Me?" Sophia was stunned. "But there must be someone else who can take Mrs. Bridgewell's place!"

"According to my mother, no. She has asked for your assistance."

"I cannot! That is, I have no experience in taking care of something like this."

"You do quite well at managing the servants here."

"*Three* servants," Sophia said in agitation. "When your mother must have dozens and dozens."

"About fifty," he told her in a deliberately offhand manner, as if the number were of little significance.

"Fifty! I can't be in charge of fifty people! Surely there is someone far more suitable than I."

"Perhaps if the housekeeper's departure had been less precipitate, they would have found someone else. As it is, you are my mother's best hope."

"I pity her, then," she remarked with great feeling.

He laughed suddenly. "It is only a party, Sophia. If all goes well, my mother will no doubt take the credit for everything. If it proves to be a disaster, we'll blame it all on the absent Mrs. Bridgewell. There is nothing for you to worry about."

"But what about you? Who will take care of you and manage things here while I am gone?"

He reached out and fingered the white collar at the neck of her dark blue dress, the back of his knuckle brushing the tender underside of her chin. "It appears

I will have to make do without you." His voice lowered to an intimate pitch. "I expect it will be a long week indeed."

Standing so close to him, Sophia could smell the tang of his shaving soap, the touch of coffee on his breath. "Will your entire family be there?" she asked warily. "Including your brother and his wife?" The prospect of abiding beneath the same roof as Matthew was distinctly unappealing.

"I doubt it. Matthew and Iona prefer the pleasures of town life—the country is too quiet for them. I expect they will wait until the weekend, and arrive at the same time as the other guests."

Sophia considered the situation carefully. There seemed to be no graceful way to refuse Ross's mother. She sighed in consternation at the Herculean mission that had been set before her. "I will go," she said tersely. "I will do everything in my power to make your grandfather's party a success."

"Thank you."

His hand slid around the back of her neck, and his fingers brushed over the braided coil pinned at her nape. His fingertips found a few delicate wisps of hair and stroked gently.

Sophia drew in an unsteady breath. "I will pack my things."

His thumb traced a slow, tiny circle on the side of her neck. "Aren't you going to kiss me good-bye?"

She licked her dry lips. "I don't think it is wise for us to . . . to do that anymore. It is not appropriate. This separation is a timely one, as it will allow us to go back to the way things were—"

"Don't you like kissing me?" He picked up a stray lock of hair on her neck and fingered it lightly.

"That is not relevant," Sophia heard herself say. "The point is, we shouldn't."

His eyes glinted with challenge. "Why?"

"Because I think . . . I am afraid . . ." She gathered her courage before blurting out, "I cannot have an affair with you."

"I have not asked for an affair. What I want from you is—"

Impulsively Sophia put her hand to his lips. She did not know what he had been about to say, but she did not want to hear it. Whatever his intentions were, she would die if he put them into words. "Don't say anything," she begged. "Let us be separate for a week. After you take some time to reflect, I am certain that your sentiments will change."

His tongue touched the seam between her fingers, and her hand jerked away. "Are you?" he asked, lowering his head.

His lips brushed over hers in a communion of moisture and warmth that filled her with unbearable pleasure. She felt the tip of his tongue against her bottom lip, softly teasing, and her resistance melted away. Gasping, she strained upward, and was caught against his hard body, one of his hands fitting beneath her buttocks. Her arms wrapped around his neck, and she kissed him hungrily. She was unable to deny the attraction between them, which was, of course, the point that Ross was now intent on making. He rewarded her response with an even deeper kiss, his tongue sliding past her teeth, until she sagged against him in helpless pleasure.

Suddenly she was released. Stunned, Sophia put her fingers to her damp mouth.

Ross looked arrogant and amused, his own face flushed. "Good-bye, Sophia," he said, his voice thick. "I will see you in one week."

The vehicle provided by the Cannons was by far the most luxurious Sophia had ever ridden in, with French windows and velvet curtains, the dark-green-lacquered exterior decorated with gold-leaf scrolls, the interior upholstered in glossy brown leather. The well-sprung carriage traveled jauntily over the twenty-five-mile distance between London and Berkshire.

Although the prospect of arranging the weekend party was intimidating, Sophia was eager to see the country estate where Ross had spent his childhood. The county of Berkshire and its environs were just as he had described them, with abundant pasturelands, fertile woods, and small towns with bridges arching over the Kennet and Thames rivers. The smells of freshly turned sod, river breezes, and grass mingled to create a pleasantly earthy fragrance.

The carriage turned off the great road onto a much smaller one, the wheels bouncing and jolting as the paving became ancient and uneven. As they approached the town of Silverhill, the scenery became even more picturesque, with fat sheep grazing in the meadows and half-timbered cottages dotting the green countryside. The road led through a series of timeworn gates covered in ivy and roses. The carriage skirted the periphery of Silverhill and started down a long private avenue. They passed through the stone gates of the Cannon estate, which Ross had told her was about fifteen hundred acres in size.

Sophia was impressed by the beauty of the land, which featured groves of oak and beech, and an artificial lake that sparkled beneath the cool blue sky. Finally the outlines of a Jacobean mansion rose before her, its roofline arching in a profusion of turrets and gables. The rubbed-brick facade of the home was so magnificent that Sophia felt a painful jab of anxiety in her stomach.

"Oh, Lord," she whispered. The towering entrance of Silverhill Park Manor was fronted by fifteen-foot-high hedges and bordered by a terraced walk featuring huge beds of primrose and rhododendron. A row of immense Oriental plane trees led the way to an orangery on the south verge of the walk. In Sophia's most extravagant dreams, she had never expected the Cannons' country estate to be so imposing.

Two thoughts assailed her at once. First, why would a man with this kind of wealth consign himself to live in the Spartan quarters at Bow Street? And second, how was she going to survive the next seven days? Clearly, she was wholly inadequate to the task that lay before her. She was too inexperienced to direct an entire regiment of servants. They would not respect her. They would not listen to her.

Sophia clasped her hands over her stomach, feeling sick.

The carriage stopped before the central entrance. White-faced but resolute, Sophia accepted the footman's assistance from the carriage and accompanied him to the door. A few knocks of his gloved hand, and the oak-paneled door opened in well-oiled silence.

The stone-floored entrance hall was immense, with a grand central staircase that split on the second landing and led to the east and west wings of the mansion. The walls were covered with gigantic tapestries woven in apricot, dark gold, and faded blue. Sophia was interested to see that two sets of receiving rooms flanked the entrance hall. The set on the left was decorated in a masculine style, with elegant dark furniture and blue tones, whereas the set on the right was predominantly feminine, the walls covered with peach silk, the furniture delicate and gilded.

A butler showed Sophia to the peach receiving room, where Sir Ross's mother awaited.

Mrs. Catherine Cannon was a tall and elegant woman, dressed in a simple day gown, with shimmering amethyst combs in her upswept gray hair. Her face was angular, but her green eyes were kind. "Miss Sydney," she exclaimed, coming forward. "Welcome to Silverhill Park. Thank you for rescuing me from a terrible disaster."

"I hope I may be of some use," Sophia said as the older woman took her hands and pressed them warmly. "I explained to Sir Ross, however, that I have little experience in these matters—"

"Oh, I have every faith in you, Miss Sydney! You strike me as a very capable young woman."

"Yes, but I—"

"Now, one of the maids will show you to your room so that you may freshen up after that long carriage ride. Then we will walk through the house, and I shall introduce you to the servants."

Sophia was shown to a small but serviceable room that had belonged to the former housekeeper of Silverhill Park. She exchanged the white collar of her dark dress for a fresh one, brushed her skirts and shook the dust from them, and washed her face with cool water. As she returned downstairs, she marveled at the loveliness of her surroundings; the ceilings of interlaced ribs and painted panels, the galleries filled with sculpture, and the endless rows of windows providing lush views of the gardens outside.

Rejoining Catherine Cannon, Sophia accompanied her on a tour of the house, doing her best to commit every detail of the place to memory. She was vaguely puzzled by the way Ross's mother treated her, which was with far more solicitude than a servant merited. As they strolled through the house, Mrs. Cannon told her stories about Ross—that as a boy, he had been given to playing pranks on the butler and wheeling his friends about on the gardener's flat-barrow.

"It seems that Sir Ross was not always serious and solemn, then," Sophia commented.

"Heavens, no! That came only after his wife passed away." Mrs. Cannon's mood changed suddenly, her lips taking on a regretful softness. "Such a tragedy. Devastating to all of us."

"Yes," Sophia said softly. "Sir Ross told me about it."

"He did?" Catherine came to a halt in the middle of a huge drawing room papered in a white-and-gold French-flocked design. She regarded Sophia with an arrested stare.

Sophia returned her gaze uneasily, wondering if she had said something wrong.

"Well," Mrs. Cannon murmured with a faint smile. "I have never known my son to mention a word about Eleanor to anyone. Ross is an unusually private man."

Feeling that Mrs. Cannon was perhaps drawing some conclusion that should not be drawn, Sophia tried to remedy the woman's misunderstanding. "Sir Ross mentioned a few things about his past during his fever. It was only because he was weary and ill—"

"No, my dear," came Catherine's gentle reply. "My son obviously trusts you, and values your company." She paused and added cryptically, "And any woman who is able to draw my son away from that sordid world of Bow Street will have my blessing."

"You are not pleased by his position as Chief Magistrate, Mrs. Cannon?"

They resumed their stroll through the drawing

room as Ross's mother replied, "My son has given ten years of his life to public service and been remarkably successful. Naturally I am quite proud of him. But I feel the time has come when Ross should turn his attention to other matters. He must marry again, and sire children. Oh, I am aware of the impression Ross gives that he is somewhat cold-natured, but I assure you, he has the same needs as any man. To be loved. To have a family of his own."

"Oh, he is not cold-natured at all. Any child would be quite fortunate to have such a father. And I'm certain that as a husband, Sir Ross would be—" Suddenly realizing that she was chattering like a parrot, Sophia snapped her mouth shut.

"Yes," Catherine said with a smile. "He was an excellent husband to Eleanor. When he marries again, I am positive that his bride will have few complaints." Seeing Sophia's discomfort, she spoke in a brisk manner. "Shall we go to the formal dining room? It is sided by a serving room—quite a convenient area to keep the dishes hot during a long supper."

During the day, Sophia was so busy that she had little time to think about Ross. However, there was no escape from the longing and desolation that filled the quiet evening hours. Utterly defeated, she admitted to herself that she had fallen in love with the man she had wanted to ruin. She had been vanquished by her own heart. There was nothing to do but abandon her plans for revenge. There would be no seduction . . . no tainted victory. She would leave her position at Bow Street as soon as possible and try to go on with the rest of her life.

Her new resolve left her feeling drained but peaceful, and she concentrated on the coming weekend party with wan determination.

Twenty-five bedrooms in the main house would be occupied with guests, as well as another dozen in the nearby gatehouse reserved for the use of bachelors. Families from Windsor, Reading, and surrounding towns would attend the masked ball on Saturday night, bringing the number of guests to three hundred and fifty.

Unfortunately, the written notes and plans left by the former housekeeper, Mrs. Bridgewell, left much to be desired. Wryly Sophia reflected that the absent Mrs. Bridgewell had probably been far more concerned with her own romantic affairs than with the upcoming weekend party. Sophia busied herself with taking inventory of the china and flatware, the contents of the butler's pantry and wine cellar, the larders and linen closets. Consulting with both the cook and Mrs. Cannon, Sophia made notes on menu suggestions, and the proper china for each course. She met with the butler and the master gardener, and laid out plans for a score of housemaids. The village butcher, grocer, and milkman came to call and took Sophia's written orders for the approaching celebration.

In the midst of this activity, Sophia made the acquaintance of Mr. Robert Cannon, the elderly gentleman whose ninetieth birthday was the cause of all the excitement. Ross's mother had tried to prepare Sophia for his outspokenness. "When you meet my father-in-law, I should not wish you to be disconcerted by his manner. As he has aged, he has become quite blunt. Do not be put off by anything he says. He is a dear man, if a trifle lacking in discretion."

Walking back from the icehouse, set apart from the main house, Sophia saw an old man sitting beneath a canvas awning in the rose garden. A small table laden with refreshments had been placed beside him. His chair had been fitted with a leg rest, and Sophia recalled Mrs. Cannon mentioning that her father-in-law was often troubled by gout.

"You, girl," he said imperiously. "Come here. I have not seen you before."

Sophia obeyed. "Good morning, Mr. Cannon," she said, dipping into a respectful curtsy.

Robert Cannon was a handsome old man with a ruff of silver hair and a craggy but distinguished face. His eyes were a steely blue-gray. "I suppose you are the girl my daughter-in-law told me about. The one from Bow Street."

"Yes, sir. I hope very much that I may help to make your birthday celebration satisfactory—"

"Yes, yes," he cut in impatiently, waving his hand to indicate that the event was trivial nonsense. "My daughter-in-law will seize on any excuse for a party. Now, you will tell me exactly how things stand between you and my grandson."

Caught completely off guard, Sophia stared at him openmouthed. "Sir," she said cautiously, "I am afraid I do not understand your question."

"Catherine says that he has taken an interest in you—which is a welcome piece of news. I want to see my family line continue, and Ross and his brother are the last of the Cannon males. Has he come up to scratch yet?"

Sophia was too shocked to reply quickly. How in the world had he arrived at such a conclusion? "Mr. Cannon, you are entirely mistaken! I—I have no intention of . . . of . . . and Sir Ross would not . . ." Her voice trailed into silence as her mind searched futilely for words.

Cannon regarded her with a skeptical smile. "Catherine says you are a Sydney," he commented. "I knew your grandfather Frederick quite well."

The revelation astonished her further. "You did? You were friends with my grandfather?"

"I didn't say that we were friends," Cannon replied crustily. "I only said that I knew him well. The reason we did not get on was that we both fell in love with the same woman. Miss Sophia Jane Lawrence."

"My grandmother," Sophia managed to say. She shook her head in wonder at the unexpected connection to her family's past. "I was named after her."

"A lovely and accomplished woman. You resemble her, although she was a bit more refined in appearance. She had a regal quality that you lack."

Sophia smiled suddenly. "It is difficult to be regal when one is a servant, sir."

His blue eyes remained on her, and his rugged face seemed to soften. "You have her way of smiling. Sophia Jane's granddaughter, a servant! The Sydneys have fallen on hard times, eh? Your grandmother would have done better to marry me."

"Why didn't she?"

He gestured to a nearby chair. "Come sit by me, and I will tell you."

Sophia cast an anxious glance at the main house, thinking of the work that had to be done.

The old man made a surly sound. "That can wait, my girl. After all, the weekend is supposed to be in my honor, and here I am, set out to pasture. I wish for a few minutes of your company—is that too much to ask?"

Sophia promptly sat.

Cannon settled back in his chair. "Your grandmother Sophia Jane was the loveliest girl I had ever seen. Her family was not wealthy, but they were of good blood, and they desired their only daughter to marry well. After Sophia's come-out, I dedicated myself to winning her hand. Her lack of a substantial dowry was no obstacle, as the Cannons are a family of means. But before I could persuade the Lawrences to agree to a betrothal, your grandfather Lord Sydney made an offer for her. I could not compete against the allure of his title. Although the Cannon name is distinguished, I am not a peer. And so Sophia Jane went to Lord Sydney."

"Which of you did my grandmother love?" Sophia asked, fascinated by the piece of family history that she had never been aware of.

"I am not quite certain," Cannon replied thoughtfully, surprising her. "Perhaps neither of us. But I suspect that in time, Sophia Jane may have come to regret her choice. Lord Sydney was a pleasant enough fellow, but there never seemed to be much depth below the surface. I was a far better catch."

"And modest, too," Sophia said, laughing suddenly.

Cannon seemed to enjoy her impudence. "Tell me, child, were your grandparents content in their marriage?"

"I think so," Sophia said slowly. "Although I do not recall seeing them together very often. They seem to have led separate lives." She fell silent, reflecting on the past. In retrospect, her grandparents had not seemed especially affectionate with each other. "Fortunately, you found another love," she remarked, trying to put a happy end to the story.

"No, I didn't," Cannon returned bluntly. "I admired my wife, but my heart was always with Sophia Jane." His eyes glimmered suddenly. "I love her still, though she is long gone."

Sophia felt a surge of melancholy as she reflected on the statement. No doubt that was how Sir Ross would always feel about his wife, Eleanor.

She did not realize that she had spoken the words aloud until Robert Cannon replied with a snort of irritation. "That fragile flower! I never understood my grandson's attraction to her. Eleanor was a winsome girl, but my grandson needs a vital woman who will bear him strong sons." He gave Sophia a measuring gaze. "You look as though you're up to the task."

Alarmed by the turn the conversation was taking, Sophia stood hastily. "Well, Mr. Cannon, it has been a pleasure to meet you. However, if I do not attend to my responsibilities, I fear for the outcome of your party." She added a flirtatious note to her voice. "To my regret, I am not being paid to converse with handsome gentlemen, but rather to work."

It was evident that Cannon tried to maintain his scowl, but he let out a chuckle. "You do favor your grandmother," he commented. "Very few women are able to say no to a man in a way that flatters his vanity."

Sophia curtsied to him once more. "I bid you a very happy day, sir. But I must tell you again, you are mistaken about Sir Ross. There is absolutely no possibility of a marriage proposal, nor would I accept one from him."

"We shall see," he murmured, and lifted his glass of lemonade as she hurried away.

Chapter 9

Sophia rubbed her weary eyes as she looked at her book of notes. It was Friday morning, and soon the guests would arrive. Servants from various households had already come ahead with trunks and valises to make things ready for their masters and mistresses. She sat at the large wooden table in the stillroom, which was adjacent to the kitchen. The stillroom had long ago been used to brew medicines for the household, but now it served to store dried herbs, marchpanes, spice-breads, and conserves.

"Now, Lottie," Sophia said to the head housemaid, who was responsible for disseminating her instructions to the other housemaids, "I've told you the schedule for when and how the rooms should be cleaned after the guests arise each morning."

"Yes, miss."

"Just remember that when you go to the bachelors' lodgings at the gatehouse, do not let any of the maids venture into a room alone. They must work in pairs."

"Why, miss?"

"Because one of the bachelors might be overcome by what was once described to me as 'early-morning passion.' They are likely to take advantage of a female servant and make unwanted advances, or even worse. That will be far less likely if the girls work together."

"Yes, miss."

"Now, as some guests will arrive this morning, you must lay out fresh cards in the card room. I suppose a few gentlemen may want to visit the fishing pavilion at the lake—would you please ask Hordle to set out chairs, tables, and some wine?"

"Miss Sydney . . ." Lottie began, then looked over Sophia's shoulder and giggled. "Oh, lor!" Placing a hand over her mouth, she tittered in abashed amusement.

"What is it?" Sophia asked. She turned in her chair, then sprang to her feet when she saw Sir Ross's tall form in the doorway of the stillroom. Her heart pounded at the sight. He looked virile and stunningly handsome in a rich blue coat and fawn-colored trousers.

"I will go speak wi' Mr. 'Ordle," the housemaid said, still giggling as she rushed from the room.

Staring into Ross's smiling gray eyes, Sophia moistened her lips. He could not have been at Silverhill Park for long—he must have come to find her as soon as he had arrived. The weeklong separation had only intensified her feelings for him, and she had to stiffen her spine to keep from throwing herself at him. "Good morning, Sir Ross," she said breathlessly. "You . . . you look well."

Ross approached her, one large hand lifting to the side of her face. His fingertips rested briefly on the curve

of her cheek. "You are even lovelier than I remembered," he murmured. "How have you been, Sophia?"

"Quite well," she managed to say.

"My mother cannot speak highly enough of you.
She is very pleased with your efforts."

"Thank you, sir." Sophia lowered her lashes, afraid
that her violent longing was all too easy to read. Feeling
miserable, she drew away and wrapped her arms
around herself. "Have you learned anything about the
dress?" she asked, hoping to restore her self-control.

He understood at once that she was referring to the
lavender ballgown. "Not yet. Judging from the make
and fabric, Sayer has narrowed the possibilities to three
dressmakers. I am going to question each of them personally when I return to London."

"Thank you." She gave him a small smile. "I must
offer you some recompense. You must garnish my
wages, or—"

"Sophia," he interrupted with a scowl, as if she had
insulted him. "I would not accept any payment from
you. It's my responsibility to protect you and the others
who work for me."

Sophia was nearly undone by his words. "I must return to my work," she said gravely. "Before I do, is there
something you want, Sir Ross? Some refreshments, or
perhaps coffee?"

"Just you."

The quiet statement made her knees weak. Sophia
struggled to keep her voice calm. As if her mouth were
not dry with longing. As if her body were not thump-

ing with desire. She strove to change the direction of the conversation. "How is your shoulder, sir?"

"It's healing well. Would you like to have a look?" His fingers went to the knot of his cravat, as if he were willing to undress for her right there. Sophia shot a startled glance at him, and saw from the glint in his eyes that he was teasing.

If she was ever going to put a stop to the attraction that had developed between them, it would have to be now. "Sir Ross, now that you are well again, and I have had a few days to consider our . . . our . . ."

"Relationship?" he supplied helpfully.

"Yes. I have reached a conclusion."

"What conclusion is that?"

"A . . . an intimate association would not be wise for either of us. I am content to be your servant, nothing more." She faltered only a little as she finished her recitation. "From now on, I will not welcome any advances from you."

His smoky gaze held hers. Finally he spoke in a gentle murmur. "We'll discuss the matter later. After the weekend. And then you and I are going to come to an understanding."

Breathing in shallow gulps, Sophia turned to busy herself with the articles on a nearby shelf. Her fingers encountered a sheaf of dried herbs, and her fingers fumbled with the crackling leaves, inadvertently crumbling them. "I will not change my mind."

"I think you will," he said softly, and left.

* * *

Noblemen, politicians, and professional men moved through the circuit of common rooms and out to the gardens in back. Groups of ladies played cards, gossiped over needlework or magazines, or went on walks along the neat graveled pathways outside. The gentlemen gathered in the billiards room, read newspapers in the library, or strolled to the pavilion at the lake. It was a warm June day, the breeze insufficient to atone for the unseasonable strength of the sun.

Behind the scenes, the servants were busy cleaning, preparing food, and pressing and airing the many changes of clothes that would be needed for each day of the house party. The kitchen was steaming and fragrant, the bread ovens filled with baking dough, the spit-jacks turning roast fowls, joints of beef, and large hams. Under the direction of the cook, kitchen maids wrapped trussed quails with vine leaves and bacon, then threaded them on skewers. The quail would be offered as a late-afternoon luncheon to satisfy the guests' appetites until supper was served at ten o'clock.

Pleased that everything was running smoothly, Sophia went to the large windows at the top of the grand staircase and watched the guests mingling on the terraced lawn below. She located Ross at once. His dark form was easy to distinguish from the others. Although he wore his authority comfortably, he was a man of almost legendary accomplishments, and the guests were clearly in awe of him.

Sophia felt a prickle of jealousy as she saw the way

the women fluttered around him in nervous excitement, how they chattered and smiled and sent him flirtatious glances. Apparently Ross's reputation as a chaste-living gentleman did not dampen feminine ardor, but rather fanned it into vigorous flame. Sophia was certain that many women present, no matter what their age or circumstance, would have loved to claim that they had managed to snare the elusive widower's interest.

Sophia's thoughts were interrupted by the sound of footsteps on the marble staircase. She turned from the window to view a pair of footmen carrying an extremely large trunk, their faces reddened from the exertion. Matthew Cannon followed them, escorting a slender and very pretty blond girl. Neither of them seemed to notice Sophia until they reached the landing.

Dipping into a curtsy, Sophia murmured, "Good afternoon, Mr. Cannon."

Matthew regarded her with obvious surprise. Amused, Sophia realized that he had not been told that she was here. But of course, matters involving servants would certainly be of no interest to him.

"What are you doing here?" he asked rudely.

She kept her gaze submissively lowered as she replied, "I was summoned by Mrs. Cannon to help with the preparations for the party, as the previous housekeeper left rather precipitately."

The young blond woman looked up at Matthew. "Who is she?"

He gave a dismissive shrug. "Only my brother's servant. Come, Iona, it is unseemly for us to dawdle on the landing."

As the pair left, Sophia observed them with interest. Matthew's wife was a classic English beauty, golden and fair, her eyes pale blue, her mouth as small and red as a rosebud. Iona seemed cool and remote, as if she were incapable of ever being in a temper. Sophia felt sorry for her. Marriage to a spoiled brat like Matthew could not be easy.

Much later in the evening, the guests proceeded into the dining room, which was dominated by a marble inglenook fireplace. Great stone arches framed a series of pre-Raphaelite stained-glass windows that glittered in the blaze of candlelight. Sophia concealed herself from view as much as possible, occasionally conferring with the footmen as they served the eight-course meal, which included braised beef, John Dory fish, roast hare and teal, and pheasant sausage. After a lengthy succession of removes, a selection of jellies, cakes, and ices was served.

At the conclusion of supper, the footmen removed all the dishes and used clean silver knives to scrape any crumbs from the tablecloth. The ladies withdrew for coffee in the drawing room. Although most of the gentlemen remained at the table for port and masculine conversation, a few headed to the billiards room for a smoke. Following a half hour of segregation, the entire crowd rejoined in the drawing room for tea and entertainment.

Sophia entered the room discreetly and glanced at Catherine Cannon to see if she was satisfied. As their gazes met, Catherine smiled and gestured for Sophia to come to her.

Sophia obeyed quickly. "Yes, Mrs. Cannon?"

"Sophia, the guests wish to play a game of murder."

"Ma'am?" Sophia asked, mildly startled.

Catherine laughed at her expression. "Murder is all the rage just now—haven't you heard of it? The players draw slips of paper from a bowl to see what parts they are to take. One slip says 'murderer,' another is labeled 'investigator,' and all the rest are potential victims. The house must be darkened, and everyone goes to hide. The murderer goes about finding his victims, while the investigator tries to discover his—or her—identity."

"Like hide-and-seek."

"Exactly! Now, Sophia, take one or two of the maids and darken the house. And tell the servants to go about their work without getting in the way of the players."

"Yes, Mrs. Cannon. May I ask which areas of the house are to be dimmed?"

One of Catherine's companions, a middle-aged woman with an elegant sweep of red-gold hair, answered disdainfully. "The whole of it, of course! The game would not be nearly as exciting if we couldn't use the whole house."

Ignoring the woman, Sophia lowered her head and murmured to Catherine, "Mrs. Cannon, may I suggest that the kitchen remain lighted, as the scullery maids have a great deal of washing up to do?"

Catherine's green eyes sparkled with amusement. "A wise suggestion, Sophia. You may keep the kitchen lit. Now hurry, please, as I fear many of the guests are impatient to begin."

"Yes, ma'am."

As Sophia walked away, she heard the red-haired woman say to Catherine, "I don't fancy her manner, Cathy. Rather proud, if you ask me. Not at all appropriate for a housekeeper."

Sophia's ears burned when she heard herself being criticized. "No one asked for your opinion," she muttered beneath her breath. Try as she might, she could not stop herself from thinking bitterly that if fate had been kinder, she might have been a guest this very evening. She had been born the social equal of these people, and she had little patience for their pretensions. In fact, her blood was bluer than the Cannons', though that was of no consequence now.

After directing the housemaids to darken the rooms, Sophia went to turn down the lamps in one of the upstairs receiving rooms. Moonlight glowed through the window, and she began to draw the velvet panels over the glass panes.

Someone entered the room. Sophia hesitated in a pool of moonlight as she turned toward the visitor. At first glance, the man's shadowed form reminded her of Ross, and her heart jolted with anticipation. But the sound of his voice caused her spirits to plummet abruptly.

"What a clever little cat you are," Matthew Cannon

declared contemptuously. "Wriggling your way into my brother's life, and now into my family's home. You must be quite pleased with yourself."

Sophia strove to sound emotionless despite a flare of outrage. What right had he to follow her up here and insult her? "I do not know what you mean, Mr. Cannon. I only hope that I have pleased your mother."

He gave a guttural laugh. "I'm sure you have. No doubt you've pleased my brother as well, in more ways than one."

"Sir?" She pretended not to understand his meaning and began to leave. "Please excuse me—"

However, he moved in front of the doorway, blocking her exit. His face rounded with a nasty smile. "Ross must have been an easy target," he commented. "After all these years of living as a monk, my brother must have fallen on you like a starving dog with a bone."

"You are mistaken," she said shortly. "Please let me pass, Mr. Cannon."

"And now you appear to have him well in hand," he sneered. "It's the talk of the family. My mother even claims that . . . well, never mind. I won't dignify her foolish speculations by putting them into words. Just understand one thing, you grasping light-skirts—you will never be part of this family." As he moved closer, the shadows played over his half-raised hands and made them look like claws.

"Such a thought has never entered my mind," Sophia said. "I believe you are the worse for drink, sir."

Her denial seemed to mollify him. "As long as you

harbor no illusions of ever becoming a Cannon, I have no quarrel with you. In fact . . ." He gave her a glance ripe with speculation, his mouth becoming heavy-lipped. "You'll soon tire of my brother's attentions, if you haven't already. He's too saintly to offer real passion to a woman. There's no excitement in going to bed with such bland fare, I'll wager. Why not try a man who can give you some variety?"

"That would be you, I suppose," Sophia replied acidly.

Matthew spread his hands wide and gave her a knowing smirk. "Unlike that paragon you work for, I know how to please a woman." He laughed deep in his throat, then spoke in a confidential murmur. "I could make you feel things you've never imagined. And if you satisfy me, I'll reward you with all the trinkets a woman could desire. It is a far better lot than you have now, is it not?"

"You disgust me."

"Do I?" He came forward in two strides and grasped the back of her head, his fingers sinking painfully into her pinned-up hair. "Then why are you trembling?" he murmured, his mouth hovering above hers. "You're excited, aren't you?"

She twisted away, making a sound of revulsion. They scuffled briefly, and then Matthew froze as someone else entered the room. To Sophia's horror, she realized that the intruder was Ross. Although the room was dim, his light eyes shone like a cat's. His gaze touched first on Matthew, then settled on Sophia. "What are you doing here?" he asked roughly.

"I was looking for a place to hide," Matthew retorted, releasing Sophia abruptly. "Unfortunately, your precious Miss Sydney decided to make her attentions known to me. As I predicted, she's nothing but a harlot. I wish you joy of her." He left at once, the door hanging ajar in his wake.

Sophia remained frozen, staring at Ross's huge, dark form. The tense silence was fractured by the sounds of partygoers giggling as they scurried through the house in search of concealment.

"What happened?" Ross asked quietly.

She opened her mouth to tell him the truth, but suddenly a chilling thought occurred to her. Matthew Cannon had just given her the perfect excuse to break things off between herself and Ross. Cleanly. Completely. If Ross believed she had tried to seduce his brother, he would entertain no further interest in her. He would let her go without a second glance. And that would be infinitely easier than the alternative—the arguments, the confessions about the past and how she had planned to ruin him, the pain in Ross's face as he realized that he had sent her brother to his death. Perhaps it would be best to make him think that he had never really known her, that she was unworthy of affection or trust. That he was fortunate to be rid of her.

Summoning all her strength, Sophia made her voice cool and steady. "Your brother just told you."

"You tried to seduce him?" Ross asked incredulously.

"Yes."

"Like hell you did!" He grabbed her much as his brother had, his hand closing around her nape, the other seizing the back of her dress. "What is going on? I don't play games, and I won't tolerate them from you."

She hung helpless in his grasp, her face turned away. "Let me go. It doesn't matter what you believe. The truth is that I don't want you! Now take your hands off me!" She shoved against the muscular bulk of his shoulders, then realized that she had pressed the site of his injury. Ross grunted with discomfort but did not loosen his grip. His wine-scented breath burned her like steam.

"Someone will come in here," she gasped.

Ross didn't seem to care. His hand urged her head back, exposing the white length of her neck. As their bodies crushed together, Sophia felt the hard thrust of his erection even through the heavy weight of her skirts. He licked at her lips, then sealed his over hers and consumed her with a blatantly lustful kiss. The pleasure of it engulfed her in a hot tide. A whimper rose in her throat, and she writhed against him helplessly.

Ross cupped her breast over the tight bodice of her gown. "You can't lie to me," he muttered against her ear. "I know you too well. Tell me the truth, Sophia."

Sophia sagged against him in despair, utterly lost. She was no longer in control of her words or actions. Emotion came crashing over her, breaking over her soul until it was washed as clean as a sand-scoured beach. "I can't," she said, her voice shattered. "Because the truth will make you hate me, and I couldn't bear that."

"Hate you?" he asked thickly. "Good Lord, how could you think that? Sophia—"

Ross stopped and inhaled sharply as he saw the tears pooling in her eyes. Suddenly his mouth was on hers, hard and demanding, and he fumbled with her clothes as if wanting to rip away every layer between them. She succumbed to his lips and hands, drowning in sensation, all thought submerged in an ecstasy of surrender. He drew her tongue inside his mouth, playing with the silky underside. Losing her balance, Sophia clung harder to his neck. He was the only solid thing in a world that had become volatile and unstable. Suddenly she felt the carpeted floor against her back, and she realized what he meant to do. "Oh, no," she whispered, but he silenced her with another of those sweet, shocking kisses while his large body settled over hers.

He pulled the front of her gown up to her waist and tugged at her drawers. Sophia writhed as she felt Ross's hand close on the top of her leg, above the tightly cinched garter. His thumb stroked the thin, hot skin, moving higher and higher until it reached the thatch of crisp, curly hair.

Somewhere in the house, a woman squealed in pretend fright as the murderer made his rounds. The little shriek caused a round of smothered laughter from the game-players.

"They'll find us," Sophia said, wriggling frantically beneath him. "Don't, you mustn't . . ."

His fingers slid tenderly into the cleft between her thighs, the pad of his thumb drawing upward to circle the hood of her sex. She groaned and trembled while his fingers entered her with gentle skill, and his mouth consumed hers with desperate fervor.

"We can't," Sophia moaned. "Not here—"

He hushed her with his mouth and caught her head in the crook of his arm. His fingers withdrew, and she felt him opening the front of his trousers. He mounted her, using his thighs to widen the angle between her legs. Turning her face against the bulging muscle of his upper arm, Sophia breathed in shallow pants, her body rigid with anticipation.

His large hand slipped beneath her bottom. "Relax," he whispered. "I'll be gentle. Just open to me. That's it . . . yes . . ." And he began to enter her with exquisite care, stretching her, filling her with silk and heat and impossible sensation.

Footsteps hastened past the door . . . the sounds of gleeful laughter . . . guests searching for new places to hide.

They were going to be caught. Sophia reared upward in panic, fighting wildly in a sudden effort to free herself. Ross withdrew from her, the weight of his erection sliding wetly from her body. Panting hard, he pinned her wrists to the carpet. "Hush," he breathed in her ear.

". . . shall we try in here?" a female asked as she paused just outside the door.

"No," came an answering male voice. "Too obvious. Let's go down the hall . . ."

Their footsteps retreated from the threshold, and Sophia rolled away from Ross the moment he released her wrists. She staggered to her feet and jerked at her clothes to rearrange them. Her face burned as she bent to tug her drawers upward and tie the dangling tapes at her waist. Her limbs were shaking from nerves and fear. Her body ached with unspent passion. She had never known such need, an unquenchable fire that burned with maddening ferocity.

Ross fastened his trousers and approached her from behind. The gentle clasp of his fingers on her shoulders made her flinch. She wanted to seize his hands and pull them to her breasts and beg him to give her the relief she craved. Instead she stood as stiffly as a statue while he nuzzled into her disheveled hair.

"Obviously I haven't done this for a while." Irony washed through his voice. "My sense of timing used to be much better."

"We shouldn't have gone so far," she said through lips that felt swollen. "It was f-fortunate that we were not able to finish."

His hands tightened on her shoulders. "I'm going to finish it soon, by God. I'll come to your room later."

"No," she said instantly. "My door will be locked. I-I don't want to discuss this, ever. As far as I'm concerned, it never happened."

"Sophia," he murmured, "there is only one thing you can do to keep me from your bed—and that is to tell me that you don't want me."

Ross waited with calculated patience while Sophia struggled until her chest felt as if it would burst. Every time she tried to speak, her throat closed, and her shoulders quivered within the supportive frame of his hands. "Please," she finally whispered, although she had no idea what she was asking him for.

His palm slid across her collarbone and pressed to the center of her chest, where her heartbeat could be felt through the thick fabric of her gown. "We'll have our reckoning soon," he said gently. "There is nothing to be afraid of, Sophia."

She pulled away from him with a sharp jerk. "There is," she said hoarsely, striding away from him. "You just don't know it yet."

Chapter 10

Sophia fled to her room and tried to restore herself. She washed with cold water, scrubbing her face until it was pink. After brushing her hair and pinning it in an excruciatingly tight coil, she returned to her duties, feeling dazed and frantic.

The murder game was soon declared over, and the guests proceeded to entertain themselves with a guessing game in which they gave imitations of classical statuary. Howls of laughter greeted each effort. Having received no education in art history, Sophia could not understand why the company seemed to find the game so uproarious. Absently she bade the footmen to clear away the tea dishes and port glasses. The kitchen scullery was crowded with maids washing flatware, crystal, and hundreds of plates. Thankfully, the other servants seemed too busy to notice Sophia's distracted manner.

As the hour of two o'clock approached, most of the guests retired for the evening, heading to their rooms where valets and ladies' maids waited to assist them.

Exhausted, Sophia supervised the cleanup of the common rooms, and praised the servants for a job well done. She finally went to her room, carrying a tinplate lantern fashioned in the shape of a cup with a pattern of punched holes. Although she was outwardly calm, her hand shook until the lantern caused brilliant dots to flutter across the wall like a cloud of fireflies.

When she reached her room, she closed the door and carefully set the lantern on the small rustic table in the corner. Only now, in the privacy of the bedroom, could she allow her tightly suppressed emotions to escape. Clutching the edge of the table for support, she bowed her head and sighed shakily. She stared at the tear-blurred light before her, reliving the moments of rapturous intimacy in Ross's arms.

"Ross," she whispered, "how can I leave you?"

A voice came from the shadows. "I will never let you leave me."

She whirled around, a cry caught in her throat. The uncertain light from the tinplate lantern played over the hard contours of Ross's face. He lounged on the small bed, so still and quiet that she had not seen him when she entered the room.

"You frightened the wits out of me!" she exclaimed.

He smiled slightly, unfolding his long frame from the bed. "I'm sorry," he murmured, coming to her. His fingertips drew through the wet trails on her cheeks. "Why the talk of leaving? I didn't mean to upset you earlier. It was too soon—I shouldn't have approached you that way."

That comment brought a fresh, stinging surge of salt water to her eyes. "It's not that."

He reached around to the back of her head and unfastened her hair, dropping the pins to the floor. "Then what is it? You can tell me anything." His fingers stroked her scalp and spread her hair over her shoulders in a rippling stream. "You must realize that by now. Tell me, and I'll make it all better."

The words made Sophia want to throw herself at him and weep and howl. Instead she closed her expression and glanced away from him. She forced words through her stiff lips. "Some things cannot be made better."

"What things?"

She wiped her palm over her cheeks and set her jaw to keep it from quivering. "Please don't touch me," she said in a raw whisper.

He ignored the plea and slid his arm around her, bringing her against his broad chest. "You know how stubborn I am, Sophia." His hand settled at the small of her back. Although his grasp was light, she knew that it would be impossible for her to break free. His lips brushed over her forehead as he spoke. "I'm going to get the truth out of you sooner or later. Save us both time and tell me now."

Despairing, she realized that Ross was going to persist until he had the answers he wanted, unless she found a way to stop him. "Please leave my room," she said distinctly. "Or I am going to scream and tell everyone that you are forcing yourself on me."

"Go ahead." Ross waited, relaxed and calm, while she quivered with tension. A faintly arrogant smile touched his lips. "You may as well learn now that it's useless to try and bluff me."

"Damn you," she whispered.

"I think you want to tell me." He nuzzled the top of her head. "I know that you've kept secrets from me since you first came to Bow Street. It's time to bring them to light, Sophia. Afterward there will be nothing left to fear."

Sophia gripped the hard muscles of his arms and breathed jerkily. It was finally time to confess. She would have to tell Ross everything, and face the consequences. Vehement sobs pushed from her throat . . . abraded cries of ruined vengeance and hopeless love.

"Don't," Ross murmured, gathering her protectively against his chest. "Don't, Sophia. Sweetheart. It's all right."

His tenderness was too much for her to bear. Sophia fought her way out of his arms and stumbled to the bed. She sat and blindly held up a hand to keep him at bay. The gesture, frail though it was, served to hold him back. He stood in the shadows, his large form nearly blocking out the glimmer of the tinplate lantern.

"I can't tell you if you touch me," she said hoarsely. "Just stay there."

Ross was still and silent.

"You know about the months after my parents died," Sophia said in a wretched whisper, "when John and I were caught stealing. And I was taken in by my cousin Ernestine."

"Yes."

"Well, John would not go. He ran off to London instead. He continued to . . . to steal and do bad things, he . . ." She squeezed her eyes shut, but tears kept welling from beneath her lashes. "He fell in with a gang of pickpockets. Eventually he was arrested and charged with an act of petty thievery." She rubbed her hands over her streaming face and sniffled.

"Here," Ross muttered, and she saw from the edge of her vision that he was extending a handkerchief. His face was grim, revealing how difficult it was for him to witness her distress and not be able to touch her.

Accepting the handkerchief, Sophia mopped her face and blew her nose. Wearily she resumed her story. "He was taken before a magistrate who sentenced him to a year on a prison hulk. It was an unusually harsh sentence for such a trivial crime. When I learned of what had happened to my brother, I thought of going to London to visit the magistrate and plead with him to reduce the severity of the punishment. But by the time I reached the city, John had already been taken to the hulk."

A curious numbness came over her, making it easier to talk. It was as if she had suddenly become detached from the scene, watching as if a play were being enacted before her. "I was in torment for months, thinking every minute of my brother, wondering what he was suffering. I was not so sheltered that I didn't have some idea of what occurs on prison hulks. But no matter what happened to him in that place, I promised myself that I would take care of him and heal him afterward. If only he would live."

A long, emotion-fraught silence passed.

"But he didn't," Ross finally said.

Sophia shook her head. "Cholera. The hulks were always riddled with one disease or another . . . it was only a matter of time before John became ill. He did not survive. He was buried in a mass grave near the ship, without any stone or marker. I . . . I have never been the same since I was told. John's death has underpinned every emotion, every experience, every thought and desire I've had in my adult life. I have lived with constant hatred for years."

"Hatred of whom?"

She looked at him then, her expression incredulous. "Of the man who sent him there. The magistrate who took no pity on an orphaned boy and sentenced him to certain death."

The shadows obscured most of Ross's face, except for the gleam of his narrowed eyes. "His name," he demanded in a tightly leashed voice that betrayed his hideous suspicions.

Sophia's numbness lifted away, leaving her as raw as an open wound. "It was *you*, Ross," she whispered. "You sent John to the prison hulk."

Although he remained still, she sensed the tremendous impact of her words, the ripple of shocked anguish beneath his facade. She knew that he was trying to dredge rapidly through the past, to remember one out of the thousands of cases that had come before him on the bench.

The rest of the confession drained out of her like poison. "I wanted revenge against you," she said dully. "I thought that if I could persuade you to employ me, I would find ways to undermine you. For a while I copied parts of various files in the criminal records room, looking for anything that would discredit you and the runners. But that wasn't all of my plan. I also wanted to hurt you in the deepest way possible. To . . . to break your spirit as mine had been broken. I wanted to make you fall in love with me so that I could injure you in a way that you would not recover from. But as it turned out . . ." A jagged laugh escaped her. "Somehow all that hatred has vanished. And I have failed utterly."

She was silent then, closing her eyes to avoid the sight of his face. She waited for his contempt, his anger, and, worst of all, his rejection. Silence fell gently around her. Aching, annihilated, she waited for fate to deliver its final blow. As the quiet continued, she felt almost dreamlike, wondering if Ross would simply leave the room and let her crumble in despair.

She was not aware of any movement, but suddenly Ross was standing behind her, his hands settling on her shoulders, fingertips touching the base of her throat. With no effort at all, he could choke the life from her. She almost wanted him to. Anything to escape the desolation that saturated her. Docile and hopeless, she swallowed against the featherlight pressure of his fingers.

"Sophia," he said without inflection, "do you still want revenge?"

A breath clogged in her throat. "No."

His fingers began to move then, caressing the sides and front of her throat, drawing sensation to the surface of her skin. She began to gasp beneath the life-giving touch, her head lolling back helplessly until it rested against the hard surface of his stomach. Puppet-like, she could not seem to move without the animation of his hands.

He spoke again. "When did you change your mind?"

God help her, she could withhold nothing from him now. He would strip her of all pride and leave her decimated. Sophia fought to keep silent, but his stroking fingers seemed to coax the words from her unwilling throat. "When you were hurt," she said brokenly. "I wanted to help you . . . I wished that no harm would ever come to you again. Especially not from me." She was breathing too hard to speak. A whimper came from the bottom of her lungs as she felt his warm fingers slip into the bodice of her gown. He cupped her breast and softly circled the nipple until it tightened into a hard bud. It seemed that he touched her not with the intention to arouse, but to recall the intimacy that had existed between them just a few hours earlier. Heat danced over her skin, and she leaned back against him more heavily, her body robbed of strength.

Ross sat on the bed and carefully turned her toward

him. As Sophia lifted her gaze, she saw that his lips were tight with pain, as if he had suffered a body blow. "I don't know what happened in the past," he said huskily. "I don't remember your brother. But I promise you that I will find out exactly what occurred. If it turns out that I am guilty of your accusations, I will accept the blame, and everything that comes with it." His hands continued to play over her breast, as if he couldn't keep from touching her. "For now, I will ask only one thing of you. Stay with me until I uncover the truth. Will you do that, Sophia?"

She nodded with a shuddering sound of assent.

He pushed the wet strands of hair away from her cheeks. Leaning forward, he covered her mouth with his in a hard, warm kiss. Sophia fought to think above the pounding of her heart. "But the way I deceived you . . ." she said unevenly. "You can't possibly want me now."

"What makes you think I have any more control over this than you do?" he muttered. He pulled her close, hugging her to his strong body, and she shivered as immeasurable relief flooded her. Ross knew the truth, and he had not rejected her. This fact was difficult for her mind to encompass. She buried her face in his coat, which held a trace of tobacco from the smoke-filled billiards room.

He cradled her gently. "Those feelings you've carried with you for years . . . it won't be easy to let them go."

"They're already gone." Sighing, she rested her head on his shoulder. "All this time I wanted revenge against someone who didn't exist. You are nothing like the man I expected you to be."

"Portly and old, with a wig and a pipe," he said, recalling what she had said the first day they met.

Sophia smiled wearily. "You have ruined my plan every step of the way by making it impossible for me not to care for you."

The statement seemed to bring Ross no pleasure. "What if it turns out that I did indeed send your brother to his death?" His eyes were dark and troubled. "When I became a member of the judiciary ten years ago, I had no practical experience. For a while I modeled my judgments after those of the magistrates who had gone before me. I thought it best to follow the procedures they had already initiated. It was only later that I heeded my own instincts and began to run the court as I wished. I have no doubt that I was too harsh on many of the defendants who came before me in those early days." His deep chest moved with a taut sigh. "Even so, I cannot fathom that I would have sent a mere pickpocket to a prison hulk."

Sophia was helplessly silent.

His fingertips traced gently over the slender wings of her eyebrows. "I have never allowed myself to wish that I could change the past. Such thoughts are futile, and the regrets would drive me insane. But this is the first time that my entire future has hung in the balance, depending on some mistake I may have made years ago." He raised himself on one elbow, a swath of dark hair falling over his forehead as he looked down at her.

"How can I ask you to forgive me for your brother's death? There is no way I could atone for it. But the thought of losing you is something I can't endure."

"I have already forgiven you," she whispered. "I know what kind of man you are. You punish yourself far more harshly than anyone else could. Besides, how could I withhold my forgiveness when you have offered yours so freely?"

He shook his head with a rueful smile. "Whatever your original intentions were, you've done nothing but take care of me."

"I was trying to make you fall in love with me," she said. "Then I was going to break your heart."

"I have no objection to the first half of the plan," he informed her dryly. "Though I wouldn't care much for the second half."

A wobbly smile curved her lips. She put her arms around his neck and buried her face against his throat. "Neither would I."

Ross kissed her gently, and it seemed the passion between them was underlaid with an understanding that the path to happiness would not be easy for them. It would require forgiveness, and compromise, and blind trust. Sophia tried to intensify the kiss, but he drew back and clasped her head in his hands.

"I'm not going to stay with you tonight," he murmured, his thumbs stroking her temples. "When we finally sleep together, I don't want there to be any regrets afterward."

"I won't regret anything," Sophia told him earnestly.

"Now I know that you won't blame me for what I tried to do to you. That was what I feared most. Please stay with me tonight."

He shook his head. "Not until I find out the truth about your brother's death. Once we are in possession of all the facts, we can decide what is to be done."

She turned her face against his hand and kissed the warm interior of his palm. "Make love to me. Make me forget every moment of my life before you."

"Oh, God." Ross released her with a savage groan and left the bed as if it were a torture rack. "I want you more than I can bear. Don't make this even more difficult."

Sophia knew that she should help him in his resolve, but she couldn't seem to keep herself from saying recklessly, "Come lie with me. We won't sleep together, if that is what you want. Just hold me for a while."

He growled in frustration and headed to the door. "You know what would happen if we tried that. In about five minutes I would have you on your back with your heels in the air."

The crude image caused her stomach to tighten deliciously. "Ross—"

"Lock the door behind me," he muttered, opening the door and crossing the threshold without a backward glance.

After sleeping until late morning, Ross's brother decided to spend the day playing cards at the lakeside pavilion. However, before Matthew was able to exit through the French doors at the rear of the mansion, Ross snared him.

"Hello, Matthew," Ross said pleasantly, resting a hand on his brother's shoulder. As Matthew attempted to pull away, his grip tightened into an unbreakable clamp. "I see you've finally arisen. Why don't you join me in the study? I have a sudden desire for your company."

Matthew stared at him warily. "Perhaps later, brother. I must act as host to my friends. You would not want me to be rude, I'm certain."

Ross gave him a chilling smile. "They can make do without you for a while." His cold gaze swerved to the three young men who had accompanied Matthew. "Proceed with your plans, gentlemen. My brother will join you later." Hauling a protesting Matthew back inside, Ross ushered him down the hall to a private study.

"What the hell is going on?" Matthew demanded, trying without success to pry himself free of Ross's grip. "Dammit, let go—you're ruining my coat!"

"In here," Ross commanded, pushing him inside the study and closing the heavy oak door to afford them some privacy.

Clearly nettled, Matthew made a great show of smoothing his lapels and sleeves.

Ross glanced around the study, which had been left exactly as their father had arranged it. The cozy masculine room was small and lined with oak bookcases. A

French drop-leaf table and a writing chair were positioned in front of a trio of windows. Remembering how often he had seen the elder Cannon writing correspondence or poring over account books at that desk, Ross scowled. He could not help feeling that he had failed his father by allowing Matthew to become the spoiled, selfish creature that he was.

Matthew frowned. "You're looking at me as if I'm some cutpurse you're about to dispatch to Newgate."

"Newgate would be a pleasure palace in comparison to the place I'd like to dispatch you to."

Hearing the grim fury in Ross's voice, Matthew heaved a great sigh. "All right, I apologize for last night—I suppose Miss Sydney has offered her version of the story, casting herself as the virtuous victim. And I will admit, I was somewhat the worse for drink. My friend Hatfield had opened a damn fine brandy, and it went to my head." Adopting an air of indifference, Matthew wandered to the well-worn globe in the corner and spun it idly.

"That isn't good enough, Matthew. Yes, I intend to discuss your behavior of last night, but first we will deal with another matter that has presented itself."

Matthew looked surprised. "What do you mean?"

"I had a meeting with Mr. Tanner this morning."

"Who is Tanner?"

Ross shook his head in annoyance. "Our estate agent. The man who has managed our land and properties for the past ten years."

"And you've already met with him this morning?

Good God, do you ever rest? The last thing I want to discuss is some trivial business matter—"

"It's not trivial," Ross interrupted curtly. "And it doesn't concern business. It appears that one of our tenants has approached Tanner with the complaint that his unmarried daughter is several months pregnant."

Matthew's expression became guarded. "What has that to do with me, if some peasant wench is carrying a bag pudding?"

"Her family claims that you are the father." Ross watched his brother's face closely, and his heart sank as he saw the look of guilt in Matthew's gray-green eyes. A curse escaped his lips. "The family's name is Rann. Did you seduce the girl or not?"

Matthew's face twisted into a surly grimace. "It was not seduction. It was mutual desire. She wanted me, I obliged her, and no one was the worse for it."

"No one was the worse?" Ross repeated incredulously. "Tanner says the girl is not yet sixteen, Matthew! You've taken her innocence and given her a fatherless babe—and betrayed Iona in the process."

Matthew looked unrepentant. "Everyone does it. I could name you a dozen men who have taken their pleasure outside the marriage bed. A bastard child is an unfortunate consequence—but that is the girl's concern, not mine."

Somewhere in the midst of his fury, Ross was shocked at his brother's callousness. It was not lost on him that Matthew had done exactly what Sophia's lover had done to her—used her, deceived and abandoned her. "My God," he said softly. "What am I to do with you? Have you no conscience? No sense of responsibility?"

"Conscience and responsibility are your preserves, brother." Matthew spun the globe again; it nearly teetered off its axis. "You've always been held up to me as an example of supreme morality. Sir Ross, the paragon of manhood. No one on earth could live up to the standards you set, and I'll be damned if I'll even try. Besides, I don't envy you your sterile, joyless life. Unlike you, I have some passion—I have a man's needs—and, by God, I'll indulge them until I'm in my grave!"

"Why don't you indulge them in your wife?" Ross suggested acidly.

Matthew rolled his eyes. "I was bored with Iona a month after we were married. A man can't be expected to be satisfied with one woman forever. As they say, variety is the very spice of life."

Ross was sorely tempted to blister his ears with a scalding lecture. However, the obstinate set of Matthew's jaw made it clear that he was going to remain stubbornly unrepentant. He would never willingly face the consequences of his actions.

"Exactly how much 'variety' have you enjoyed?" Seeing Matthew's blank look, Ross clarified his question impatiently. "How many women have you seduced besides the Rann girl?"

A vaguely smug expression settled on Matthew's face. "I can't be certain . . . nine or ten, I suppose."

"I want a list of their names."

"Why?"

"To discover whether or not you have fathered any other bastard children. And if so, you are going to provide for their support and education."

The younger man sighed grumpily. "I don't have any money to spare—unless you give me an advance on my allowance."

"*Matthew*," Ross said, his gaze menacing.

Matthew held up his hands mockingly. "All right, I yield. Scour the countryside for my illegitimate offspring. Take away what little money I have. Now, may I join my friends?"

"Not yet. There is something you should know. From now on, I will ensure that your indolent way of life is over. No more lounging at the club and drinking all day; no more gambling or chasing women. If you attempt to visit your usual haunts, you'll find that you are no longer welcome. And you will be refused credit wherever you go, for I will make it clear to shopkeepers and list-makers alike that I will no longer be responsible for your debts."

"You can't do that!" Matthew burst out.

"Oh, but I can," Ross assured him. "From now on, you are going to work for your allowance."

"Work?" The word seemed unfamiliar to Matthew. "Doing *what*? I'm not qualified to work—I am a gentleman!"

"I will find something appropriate for you," Ross promised grimly. "I am going to teach you responsibility, Matthew, no matter what it takes."

"If Father were still alive, this would never happen!"

"If Father were still alive, this would have happened years ago," Ross muttered. "Unfortunately, much of the blame is mine. I've been too busy at Bow Street to pay attention to your activities. That is going to change, however."

A string of curses issued from Matthew's lips as he moved to a cabinet and rummaged for a glass and a decanter. Pouring himself a brandy, he tossed it down as if it were medicine, then refilled the glass. The liquor appeared to brace him. Taking a few long breaths, he glared into Ross's implacable countenance. "Are you going to tell Iona?"

"No. But neither will I lie to her if she ever comes to me with questions about your fidelity."

"Good, then. My wife will never ask—she does not want to hear the answers."

"God help her," Ross muttered.

After taking another swallow of brandy, Matthew swirled the liquid in his glass and gave a moody sigh. "Is that all?"

"No," Ross said. "We have one more issue to address— your behavior toward Miss Sydney."

"I've already apologized for that. I can't do any more than that . . . unless you would like me to open a vein?"

"That won't be necessary. What I wish to emphasize is that you are to treat her with absolute respect from now on."

"There is only so much respect I am going to show a servant, brother."

"She isn't going to be a servant for much longer."

Matthew raised an eyebrow in mild interest. "You're going to dismiss her, then?"

Ross gave him a hard, purposeful stare. "I'm going to marry her. If she will have me."

Matthew stared back with total incomprehension. "Holy Mother of God," he said raspily, and stumbled to the nearest chair. He sat down heavily, the whites of his eyes on full display as he regarded Ross. "You're serious. But that is madness. You would be a laughingstock. A Cannon marrying a servant! For the sake of the family, find someone else. She is only a woman—there are a hundred others who could easily take her place."

It took all of Ross's will to keep from doing his brother bodily harm. Instead he braced his hands on the desk, closed his eyes for a moment, and battened down his temper. Then he turned and sent Matthew a gaze filled with black fire. "After all the years I've spent alone, you ask me to reject the one woman who makes me complete?"

Matthew seized on his words. "That is my point. After so many celibate years, you're half mad from deprivation. Any woman would seem desirable. Believe me, that creature is not worthy of your affection. She has no sophistication, no style, no family. Take her as a mistress, if you fancy her. But I advise you not to marry her, because I guarantee that you will soon tire of her, and then you'll be well and truly shackled."

Abruptly Ross's anger died. He felt nothing for his

brother except pity. Matthew would never find true
love or passion, only hollow imitations. He would
spend the rest of his life feeling dissatisfied, never
knowing how to fill the emptiness inside. And so he
would turn to artificial pleasures, and try to convince
himself that he was content.

"I will not attempt to presuade you of Sophia's
worth," Ross said quietly. "However, if you say one
word to her that could be construed as critical or con-
descending, I will castrate you. Slowly."

Chapter 11

Simple black or white silk masks were provided for the guests who had not brought one for the Saturday evening ball. But most of the company were wearing beautiful creations that had been designed especially for the event. Sophia was dazzled by the array of masks adorned with feathers, jewels, embroidery, and hand-painted motifs. People mingled and flirted audaciously, enjoying the anonymity that their disguises afforded. The unmasking would occur at midnight, after which a lavish supper would be served.

Peeking around the doorway of the drawing room, Sophia smiled in satisfaction at the splendid sight of guests dancing a formal minuet, executing bows and curtsies with practiced grace. The ladies all wore gowns in fashionably rich colors, while most of the gentlemen were striking in their schemes of black-and-white evening wear. Freshly waxed and polished floors reflected the sparkling light of the chandeliers, bathing the assemblage in an almost magical glow. The air was thick with flowers and perfume, relieved by the evening breeze that drifted in from the conservatories and anterooms.

The series of rooms beyond the drawing room were filled with guests who played cards or billiards, drank champagne, and partook of small delicacies such as oyster pâté, lobster tarts, and cakes soaked in rum. Thinking of the meal to come, Sophia decided to return to the kitchen and make certain that everything was going according to schedule. Discreetly she slipped outside to a walk that skirted the side of the house. The night air was cool and springlike, and she sighed in relief, pulling at the snug collar of her dark gown.

Passing an open conservatory lined with columns, Sophia was surprised to note that it was occupied by the elderly Mr. Cannon, positioned in his wheeled chair to view the ball through a large window. A footman waited nearby, evidently having been recruited to attend the crusty old gentleman.

Sophia approached him with a hesitant smile. "Good evening, Mr. Cannon. May I ask why you are sitting out here alone?"

"Too much noise and bother in there," he replied. "Moreover, the fireworks will start at midnight, and this is the best place from which to view them." He eyed her speculatively. "In fact, you shall watch them with me." Turning to the footman, he said brusquely, "Go fetch some champagne. Two glasses."

"Sir," Sophia said, "I'm afraid I cannot—"

"Yes, I know. You have responsibilities. But this is my birthday, and therefore I must be humored."

Sophia smiled wryly as she sat on the stone bench beside his chair. "If I am seen drinking champagne and watching fireworks with you, I will probably be dismissed."

"Then I will hire you as my companion."

Still smiling, Sophia folded her hands in her lap. "Are you not going to wear a mask, sir?"

"Why would I wear a mask? I'm hardly going to deceive anyone, sitting in this contraption." Viewing the dancers through the window, Cannon snorted derisively. "I didn't like masked balls when they were in fashion forty years ago, and I like them even less now."

"I wish I had a mask," she mused with a thoughtful smile. "I could do or say whatever I liked, and no one would know me."

The old gentleman's gaze moved over her. "Why are you wearing plain broadcloth on such an evening?" he asked abruptly.

"There is no need for me to wear a fine gown."

He made a scoffing sound. "Nonsense. Even Mrs. Bridgewell wore a good black satin on special occasions."

"I have no gowns more elegant than this, sir."

"Why not? Isn't my grandson providing a decent salary?"

Their conversation was interrupted as the footman reappeared with a tray of champagne. "Ah, good," Cannon said. "Is that the Rheims? Leave the bottle here, and go be of use to someone inside. Miss Sydney will keep me company."

The footman complied with a submissive bow. Sophia accepted the glass of champagne from Mr. Cannon, holding it by the stem and regarding the light amber liquid curiously.

"Have you drunk champagne before?" the old man asked.

"Once," Sophia admitted. "When I lived with my cousin in Shropshire, a neighbor gave me a bottle of champagne that was not quite finished. It had gone flat by then, and I was disappointed by the taste. I expected it to be sweet."

"This is French champagne—you will like it. See how the bubbles rise in vertical lines? That is the sign of a good vintage."

Sophia brought the shallow glass to her face and enjoyed the cool, tickling sensation as the bubbles burst near her nose. "What makes it sparkle?" she asked almost dreamily. "It must be magic."

"Actually, it is a process of double fermentation," he informed her, his tone so flat and dry that he reminded her of Ross. "The 'devil's wine,' it is called, because of its explosive nature."

Sophia took an experimental sip of the dry, effervescent vintage and wrinkled her nose. "I still don't like it," she said, and the old man chuckled.

"Try it again. You will acquire the taste for it eventually."

Although she was tempted to point out that she would never have the opportunity to acquire such a taste, Sophia nodded obediently and drank. "I like the shape of the glass," she commented while the champagne trickled down her throat.

"Do you?" A mischievous sparkle entered his eyes. "That style is called the coupe. It was modeled after Marie Antoinette's breast."

Sophia gave him a reproving glance. "You are wicked, Mr. Cannon," she said, and he cackled in delight.

A new voice entered the conversation. "It was *not* modeled after Marie Antoinette's breast. Grandfather is trying to shock you." The speaker was Ross, austerely handsome in his evening clothes, a black mask dangling in his fingers. His teeth flashed in a smile so easy and charming that Sophia's breath caught. There was no man who could equal him tonight, no one who possessed his mixture of elegance and rugged masculinity.

Trying to conceal her reaction to him, Sophia took a deep swallow of cold champagne, and choked on the icy burn. "Good evening, Sir Ross," she said hoarsely, her eyes watering. She stood awkwardly, looking for a place to deposit her half-filled glass.

"Well, Grandfather," Ross continued, "I should have known you would be doing your best to corrupt Miss Sydney."

"I would hardly call a good bottle of Rheims *corruption*," Cannon replied defensively. "Why, it is a health tonic! As the French say, champagne is the universal medicine."

"That is the first time I've ever heard you agree with the French, sir." The amusement lingered in Ross's eyes as he caught Sophia's wrist, preventing her from leaving. "Stay and finish your champagne, little one," he said softly. "As far as I'm concerned, you may have anything you desire."

Flushing, Sophia tugged at her wrist, conscious of the elderly man's attention on them. "I desire to return to my duties, sir."

To her disbelief, Ross lifted her hand to his mouth and kissed her palm, right in front of his grandfather. Their relationship couldn't have been more clear if he had proclaimed it from a podium.

"Sir Ross," she said softly, shocked.

He held her gaze deliberately, informing her silently that he was no longer going to conceal his feelings for her.

Unnerved, Sophia handed her glass to him. "I must go," she said breathlessly. "Please excuse me." As she left with great haste, Ross remained with his grandfather, watching her so intently that she could feel the heat of his gaze on her back.

Glancing at his grandfather, Ross raised his brows expectantly. "Well?"

"It is a good match," Cannon said, pouring more champagne with obvious relish. "She is a pleasant girl without pretensions. Much like her grandmother. Have you sampled her charms yet?"

Ross smiled at the abrupt question. "If I had, I wouldn't tell you."

"I think you have," the old man said, regarding him over the rim of the glass. "And if she is anything like her grandmother was, you had a fine time indeed."

"You old fox. Don't say that you and Sophia Jane . . . ?"

"Oh, yes." The memory appeared to be a delicious one. Lost in private reflections, Cannon gently rolled the stem of the champagne glass between his time-worn fingers. "For years I've loved her," he said softly. "I should have tried harder to win her. Don't let anything come between you and the woman you love, my boy."

The smile vanished from Ross's face, and he replied gravely, "No, sir."

As Sophia strode across the stone-and-marble-paved floor of the great hall, she saw a dark figure detaching itself from the shadows of a domed alcove. It was a man wearing a black silk mask, dressed in evening wear like the other guests. He was young and strapping, with broad shoulders and a slim waist—the same unusually powerful build that most of the Bow Street runners possessed. What was such a man doing far away from the drawing room? Sophia paused uncertainly. "Sir? May I assist you?"

He took a long time to respond. Finally he approached, stopping within an arm's length of her. The eyes behind the mask were a bright jewel-blue, mesmerizing in their intensity. When he spoke, his voice was low and hoarse. "I've been looking for you."

Puzzled, Sophia tilted her head as she gazed at him. Something about him made her uneasy, her nerves thrilling with a sense of dangerous awareness. The mask concealed most of his face, but there was no disguising the bold jut of his nose or the generous shape of his mouth. His brown hair was short and neatly brushed, and his skin was unusually swarthy for a gentleman.

"How may I help you?" she asked cautiously.

"What is your name?"

"Miss Sydney, sir."

"You are the housekeeper here?"

"Only for tonight. I work for Sir Ross Cannon at Bow Street."

"Bow Street is too dangerous a place for you," he said, sounding annoyed.

He was drunk, she thought, and inched backward.

"You are a spinster?" he asked, following her slowly.

"I am unwed," she acknowledged.

"Why would a woman like you remain unmarried?"

The questions were strange and inappropriate. Uneasily Sophia decided that it would be wise for her to leave as soon as possible. "You are kind to spare me your concern, sir. However, I have duties to attend to. If you will excuse me—"

"Sophia," he whispered, staring at her with what seemed to be longing.

Startled, she wondered how he knew her first name. She stared at him with wide eyes, but then a sudden noise distracted her. It was the sound of laughter and cheering, accompanied by a vigorous swell of music and a cacophony of fireworks explosions. Bursts of brilliant light lit the sky and flickered through the windows. It must be midnight, Sophia realized. Time for the unmasking. Automatically she looked toward the sound.

The stranger moved behind her, so swift and silent that she did not sense him until she felt something cold drop on her chest. She reached up and fumbled at the foreign weight, then heard a smooth click as something was clasped around her neck.

"Good-bye," came a warm whisper near her ear.

By the time she had turned around, he was gone.

Dumbstruck, Sophia put both hands to her chest and felt a web of stones and precious metal. A necklace. But why would a stranger do such a thing? She was bewildered and terrified, her feet carrying her swiftly outside. She pulled at the heavy necklace, searched for the clasp, but could not seem to unshackle herself.

Anxiously Sophia rushed to the open conservatory, where she had left Ross and his grandfather. A crowd had gathered around them, with many more coming from the ballroom. Rockets filled the sky with clusters of brilliant color, forming shapes of trees and animals, while rain-fire drifted downward through billows of smoke. The scene was chaotic and deafening.

Sophia stood huddled against the side of the house, her hands ineffectually trying to cover the rich glitter at her throat. Although Ross could not possibly have seen or heard her, his head turned as if he sensed she was there. At the sight of her starkly pale face, he reacted instantly. He moved through the cheering crowd, his gaze never leaving her, and he reached her in a few strides. The noise made it impossible for them to speak.

Ross took one of her hands and gently pulled it from her throat, exposing the mass of diamonds. His eyes narrowed at the sight. Sophia tugged helplessly at the heavy collar, trying to remove it. Suddenly she felt his warm fingers behind her neck. The clasp was unfastened, and the weight of gold and jewels slid away from her throat. Pocketing the necklace, Ross took her hand and drew her inside the house.

He did not stop until they reached the blue parlor adjoining the central hall. After the earsplitting noise and jubilant brilliance of the fireworks, the quietness of the room was almost shocking. "What happened?" Ross asked tersely, closing the door.

Sophia tried to explain in a coherent fashion. "I was going to the kitchen, and a man stopped me. He was wearing a mask. He said he had been looking for me. I am certain I have never met him before, but somehow he knew my name." Unsteadily she described the odd conversation that had taken place, and then the stranger's astonishing act of clasping the diamond necklace around her throat before disappearing.

As she spoke, Ross stroked the side of her neck lightly, as if he were erasing the other man's touch. "What did he look like?"

"He had brown hair and blue eyes. And he was tall, though not quite so tall as you. At first I thought he was one of the runners. He had a powerful build, and he even seemed to move in the way they do—that is, he seemed unusually agile for his size. He was dressed in fine clothes, just like the party guests ... but I don't think he was one of them."

"Did he have any scars or marks?"

Sophia shook her head. "Not that I could see."

Grimly Ross extracted the necklace from his pocket and spread it on a mahogany table. Standing close by his side, Sophia stared at the piece in awestruck dismay. She had never seen anything so magnificent, a glittering collar woven of strings of diamond flowers and emerald leaves. "Is it real?" she whispered.

"Those jewels are not made of paste," came his flat reply.

"It must be worth a fortune."

"Three or four thousand pounds, I would guess." Ross's assessing gaze traveled over the necklace. "Your admirer is either a very wealthy man or an accomplished thief."

"Why is this happening to me?" Sophia whispered. "I've done nothing to encourage anyone's interest. What does he want? Why would a stranger do something like this?"

Hearing the note of panic in her voice, Ross bent and kissed her temple reassuringly. "I intend to find out. Don't be afraid—I won't let anything happen to you."

She closed her eyes and breathed in his familiar scent, gaining comfort from his solid strength.

"Come," he murmured. "I'll take you to the kitchen."

"And then?"

"I'm going to recruit some of the footmen to help me search the grounds, in case your stranger is still lurking about. Though I doubt he would be such a fool." Reaching for the necklace, Ross dropped it back into his pocket. "A necklace like this didn't appear from thin air . . . it is unique and valuable. I suspect it won't be difficult to trace its origins. Which leads to an interesting conclusion. Your admirer wants you to discover his identity—otherwise he wouldn't have given you such a telling piece of evidence."

"Do you think he is the one who sent me the lavender gown?"

"I assume so." Ross's mouth was set in an impatient line, betraying his eagerness to go hunt for the mysterious guest. However, as he glanced at Sophia's tense face, he stopped and took her into his arms. He pulled her against his body until her toes nearly left the floor. A muscular arm hooked around the back of her neck as his lips descended to hers in a possessive kiss.

At his silent command, Sophia parted her own lips and yielded to his sensuous exploration. The kiss turned demanding, his tongue ravishing slowly, his thigh intruding between her legs. All rational thought, all trace of worry, burned to ashes. There was only Ross, his mouth and hands reminding her of the scorching intimacy they had shared the previous night. Her knees weakened, and she began to gasp, her hands searching restlessly over the back of his coat. She was possessed with a terrible urge to rip at his clothes, and at her own, until they were both naked.

"Ross," she moaned, her neck arching as his tongue traced an intricate pattern on her throat.

He lifted his head and smiled in masculine satisfaction when he saw the passion-softened curve of her lips and the haziness of her blue eyes. "You're mine, Sophia . . . and I will never let anything happen to you. Do you understand?"

She nodded dazedly, wobbling a little as he slid a supportive arm around her and guided her from the room.

The mysterious stranger was nowhere to be found on the grounds at Silverhill Park, which Ross had expected. However, the clue he had left behind would eventually lead to his capture. Ross was impatient to return to Bow Street and launch an investigation into the matter. The thought that someone had chosen to stalk Sophia in this untoward fashion provoked his most primitive male instincts. He would not be satisfied until he had cornered the bastard, seized him in a choke-hold, and pried a detailed confession from him.

Thankful that the party would be over on the morrow, Ross bade his valet to pack most of his belongings in preparation for an early departure. While the man was folding clothes and laying them neatly in the trunk, Ross wandered around the darkened mansion. A few pockets of activity remained: a couple embracing in a shadowy corner, a card game in the billiards room, men lounging in the library with half-finished cigars.

Sophia was probably in her room by now. Ross

longed to go to her. He had never been in such a disturbing situation before, having wounded someone he cared for, wondering how to make amends, realizing there was nothing he could do. Nothing short of raising John Sydney from the dead would make things right.

The fact that Sophia had forgiven him afforded no relief. The knowledge of his past actions would always exist between them. With a harsh sigh, Ross continued to walk aimlessly, reflecting on the events of the past twenty-four hours. His feelings for Sophia had so intensified that he could settle for nothing less than complete possession of her. He wanted her permanently, irrevocably. If she accepted him, he would try to make her so happy that the memory of her brother would not interfere with their feelings for each other.

He found himself in front of the housekeeper's door near the kitchen, the small room where Sophia was staying. Twice his hand raised to knock at the wood panel, then dropped without striking the surface. He knew that he should go back to his own room and wait patiently until he had uncovered the truth about the past. He should think of her needs rather than his own. But he wanted her so badly that scruples and conscience didn't matter anymore. Torn between duty and desire, he stood at the door with clenched fists, his body seething with sexual heat.

Just as his reluctant conscience prompted him to leave, the door opened, and Sophia's heavy-lashed blue eyes stared into his own. She was dressed in a prim nightgown, high-necked with a row of buttons. He wanted to unfasten them slowly, trace his tongue over every inch of pearly skin.

"Are you going to stand there all night?" Sophia asked softly.

Ross braced his hand on the doorjamb, his gaze raking over her. Desire exploded inside him, making it difficult for him to think straight. "I wanted to see if you were all right."

"I'm not," she said, one small hand catching at the front of his waistcoat and tugging him forward. "I'm lonely."

Breathing hard, Ross let her pull him into the room. He closed the door and looked down at Sophia's serious face. Her lips were plum-colored and velvety in the soft candlelight. "There are reasons why we should wait," he began gruffly, giving her one last chance to retreat. But the words were knocked from his throat as she pressed her slim body against his, standing on her toes to mold herself against him.

"For once, don't do the right thing," Sophia whispered, her silken arms sliding around his neck. He felt the delicate nip of her teeth on his earlobe just before she whispered tenderly, "I dare you."

The few memories Sophia had of her first lover were soon dispelled like smoke in the air as she was consumed by the deliberate fire of Ross's caresses. He undressed both of them leisurely, pausing often to possess her mouth with languid kisses. Bemused, Sophia wondered how a man who conducted his life at such a breakneck pace could make love so slowly, as if time had lost all meaning. When he finally removed her chemise and she was naked, she pressed herself against his body with a whimper of relief. His skin was warm and satin-smooth, his chest covered with thick black hair that tickled her breasts. She felt the strong upthrust of his sex against her belly, and she touched it cautiously, still very much a novice in the art of lovemaking.

The shaft was ridged with veins, the thin silken skin slipping a little over the steely hardness beneath. At the hesitant clasp of her fingers, the heavy organ moved as if it had a will of its own. Sophia's breath stopped. "Oh."

Ross's voice was thick with desire and something that sounded suspiciously like laughter. "Don't be afraid." He guided her fingers to the head of the shaft. "This is where it is most sensitive."

She stroked and played with the broad tip, and the small slit in the center, until she felt a drop of moisture emerge. It made his skin slippery, and she circled the head with her fingertips before sliding down to explore the tight, cool pouch nestled beneath.

Suddenly he caught her wrist in a gentle grasp. "That's enough for now," he said raspily.

"Why?"

"Because I'm about to lose my self-control."

"That was my intention," she said, and he laughed low in his throat.

"We're going to do this my way," he murmured, scooping her up and depositing her on the narrow bed. "And I intend to make it last a long time."

Ross's body settled beside hers, more than six feet of hard, powerful male, and she rolled toward him with trembling eagerness. He pushed her back down and bent over her, his hot breath fanning her breast. The tip of his tongue teased her nipple, and she grasped his broad shoulders, straining upward in supplication. He nibbled and sucked lightly at the hardening peak, then moved to the other breast, making her writhe beneath him.

"Ross," she said desperately.

"Mmm?"

"I need more . . . more . . ." She felt his hand descend to her stomach, and her hips lifted in an eloquent arch.

He raised his head, his passion-bright eyes glinting with satisfaction when he saw the flush on her cheeks. She moaned in gratitude as his fingers slid through the triangle of curls, finding the feminine crest that ached so sweetly. To her dismay, the touch was only fleeting. "Oh, Ross, don't stop, please—"

"I want something else." He slid much lower, trailing kisses along her body until his shoulders lodged between her thighs.

Sophia felt his lips descend to the inside of her thigh. Suddenly realizing what he meant to do, she jerked and struggled upward to a half-sitting position. "Wait," she gasped, catching his dark head in her hands. "Wait. Not there."

His hand moved along the outside of her leg in a soothing stroke. "Haven't you done that before?"

"Of course not—I didn't even imagine that someone would—" She stopped and regarded him with a perplexed frown. "I doubt that Anthony even knew about such a thing."

Laughter rumbled in his chest, and he kissed her knee. "I wanted to do this to you the first day we met."

"You did?" she asked in complete astonishment.

"Right there in my office. I wanted to throw you across my desk and put my head under your skirts."

"No," Sophia said skeptically, unable to believe that beneath his remote exterior, he could have been thinking such a thing. "But you were so dignified!"

"As dignified as a man with a full-blown cockstand could be."

"Truly? But how—" She gasped as his head dropped between her thighs once more. "Oh, Ross, wait—"

"After tonight," came his velvety murmur, "you're going to forget all about Anthony."

She felt his fingers pressing her swollen folds open, his tongue touching the delicate peak between them. Her elbows collapsed, and she felt back to the mattress with a groan, staring blindly into the darkness. Oh, God, he was *licking* her, in long, sinuous laps that made her body quiver with desperate excitement.

She could not stop the motion of her hips, rising upward in repeated surges. His hands slid beneath her, guiding her rhythm while his tongue strummed, bathed, flirted. Just as the sensations coalesced in an unendurable peak, Ross lifted his head and levered his body over hers.

"Oh, God," Sophia whimpered, left suspended on the brink of climax. "Please, *please*—"

He entered her with a deep flex of his hips. Sophia cried out, her muscles instinctively grasping at the gentle but relentless intrusion. She was stretched tight, unable to take any more. Desperately she struggled to accommodate him, but it seemed impossible.

His mouth brushed over hers, and he whispered, "Easy. I won't hurt you. Relax, sweetheart." His hand slid between their bodies and she felt him stroke her while he pressed forward in slow nudges, his every movement careful and easy. Each plunge of his shaft drew a moan from her throat, and she bit her lip to hold in the sounds. Suddenly he was all the way inside her, gliding full and deep, burying every inch of his sex.

He withdrew almost to the head of his shaft, then submerged the entire length with excruciating slowness, his chest hair teasing her nipples, his flat stomach brushing over hers. She writhed upward, her hips pushing into his long, pleasuring thrusts until she begged frantically, "Please don't be gentle, don't, *don't*, do it harder, *please*—"

His mouth covered hers, muffling her cries. Her body shook with violent spasms, gripping the hard organ inside her until Ross let out a groan and seized her hips with both hands, spending his own passion.

As her body continued to twitch and jerk with delight, Ross cradled her in his arms and kissed her again. Filled with his tongue and his sex, she felt another wave of sensation roll over her, and she moaned and shivered with a second climax.

After a long time Ross moved onto his side, taking care not to crush her. Sophia stretched luxuriously against him. "Ross . . ." she murmured drowsily. "I want to tell you something. Perhaps you won't believe me, but it's true."

"Yes?"

"I couldn't have gone through with it."

"You mean, breaking my heart? Yes, I know that."

"You do?"

He smoothed the reckless profusion of her hair and spread it over his chest. "It's not in your nature to hurt anyone. You could never have brought yourself to betray me."

Sophia was astonished by his belief in her. "How can you be so certain?"

"You are very easy to read." He played lightly with the lobe of her ear. "I've known for a while that you cared for me. But I wasn't certain how much until yesterday morning, when you saw me after we'd been apart for a week. Your face showed everything."

Perturbed by the revelation, Sophia sat up and leaned over him, her bare breasts half concealed by the wild locks of her hair. "If I am so transparent, then what am I thinking now?"

Ross studied her for a moment, and a slow smile

curved his lips. "You're wondering how soon I'm going to make love to you again." Before she could reply, he pulled her farther atop his body, settling her legs on either side of his hips. To her astonishment, his sex stirred into vibrant life, springing hard against her vulnerable flesh. "And this is your answer," he murmured, pulling her head down to his.

Exhausted by the tumultuous weekend, Sophia cuddled on Ross's lap and dozed for most of the carriage ride back to London. Staring at the sleeping face on his shoulder, Ross marveled at the momentous change that had taken place in his life. He had become so accustomed to solitude that he had forgotten what it was like to need someone this way. Now all the desires that he had suppressed for so long—for sex, for affection and companionship—had been freed with a vengeance. It troubled him that Sophia had such power over him, a power that he himself had given her. God help him when she realized it. Yet he could not bear to withhold anything from her.

Her body bounced in his lap with each jolt of the carriage, arousing him and filling his mind with idle fantasies. Gently he held Sophia's head against his chest and watched the alterations of her expression as she slept: the tiny frown that gathered between her dark brows, the restless twitch of her mouth. It seemed that her dreams were far from peaceful. He stroked the side of her face and murmured quietly, and her frown smoothed away. Unable to help himself, Ross slid his hand to her breast and molded his fingers over the voluptuous curve. Even in sleep she responded to him, arching with a drowsy murmur. He pressed his lips to her forehead, and cradled her as she stretched and yawned.

"I'm sorry," he said, staring into the slumbrous depths of her eyes. "I didn't intend to wake you."

She blinked sleepily. "Are we almost there?"

"A half hour at most."

Her gaze turned wary. "What will happen tomorrow?" she asked.

"I'm going to find out if I was the man who sent your brother to the prison hulk all those years ago."

Her fingers slipped inside his waistcoat, seeking the warmth of his body. "Whatever you discover will not matter."

"Of course it will," he said gruffly.

"No." She levered herself upward. Her hand curved around his neck, and she applied her lips to his, exploring daintily, her tongue lapping into the warmth of his mouth. Ross remained stalwart for precisely five seconds, then responded to her tender witchery with a low groan. Her taste mingled with his, the kiss becoming full and deep as he immersed himself in her sweetness.

"Sophia," he said, tearing his mouth free. Although it was not the time or place he had planned, he could not prevent the words that escaped him. "I want to marry you."

She was very still, her face scant inches from his. Clearly, she had not expected such a proposal. Agitation caused her lashes to flutter, and she touched the tip of her tongue to her upper lip. "Gentlemen in your position don't marry servants."

"It has been known to happen."

"Yes, and the men who make such mistakes are exposed to ridicule and sometimes even ostracism. And you are very much in the public view—oh, your critics would be merciless!"

"I've been publicly criticized too many times to count," Ross said firmly. "I am well used to it by now. And you are carrying on as if I am a peer of the realm, when I am no more than a professional man."

"A professional man from a wealthy family with ties to the aristocracy."

"Well, if we are to start defining ourselves, I should point out that you are the daughter of a viscount."

"But I was not reared as one. After my parents died, I had no further education. I can't ride a horse, or dance, or play an instrument. And I was taught nothing of etiquette and aristocratic manners—"

"None of that matters."

She laughed in disbelief. "Perhaps not to you, but it does to me!"

"Then you will learn whatever is necessary."

Sophia fidgeted with a loose fold of his shirt. "I cannot marry you."

"Does that mean you don't want to?" His lips grazed the silken edge of her hairline and drifted to her temple.

"Your family would not approve of a marriage between us."

"Yes, they would." He kissed her throat. "My mother has made it clear that she will accept you with open arms. The rest of the family—aunts, uncles, and cousins—will follow her lead. And my grandfather has practically ordered me to propose to you."

"No!" Sophia exclaimed, astonished.

"He said that you were as pretty a miss as could be found anywhere. According to him, you are fertile ground for sowing, and I had better go about it right away."

"Good Lord!" Sophia was torn between laughter and dismay. "I can only imagine what else he said."

"He told me about his lifelong love for your grandmother, and how he wished that he had simply kidnapped Sophia Jane and eloped with her. He has lived with that regret for decades. God spare me from having to do the same."

Sophia's delicate face turned pensive. "I will stay with you for as long as you want me. Perhaps the best solution is that I become your mistress."

Ross shook his head decisively. "That is not what I need, Sophia. I'm not the kind of man who keeps a mistress. And you're not the kind of woman who would be happy with such an arrangement. There is no reason to make our relationship into something shameful. I want you to be my wife."

"Ross, I can't—"

"Wait," he murmured, sensing that he had pressed his advantage too soon. He should have waited patiently for the right time. "Don't give me an answer. Just consider the idea for a while."

"I don't need to consider it," she responded. "I really don't think—"

He covered her mouth with his, silencing her for a long time, so that she forgot what she had intended to say.

Chapter 12

Ross headed to Bow Street No. 3 immediately upon their arrival. Morgan had agreed to take up temporary residence at the public office during Ross's three-day absence, and the light at his desk was burning as evening settled over London. When Ross crossed the threshold, Morgan glanced up from his work and sighed in patent relief.

"Thank God you're back."

"Has it been that bad?" Ross regarded him with a slight smile, standing with his hands thrust into his coat pockets. "Did anything out of the ordinary occur?"

"No, just the usual." Morgan rubbed his eyes with the pads of his fingers, looking weary. "We served ten warrants, arrested a deserter, and investigated a murder at the thieves' kitchen on the east side of Covent Garden. And we looked into the matter of an escaping codfish from Lannigan's."

"A what?"

Despite Morgan's obvious weariness, a smile tugged at his wide mouth. "It seems that a young lad named

Dickie Sloper took a fancy to a particular codfish at the shop. Dickie fastened a hook to the gills, attached the other end of the line to the button of his inexpressibles, and walked away. The fishmonger was understandably alarmed when he saw the cod jump off the table and slide out the door, seemingly of its own accord. When young Dickie was caught, he swore that he was innocent and the fish was willfully following him."

Ross snorted with laughter. "Will Lannigan press charges?"

"No. The fish was recovered in its entirety, and Lannigan was satisfied after Dickie spent the night in the Bow Street strong room."

Ross regarded Grant with an irrepressible smile. "Well, it appears that Bow Street can manage without me after all."

The assistant magistrate gave him a sardonic glance. "You wouldn't say that if you could see the work that has accumulated on your desk. The pile is as high as my chest. I've done my damnedest, but I couldn't keep up with it. And now that you're here, I'm going home. I'm tired, hungry, and I haven't bedded my wife in days. In other words, I've been living as you do, and I can't stand another bloody minute of it."

"Wait," Ross said, turning serious. "I have come to ask a personal favor of you."

Ross had never made such a request before. Morgan stared at him with a new alertness, settling back in his chair. "Of course," he said without hesitation.

Approaching the desk, Ross withdrew the diamond-

and-emerald necklace from his pocket and laid it gently on the scuffed mahogany surface. Even in the uncertain lamplight, the jewels glittered with unearthly brilliance.

Morgan's stunned gaze met his before returning to the necklace. His lips pursed in a quiet whistle. "Sweet Jesus. Where did that come from?"

"That is precisely what I want you to find out."

"Why not assign one of the runners? Sayer could easily handle such a task."

"Not as quickly as you," Ross replied. "And I want answers soon." Although Morgan had spent the better part of a year on the bench, he still had more experience and ability than any of the runners. No one knew his way around London as Grant Morgan did, and Ross trusted him to take care of the matter expediently.

"How did the necklace come into your possession?" Grant asked, and Ross explained the details. The assistant magistrate gave him a long, thoughtful look. "Miss Sydney is unharmed?"

"She is fine, other than being understandably anxious. I want this matter resolved immediately, to spare her needless worry."

"Of course." Picking up a penholder, Morgan tapped it repeatedly on the desk in a rapid staccato that belied his impassive facade. "Cannon," he said quietly, "I suppose you've considered the possibility that Miss Sydney may be involved with someone. These gifts could likely have come from a paramour."

Ross shook his head even before the other man had

finished speaking. "No," he said firmly. "She has no paramour."

"How can you be certain?"

Annoyed by his friend's persistence, Ross scowled. "Because I am in a position to know."

"Ah." Grant seemed to relax, setting down the penholder and lacing his fingers together across his midriff. He pinned Ross with a glance of mingled speculation and amusement. "You've finally bedded her, then."

Ross wiped his face of all expression. "That has no relevance to the matter of the necklace."

"No," Morgan said easily, seeming to enjoy Ross's discomfort. "But it has been a long time for you, hasn't it?"

"I didn't say that I had bedded her," Ross said curtly. "I have the utmost respect for Miss Sydney. Moreover, it would be entirely inappropriate for me to take advantage of a woman who is in my employ."

"Yes, sir." Grant paused before asking with a straight face, "So . . . how was it?" He grinned as Ross sent him a warning look.

To Ross's disgruntlement, Morgan's comment about the pile on his desk was an understatement. Reports, files, correspondence, and assorted documents formed a precarious mountain. He sighed heavily as he entered his office. Not long ago he would have thought nothing of such a pile. Now it seemed ridiculous for one man to handle so much. A year earlier, he had accepted commissions to serve as the justice for Essex, Kent, Hertfordshire, and Surrey, in addition to the responsibilities he already had for Westminster and Middlesex. It had made him the most powerful magistrate in England, and he had taken satisfaction in the increasing reach of his authority. Until now. Now he wanted to ease back from the relentless flood of responsibility and have a private life. He wanted a wife, a home . . . even children someday.

He did not know any man who would willingly assume his post at Bow Street, not even Grant. Although Morgan was ambitious and dedicated, he would never allow his profession to take precedence over his marriage. Ross would simply have to obtain help in the administration of the Bow Street office, since it was too much for one man to handle. At the very least, he would have to fill his commission with three more justices, and hire a half-dozen additional runners. Moreover, it would be necessary to open two or three additional magisterial offices in Westminster. Picturing the reception *that* would get in Parliament, along with the accompanying requests for financial grants, Ross smiled darkly.

His smile faded as he rummaged through his desk for the key to the criminal records room. Locating it, he went down the hall and unlocked the door, then entered and set a lamp on a table. The room smelled of dust and vellum, tiny motes floating lazily through the lamplight. After a brief search, Ross found the drawer most likely to contain the file for John Sydney. Filled with equal parts of dread and resolution, he paged through sheaves of documents, but he could find nothing pertaining to the case of a pickpocket named Sydney.

Closing the drawer, Ross considered the row of cabinets thoughtfully. Apparently Sydney's case had been too insignificant to warrant an entire file. However, the boy must have been mentioned in the court records. A frown settled between Ross's brows as he turned toward another cabinet and opened it decisively.

A quiet voice interrupted his search. "I've already looked there."

He glanced at the doorway and saw Sophia's slender figure. She came forward, the light playing on her exquisite features. A melancholy smile curved her lips. "I have searched through every drawer and file in this room," she murmured. "There is no mention of John."

Guilt and concern assailed him, but Ross kept his face impassive while he considered the problem. "The court records dated before the past ten years have been moved to a storage room on the top floor. I will go find them now."

"Later," Sophia said gently. "You can ask Mr. Vickery to locate them tomorrow."

Understanding that she was no more eager than he to find the information, Ross approached her and hooked an arm around her waist. She yielded at once as he brought her hips against his. He lowered his mouth to her throat and searched with his tongue until he felt the throb of her pulse. "And in the meantime?" he asked, urging her into the rock-hard shape of his erection.

She circled her arms around his neck and rubbed her lips over his in the barest promise of a kiss. "In the meantime, I am going to keep you very busy."

"My room or yours?" he asked.

Sophia gave a breathless laugh as she remembered the last time he had asked her that question, right there in his office. "Which would you prefer?"

Lowering his mouth to her ear, he whispered, "My bed is bigger."

Brilliant sunlight streamed into the room, for they had forgotten to close the curtains the previous evening. Still half asleep, Sophia reflected that the sun must be very strong to cut through the haze of coal smoke that hovered over the city.

There was movement beside her, and she rolled onto her side, pushing up on one elbow. Ross stretched lazily as he awakened, tangled black lashes lifting to reveal drowsy gray eyes. He was so handsome with his hair disheveled and his face still sleep-flushed that Sophia nearly caught her breath.

Ross had been insatiable during the night. He had touched, kissed, and tasted every inch of her body, his hands gentle, his mouth insistent. The intimate memories filled her with wonder, and she felt her face turning pink. Moving experimentally, she discovered that the muscles on the inner sides of her thighs were sore, as well as her shoulders and the back of her neck.

Seeing her slight grimace, Ross sat up and leaned

over her, a frown crossing his forehead. "Did I hurt you last night?"

She laid her hands on his forearms, stroking the hair-roughened surface of his skin. "It's nothing that a hot bath won't cure."

No one would have recognized the reserved, authoritative Bow Street magistrate if he had been seen gazing at her with such tenderness. "You are beautiful in the sunlight," he said huskily.

Sophia's smile was immediately extinguished as she awakened fully and saw how the daylight reflected incandescently off the snowy bed linens. A chill of anxiety settled over her. "We've slept late," she said in dawning horror. "I can't believe it. Both of us are always awake before everyone else, at the break of dawn, and now . . . My God, it's practically midday!"

She reared upward in panic, and he pressed her back down to the mattress. "Hold still," he murmured. "Take a deep breath."

"Everyone is awake," she said, staring at him with wide eyes. "It is well past breakfast time. Oh, Lord, I have never slept late before!"

"Neither have I."

"Well, what are we to do?"

"I suppose we could get out of bed and put our clothes on." He didn't sound particularly enthralled by the idea.

Sophia moaned in increasing misery. "The servants, clerks, constables, and runners—they all know that we are together in your room." Snatching at a corner of the sheet, she pulled it over her face, wishing she could hide forever. "They know what we've been doing. Oh, don't you dare laugh!"

Ross did his best to oblige her, but his eyes were bright with amusement. "Unfortunately, we have ruined the opportunity for discretion. The only thing left to do is go about our work as usual."

"I can't," Sophia said, her voice muffled. "The thought of facing everyone . . ."

The sheet was inexorably pulled away, although Ross had to forcibly uncurl her fingers from the handfuls of white linen. "You don't have to face anyone," he told her. "We'll just stay here all day."

She frowned up at him. "I wish you would be serious!"

A chuckle stirred in his throat. "I *am* serious," he told her, and she wriggled impatiently beneath him.

"Ross, we must rise now!"

"I've already risen," he assured her, bringing her hand to the turgid length of his erection.

She gasped and jerked her fingers away. "If you think I'm going to do *that* with you now, in *broad daylight*, while everyone knows we're up here—"

He gave a suggestive laugh and spread her beneath him.

"Do be quiet!" Sophia whispered sharply, managing to flip over and crawl to the edge of the bed. "Someone will hear—oh!" She gasped as she felt the playful nip of his teeth on her right buttock.

Catching her by the waist, Ross dragged her backward and began to kiss the naked length of her spine, starting at the small of her back and working his way upward.

"I am sore," she protested, although a ripple of pleasure went through her body when he nibbled at a sensitive place beneath her shoulder blades.

Levering himself higher, he whispered at the nape of her neck, "I'll be gentle. Just once more, Sophia."

The feel of his mouth made her shiver weakly. "I . . . I hope this isn't usual for you. Three times last night, and again this morning . . . it won't be like this all the time, will it?"

"No." He pushed a pillow beneath her hips to angle them higher. "I've just been deprived for a while. Eventually I'll have my fill, and slow down to once a night."

"How long is 'eventually'?" she asked, and he laughed softly.

Her cheek pressed against the mattress and her eyes closed. "Ross," she moaned, flinching as he slid two fingers into her swollen sheath. He became even more gentle, his fingers barely moving while they remained deep inside her. His lips wandered from her neck to the side of her throat, his kisses as light as butterfly wings, his warm breath fanning on her skin in a way that made her shiver. The sensations gathered and intensified, until Sophia released a whimpering breath and tried to turn over.

"Don't move." His hot whisper collected in the shell of her ear.

"But I want you," Sophia said, writhing as his fingers eased further inside. It was torture to lie pinned there with his weight poised above her, feeling the teasing brush of his chest hair against her back. The tip of his tongue ventured into the hollow behind her earlobe, and she writhed and groaned, her inner muscles clenching hungrily around his knuckle. Her empty hands grasped for purchase, found the edge of the mattress, and clutched until her fingers turned white.

Suddenly she felt his legs push between hers. "Open your thighs," Ross murmured. "Wider . . . yes, sweet, sweet . . ."

His fingers withdrew and the head of his shaft eased forward. The hard length of him filled her completely, while his hands pulled her hips even higher, adjusting the fit with meticulous care. Once inside her, he barely thrust at all, just held himself deep and tight while his hand slipped beneath her body. Searching the moist curls between her thighs, he found the nub that throbbed so eagerly.

He moved in deep nudges that corresponded to the caress of his fingers, refusing to give her the long thrusts she craved. His restraint made her wild. Burying her face in the mattress, she smothered her involuntary cries as her hips churned upward. Heat curled in her abdomen and radiated outward in hectic ripples. Every part of her being was focused on the place where he joined her, the thick pulsing organ that pleasured her until her senses were spurred into an ecstatic explosion.

The shuddering contractions wrapped around his

sex, and Ross groaned loudly against her back, letting the climax flow over him, drain and deliver him. Breathing hard, he hung over her until his arms trembled. Collapsing onto his side, he kept her with him, still enclosed in the depths of her body. Bathed in sunshine, they lay amid the tangled sex-scented bedclothes.

A long time passed before Ross spoke. "I'm going to send for a bath. We both need one."

Sophia turned and buried her face against his hairy chest. "At this rate, we'll be here all day," she muttered ruefully.

"I can only hope so," he replied, tilting her face upward with his fingers to steal another kiss.

To Sophia's surprise, the employees at Bow Street strove to pretend that nothing unusual had happened. No one was quite able to meet her eyes, and it was clear that they were all bursting with curiosity. However, their collective respect for Ross—not to mention the fear of risking his wrath—kept them from uttering even one word about the fact that Sophia had obviously shared his bed.

Mr. Vickery was given the task of finding any mention of John Sydney in the court records dating beyond ten years earlier, although Ross did not explain any particulars of the request to him. The process was a laborious one, requiring the clerk to scrutinize page after page of faded notes, and he would probably need several days to peruse all the necessary records. "Sir Ross," Vickery remarked with a great deal of interest, "one can't help but notice the last name of the defendant. May I know if he was related in some manner to Miss Sydney?"

"I would rather not say," Ross replied quietly. "And I would ask that you keep his name private, and do not mention the records search to anyone else at Bow Street."

"Not even to Sir Grant?" Vickery's surprise was evident.

"No one," Ross emphasized, giving the clerk a meaningful stare.

While Vickery conducted his search, Sophia helped Ross with a deluge of work. In addition to his usual responsibilities, he was engaged in planning a series of raids at the outskirts of London to clear out hives of vagrants. Furthermore, he was unexpectedly called upon to act as arbitrator in an impassioned demonstration for higher wages staged by a majority of London tailors.

Amused and sympathetic, Sophia listened to Ross's grumbling as he prepared to leave the office. "Will it take long to resolve the dispute?" she asked.

"It had better not," he said darkly. "I'm in no mood to tolerate hours of squabbling."

She smiled into his scowling face. "You will be successful. I have no doubt that you could persuade anyone to agree to anything."

His expression softened as he drew her against his tall form and bent to kiss her. "You're proof of that, aren't you?" he murmured.

Just as Ross began to take his leave, however, Mr.

Vickery knocked at the door. Sophia went to open it, and her stomach did a peculiar flip when she saw the triumphant glow on the clerk's face. He held a yellowing records file in his hands. "Sir Ross," he said with visible satisfaction, "by a stroke of luck, I have found the information you requested. It could have taken weeks, but somehow I happened upon the right box before I was even a quarter of the way through the records. Now, perhaps you might tell me why—"

"Thank you," Ross said evenly, stepping forward to accept the file. "That will be all, Vickery. You have done well."

The clerk's face was etched with disappointment as he realized that no further information would be forthcoming. "Yes, Sir Ross. I suppose you will read it after you return from the tailors' dispute—"

"The tailors can wait," Ross said firmly. "Close the door when you leave, Mr. Vickery."

Obviously perplexed at why an ancient court record would take precedence over the tailors' demonstration, the clerk complied slowly.

The quiet click of the door caused Sophia to flinch. She stared in morbid fascination at the file in Ross's hands, the blood draining from her face. "You don't have to read it now," she said scratchily. "You should attend to your responsibilities."

"Sit down," Ross murmured, coming forward to rest his hand on her shoulder. Obeying the gentle pressure, she sank into the nearest chair and gripped the arms tightly. Her gaze locked on his impassive face as he went to his desk and spread the tattered file across the scarred mahogany surface. Still standing, Ross braced his hands on either side of the court records and leaned over them.

The silence in the office was smothering as his gaze scanned the pages. Sophia fought to keep her breathing steady, and wondered why she should be so nervous. After all, she was fairly certain what the records would reveal, and as she had said to Ross, it no longer mattered. She had forgiven him, and had found a measure of peace in the process. However, her body felt like a watch that had been wound too tightly, and she dug her nails into the chair arms when she saw the frown that pulled at Ross's forehead.

Just as Sophia thought she would go mad from the tension, Ross spoke with his gaze remaining on the court records. "I remember it now. I was the sitting magistrate that day. After hearing the case, I sentenced John Sydney to ten months on a prison hulk. Considering his crime, it was by far the lightest punishment I could deliver. Anything less would have aroused such public outrage that I would have been forced to step down from the bench."

"Ten months on a prison hulk because of picking someone's pocket?" Sophia asked incredulously. "Surely the punishment far outweighed the crime!"

Ross did not look at her. "Your brother was not a pickpocket, Sophia. Nor had he fallen in with a group of petty thieves. He was a highwayman."

"A highwayman?" She shook her head in bewilderment. "No. That isn't possible. My cousin told me . . ."

"Either your cousin was not aware of the truth, or she thought it was kinder to keep it from you."

"But John was only fourteen!"

"He had joined a gang of highwaymen and embarked on a string of increasingly violent robberies, until all four were brought before me and accused of murder. For some reason Sydney never mentioned his title—he identified himself as a commoner."

Sophia stared at him blankly.

Ross met her gaze then, his face impassive as he continued in a monotone. "They stopped a private carriage containing two women, a small child, and an elderly man. Not only did they rob the ladies of their watches and jewelry, but one of the highwaymen—Hawkins—took a silver sucking-bottle from the child. According to the women's testimony, the child began to wail so piteously that his grandfather demanded the return of the silver bottle. A scuffle ensued, and Hawkins struck the old man with the butt of his pistol. The grandfather fell to the ground, and whether he died of the injury or his excitation is not clear. By the time the gang was captured and brought before me, public sentiment was greatly aroused against them. I bound the older three over for trial, and they were condemned and executed in short order. However, in light of John Sydney's youth and the fact that he had not personally attacked the old man, I managed to give him a lesser sentence. I had him sent to the prison hulk—which earned a great deal of public fury and criticism, as most were calling for his death."

"None of that sounds like my brother," Sophia whispered. "I don't think John would have been capable of such crimes."

Ross replied with great care. "A young man would not be able to survive in the London underworld unscathed. I suspect your brother was hardened from his experiences in the rookeries and flash houses. Anyone would be corrupted by such a life."

Sophia felt nauseated by the revelations, not to mention painfully ashamed. "All this time I've blamed you for injustice," she managed to say, "when you actually did the most you could to help him."

Ross contemplated the fragile parchment before him, his long fingers brushing over the faded script. "I remember there seemed to be something in him worth saving," he said absently. "It was apparent that he had become involved in something beyond his ability to control." Ross's gray eyes narrowed as he continued to stare at the court documents. "Something about this case troubles me," he murmured, "I have overlooked something . . . I sense there is some connection that has yet to be made, but I'm damned if I can figure it out."

Sophia shook her head slowly. "I'm so sorry."

His lashes lifted, and his gaze turned warm. "For what?"

"For intruding in your life . . . for seeking vengeance

when none was deserved . . . for putting you in an impossible position." She stood up with a great effort, her head pounding, her throat blocked, so that she could hardly breathe.

Ross came from behind his desk and tried to put his arms around her, but she gently repelled the attempt. "The best thing I could do for you," she said, "is to disappear."

His long fingers clamped around her upper arms, and he moved her in a soft shake. "Sophia, look at me," he demanded urgently. A sharp note, like anger or fear, entered his voice. "Look at me, dammit! If you disappeared, I would find you. No matter how fast or how far you went. So put that thought out of your head."

Staring dazedly into his piercing gray eyes, she nodded while her mind buzzed with miserable speculation.

"Now promise me," he went on tersely, "that while I'm gone today, you will not do anything foolish. Stay here, and when I return we will sort things out. All right?" When she didn't respond, he lifted her until her toes barely touched the floor. "All right?" he repeated in a meaningful tone.

"Yes," she whispered. "I'll wait for you."

Chapter 13

With Ross gone for the day, there was little Sophia could do in the office, so she decided to take inventory of the kitchen larders. The new information about her brother and his tainted past was unexpected and sickening; she could hardly think straight. She went about her tasks mechanically, feeling defeated and weary, until finally something jolted her from the numbness.

A foul smell emanated from the slate shelf of the wet larder, and Sophia gasped in disgust as she searched for the source of the odor. "My God, what is that?" she asked. Eliza hobbled to the door of the larder to watch her.

It did not take long for Sophia to discover that the putrid smell belonged to a salmon that was long past its prime. "We could soak it in vinegar and limewater," Eliza suggested hesitantly. "That will take away most of the smell—if it's not too far gone, that is."

Sophia gagged as she threw a cloth over the slimy

mess and lifted it from the shelf. "Eliza, *nothing* could salvage this fish. 'Far gone' is a distant memory . . . it is foul from head to tail."

"Here, I'll wrap it," the cook-maid muttered, fetching a day-old newspaper. Expertly she bound the salmon until its odor was safely smothered.

Sophia watched her with annoyance. "Lucie bought the fish at Lannigan's only this morning, didn't she?"

Eliza nodded. "He told her it was fresh."

"Fresh!" Sophia exclaimed with a cynical snort.

"I'll have her take it back, then." Eliza frowned. "Except that I sent her out to fetch nasturtium seeds for pickling."

"I will take it back myself," Sophia said decisively, knowing that Eliza's knee was not sufficiently healed to allow for a walk to the fishmonger's shop. She welcomed the opportunity to exercise her legs and perhaps clear her mind. "I have a few things to say to Mr. Lannigan. How dare he send such a poor excuse of a salmon to Sir Ross's household!"

"Miss Sydney, I think you will have to wait. Ernest can't go with you, as he has gone about some errands for Sir Grant."

"I will go alone, then. It isn't far, and I will return before anyone knows I've been away."

"But Sir Ross has said many times that you are always to take a companion when you go out. If anything happens to you . . ." Eliza nearly shuddered.

"Nothing will happen to me. It's not as if I am venturing into a rookery. I am merely visiting the fishmonger."

"But Sir Ross—"

"You let me handle Sir Ross," Sophia murmured as she went to fetch her bonnet.

Faced with Sophia's righteous indignation, and her reminders of all that Sir Ross had done for him in the past, Mr. Lannigan was full of apologies. " 'Twas a mistake," he mumbled in his thick Cockney accent, his gaze chasing all around the shop to avoid hers. Embarrassment mottled his meaty face. "Why, I newer would send a salmon what's gawn awf to Bow Street! To try an' chisel Sir Ross . . . why, I'd be off me nob to do such a thing, wouldn' I?" His expression lightened as a possible explanation occurred to him. " 'Twas that feather 'eaded Lucie . . . she took the *wrong fish*, she did!"

"Well, then," Sophia replied crisply, "I would like to exchange it for the correct fish, please."

"Yes, miss." Taking the paper-wrapped package from her, he sped with alacrity to the back of the shop, muttering to himself. "Only the best for Sir Ross, that's whot I allus say . . ."

While she waited for the new salmon to be wrapped, Sophia became aware of a minor commotion outside the shop. Curious, she went to the small, thick-paned window and watched as an excited crowd gathered around the entrance of the building across the street.

"I wonder what they are looking at."

Lannigan answered with a note of something that sounded oddly like pride. "Gentry's on the 'unt again."

"Nick Gentry?" Sophia glanced over her shoulder at the fishmonger, her brows lifting in surprise. "He is trying to capture someone, you say?"

Lannigan smoothed out a rectangle of brown paper and laid the fish reverently at one end. "Like a fox, Gentry is—the cleverest an' mos' fleet-footed thief-taker since Morgan, an' that's the truf." Expertly he tucked the fish neatly into its paper casing.

Returning her attention to the scene outside the window, Sophia surmised that the crowd was waiting for the infamous Gentry to exit the building. "Mr. Gentry may be a thief-taker," she said pertly, "but he is also a criminal. I would not insult Sir Grant by making such a comparison, as he is the most honorable of men."

"Yes, miss." Lannigan knotted a string around the parcel with a flourish. "But Gentry's a rum cove, jus' the same."

Sophia was puzzled by the public's intense admiration of the man. How could his magnetism and reputed charm blind the masses to his corruption?

Coming over to the window, Lannigan handed her the wrapped fish. "Miss Sydney, did ye 'ave a look at Gentry when 'e was taken to Bow Street?"

"No, actually." Sophia frowned pensively, remembering Ross's fury when she had burst into the strong room, where she'd seen only the back of the notorious crime lord. "Although I was there at the time, I never saw him."

" 'Is carriage is stopped jus' around the corner," Lannigan informed her slyly. "If ye wait there, ye can set yer blinkers on 'im."

Sophia forced herself to laugh lightly. "Oh, I have better things to do than wait for a glimpse of a scoundrel like Nick Gentry."

But after she left the shop, she hesitated and glanced down the alley, her gaze falling on a black-lacquered carriage heavily ornamented in gold. The coach-and-six was exactly the sort of extravagant but tasteless equipage that would be purchased with ill-gotten gains. A driver waited on the box, his face bored and weary beneath a high-crowned hat, while an armed footman stood beside the door.

Sophia was not certain why her curiosity about Gentry was so strong. Perhaps it was the fact that Ross hated the man so profoundly. Gentry was the opposite of everything Ross believed in. Although the man professed to be a professional thief-taker, and therefore on the side of the law, he was in actuality a black-hearted criminal. Blackmail, informing, organizing crime, framing, and outright thievery—these were all evils that had been committed by Nick Gentry. He was an outrage to morality. Yet most people considered him heroic, and those who did not were afraid to cross him.

As Sophia reflected on all the transgressions ascribed to Gentry, she saw that the crowd across the street had parted to allow a single tall figure to pass through. He had an arrogant way of walking, a jaunty confidence that showed in the set of his shoulders and in his loose, easy stride. As he strolled past onlookers, hands reached out to pat him on the shoulders and back, and hearty cheers sounded in his wake.

" 'Ere's a right cove, our Gentry!"

"Hurrah for Black Dog!"

Black Dog? Sophia wrinkled her nose in distaste at the nickname. Flattening herself against the side of the building, she watched as the people followed Gentry on his way to the carriage. As the thief-taker approached, Sophia was surprised to see that he was young and handsome, with a long, straight nose and elegant, clean-edged features and vivid blue eyes. Similar to the Bow Street runners, he possessed a distinctive physical confidence. It was clear that he was filled with what was politely referred to as "animal spirits." His hair was a rich dark brown, and his skin was very tan, making his teeth look startlingly white as he grinned. For all his apparent good humor, however, there was a strange coldness about him . . . an obvious potential for savagery that made Sophia shiver despite the warmth of the day.

The armed footman opened the carriage door, and Gentry moved toward it with a ready stride. But for some reason he paused before stepping inside, his hand braced lightly on the black lacquer. He went very still, as if he were listening to a sound that no one else could hear. His shoulders stiffened, and he turned slowly, his gaze falling right on Sophia. Startled, she stared back at him, trapped by the intensity of his expression.

The crowd, the street, the sky—all seemed to disappear, leaving only the two of them. Abruptly Sophia recognized him as the mysterious stranger at Silverhill Park, the one who had given her the diamond necklace. But how could that be? What could a man like Nick Gentry want with her? The wrapped fish dropped from her nerveless hands, and she breathed jerkily.

Frozen, she stared as he walked toward her, his face pale beneath its tan. He stopped before her, began to reach for her, then hesitated, while his gaze remained locked with hers. Then he appeared to make a decision. He caught her wrist in his large hand, his fingers wrapping over her hammering pulse.

"Come with me," he said, his soft voice undercutting the noise of the crowd. "I won't hurt you."

Stunned that he had dared to touch her, Sophia resisted the gentle urging, the blood draining from her face. She tugged at her imprisoned wrist. "Let go," she said tightly. "If anything happens to me, Sir Ross will kill you."

He drew closer, his lips at her ear. "Would you like to know what happened to John Sydney?"

She jerked backward, nearly knocking her head against the wall. "What do you know about my brother?"

A corner of his mouth lifted in the hint of a mocking smile. "Come."

The sight of Nick Gentry plucking a pretty woman from the onlookers entertained them tremendously. Laughing and clapping, they surged around the carriage as Gentry pulled Sophia inside. Frightened yet intensely curious, she half sat, half fell against the leather-upholstered cushions. The door was closed, and the vehicle lurched as the team of six moved forward. The carriage rounded the street corner and gained momentum, accelerating to a reckless hurdle through the streets.

"Where are we going?" Sophia asked tensely. "And why did you mention my brother's name? And why did you give me the gown and the necklace, and—"

Gentry held up his hands in a gesture of mock self-defense. "Wait. I'll explain. Just . . . wait."

He reached for a polished wood compartment beside the door and withdrew a glass and a small decanter of amber liquid. Either the jouncing of the carriage made it difficult for him to pour, or his hands were strangely unsteady, for he seemed unable to accomplish the task. Giving up with a curse, he lifted the spirits to his mouth and drank straight from the decanter.

Carefully he replaced the articles in the compartment and settled his large hands on his knees. "We're going to my home on West Street. Near Fleet Ditch."

Sophia could not prevent a quiver of distaste. The location was one of the most foul and dangerous in London, home to robbers and fugitives, conveniently located near the prisons of Newgate, Ludgate, and the Fleet. The huge sewer named Fleet Ditch spread its stench extravagantly through the twisted lanes and alleys that surrounded it.

"You'll be safe with me," Gentry said shortly. "All I want is to talk with you in privacy."

"Why me?" she demanded. "What have I done to attract your attention? We've never met, and I am certain that we have no acquaintances in common."

"You'll understand after I explain a few things."

Huddling in the corner of the seat, Sophia sent him a cold glare. "Explain, then. And afterward you will return me safely to Bow Street."

Gentry's white teeth gleamed as he appeared both amused and admiring of her fearlessness. "Agreed," he said quietly. "Very well. What I wish to talk about are the last days of John Sydney."

"You knew my brother?" Sophia asked warily.

He nodded. "I was on the prison hulk where he died."

"Why should I believe that?"

"What reason would I have to lie about it?" Something in his eyes compelled her to accept his claim. The words plucked painfully at the inner wound that John's death had left. No one had ever told her what her beloved younger brother had suffered on the prison hulk, or how he had died. She had always longed to know, but now that the information seemed to be forthcoming, she was filled with dread.

"Go on," she said hoarsely.

Gentry spoke slowly, allowing her time to digest the

information. "We were on the *Scarborough*, anchored on the Thames. Six hundred convicts were housed below the decks, some in iron cells, some shackled to iron shafts embedded in oak planks. Most of us were fitted with a ball and chain around one leg. Thieves, murderers, pickpockets—no matter how great or small the crime, we were all subjected to the same treatment. The younger boys, such as John and myself, got the worst of it."

"In what way?" Sophia brought herself to ask.

"We were chained beside men who had been deprived of . . ." He paused, apparently searching for a proper word that she would understand. "Men who hadn't 'known' a woman in a long time. Do you understand what I mean?"

She nodded cautiously.

"When a man is brought to that state, he is willing to do things that he would not ordinarily do. Such as attack more vulnerable creatures than he . . . and subject them to . . ." He paused, his mouth twisting. His gaze became very distant, as if he were looking through a window at some unpleasant sight. He seemed removed from the memories, detached and somewhat contemplative. "Unspeakable things," he murmured.

Sophia was silent with anguished horror, while one part of her mind summoned the question . . . why would Nick Gentry confess something so private and agonizing to a woman he didn't know?

He continued, his voice low and matter-of-fact.

"The prisoners were starved, filthy, choking on the foul air, riddled with prison fever. They kept us all together—the living, the dying, the dead. Every morning the bodies of those who hadn't survived the night were taken to the top deck, carried ashore, and buried."

"Tell me about my brother," Sophia said, fighting to keep her voice from trembling.

Gentry's gaze met hers, and she was struck by how vibrant and hopelessly blue his eyes were. "John became friends with a boy who was nearly his own age. They tried to protect each other, helped each other when possible, and talked of the day when they would be released. Although it was selfish, John dreaded the day that the boy would be released. That day was not long in coming. And when his friend was set free, John knew he would be alone again."

Pausing, he raked a hand through his thick brown hair, disheveling the gleaming locks. It seemed increasingly difficult for him to speak. "As fate would have it, a fortnight before John's friend was to be released, there was an outbreak of cholera on the ship. John's friend took ill, and despite his efforts to care for him, the boy died. Which left John in a rather interesting position. He reasoned that since his friend was already dead, there was no harm in taking his place."

Sophia was utterly bewildered. "What?" she asked faintly.

He did not look at her. "If John assumed the boy's identity, he would gain release in a matter of days, rather than staying another year on the prison hulk. And there was no doubt that John would not have lasted that long. So in the night, he switched clothes with the boy's corpse, and when morning came, he volunteered the body as belonging to John Sydney."

The carriage rolled to a halt, and the putrid stench of Fleet Ditch began to seep inside. Sophia's heart beat with terrible force, seeming to drive the air from her lungs. "But that doesn't make sense," she said woodenly. "If your story is true, then—" She broke off suddenly, aware of an high-pitched buzzing in her ears.

As Gentry stared at her, the coldness seemed to leave his face, and his chin shook as if he were struggling to master overpowering emotions. He set his jaw and forced out more quiet words. "The name of the dead boy was Nick Gentry."

Suddenly Sophia burst into violent tears. "No," she sobbed. "It's not true. Why are you doing this to me? Take me back to Bow Street!"

Through the hot, watery blur, she saw his face draw closer. "Don't you know me, Sophia?" came his anguished whisper. He shocked her by sinking to the floor and clutching handfuls of her skirts, his dark head buried against her knees.

She was dumbstruck as she stared at the hands tangled in her skirts. A harsh sob lodged in her throat as she touched the back of his left hand. There was a small, star-shaped scar in the center. It was the same scar that John had gotten in childhood, when he had carelessly brushed it against a fireplace iron still hot from the coals. Tears continued to slip down her cheeks, and she covered the mark with her own hand.

His head lifted, and he stared at her with eyes that she now recognized were exactly like her own. "Please," he whispered.

"It's all right," she said unsteadily. "I believe you, John. I do know you. I should have seen it at once, but you are much changed."

He responded with a sorrowful growl, struggling to contain his feelings.

Sophia felt her own face contort with a confounding mixture of joy and wretchedness. "Why didn't you come to me years ago? I've been alone for so long. Why have you stayed away and let me grieve for you?"

He scrubbed the sleeve of his coat over his eyes and let out a shuddering breath. "We'll talk inside."

The footman opened the carriage door, and Gentry— John—swung down easily and reached for Sophia. She put her hands on his shoulders, felt him grasp her waist, and he lowered her with great care to the ground. However, her knees quivered like jelly, and she was surprised when her legs began to collapse.

Gentry caught her at once, his hands hooking beneath her arms. "Steady. I've got you. I'm sorry— you've had a shock."

"I'm all right," she said, feebly trying to push him away.

Maintaining a supportive arm behind her back, Gentry guided her toward the house. It was a converted building that had once been a tavern. Sophia could not help gaping at her surroundings, which looked like something out of a nightmare. This was an area of London that even the bravest runners would have avoided at all cost. The people who skulked through tortuously twisted streets hardly seemed like humans. They were gray-faced and filthy, almost ghostlike in their tattered clothes.

Vermin scuttled over piles of refuse in the street, while the aromas of cesspools and drains combined with the fumes from a nearby slaughterhouse into a smell so rank that it actually caused her eyes to water. There was noise and tumult everywhere; cries of beggars and urchins, sounds of pigs and chickens, drunken brawls, even the occasional crack of a pistol.

Glancing at her face, Gentry smiled faintly at her reaction to the place. "It's not exactly Mayfair, is it? Don't worry, you'll get used to the smell in no time. I hardly notice it now."

"Why do you choose to live here?" she asked, nearly gagging on the foul air. "People say you have money. You must be able to afford something better than this."

"Oh, I have high-kick offices in town," he assured her, "where I meet with wealthy clients or politicians and such. But this area is where all the flash houses and prisons are, and I need easy access to them." Seeing her confusion at the Cockney slang, he explained further as he guided her up a flight of rickety stairs. "Flashes are successful thieves. They live in flash houses, where they are somewhat safe from the law and are free to gamble, drink, and make plans."

"And you are the most successful flash of all?" Sophia asked, accompanying him through an astonishing maze of secret corridors, staircases, and dark recesses.

"Some would say so," he replied with no trace of shame. "But most of the time I am a thief-taker—and a damned good one, too."

"You were not meant to live like this," she murmured, appalled at what had become of her brother.

"And you were meant to be a servant?" he pointed out sardonically. "Don't sit in judgment, Sophia. We've both done what was necessary to survive."

They approached a heavy door at the end of a cramped passageway, and Gentry reached to open it for her.

As Sophia stepped inside, she was stunned to find an elegantly decorated set of rooms. Papered walls were covered with gold-framed Baroque looking glasses and fine paintings. The French furnishings were heavily gilded and upholstered in brocade, and the windows were swathed in blue-gray velvet.

Stunned to find such elaborate rooms in a ram-shackle building, Sophia glanced at her brother with wide eyes.

He smiled casually. "Just because I have to stay on West Street doesn't mean I have to live badly."

Feeling weak after receiving what was surely the greatest shock of her life, Sophia made her way to an overstuffed chair. Gentry went to a sideboard, poured two drinks, and brought one to her. "Have some of this," he said, pressing a glass into her hand.

She obeyed, grateful for the smooth burn of the brandy as it slid down her throat. Her brother sat beside her, tossing down his drink as if it were water. His gaze fastened on her, and he shook his head with apparent wonder. "I can't believe you are really here. For years I've thought about you, never knowing what had become of you."

"You could have let me know that you were still alive," she said crisply.

His face was suddenly expressionless. "Yes, I could have."

"Why didn't you?"

He stared at a stray drop of brandy in his empty glass, rolling the vessel gently in his long fingers. "The main reason was that you were better off not knowing. My life is dangerous, not to mention unsavory, and I didn't want you to bear the shame of having a brother like me. I was certain that you would have married a long time ago, to some decent man in the village. I thought you would have had children by now." His voice became edged with baleful ire. "And instead you're a *spinster*!" He made the word sound like a curse. "For God's sake, Sophia, why are you a damned servant? At *Bow Street*, of all places!"

"Who would have wanted to marry me, John?" she asked ironically. "I had no dowry, no family, nothing to recommend me except an attractive face, which I can assure you held no great value for the farmers and workmen in the village. The only offer of marriage I ever received was from the local baker, a fat old man who was nearly twice my age. Working for Cousin Ernestine was far more appealing. And as for Bow Street . . . I like it there."

She was tempted to tell her brother about her short-lived affair with Anthony, how she had been ill-used and betrayed. However, in light of his wicked reputation, she decided to keep that matter private. For all she knew, he would arrange to have Anthony killed or tortured in some way.

Gentry made a scornful noise at the mention of Bow Street. "It's no place for you," he scoffed. "Those runners are no better than the thugs who work for me. And if that coldhearted bastard Cannon has mistreated you, I'll—"

"No," Sophia cut in hastily. "No one has mistreated me, John. And Sir Ross is very kind."

"Oh, of course he is," Gentry said with purest sarcasm.

The reminder that her lover and her brother were sworn enemies caused a stab of pain in her chest. This was going to change everything, she thought with sick trepidation. Ross had overlooked so much about her. But the fact that her brother was Nick Gentry, the man Ross despised most . . . well, that could not be dismissed. The situation was so dreadful and strange that she felt a wobbly smile touch her lips.

"What are you thinking?" Gentry asked.

She shook her head, the smile vanishing. There was

no need for him to know about her romantic relationship with the Chief Magistrate of Bow Street. Not when that relationship was very possibly finished. Managing to shove the despairing thoughts to the back of her mind, she studied her brother intently.

The promise of handsomeness that she had seen in his boyhood had been more than fulfilled. At twenty-five, he possessed a sleek, hard-boned grace that reminded her of a tiger. His features were dramatic, precisely angled, the chin sharply defined, the nose jutting in a straight, strong line. The thick arcs of his eyebrows surmounted a remarkable pair of eyes. They were of a shade of blue so dark that the black pupils nearly vanished into the intense irises. However, the extravagant masculine beauty of his face did not conceal a ruthlessness that troubled her deeply. Gentry seemed capable of almost anything, as if he could lie, steal, or even kill without a flicker of remorse. There was no softness in him, and Sophia guessed that any sense of mercy or compassion had been driven from him long ago. But he was still her brother.

Wonderingly, she lifted her hand to the side of his face. He remained still beneath her cradling fingers. "John, I never allowed myself to hope that you were still alive."

Gently he took her hand from his face, as if he found it difficult to tolerate another person's touch. "I was shocked when I saw you in the Bow Street strong room," he muttered. "I knew who you were at once, even before I heard your name." His jaw flexed tightly.

"When that bastard Cannon shouted at you, it was all I could do to keep from ripping his throat out—"

"No," she interrupted swiftly. "He was concerned for me. He was trying to protect me."

The ferocious glitter remained in his eyes. "You were born a lady, Sophia. No one has the right to treat you like a servant."

A weary, rueful smile pulled at her lips. "Yes, I was born a lady . . . and you were born to be a gentleman. But no one would mistake us for members of first society now, would they?" When he refused to respond to the comment, she continued. "I have heard terrible things about you. Or rather, about Nick Gentry."

"Call me Nick," he said flatly. "John Sydney no longer exists. I remember very little of my life before I was sent to the prison hulk. I don't *want* to remember." A cold grin flashed across his face. "I'm not guilty of half the things I'm accused of. But I encourage the rumors, and I never deny even the worst of them. It suits me to have an evil reputation. I want people to regard me with fear and respect. Good for business."

"Are you saying that you haven't stolen from people, and framed and betrayed and blackmailed—"

Gentry interrupted her with a sound that expressed pure annoyance. "I'm not a saint."

Despite Sophia's distress, she almost wanted to laugh at the understatement.

His eyes narrowed. "I only take advantage of people who are so dull-witted that they *deserve* to be badly used. Besides, I never get credit for the good I've done."

"Such as?"

"I'm a damned good thief-taker. My men and I have captured almost twice as many criminals as Sir Ross and his runners."

"People say that you sometimes manufacture evidence. That you use evil methods to force confessions that may not be true."

"I do what needs to be done," he said flatly. "And if the criminals I arrest are not guilty of one particular crime, they are usually guilty of at least a dozen others."

"But why don't you—"

"Enough," he said shortly, standing and striding back to the sideboard. "I don't want to talk about my work."

Sophia watched as he poured another brandy and drank it in a few careless gulps. She could hardly believe that this truculent stranger was her brother. "Nick," she said, testing his name on her tongue. "Why did you give me those presents? It nearly drove me mad, wondering who had sent them. And I was terrified that Sir Ross would think I was carrying on with a secret lover."

"Sorry," he muttered, flashing her a contrite smile. "I wanted to be a—a benefactor. To give you the things you deserve. I never meant for us to meet. But the need to see you became so strong that I couldn't bear it any longer."

"And that is why you approached me at Silverhill Park?"

He gave her the smile of a naughty schoolboy. "I

liked the idea of doing it under Cannon's nose. And I knew I could slip in and out of a large crowd without being caught. The masquerade made it almost too easy."

"Was that necklace stolen?"

"Of course not," he said indignantly. "I bought it for you."

"But what am I to do with such a necklace? I could never wear it!"

"You will wear it," he said. "I have a fortune, Sophia. I'm going to buy you a house somewhere . . . France or Italy . . . where you can live like a lady. I'll give you an account so that you'll never have to worry about money again."

Her mouth hung open as she stared at him. "John . . . *Nick* . . . I don't want to live abroad! Everything that holds value for me is here."

"Oh?" His voice became dangerously soft. "What would keep you here?"

Chapter 14

The roar of angry demonstrators penetrated the walls of the Red Lion tavern on Threadneedle. A crowd huddled inside, necks craning for the best view of the table where Ross sat with the tailors' and employers' representatives. During the first hour of negotiations for imposing new wage structures, Ross had listened to grievances from both sides. As tempers were running high, Ross deduced that the debates would last through the afternoon and well into the night. Thinking momentarily of Sophia and how much he wanted to go home to her, he fought to suppress his impatience.

A buxom waitress who had soaked herself in cologne water to mask other, far more pungent scents sidled up to Ross with the jug of coffee he had requested. " 'Ere you are, Sir Ross," she purred, deliberately brushing one massive breast against his shoulder as she leaned over him. "Whot else for yer appetite, sir? Some Welsh rabbit or apple puffs?" She put her broad face next to his and said meaningfully, "Ye can 'ave *anyfing* ye wants, Sir Ross."

Accustomed as he had become to such invitations during the past few years, Ross gave her a polite but cool smile. "You're very kind, but no."

She made a little face, pouting in disappointment. "Later, mayhap." As she walked away, her hips swung like a pendulum.

One of the tailors' representatives, a fellow named Brewer, regarded him with a sly smile. "I see what you're about, Sir Ross. Pretend you don't want a woman, and she'll work all the harder to attract you, eh? You're a canny one . . . I'll wager you understand them quite well."

Ross grinned suddenly. "There are two things a man should never do, Brewer—keep a woman waiting, and claim to understand her."

As the tailor chuckled, Ross's attention was caught by the sight of a huge figure entering the tavern. It was Sir Grant Morgan, his dark head rising far above the crowd's, his keen gaze scanning the room. Finding Ross, he pushed his way unceremoniously through the gathering. People hastened to move aside, having no desire to be trampled by the grim-faced giant.

Knowing at once that something was untoward, Ross stood to meet the assistant magistrate as he approached. "Morgan," he said curtly, "why are you here?"

"The necklace," came the former runner's succinct reply, in a tone so low that no one else could hear. "I found the jeweler who made it—Daniel Highmore, of Bond Street. I made him tell me who purchased it."

Ross experienced a savage thrill of anticipation at

the prospect of finally identifying Sophia's stalker. "Who?"

"Nick Gentry."

Ross stared at Morgan blankly. His initial astonishment was quickly replaced by an elemental, purely masculine urge to kill. "Gentry must have seen Sophia while he was at Bow Street. When she came down to the strong room. By God, I'm going to tear him limb from limb!" Becoming conscious of the host of interested gazes fastened on them, all clearly speculating as to what they were discussing, Ross strove to keep his voice quiet. "Morgan, take over the negotiations. I'm going to pay a visit to Gentry."

"Wait," Morgan protested. "I've never arbitrated a professional dispute before."

"Well, now you're going to learn. Good luck." With that, Ross strode through the tavern and headed outside to where his horse was tethered.

Sophia did not know what to make of her brother. As they talked, she tried to understand the man John had become, but he was a complex figure, seeming to have little regard for his own life or anyone else's. "The greater the rogue, the greater the luck" was a saying she had heard at Bow Street—it explained the jaunty defiance of many of the criminals brought before the bench. And it certainly described Nick Gentry. He was definitely a rogue, alternately charming and callous, an ambitious man who had inherited blue blood but had received no land, education, wealth, or social connections along with it. Instead he sought power through corrupt avenues. It seemed that his criminal success had made him as savage as he was smart, as cruel as he was confident.

Hesitantly she told him about her years in Shropshire, her desire to avenge his "death," and her plan to come to London and destroy Sir Ross Cannon.

"How in hell were you planning to do that?" Gentry asked mildly, his gaze sharp as it rested on her face.

Sophia colored, and answered with a half-truth. "I was going to try to uncover damaging information in the criminal records room." Although she would have liked to be completely honest, her instincts warned that it would be foolish to tell him about her affair with Sir Ross. They were, after all, bitter enemies.

"My clever girl," Gentry murmured. "You have access to the Bow Street criminal records?"

"Yes, but I—"

"Excellent." He sat back in his chair, idly studying the tips of his boots. "There are some things you can find out for me. I can make use of your presence at Bow Street."

The suggestion that he wished to use her for his own purposes, probably criminal ones, caused Sophia to shake her head decisively. "John, I will not spy for you."

"Just a few little things," he murmured with a cajoling smile. "You want to help me, don't you? And I'll help you. We'll both have our revenge against Cannon."

She let out an incredulous laugh. "But I only wanted

revenge because I thought he had sent you to your death on the prison hulk."

Gentry scowled. "Well, Cannon *did* send me there, and it was no bloody thanks to him that I survived!"

"Anyone else would have dispatched you to the gallows without a second thought," Sophia pointed out. "After what you did—robbing that carriage, causing that poor old man's death . . ."

"It wasn't me that gave him a knock on the head," Gentry said defensively. "I was only out to rob the old cheeser, not kill him."

"No matter what your intentions, the result was the same. You were an accomplice to murder." Staring into his stony face, Sophia softened her tone as she continued. "But the past cannot be changed. All we can do is deal with the future. You can't really mean to go on this way, John."

"Why not?"

"Because you are not invulnerable. You will make a mistake sooner or later, one that *will* have you swinging on the gallows. And I could not bear to lose you a second time. Besides, this is not the life for you. You were not supposed to—"

"It is *exactly* the life for me," he cut in tersely. "Sophia, whatever memories you have of me don't apply now. Do you understand?"

"No," she said stubbornly. "I don't understand how you can live like this. You are better, more worthy, than this."

Her words earned a peculiar mirthless grin. "That shows what you know." He stood and went over to the fireplace, bracing a large hand on the white marble mantel. The firelight played over his hard young features, striping them with black and gold. After a moment's contemplation, he turned toward her. His expression was intent, but his tone was deceptively lazy. "Let's talk about Bow Street some more. You say you can get into the criminal records room. It so happens that I need some information—"

"I've already told you no. I won't betray Sir Ross's trust in me."

"You have for the last two months," he said irritably. "What's stopping you now?"

Sophia realized that he was not going to be satisfied until she told him the truth.

"Nick," she said carefully, "there is a . . . a certain relationship that has developed between Sir Ross and myself."

"My God." He raked his hands through his hair distractedly. "You and he . . ." Words seemed to fail him.

Understanding the unspoken question, Sophia gave him a cautious nod.

"My sister and the Monk of Bow Street," Gentry muttered in disgust. "A fine revenge this is, Sophia! Jumping into bed with the man who nearly killed me! If that's your idea of retribution, I've got a few things to explain to you."

"He has asked me to marry him."

Gentry's eyes flashed with astonished fury, and he

seemed to stop breathing. "I'd rather see you dead than marry the likes of him."

"He's the best man I've ever known."

"Oh, he's a damned paragon!" Nick said caustically. "And if you marry him, he'll never let you forget it. He will make you believe that you're not good enough for him. You'll be crushed by his damned honor and respectability. Cannon will make you pay a thousand times over for not being perfect."

"You don't know him," she said.

"I've known him a damned sight longer than you have. He's not human, Sophia!"

"Sir Ross is forgiving and kind, and he is well aware that I am not perfect."

Suddenly her brother stared at her in a calculating way that made her uneasy, his dark brows lowering at the inner corners in a devilish slant. "You're very sure of him, then," he remarked silkily.

She met his gaze with earnest resolution. "Yes."

"Then let's put your faith to the test, Sophia." Nick casually rested an elbow on the mantel. "You'll get that information I want from the criminal records room. *Or* . . . I will tell your steadfast, oh-so-forgiving lover that he has proposed marriage to the sister of his worst enemy. That Sophia and the despicable Nick Gentry have the same blood flowing through their veins."

Sophia nearly reeled backward in shock. "You're blackmailing me?" she said in an airless whisper.

"It's up to you. You can get me what I want . . . or

you can take the risk of losing Sir Ross. *Now* how much faith do you have in his forgiveness?"

Sophia couldn't speak. A thought blazed through her mind: *Dear Lord, will the past always return to haunt me?*

"Do you want me to tell him that I'm your brother?" he prodded.

She just couldn't be certain. She knew that Ross was everything she had claimed and more. And once he learned of her relationship to Nick Gentry, he would try to find a way to overlook yet another terrible fact about her. But this might be the straw that broke the camel's back. There was a chance that Ross might never be able to look into her eyes without remembering that she was the sister of his hated adversary.

And suddenly Sophia realized that she would die before letting that happen. She could not survive Ross's rejection, not now, after they had become so close. She could not take a risk—she had too much to lose.

Her voice came out in a croak. "No."

Strangely, Gentry's eyes seemed to flicker with disappointment, almost as if he had hoped that she would defy him. "I thought so."

Sophia stared at her brother intently, wondering if he was playing games with her. "You couldn't really bring yourself to blackmail me," she said, though she couldn't prevent the wobble of uncertainty in her tone.

He gave her a callous smile. "There's only one way to find out, isn't there?"

Before she could reply, the door vibrated with an imperative thump, and a muffled voice asked for entrance. Obviously annoyed, Gentry went to let the man in. The visitor was one of the most peculiar creatures Sophia had ever seen, a heavyset man with bulbous features and a distinctive lavender pallor. The blue-black shadows on his bristly cheeks contributed to his grimy, dark appearance. Sophia wondered how many of these strange underworld figures must work for her brother.

"Blueskin," Gentry greeted his henchman.

"Someone's come looking for ye," the man muttered. "The Monk 'isself."

"Cannon?" Gentry asked incredulously. "Damn his eyes, he just raided the place in February! What in the bloody hell is he hoping to find?"

" 'Tis no raid," Blueskin replied. " 'E's come alone."

Sophia shot to her feet in alarm. "Sir Ross is here?"

"It appears so," Gentry said in disgust, motioning for Sophia to follow him. "I'll have to see him. You can go with Blueskin out the back way before Cannon has a look at you."

Blueskin interrupted. "D'ye want me to 'ave the boys throw 'im out, Gentry?"

"No, idiot. Then he'll come back with a hundred constables and take the place apart brick by brick. Now, take this woman back to Bow Street. Anything happens to her, and I'll slit you from ear to ear." Nick returned his attention to Sophia. "About those criminal records—I want you to find out what Cannon may have learned from a man named George Fenton when he was held for questioning two weeks ago."

"Who is Fenton?"

"One of my spruce prigs." Seeing her confusion, he clarified impatiently. "A highly trained thief. I need to know what Fenton told Cannon—if he stayed loyal to me and kept his gob shut."

"Yes, but what will happen to Mr. Fenton if it turns out—"

"That's not your concern," he replied, pushing her toward the back door. "Now go quickly, before Cannon finds us together. Blueskin will keep you safe."

Less than a minute after Sophia had left, Cannon shoved his way inside the apartment. Nick sat in his chair by the hearth, stretching out in a provokingly idle position, as if it were of little concern to him that the Chief Magistrate of Bow Street had just invaded his home. Cannon approached him and stopped just a few feet away, his eyes appearing oddly light in his wrath-darkened face.

Despite his animosity toward the Chief Magistrate, Nick had to concede a certain grudging respect for him. Cannon was smart, seasoned, and powerful . . . a man's man. And he possessed an unyielding morality that fascinated Nick. A man handicapped by principles, who could accomplish all that Cannon had, was someone to be reckoned with.

The air was alive with challenge and aggression, yet they both managed to converse in a normal tone.

"You gave the necklace to Miss Sydney," Cannon said without preamble.

Nick inclined his head in mocking commendation. "You found that out damned quickly."

"Why?" The magistrate looked as though he wanted to tear him apart piece by piece.

Shrugging, Nick offered a casually spoken lie. "I've fancied the little muff ever since I saw her at Bow Street. I want a chance at her after you're finished."

"Stay away from her." Cannon's words were quiet but fatally sincere. "Or I'll kill you."

Nick threw him a cold grin. "Apparently you're not done with her yet."

"I'll never be done with her. And the next time you send her a gift, I'll personally shove it up your—"

"All right," Nick interrupted in rising irritation. "Warning taken. I won't bother your fancy piece. Now get the hell out of my house."

Cannon stared at him with a lethal dispassion that would have alarmed any other man. "It's only a matter of time before you overreach yourself," he said softly. "One of your schemes will fall through. Some piece of evidence will implicate you. And I'll be there to watch you hang."

Nick smiled thinly, reflecting that Cannon wouldn't

be so smug if he knew that Sophia was his sister. "I'm sure you will," he muttered. "But don't expect to take any satisfaction in my death. You may even come to regret it."

A look of puzzled speculation crossed the older man's face, and then he contemplated Nick with narrowed eyes. "Before I leave," he growled, "I want you to explain something. The gown you sent to Miss Sydney . . . she claims it is almost identical to one that her mother once possessed."

"Is it?" Nick asked lazily. "That's an interesting coincidence."

It was clear that behind Cannon's set face, his mind was busy sifting through questions. "Yes," he agreed. "Very interesting."

And to Nick's relief, the magistrate left his rooms without another word.

As soon as Sophia returned to Bow Street, she took advantage of Ross's absence and went to the criminal records room. It was an ideal time to search for the information her brother had requested, since Vickery and the other clerks had gone to a local tavern for a supper of beef and ale. The offices would remain largely unoccupied until one of the assistant magistrates returned to prepare for the evening court session.

Sophia's slender fingers combed rapidly through the file drawer as she hunted for the notes that had been taken during George Fenton's questioning. A single lamp illuminated the small room, providing barely enough light for her to read.

Eventually her attention was caught by a particular page, and she held it closer. There were references to both Nick Gentry and George Fenton. Realizing that she had found what she was seeking, Sophia folded the page and began to tuck it into her sleeve.

Suddenly she heard footsteps, and the sound of the doorknob turning. She had been caught. Her heart propelled upward in one great choking lump, and she shoved the page back into the drawer and slammed it shut just as the door swung open.

Ross stood there, his lean face shadowed and impassive. "Why are you in here?"

Apprehension swamped her, and she moistened her lips nervously. Certainly Ross could see how white her face was. She knew that she was the very picture of guilt. Desperately she seized on the first lie she could think of.

"I was . . . trying to replace information I had taken from the files, back when I was hoping to discredit you and the runners."

"I see." His face softened as he approached her. He took her chin in his hand, his fingers stroking the soft space beneath her jaw. Sophia forced herself to meet his gaze, although her soul cringed at deceiving him. A caressing smile touched Ross's lips. "There is no need to look so guilty. You didn't harm anyone."

He began to spread light, wandering kisses over her

face. "Sophia," he murmured, "Morgan found out to-day who sent you the necklace."

Drawing back, Sophia tried to look as though she didn't already know the answer. "Who is it?" she asked unsteadily.

"Nick Gentry."

Her heart began to pound with uncomfortable force. "Why would he do that?"

"This afternoon I paid a visit to Gentry, to ask him that question. Apparently he had taken an interest in you, and wishes to become your protector in the event that our relationship ends."

"Oh." Unable to meet his gaze any longer, Sophia pressed herself against him, hiding her face against his shoulder. Her voice was muffled by his coat. "Did you tell him that would never happen?"

His arm slid around her. "Gentry won't bother you again, Sophia. I'll make certain of it."

If only that were true, she thought miserably, caught in a violent welter of feelings. She was furious at her brother for putting her in this terrible position, yet she still loved him and believed there was goodness in him. She was certain that he was not completely beyond re-demption. On the other hand, there was not much to recommend about a man who was willing to blackmail his own sister.

The temptation to confide in Ross was overwhelm-ing, and she bit her lip to contain the words that bat-tled frantically inside her. Only the chilling fear of losing him kept her silent. Trembling from distress and frustration, she leaned harder against his supportive body.

Feeling her shake against him, Ross made a soothing sound. His warm breath feathered the delicate crevices of her ear as he nuzzled her. "You're not afraid, are you?" His arms surrounded her. "Sweetheart, there's no reason to be upset. You're safe."

"I know," she said, her teeth chattering. "It's just that the past few days have been a bit of a strain."

"You're tired," he murmured. "You need a hot brandy, and a relaxing bath, and a night of sleep—"

"I need *you*." Sophia grasped his collar and tugged his head down, straining hungrily to reach his lips.

At first Ross was reluctant, returning her kiss with restraint. "Easy," he whispered when their mouths parted. "You don't want this right now—"

She crushed her lips against his, pushed her tongue into the dark sweetness of his mouth, until his resistance crumbled and he began to breathe harshly.

"*This* is what I want," she whispered, pulling his hand to her breast. "Please. Don't deny me, Ross."

With objections still poised on his lips, he cradled the weight of her breast and bent his head to kiss her throat. Rapidly his concern was replaced by desire. A groan of pure lust escaped him, and he reached down to clamp her bottom in his hands. He lifted her onto the top of the file drawers, his mouth continuing to devour hers. Sophia sat and parted her stocking-clad legs

with shameful eagerness, allowing him to stand between them.

"We can't do this here," Ross muttered, his hand
searching inside the rustling mass of her skirts. "If a
clerk should walk in and see—"

."I don't care." She pulled his head to hers again.

Their mouths meshed and clung until they were
both robbed of breath. Sophia moaned as his fingers
slid past the slit of her drawers, gently fondling her
moistening flesh. "I want you," she gasped, her hand
descending to press on his.

"Sophia . . ." Ross ground out the word against the
side of her neck. "Let's go to my room . . ."

"Now," she insisted. Greedily she fumbled with the
front of his trousers to free his straining erection.

Abandoning all attempts to dissuade her, Ross
helped her with a muffled laugh. "Insatiable minx," he
accused, sliding her hips to the edge of the cabinet. He
entered her in a smooth, deep plunge that made her
gasp. "*There* . . . will this satisfy you?"

"Yes. Yes . . ." She leaned back helplessly against his
arm.

Supporting her back and buttocks, Ross lifted her
completely off the cabinet, keeping her fully impaled.
He brought her to the door and pinned her against it,
allowing her legs to dangle helplessly on either side of
his hips. Sophia moaned as he thrust at exactly the
right angle, stroking inside her, rubbing against the
most sensitive part of her sex.

"Sophia," he growled, his rhythm unceasing, "I want an answer now."

Panting, she stared at him in bewilderment. "An answer?"

"I want you to say you'll marry me."

"Oh, Ross . . . not now. I want to think some more."

"Now," he insisted, suddenly holding still inside her. "Do you want me? A simple yes or no will suffice."

She clutched at his shoulders while her body throbbed with longing. "Don't stop. Don't."

His brilliant gray eyes stared into hers as he resumed his thrusting at a torturously slow pace . . . the deep, prolonged drives that he knew would drive her mad. "Yes or no?"

"I won't answer that question now," she said, writhing uncontrollably. "You will have to wait."

"Then so will you." His mouth caught hers in a hard, wet kiss. "We'll wait just like this," he whispered. "And I vow, Sophia, that your toes are not going to touch the floor until I have my answer." He rocked against her gently, his sex penetrating even deeper than before.

A sob rose in her throat. She was so close, her body primed for release, her emotions strained beyond bearing. Nothing mattered but him. In one reckless, greedy, soul-anguished moment, she chose what she wanted most. Her mouth moved against his, pressing a silent word to his lips.

"What?" he asked urgently, drawing his head back to look at her. "What did you say?"

"I said yes," she moaned. "*Yes.* Ross, please help me, please—"

"I'll help you," he whispered tenderly, and muffled her cries with his mouth as he gave her exactly what she needed.

Chapter 15

Following a simple wedding ceremony in the private chapel on the Silverhill Park estate, Ross's mother hosted a ball that was attended by guests from at least three counties. Sophia tried not to be overwhelmed by the surfeit of attention. Countless newspapers and magazines had published information concerning Sir Ross Cannon's bride, where and when the wedding would take place, and even where they were to live. Gossip raged in salons, coffeehouses, and taverns. The revelation that Sir Ross's new wife was the daughter of a viscount added more spice to the story, for it was also known that she had worked for him at Bow Street.

Sophia was gratified by the Cannons' ready acceptance of her, and especially by the warmth that his mother displayed. "My friends have asked me to describe you," Catherine had told her the day before the wedding. Assorted guests sat in the parlor, some playing games at the card table, some strolling arm in arm through the circuit of family rooms. A few women were engaged in needlework, while gentlemen sat with newspapers and conferred on the day's events. "Naturally," Catherine continued, "they are all exceedingly curious about what kind of woman would manage to capture Ross's heart."

"His *heart* isn't the part of his anatomy that she's captured," Matthew muttered nearby.

Catherine turned toward him inquiringly. "What did you say, darling?"

He managed to produce an insincere smile. "I said my brother has indeed been captured. One can hardly recognize him for that witless grin he has taken to wearing." A few guests laughed upon overhearing the comment, as the change in Sir Ross's usually remote demeanor had been generally remarked upon. Many had agreed that it had been a very long while since Sir Ross had seemed so lighthearted and relaxed.

As Matthew spoke, Ross entered the parlor and went over to Sophia. Picking up her hand, which was resting on the curved back of the settee, he lifted it to his lips and whispered, "Shall I tell them why I'm smiling?"

The wicked gleam in his eyes reminded Sophia of the passionate interlude they had shared the previous night, when he had sneaked into her room and joined her in bed. She frowned at him while her cheeks colored. Laughing at her discomfiture, Ross seated himself beside her on the settee. "And how do you describe my fiancée to your friends, Mother?" he asked Catherine, picking up the threads of the conversation.

"I tell them that she is the most delightful young woman I have ever met. Not to mention lovely."

Catherine glanced at Sophia's peach-colored gown with an approving eye. "Is that a new dress, dear? The color is most becoming."

Sophia did not dare glance at Ross. The subject of her clothes had provoked a heated argument between them just a few days earlier. Because Ross had insisted on marrying her so quickly, there had been no time for Sophia to have new gowns made. And since he was a man, he had not given a single thought to her trousseau. The only clothes Sophia possessed were the dark dresses she had worn at Bow Street, all of them made with coarse fabric and no embellishments. She had cringed at the thought of being wed in one of those drab garments and then attending a ball in it. Therefore she had approached Ross with some trepidation and asked for the return of the lavender-silver gown.

"As you no longer require it for an investigation," she had told him in his office, "I would like to have it back, please."

Ross had received the request with disgruntled surprise. "What do you need it for?"

"It is the only suitable gown I have to get married in," she said calmly.

A scowl settled on his face. "You are *not* going to wear that at our wedding."

"It is a perfectly lovely gown," she persisted. "There is no reason why I can't wear it."

"Yes, there is," he countered in outrage. "It came from Nick Gentry."

Sophia returned his scowl. "No one will know that."

"*I'll* know it. And I'll be damned if I will allow you to wear it."

"Fine, then. What will you have me wear?"

"Choose a dressmaker—I will take you anywhere you wish this afternoon."

"No dressmaker will be able to make a suitable gown in three days. In fact, there is barely enough time to alter the lavender one. And I will not marry you in front of all your friends and family looking like a beggar!"

"You can borrow a gown from my mother. Or Iona."

"Your mother is nearly six feet tall and as thin as a rail," Sophia pointed out. "And *I'll* be damned if I will wear a gown of Iona's and then endure snide comments from your brother about it. Now, where have you put the lavender gown?"

Glowering, Ross leaned back in his chair and propped the heel of his boot against the side of the desk. "It's in the evidence room," he muttered.

"My gown, in the evidence room?" she exclaimed indignantly. "No doubt it has been shoved onto some filthy shelf!"

As she hurried out of the office, his curses could be heard down the hallway.

Rather than allow Sophia to wear the lavender silk, Ross had actually sent three runners out to investigate various dressmakers. Somehow they managed to find one who was willing to sell a gown that was part of another order. It would cost a fortune, the dressmaker warned, as she would probably lose one of her most valued clients as a result. Ross paid the hefty sum without a word of protest.

To Sophia's private relief, the dressmaker presented her with an exquisite pale blue gown with a flattering square-cut bodice and a fashionably low waistband. The full skirts were adorned with glittering beadwork flowers, as were the full, elbow-length sleeves. It was a magnificent creation that fitted her almost perfectly and required very few adjustments. In a display of generosity, the dressmaker had also allowed Ross to purchase two other gowns from her other client's order, so that Sophia would have day dresses to wear at Silverhill Park.

On their wedding day, Sophia wore her hair pinned in curls atop her head, with silver ribbons woven throughout. A necklace of pearls and diamonds was clasped around her neck, a gift that Ross had sent to her that very morning. She felt like a princess in the shimmering gown, the clicking weight of pearls around her neck, the heeled satin shoes on her feet. The wedding ceremony was a transcendent dream, anchored only by the warm grip of Ross's hands and the silver intensity of his eyes. At the conclusion of the vows, he bent to brand her with the possessive heat of his lips, a brief caress that contained the promise of much more.

Champagne flowed freely at the wedding banquet, an eight-course feast that was followed by a lavish ball. Sophia was introduced to hundreds of people, and before long she was weary of smiling and her ears were ringing. It was impossible for her to remember more than a few of the multitude of new faces. Some people did stand out in her memory, one of them being Sir Grant Morgan's wife, Lady Victoria. Having long been curious about what kind of woman would wed the intimidating giant, Sophia was surprised to discover that his wife was quite small of stature. Lady Victoria was also one of the most spectacularly beautiful women Sophia had ever seen, with a voluptuous figure, a profusion of vivid red hair, and a vivacious smile.

"Lady Sophia," the petite red-haired woman said warmly, "no words can express how thrilled we are that Sir Ross has finally married. Only a remarkable woman could have enticed him away from widowerhood."

Sophia returned her smile. "The advantage of the match is entirely mine, I assure you."

Sir Grant interceded, his green eyes twinkling warmly. He seemed far different from when he was at Bow Street, and Sophia observed that he basked in the presence of his wife as a cat would in sunshine. "I beg to disagree, my lady," he told Sophia. "The match holds many advantages for Sir Ross—which is obvious to all who know him."

"Indeed," Lady Victoria added thoughtfully, her gaze finding Ross's dark form as he stood in a separate receiving line. "I've never seen him look so well. In fact, this may be the first time I've ever seen him smile."

"And his face didn't even crack," Morgan commented.

"Grant," his wife scolded beneath her breath. Sophia laughed. Morgan winked at her and drew his wife away.

As the musicians played a piece by Bach, Sophia searched the crowd for a glimpse of Ross. Unfortunately, he was nowhere to be seen now. The sweet melody provided by strings and a transverse flute made her feel curiously wistful. Glancing at the glittering skirts of her gown, Sophia smoothed them with a gloved hand. She imagined the pleasure her parents might have felt if they had known she would marry a man like Sir Ross. And she had no doubt of the grief they would have suffered to learn what had become of their only son. Suddenly feeling very much alone, Sophia wished that her brother could have attended her wedding, although that was obviously impossible. He and she lived in different worlds, and there would never be a way to close the distance between them.

"Lady Sophia." A voice intruded on her thoughts, and she was confronted with the last face she would ever have expected to see.

"Anthony," she whispered, her heart dropping in a sickening plunge.

Anthony Lyndhurst was just as she had remembered, handsome and blond, wearing a self-important smile. Sophia could not believe that he had the gall to approach her. Stricken, she did not curtsy in response to his bow.

"My congratulations on your marriage," he said softly.

It took all of Sophia's strength to conceal her turmoil. Frantically she wondered why Anthony had come and who had invited him. Was there to be no peace even on her wedding day?

"Walk with me," he suggested, indicating the long portrait gallery that branched off the drawing room.

"No," she replied in a low tone.

"I insist." He proffered his arm, making it impossible for her to refuse without causing a scene. Pasting a brittle smile on her face, Sophia rested her gloved fingers on his coat. She accompanied him to the gallery, which was far less crowded than the drawing room. "You've done quite well for yourself, Sophia," Anthony remarked. "Marrying a Cannon will give you considerable status and fortune. Well done."

She let go of his arm as soon as they stopped before a grouping of family portraits. "Who invited you?" she asked coldly.

Anthony smiled. "The Lyndhursts and Cannons are distantly related by marriage. I am frequently invited to the Silverhill estate."

"I am sorry to hear it."

He gave a brief laugh. "I see that you're still put out with me. Allow me to apologize for leaving so precipitately when last we met. I had received word of some urgent business that had to be attended to."

Contempt flared inside her. "Involving your wife, perhaps?"

He smiled a bit sheepishly, as if at a minor faux pas. "My wife had nothing to do with us."

"You asked me to marry you when you were already married. A bit deceptive, don't you think?"

"I only did that to nudge you into doing what you already wanted to do. There was a strong attraction between us, Sophia. In fact, I sense that it is has not vanished entirely."

She was astonished by the appraising glance he gave her. Good Lord, how easy it was for him to renew all the self-disgust and shame she had tried to dispel. "If you sense anything from me, it is loathing."

"Women," he replied, clearly amused. "You always say the opposite of what you mean."

"Take it as you will. But stay away from me, or you will have to deal with my husband."

"I don't think so," Anthony murmured with an insolent smile. "Cannon is a gentleman, and a cold fish besides. His kind always looks the other way."

If Sophia had not been so outraged, she would have laughed scornfully at the notion that Ross was too much of a gentleman to protest being cuckolded. "Stay away from me," she repeated, her voice unsteady despite the tight control she maintained over herself.

"You intrigue me, Sophia," Anthony remarked. "You are far more spirited and worldly-wise than you were before. The change in you is quite lovely. It bears investigation, I think."

"*Investigation?*" Her voice held utter bewilderment.

"Not now, of course, as you've just been wed. But sometime in the future, I may persuade you to renew our . . . friendship." His smile was taunting and arrogant. "I can be very persuasive, as you well know."

Sophia inhaled sharply. "There is ño possible inducement to make me spend five minutes in your company."

"Isn't there? I would hate for certain rumors about you to circulate. What an embarrassment for your husband and his family. Perhaps you should consider being pleasant to me, Sophia. If not, the consequences could prove most distressing."

She turned white with fear and rage. No doubt Anthony was enjoying the exchange, toying with her like a cat with a mouse. Whether his threats were serious or not, his efforts to set her off-balance were very effective. And she herself had given him that power by once having been stupid enough to trust him. If Anthony ever chose to tell people that he had known her intimately, she would not be able to refute his claims. An embarrassment to the Cannon family, indeed. Wretchedly Sophia contemplated the solemn portraits before her—the faces of her husband's distinguished ancestors. How ill-suited she was to join such company.

"There, now," Anthony murmured, seeming to relish her silent despair. "I see that we have reached an understanding."

As Ross brought a glass of champagne punch to his mother, he saw Sophia standing near the entrance of the portrait gallery. She was conversing with a young man whom Ross had never met. Although a casual observer could not have read the expression on Sophia's carefully blank face, Ross knew her too well.

"Mother," Ross asked casually, "who is that?"

Catherine followed his gaze. "The blond gentleman speaking with Sophia?"

"Yes."

"That charming boy is Mr. Anthony Lyndhurst, the son of Baron Lyndhurst. I have become quite attached to the family this past year. Such delightful people. You would have met them at your grandfather's birthday weekend, but the baron's sister was quite ill, and of course the family did not wish to leave her until she was out of danger."

"Anthony," Ross repeated, studying the slim, golden-haired man. There was no doubt in his mind that he was the same Anthony who had seduced Sophia.

"The youngest of three sons," Catherine informed him, "and perhaps the most accomplished of the lot. He sings in the most lovely tenor—it would give you chills to hear him."

Ross was far more interested in giving *him* chills. "Audacious bastard," he said beneath his breath. Whether Anthony was apologizing for the past or, more likely, throwing it in Sophia's face, Ross was going to set him straight on a few points.

"What did you say?" Catherine asked. "My goodness, the way you and Matthew have taken to muttering to yourselves of late, I am beginning to wonder if I have become hard-of-hearing."

Ross tore his glance from Anthony Lyndhurst for one moment. "Forgive me, Mother. I referred to Lyndhurst as an audacious bastard."

Catherine was obviously taken aback by the blunt comment. "Mr. Lyndhurst is merely chatting with Sophia, dear. There is no need to carry on as if he has done something ungentlemanly. It isn't like you to be jealous and possessive. I do hope you will not make a scene."

Instantly Ross adopted a bland smile. "I never make scenes," he said mildly.

Pacified, Catherine beamed at him. "That's better, dear. Now, if you will come this way, I want to introduce you to Lord and Lady Maddox. They have purchased the old Everleigh estate and are refurbishing the entire east—" Catherine broke off in perplexed surprise as she realized that her elder son was no longer with her. "All this mysterious dashing about!" she exclaimed to herself, vexed by his sudden disappearance. "Perhaps he has forgotten that he is not at Bow Street this evening." Shaking her head in exasperation, she drank the rest of her champagne punch and headed toward a circle of friends.

After taking his leave of Sophia, Anthony Lyndhurst wandered away from the drawing room. He paused at a massive gold-framed mirror and preened expertly. When he was satisfied that his appearance was immaculate, he strolled out to an open conservatory to have a smoke and enjoy the evening breeze. The night was dark and warm, the air laced with the rustling of leaves as well as the flexible strains of music from inside.

Filled with anticipation, Anthony considered the unexpected changes in his former light-o'-love. He had never revisited one of his paramours after he had left them. Once he was finished with a woman, he had no further interest in her. And Sophia had offered little in the way of sexual amusement, save for an innocent affection that had palled rather quickly. However, it was obvious that Sophia had received some tutoring in the intervening months. She wore the look of a well-pleasured woman, with her ripe mouth and blooming cheeks, and a sensuality in her movements that she had definitely not possessed when Anthony had known her. She seemed both elegant and sexually aware.

Surely Sir Ross had not effected such a change in her. Everyone knew him to be a cold and charmless bastard, not to mention notoriously celibate. Perhaps Sophia had taken yet another lover. The small but intriguing mystery occupied Anthony's thoughts pleasantly as he reached into his pocket for a cigar.

All at once a shadow seemed to fly at him from nowhere. Anthony had no chance to make a sound before he was brutally slammed against the wall. Paralyzed in fright, he felt something hard press against his throat—an unyielding muscular arm that threatened to crush the life from him.

"Wh . . . wh . . ." Anthony gasped, struggling helplessly against his captor. The man was large and irate, with all the restraint of a ravening animal. Anthony's bulging eyes beheld a dark visage that could have belonged to Satan himself. It took several moments for Anthony to recognize his assailant.

"Sir Ross—"

"You cowardly milksop," Cannon growled. "I know your kind. You pick your victims carefully—innocent women who have no one to protect them from gutter-scum like you. But you have finally chosen the wrong one. Find an excuse to leave Silverhill immediately, or I will smear you from here to London. And if you ever speak to my wife again, or dare to even glance in her direction, I will butcher you."

"Cannon . . ." Anthony wheezed uncontrollably. "Be . . . civilized . . ."

"I'm afraid I am nothing close to civilized where my wife is concerned."

"*Please*," Anthony choked as the blunt pressure at his throat increased.

"There is something else I should make clear," Cannon continued softly. "If you mention one word to anyone about your past with Sophia, I will personally throw you in Newgate. Of course, I can only keep you there for three days, but that will seem like a lifetime when you're locked in a cell with creatures that are more animal than human. By the time you're released, you'll be cursing your mother for bearing you."

"No," Anthony begged. "Won't say anything . . . won't bother her . . ."

"That's right," Cannon said in a malevolent whisper. "You will avoid my wife so that she forgets your very existence. Your acquaintance with the Cannons is at an end."

Somehow Anthony managed to nod, conveying acceptance in any way he could. Just as he thought he would faint, he was abruptly released. He fell to the floor, gasping and choking, rolling onto his side. When he finally managed to recover himself, Cannon's brutal form had disappeared. Shivering with terror, Anthony struggled to his feet and ran toward the line of carriages on the front drive as if he were fleeing for his life.

Sophia chatted and laughed with the guests at the ball, while inside, she felt sick and numb. A glass of champagne punch had done nothing to relax her. Anxiously she wondered where her husband was. She considered various ways to tell him about her encounter with Anthony. Certainly the news would ruin his evening as well as hers. No man wished to be confronted with his wife's paramour at his own wedding celebration.

As increasingly gloomy thoughts slunk through her mind, Sophia saw her husband approaching. He looked elegant and handsome, his dark face emphasized by a fresh white cravat. She decided he must have been relaxing with friends in the billiards room or the library, for something had evidently put him in a good humor.

"My sweet." He took her gloved hand and lifted it to his mouth.

"I haven't seen you for a while," she said. "Where have you been?"

"I had to dispose of a rodent," he said lightly.

"A *rodent*?" she repeated, perplexed. "Couldn't one of the servants have taken care of it?"

His white teeth gleamed as he laughed. "I wanted to take care of this one."

"Oh." She looked across the polished drawing room floor with a frown of worry. "Do you think there might be others scurrying around? They like to run up ladies' skirts, you know."

Still smiling, Ross slipped an arm around her waist. "My lady, the only creature that will nibble at your ankles tonight is me."

Sophia glanced around to make certain they could not be overheard. "Ross," she said unsteadily, "I-I must tell you something—"

"That your former lover is here? Yes, I know."

"How could you?" she asked in astonishment. "I've never told you his full name."

"I saw your face when he spoke to you." Ross smiled reassuringly. "It's all right. Lyndhurst can't harm you, Sophia. You're mine now."

Slowly she relaxed in his hold, acutely relieved that there would be no explosions of jealousy and no bitter accusations. What an extraordinary man Ross was, she thought with a rush of love. So many other men would have scorned her for her lack of virginity and regarded her as soiled goods. But Ross had always treated her with respect. "You mustn't refer to Anthony as my lover," she chided softly. "He gave me only pain and shame. *You* are the only lover I've ever had."

He bent his head and kissed her temple. "Don't worry, my sweet. He won't trouble you again. In fact, I suspect he has left the ball precipitately."

Something in his tone made her wonder if he had actually approached Anthony. "Ross," she said suspiciously, "about this 'rodent' you disposed of—"

"The opening march is beginning," he interrupted, pulling her with him to the mass of whirling couples.

"Yes, but did you—"

"Come—it is our responsibility to lead."

As Ross had intended, Sophia was distracted. "I'm not certain I can," she said. "I've seen the march a few times, but I've never had the opportunity to try it."

"It's very simple," he murmured, drawing her hand into the crook of his arm. "Just follow my lead."

Although their hands were gloved, Sophia felt a thrill at the pressure of his fingers. She looked up at his dark face and said with a sudden throb in her voice, "I would follow you anywhere."

Ross's thick lashes veiled his smoky eyes. She sensed his rampant desire to be alone with her. "Three hours," he said, speaking as if to himself.

"What?" she asked.

"Three hours until midnight. Then you will go upstairs, and I will follow soon after."

"Oh. Isn't that rather too early to retire from a ball such as this? I suspect some of the couples will be dancing until dawn."

"We won't be one of them," he said firmly, escorting her to the drawing room. "I can think of a much better way to spend the rest of the evening."

"Sleeping?" she said with false innocence.

Ross bent to whisper his alternative, and grinned as a wild blush rose in her face.

Chapter 16

$\mathcal{R}$oss could barely contain his annoyance upon their return to Bow Street, when all half-dozen runners gathered to congratulate him on his nuptials. The runners loudly insisted on their rights to "kiss the bride," and one after another, they bent over Sophia in a manner that was far more brotherly than amorous. However, Ross was scowling by the time he retrieved his giggling wife. He gave them all a warning stare. "Attend to your duties now."

Grumbling good-naturedly, the runners filed out of Bow Street No. 4, but not before Eddie Sayer beseeched Sophia, "Do what you can to soften his temper. You're our only hope, milady."

Laughing, Sophia threw her arms around Ross's neck and kissed his stern mouth. "There—will that serve to soften you?"

A reluctant grin curved his lips, and he kissed her possessively. "I'm afraid it's having the opposite effect. But don't stop."

She gave him a provocative glance from beneath her

lashes. "No more until this evening. You have work to do."

"Morgan will take care of it. I'll only stay long enough to attend to a few minor concerns, and then you and I are going on an errand."

"What kind of errand?" She sighed as he kissed the side of her throat, his lips traveling in a leisurely path up to her ear.

"We are going to look at something."

"Something large or small?"

"Large." He nibbled at a sensitive place on her neck. "Quite large."

"What kind of—" she began, but he silenced her with a thorough kiss.

"No more questions. Be ready to leave in an hour."

Although Sophia had expected him to be delayed by work, Ross returned for her in precisely an hour and escorted her to their carriage. She pestered him with questions, but he was maddeningly taciturn, refusing to give any hint about the nature of the mysterious errand. As the carriage traveled westward, Sophia lifted a corner of the sheer panel that covered the window and watched the scenery outside. They passed spectacular arcades and markets where luxury goods were sold, including haberdashers, goldsmiths, button-makers, perfumers, and even a feather shop bearing the intriguing title of "Plumassier."

As this was an area of London that Sophia had never visited before, she was fascinated by the masses of beautifully dressed people promenading through it.

Ladies and gentlemen of distinction visited the confectioner's to eat ices, strolled through tea gardens, or stood at the window of a print shop to view racks of decorative cards. It was a world far removed from Bow Street, and yet it was located only a short distance away.

The carriage conveyed them to Mayfair, the most fashionable location in London, where great family mansions were built in rows. They stopped in Berkeley Square, before a classically designed, triple-pedimented house. The large plate-glass windows gave the white stone facade a feeling of lightness and grandeur at the same time. One footman opened the carriage door and put down a movable step for Sophia. The other footman received a set of keys from Ross and dashed up the front steps.

"Are we visiting someone?" Sophia asked, staring admiringly at the house.

"Not precisely." Ross placed a hand at the small of her back and guided her up to the main entrance. "This house is owned by Lord Cobham, a contemporary of my grandfather's. He resides at his county seat and has decided to rent this place, as it remains unused most of the time."

"Why are we here?" She entered the cool marble hall, which was devoid of furniture or artwork. Rich blue lapis columns and doorcases contrasted crisply with the gleaming white walls.

Ross joined her, gazing upward at the gilded fretwork on the twenty-foot-high ceiling. "I thought that if this place pleases you, we might live here until our own house is built." He looked vaguely apologetic as he added, "It is unfurnished because Cobham took most of the family heirlooms with him to the country. If we take it, you will have to decorate it."

Sophia could not reply, only stared at her surroundings in amazement.

When it became clear that no immediate comment was forthcoming, Ross spoke matter-of-factly. "If you don't like the house, you have only to say so. There are other residences to consider."

"No, no," Sophia said breathlessly. "Of course I like it. How could anyone not approve? It's just that you have caught me off guard. I . . . I thought we were going to live at Bow Street."

He looked both appalled and amused by the idea. "God forbid. No wife of mine will take up residence at the public office. A place like this is more fitting, not to mention comfortable."

"It's very grand," Sophia commented doubtfully, thinking privately that the word "comfortable" would be more accurately applied to a cozy cottage or a small town house. "Ross," she said carefully, "if you spend all your time working at Bow Street, I do not think I would like to be alone in such a large place. Perhaps we could find some nice terrace on King Street—"

"You're not going to be alone." His eyes lit with amusement. "I've given enough of my life to Bow Street. I'm going to refashion the public office so that it can function without me. Then I'll recommend Morgan as the next Chief Magistrate, and step down for good."

"But what would you do?" Sophia asked in dawning worry, knowing that he was too active to settle into a life of gentlemanly indolence.

"I have more than a few reformist causes to occupy my time, and I need to take a stronger hand in running the Silverhill estate. I also plan to buy a part interest in a new railway company in Stockton, though God knows my mother will have apoplexy at such mercantile pursuits." He reached out and pulled her so close that her skirts swished around his legs and feet. His dark head lowered until their noses were almost touching. "But most of all," he murmured, "I want to be with you. I've waited long enough for this, and, by God, I'm going to enjoy it."

Sophia stood on her toes, brushing her lips against his. Before Ross could intensify the kiss, she drew back and regarded him with a saucy smile. "Show me the rest of the house," she said.

The house was unexpectedly charming, many of the rooms shaped with rounded ends and fitted with niches and built-in bookshelves. The delicate pastel walls were framed with white molding, some panels filled with the fanciful shapes of winged gryphons and other mythical beasts. Fireplaces were made of carved marble, and the floors were covered with thick-piled French carpets. Here and there an odd piece of furniture had been left: a bow-fronted chest in one room, a japanned screen in another. In a back room on the second floor, Sophia discovered an intriguing oddity, something that resembled a chair but had been constructed in a queer fashion.

"What is this?" she asked, walking around the piece, and Ross laughed.

"A chamber horse. It has been years since I've seen one of these. Not since boyhood, actually."

"What is it used for?"

"Exercise. My grandfather had one. He claimed that it strengthened his legs and slimmed his waist whenever he had indulged a bit too often."

She regarded him skeptically. "How is it possible to exercise on a chair?"

"You bounce on it." He grinned in reminiscence. "On rainy days, when there was nothing else to do, Matthew and I jumped on Grandfather's chamber horse for hours at a time." Using his hand, he pushed on the seat, which had been upholstered with at least two and a half feet of cushioning. "This is filled with springs and dividing boards. Air is expelled through the holes on the sides."

Ross sat on the chamber horse experimentally, holding the mahogany arms and resting his feet on the stepping board in front. He gave the chair a slight bounce, and the seat moved up and down with a creaking sound.

"You look ridiculous," Sophia said, giggling at the sight of the dignified magistrate on the odd contraption. "Very well, I will agree to live in this house if you promise to dispose of that thing."

His smiling gray eyes stared into hers, and he regarded her thoughtfully. When he spoke, his tone had lowered just a notch. "Don't be so hasty. You might want to use it sometime."

"I don't think so," she said, her eyes sparkling. "If I want exercise, I will take a walk."

"Do you know how to ride?"

"No, I'm afraid I can't. Neither real horses nor chamber horses."

"I'll teach you, then." His gaze traveled from her head to her toes in a single hot sweep. And then he astonished her by murmuring, "Take off your gown."

"What?" She shook her head, bemused. "Here? Now?"

"Here and now," he affirmed softly. He relaxed back in the chair, propping one foot on the stepping board. The wicked challenge in his eyes was unmistakable.

Sophia regarded him uncertainly. Although she was by no means inhibited, she was hesitant to remove her clothes in a strange house in the middle of the day, with sunlight streaming through the uncurtained windows. Cautious but amenable, she started at the fastening at the neck of her gown. "What if we are interrupted?"

"The house is empty."

"Yes, but what if one of the footmen comes in here to ask something?"

"They know better." He watched her hands alertly as

she fumbled with her bodice. "Do you need help with that?"

Sophia shook her head, feeling excruciatingly self-conscious as she stepped out of her shoes. She unfastened her dress, let it fall to the floor, and unhooked the front of her light corset. When that, too, was discarded, she was left in her knee-length chemise, cotton drawers, and stockings. A brilliant blush spread up to her hairline as she reached for the hem of the chemise and pulled it up to her waist. Pausing, she glanced at Ross's intent face.

"Go on," he encouraged.

She felt like a wanton, standing before him like one of the women who were paid to assume seductive poses at some of London's choice brothels. "If you were not my husband, I wouldn't do this," she said, and stripped off the chemise in a sudden decisive motion.

A smile played on his lips. "If you were not my wife, I wouldn't ask you to." His gaze moved over her naked upper body, lingering on the curves of her breasts and the rosy peaks of her nipples. His breathing changed noticeably, and his fingers twitched as they rested on the arm of the chamber horse. "Walk to me—no, don't cover yourself."

Sophia came to stand before him, gooseflesh rising on her skin as he touched her shoulder with a feathery stroke of his fingertips. His warm hand moved downward, tracing the shape of her breast, his thumb brushing over the nipple. She felt him pull at the tapes of her drawers, and they slid over her hips and down to the floor. Stepping out of them, she reached for her garters and stockings, but he caught her wrist.

"No," he said, his voice slightly raspy. "I like the way you look in your stockings."

Her gaze stole to the obvious bulge in his trousers. "Apparently so."

He grinned and exerted more tension on her wrist, pulling her forward. "Climb onto my lap."

Carefully she placed her stockinged foot on the stepping board; his hands clamped on her waist and lifted. She collapsed onto his lap in a giggling heap, her arms linking around his neck. The chair creaked loudly, and they sank downward several inches. "This isn't going to work," Sophia exclaimed, laughing uncontrollably.

"Cooperate," he said sternly, his eyes smiling.

"Yes, sir." Feigning meek obedience, she let him arrange her legs on either side of his lap, until her thighs were spread wide and she was left utterly vulnerable.

Gradually the giggles died in her throat. "Are you going to remove *your* clothes?" she asked, jumping a little as his hands slid to her bare bottom.

He cupped her and lifted her body upward. "No."

"But I want—"

"Shhh." He took her nipple into his mouth, drawing with sweet, hot suction. At the same time his fingers wandered high inside her thigh, until the backs of his knuckles brushed across the patch of protective curls. Every time she moved, the chamber horse bounced gently, forcing her to wrap her arms around his neck for balance.

His finger slipped inside her and stroked until she was wet and throbbing. Closing her eyes against the dazzle of sunlight from the window, Sophia rested her cheek on his thick hair. As he suckled her breast, the scratch of his beard abraded her moist flesh.

Too impassioned to wait, she reached down and tugged at the fastenings of his trousers. He caught her fumbling fingers and pushed them away. "Let me do it," he said with a soft laugh, "before you tear off the buttons."

Panting, she pressed closer to him as he unfastened the row of buttons and freed his swollen erection. With a soothing murmur, Ross positioned her over his hips, canting them to just the right angle. She sank down eagerly, gasping as he filled her completely. Her hands clutched at the fabric of his coat, fingertips digging into the smooth broadcloth.

"Hold onto me," he whispered. When she had wrapped herself around him, he picked his feet up from the stepping board and let the chamber-horse seat drop several inches in a sudden electrifying jolt. The movement forced Sophia harder onto the hilt of his shaft, and she whimpered in pleasure.

Ross smiled as he stared into her wide, unfocused eyes. Color burnished the edges of his cheekbones and the bridge of his nose, and sweat misted his skin. His thighs went taut as he braced his feet on the board once more, then let them drop again. "Is this all right?" he murmured. "Is it too much?"

"No," she gulped. "Do it again."

Obligingly he began a bouncing motion that elicited a rhythmic squeak from the chamber horse. Air rushed from the contraction and expansion of the cushions like the sighing of fireplace bellows. Sophia held on tightly, her body gripping his intimately. Each drop of the seat caused the stiff, thick shaft to push harder inside her, again, again, until the stroking, grinding motion caused her to convulse in a release that had no end.

Feeling the spasms of her body, Ross impaled her one last time and groaned in satisfaction. When at last he leaned backward with her body clasped in his arms, Sophia draped herself over him, utterly relaxed. Their bodies were still joined, and she moaned as he flexed inside her.

"I think we'll keep this chair," he murmured into her hair. "One never knows when you'll need another riding lesson."

Until the rented house was furnished with the basic necessities, Sophia and Ross resumed their residence at Bow Street No. 4. While Sophia spent much of her time purchasing goods and furniture, hiring servants, and enduring countless hours of clothes fittings, Ross made good on his promise to arrange for his retirement. Sophia knew that it would not be easy for him to relinquish the considerable power he had accumulated. However, he seemed remarkably untroubled at the prospect. His life had been confined to one narrow channel for a long time, and now it was expanding with new possibilities. He had been an exceptionally serious man, one who rarely smiled or laughed. Now he was far more apt to smile and tease, displaying a playful side that Sophia found utterly charming. And he was a sensual lover, possessing her with an unbounded intimacy that left her utterly fulfilled.

She had thought that she knew Ross quite well, having resided under the same roof with him. But she was gaining a far deeper understanding of him. Ross trusted her with his private thoughts and emotions, and he let her see him as he truly was—not a paragon, but a man with doubts and fears. He was capable of making mistakes, and he felt all too often that he had not met his own high expectations.

To Ross's frustration, his efforts to persuade the Treasury to release funds to establish public offices and hire new magistrates for Middlesex, Westminster, Surrey, Hertfordshire, and Kent had so far come to naught. It seemed the government was unconvinced that such changes were justified, and that they would prefer to pay only one man to handle the great mass of responsibilities.

"It's my own fault," Ross told Sophia grimly, sitting before the hearth in the bedroom with a glass of brandy in his hand. He drank the vintage without seeming to taste it. "I set out to prove that I could singlehandedly do it all, and now the Lord of the Treasury believes it is necessary to hire only one man as my replacement. I'm convinced that Morgan is entirely willing to succeed me as Chief Magistrate, but not at the expense of his family and personal life."

"No one but you could handle so much," Sophia said, taking the empty glass from his hand. She sat on the arm of his chair and caressed his dark hair, her fingers trailing gently over the threads of silver at his temple. "And even you were suffering under the weight of all that work, although you were too stubborn to admit it."

He looked up at her and seemed to relax slightly. "Until you appeared," he murmured. "Then I realized what was missing in my life."

"Such as food and sleep?" she suggested, her eyes twinkling.

"Among other things." His hand clasped her ankle and ventured beneath her skirts to her knee. "And now nothing is going to keep me from you."

Sophia continued to stroke his hair. "It may take some time for you to implement so many changes," she said. "There is no need for urgency on my account. Although I want you all to myself, I will wait as long as it takes."

Ross's gaze was warm as he stared up at her. "*I* don't want to wait." Tracing circles over her knee, he grinned suddenly. "It's ironic, isn't it? For years people have complained about my usurpation of power. But now that I want to leave Bow Street, no one wants me to go. The critics accuse me of abandoning my responsibilities, and the government ministers are offering me all manner of incentives to stay."

"That's because there is only one Sir Ross Cannon, and everyone knows it." Sophia drew her fingers lightly over the hard edge of his jaw. "And you're mine," she added in satisfaction.

"Yes." He turned his mouth into her palm, his eyes closing. "It has been a long, hellish day. I need something to help me forget about parliamentary funds and judicial reform."

"More brandy?" Sophia asked sympathetically, rising from the chair.

That drew a sudden laugh from him. "No, not brandy." He stood and caught her waist, urging her closer. "I had a different remedy in mind."

Anticipation curled inside her, and she linked her arms around his neck. "Whatever you wish," she told him. "As your wife, I want to be helpful."

Ross chuckled at her prim tone and nudged her toward the bed. "Oh, you will be quite helpful," he assured her, following closely at her heels.

Because Sophia was the object of much curiosity, she and Ross were invited everywhere, by politicians and professionals and even some upper-tier aristocrats. However, they accepted only a handful of invitations, for Sophia found it difficult to adjust to the new life she had stepped into. Having worked for so many years as a servant, she could not seem to interact comfortably in elevated social circles, no matter how kind her new acquaintances were. She felt awkward and stiff at most gatherings, although Ross's mother assured her that she would feel more comfortable as time passed. She found it somewhat easier to mix with "second-tier" sorts, such as Sir Grant and his wife, Victoria, and the crowd of professionals who were not nearly as rarefied as those in the first circles. These people were far less pretentious, and far more aware of ordinary matters like the cost of bread and the concerns of the poor.

Ross helped a great deal to ease her worries. He never belittled her fears or lost his patience with her. If Sophia wished to speak with him, he would interrupt whatever he was doing, no matter how important. On the evenings when they attended a soiree or went to the theater, Ross treated her with such attentiveness that other wives were moved to remark sourly that their own husbands should be half so solicitous of *their* comfort. It was the subject of much conversation, how greatly changed the Chief Magistrate was, and how such a serious-minded gentleman could have transformed into an obviously adoring husband. Sophia thought that the reason behind Ross's devotion was quite simple: having been alone for so long, he had a hard-won appreciation for the pleasures of marriage. He did not take his happiness for granted. And perhaps in some corner of his heart he feared that it all might be taken away in the blink of an eye, just as it had with Eleanor.

Frequently Ross would take Sophia for weekend visits to Silverhill Park where they attended water parties, went on picnics, or simply walked through the countryside to enjoy the fresh air and lush green views. Catherine Cannon loved to entertain, and in the summer months the mansion was constantly filled with friends and relatives. Sophia enjoyed these visits, forming a close relationship with her mother-in-law and even with Iona, her sister-in-law. Now that they had spent some time becoming familiar, Iona had thawed out considerably, although there was an ever-present sadness in her pale blue eyes. It was obvious that her melancholy stemmed from her marriage to Matthew. She even went so far as to confide to Sophia that Matthew had seemed an entirely different man before their wedding.

"He was quite charming," Iona said, her bitter expression somehow jarring on such an angelic countenance. She and Sophia sat on chairs that had been placed in front of a stone boundary wall covered with spilling roses that bloomed fiercely in the heat of high summer. In front of them, a small knot garden and an ivy-covered arch led to wide expanses of green lawn.

As Iona gazed absently into the distance, the sunlight brushed over her exquisite profile and turned her hair into a swirl of sparkling gold. "Of all the men who courted me, Matthew was the most impressive. I adored his wicked humor and, of course, his looks. He was so very charming." A humorless smile twisted her perfect lips. She paused to take a long drink of lemonade, and its sour taste seemed to linger in her mouth as she continued. "Unfortunately, I discovered later that certain men are only interested in the chase. Once the object of their desire is attained, they become indifferent."

"Yes," Sophia said, thinking of Anthony. "I have encountered that kind of man."

Iona's smile was resigned. "Of course, I am hardly

the only woman who has been disappointed in love. I have a comfortable and pleasant life. And Matthew is not a bad man, only a self-centered one. Perhaps if I could lure him to my bed often enough, I could have a child. That would be a great consolation to me."

"I hope you will," Sophia said sincerely. "And perhaps Matthew will improve. Sir Ross says that he is doing quite well with his new responsibilities." In the past few weeks, Ross had forced his younger brother to have regular meetings with the estate agent, to learn about accounting, management, farming, taxes, and all the minutiae involved in running the Silverhill estate. Although Matthew had protested long and loud, he had had little choice but to comply with Ross's dictates.

Iona used a long, perfectly filed fingernail to retrieve a fleck of dust that had settled inside the rim of her glass. "I suppose if you could cause Sir Ross to change so completely, there is a chance for my husband."

"Oh, I haven't changed him," Sophia protested.

"You most certainly have! I never thought to see Sir Ross so besotted. Before he married you, one could barely get two words out of him. Now he seems a different man altogether. It is strange—until lately, I've always been a bit frightened of him. He has a way of looking right through one. I am certain that you know what I mean."

"Yes, I do," Sophia said with a wry smile.

"And his remarkable reserve . . . Sir Ross never lowers his guard for anyone but you." Iona sighed and tucked a stray wisp of glinting hair behind her ear. "I used to think that between the two brothers, I'd gotten the better bargain. Even with Matthew's faults, at least he was warm and human, whereas Sir Ross seemed so utterly passionless. Now it has become apparent that your husband is not the cold automaton we all thought him to be."

Sophia colored as she replied, "No, he is definitely not."

"I envy you for being loved by a man who does not stray from your bed."

They sat in companionable silence for a while, each lost in her own thoughts. A bee droned lazily amid the roses, and the servants' bell clanged faintly from inside the mansion. Sophia was amazed as she reflected on how she herself had changed in such a short time. Not long ago, she had thought that what she wanted most in the world was to marry Anthony. But if she had married him, or a man similar to him, she would be exactly like Iona—bitter and betrayed, with little expectation that the future would be any better. Thank God, she thought fervently . . . thank God for not granting certain wishes, and for guiding her to a far sweeter fate.

As the warmth of the day increased, the Cannons and their guests elected to nap or relax indoors. However, Ross had never napped in his life, and the very idea of sleeping in the middle of the day was inconceivable to him. "Let's go for a walk," he suggested to Sophia.

"A *walk?* But everyone is resting comfortably inside," she protested.

"Good," he said in satisfaction. "Then we'll have the entire outdoors to ourselves."

Rolling her eyes, Sophia went to change into her lightest dress, then accompanied him on a stroll through the countryside. They walked toward the town until the steeple of the local church was visible in the distance. As they approached a grove of walnut trees, Sophia decided that she'd had quite enough exercise. Declaring that she needed to rest, she tugged Ross beneath the shade of the largest tree.

Agreeably, Ross sat with his arms around her, the neck of his shirt open to catch the occasional cooling puff of a breeze. Talking idly, they discussed subjects that ranged from the serious to the trivial. Sophia had never imagined that a man would listen to a woman as he did. He was attentive, interested, never mocking her opinions even when he disagreed with them.

"You know," she told him dreamily, lying across his lap and staring at the dark, saucer-sized leaves overhead, "I think that I enjoy talking with you even more than making love with you."

A lock of black hair fell over Ross's forehead as he looked down at her. "Is that a compliment to my conversational skills, or a complaint about my lovemaking?"

She smiled as she caressed his shirt-covered chest. "You know that I would never complain about *that*. It's just that I never expected to have this kind of relationship with a husband."

"What did you expect?" Ross asked, clearly amused.

"Well, the usual sort of arrangement. We would discuss light things, nothing improper, and we would have our separate areas of the house, and spend most days apart. You would visit my room some nights, and of course I would consult with you on certain matters . . ." Sophia paused as she saw the odd look that crossed his face.

"Hmm."

"What?" she asked, perturbed. "Did I say something that bothered you?"

"No." His expression was contemplative. "It occurred to me that you just described the kind of marriage I had with Eleanor."

Sophia sat up from his lap and smoothed her untidy hair. Ross mentioned his first wife so seldom that there were times Sophia actually forgot that he'd been married before. He seemed to belong to her so completely that she had difficulty imagining him living with another woman, loving her, holding her in his arms. Feeling a sharp bite of jealousy, Sophia strove to appear serene.

"Did you find it a pleasant arrangement?"

"I suppose I did." His gray eyes were thoughtful. "But I doubt I would be satisfied with that now. I've come to want something different in a relationship." A long hesitation passed before he murmured, "Eleanor was a good wife . . . but so very delicate."

Sophia plucked a blade of grass and examined it closely, twirling it in her fingers. She wondered what had attracted him to such a fragile, excessively ladylike creature. It seemed an ill-fitting match for a man who was so robust.

Somehow Ross was able to read her thoughts. "Eleanor appealed to my protective instinct," he said. "She was lovely and frail and helpless. Every man who ever met her wanted to take care of her."

The needles of jealousy jabbed Sophia despite her efforts to ignore them. "And naturally you could not resist."

"No." Ross propped up one knee and rested his arm on it, watching her lazily as she pulled at more bits of grass. Her tension must have been visible, for after a moment he asked softly, "What are you thinking?"

Sophia shook her head, embarrassed by the question that had come to mind, a question that was completely pointless and prying, and obviously born of jealousy. "Oh, it's nothing."

"Tell me." His hand settled over her plucking fingers. "You were going to ask about Eleanor."

She looked up at him, turning pink. "I was wondering how someone so fragile could have satisfied you in bed."

He was very still, a breeze lightly lifting the lock of hair off his forehead. The consternation on his face was easy to read. He was too much of a gentleman to answer such a question, as he would never dishonor the memory of his wife. But as their gazes held, Sophia read his unspoken reply, and it soothed her immeasurably.

Feeling reassured, Sophia turned her palm upward and slipped her fingers through his. He bent over her, his lips brushing hers in a husbandly kiss. Although he had not intended the gesture as a sexual advance, the taste of him was so intoxicating that Sophia slid her hand behind his neck and kissed him harder. Ross pulled her over his lap and took full advantage of her invitation. Her arms went around his back, fingers splaying over the hard flex of muscle. She sighed and squirmed deliciously as she felt his arousal rising beneath her.

The quiet catch of his laughter tickled her ear. "Sophia . . . you're going to cripple me."

She loved the way he looked at her, the dance of silver flame in his eyes. "I can hardly believe," she said in a passion-drowsed voice, "that a man with your appetite could have remained celibate for five years."

"I wasn't celibate the entire time," he admitted.

"You weren't?" She sat bolt upright in his lap. "You never told me that. Whom did you sleep with?"

Ross pulled the tortoiseshell comb from her hair and sifted his fingers through the rippling golden locks. "The widow of an old friend. For the first year after Eleanor died, I could not even contemplate making love to another woman. But eventually I had needs . . ." He paused, looking uncomfortable, and his hand stilled in her hair.

"Yes?" Sophia prompted. "And you renewed your acquaintance with this widow?"

He nodded. "She was similarly lonely, and also desirous of intimacy, so we met discreetly for about four months, until . . ."

"Until?"

"She began to cry one day after we . . ." A flush of embarrassment crept over his face. "And she said that she had fallen in love with me. She told me that if I did not return her feelings, she could not continue the affair, as it would be too painful for her."

"Poor lady," Sophia said, feeling genuine sympathy for the widow. "And so the relationship ended."

"Yes. And afterward I felt a great deal of guilt for the pain I had caused her. I also learned something—that as pleasant as the affair had been, it was not nearly as fulfilling without love. So I decided that I would wait until I found the right woman. That was three years ago. The time passed quickly, especially since I was occupied with work."

"But there must have been nights when you found it impossible," Sophia said. "A man of your physical nature . . ."

Ross smiled wryly, not quite meeting her gaze. "Well, there are ways a man can solve that problem by himself."

"You mean you . . ."

He looked at her then, a touch of color lingering on his cheekbones. "Haven't you?"

The canopy of leaves rustled over them, and a lone bird chirped innocently, while Sophia struggled to answer. "Yes," she finally admitted. "Not long after you were shot. You remember that morning when you kissed me and took me into your bed, and we almost . . ." Her scalding blush spread everywhere. "After that, I couldn't stop thinking about the way you touched me, and one night the feelings were so desperate that I—" Mortified, she put her hands over her face with a groan.

Ross twisted his hand in her hair and eased her head back, smiling as he kissed her. Still red-faced, Sophia relaxed in his lap and closed her eyes against the splashes of sunlight that slipped through the swaying branches overhead. His mouth possessed hers with slow, tempting kisses, and she did not protest when she felt him unfastening her clothes. His hands slipped inside the garments to fondle her breasts, hips, thighs.

"Show me," he murmured, his lips at her throat.

"Show you what?"

"How you pleasured yourself."

"*No*," she protested, giggling nervously at the outrageous request. He persisted, however, coaxing and teasing and demanding until she acceded with an embarrassed sigh. Her hand trembled as she reached down to the place he had exposed, her drawers at her knees, her skirts rucked up to her waist. "There," she said, breathing fitfully.

Ross's fingers lightly covered hers, learning the small, subtle motion. Her hand fell away, and he continued to caress her. "Like this?" he murmured.

She writhed in his lap, breathing too hard to speak.

A tender smile curved his lips as he watched her taut face. "Now, isn't this better than napping?" he asked, his fingers circling wickedly.

Suddenly lost to shame, she purred and twisted in his lap as sensations flowed over her in an endless river.

The only obstacle to Sophia's happiness was her growing concern for her brother. Nick cut a swath through London with the same cheerful carnage as always, acting alternately as a master criminal and a "thief-taker general." Society was divided in its opinion of him. Most still regarded him as a dashing public benefactor for his ability to track and arrest thieves and persuade gang members to inform on each other. However, a small but growing number of people were beginning to condemn his corrupt methods. "When Gentry enters the room," it was said, "one can smell the brimstone." It was clear that despite the power he held in the underworld, his throne was an unstable one.

After Sophia had sent Nick the information he had requested, he did not ask her for additional favors, nor was there any further mention of blackmail. From time to time he sent her notes that expressed his brotherly devotion, having an errand boy slip them to her undetected. It broke Sophia's heart to read these short letters, for her brother's lack of education was more than obvious. The words were labored and misspelled, but his fanciful intelligence and cautious love for her shone through. The notes gave her glimpses of what kind of man Nick could have become. If only his ambition and keen mind could have been turned to good purposes instead of wicked ones, she reflected sadly. Instead her brother was busy developing an extensive network of spies and informers all over London, not to mention a virtual corporation of thieves. He ran a sophisticated smuggling operation that imported huge quantities of luxury goods and distributed them with stunning efficiency. Nick was smart, bold, and ruthless, a combination of characteristics that made him a criminal mastermind. And what Ross had not admitted to Sophia—but was perfectly clear just the same—was that he wanted to bring Gentry down before he himself retired.

Soon Sophia's worry over Nick was temporarily set aside by a discovery that overwhelmed her with excitement. Before sharing the news with Ross, she had Eliza prepare one of his favorite dishes—broiled salmon with lime-and-parsley sauce—and she donned a light sea-green gown with white lace spilling from the neck and sleeves. At the end of the day, when he returned to Bow Street No. 4 after being out on an investigation, Ross was pleasantly surprised by the sight of the small table arranged by the window, with supper waiting beneath domed silver covers. Sophia had lit the room with candles, and she greeted him with a bright smile.

"This is what every man should come home to," Ross said with a grin, catching her around the waist and pressing a lusty kiss on her lips. "But why aren't we eating downstairs as usual?"

"We are celebrating something."

Ross studied her as he contemplated what the mysterious "something" could be. Gradually a cast of apprehensiveness came into his eyes, as if he suspected what she was going to tell him.

"Would you like to guess?" Sophia asked.

His tone remained relaxed. "I'm afraid I can't, my love. You may as well tell me."

She took his hand and squeezed it hard. "Nine months from now, the Cannon family will have a new addition."

To her surprise, Ross's face froze for an instant. Quickly he masked his reaction with a smile and pulled her close. "Sweetheart," he murmured. "That is good news indeed. Although it is hardly unexpected after what we've been doing for the past three months."

She laughed and hugged him tightly. "I am so happy! I've been to see Dr. Linley, and he says I'm in the best of health and there is no reason to worry about anything."

"I have complete faith in his opinion." He kissed her forehead gently. "Do you feel well?"

"Yes." Sophia drew back and smiled at him, sensing that something was not quite right, but she could not identify the problem. Ross had certainly taken the news well. However, she had expected his reaction to be a bit more enthusiastic. Well, she reasoned, perhaps it was simply the difference between men and women. After all, to most men, matters relating to childbirth and children were strictly a woman's territory.

She let him seat her at the table, and the conversation passed from the subject of her pregnancy to that of the house they were soon to move into. A nursery would have to be set up, of course, and they would need to hire a nurserymaid. While they ate and talked, Sophia kept glancing at Ross, feeling that he was keeping something from her. His eyes revealed nothing, and his face looked as if it had been cast in bronze as the candlelight slid over his hard features.

When they finished eating, Sophia stood and stretched. "It is late," she said with a yawn. "Will you come to bed now?"

He shook his head. "I'm not ready to sleep yet. I'm going outside for a walk."

"All right," she said, her smile turning uncertain. "I will be waiting for you."

Ross disappeared from their private apartments as if he were escaping prison. Frowning at his odd behavior, Sophia went into the bedroom and washed her face with cool water. As she began to undo the buttons on her bodice in preparation for a sponge bath, some instinct prompted her to go to the window. Pushing the curtain aside, she stared at the courtyard that backed both buildings of the public office. Ross was there, his dark form illuminated by the moonlight, the crisp white of his shirtsleeves contrasting with the rich gleam of his waistcoat.

Sophia was perplexed to see him holding a cigar and what seemed to be a matchbox. Ross rarely smoked, and when he did, it was a social ritual performed in the company of others. He struck a match and endeavored to light the cigar, but his hands were unsteady, and the little flame shook violently in his grasp.

He was upset, Sophia thought in amazement. Not perturbed, but actually distraught, which she had never seen in him before. Quickly she refastened her bodice and went downstairs. How foolish she had been, not to realize what the news would do to him! Ross's life had been shattered because his first wife had died in childbirth. Now it must seem as if the entire hideous experience was beginning again.

As Ross was a supremely rational man, he would know that the chances of that happening again were very slight. However, he was no different from anyone else, in that his emotions occasionally eclipsed common sense. Perhaps no one would believe it of the invincible Chief Magistrate, but he had fears of his own, and this was perhaps the greatest.

Sophia went through the kitchen and out into the courtyard. Ross's back was turned toward her, and it stiffened as he sensed her approach. He had given up the attempt at smoking and merely stood with his hands shoved deep in his pockets, his head bowed.

As she came closer, his voice emerged in a quiet growl. "I want privacy."

Sophia did not stop until she had pressed herself against his back and wrapped her arms around his midriff. Although Ross could have pulled away with ridiculous ease, he remained motionless in her grasp. Sophia's heart ached with compassion as she felt him trembling all over like a huge captive wolf, panicked by his confinement.

"Ross," she said softly, "everything is going to be fine."

"I know that."

"I don't think you do." She laid her cheek on his back and tightened her arms around his lean waist while she fumbled for the words that would comfort him. "I'm not fragile, as Eleanor was. It won't happen again. You must believe me."

"Yes," he agreed instantly. "There's no reason for worry." But the tremors continued, and there was a ragged edge to his breathing.

"Tell me what you're thinking," she said. "Your real thoughts, not what you believe I want to hear."

Ross waited so long to answer that she thought he had refused her, until he forced words out between abbreviated breaths. "I knew this would happen . . . I prepared myself . . . there is no logical reason to fear it. I want this child. I want a family with you. But no matter what I tell myself, I can't help remembering . . . Oh, God, you can't know what it was like!" His voice cracked, and she knew that the dark memories were assailing him faster than he could defend himself.

"Ross," she demanded, "turn and face me. Please."

He seemed dazed as he complied. Immediately she wrapped her arms around him, pressing herself to his big, warm body. He seized her as if she were a lifeline, his arms clamping onto her in a desperate vise.

Sophia smoothed her hands over his back and kissed

his ear. His fingers clenched in her hair and her clothes, and he gripped her while his lungs moved in shuddering sighs. Sophia placed her hands on either side of his damp, hot face and urged it to hers. His thick lashes were spiked with tears, and he seemed to be staring through the gates of hell. Tenderly she kissed his stiff lips.

"You will never be alone again," she promised. "We are going to have many healthy children, and grandchildren, and we will grow old together."

He nodded, clearly trying to make himself believe her.

"Ross," she continued, "I'm not like Eleanor in any way, am I?"

"No," he replied gruffly.

"Our entire relationship, from the moment it started until now . . . not a moment of it has been similar to what you experienced with Eleanor, has it?"

"Of course not."

"Then why do you believe it will end the same way?"

He did not answer, only crushed his lips to her temple and stood holding her in a desperate grip.

"I don't know why Eleanor had to die in such a manner," Sophia said. "It wasn't her fault, and it certainly wasn't yours. It was beyond your control. Until you stop holding yourself responsible for what happened to her, you will continue to be haunted by the past. And in punishing yourself, you will punish me as well."

"No," he breathed, clumsily stroking her hair, her neck, her back.

"Your guilt does her no honor." Sophia drew back to stare into his contorted face. "Eleanor would have hated to know that you were worse off for having loved her."

"I'm not!"

"Then prove it," she challenged, her own eyes misting with emotion. "Live as she would have wanted, and don't blame yourself any longer."

Ross huddled over her, and Sophia held him with all her strength. His beard-roughened face scraped hers as he sought her lips, found them, and kissed her almost angrily. She opened to him, accepting his passionate aggression. His hands searched her body roughly, emotion transforming into raw physical need.

"Upstairs," she said. "Please."

With a savage groan, he picked her up and headed into the house, not stopping until he had reached their bedroom.

Chapter 17

Sophia awakened alone and naked beneath the rumpled bedclothes. She had slept late, she thought groggily. There was much to do today—meetings with an interior decorator and a master gardener, and a charity luncheon to attend. But somehow the thought of all that did not bother her nearly as much as it should have.

A drowsy smile curved her lips as she rolled onto her stomach. Memories of Ross's lovemaking swirled in her head. He had reached for her countless times in the night, lavishing her with passionate attention until she had finally begged him to cease. Now she was sore everywhere, and she felt the sting of whisker burns in indecent places, and her lips were chapped and kiss-swollen. And she was utterly satisfied, her body filled with luxurious contentment.

She asked Lucie to fill a slipper-bath for her, and she took her time about selecting her clothes for the day, a peach corded silk trimmed with fluted bands at the waist and hem. When the bath was ready, she lowered herself into the steaming water with a sigh, letting the heat soothe her abraded skin and sore muscles. Afterward she dressed and arranged her hair in a newly fashionable style, parted on the right with curls pinned on the left side.

Just as she reached for a bonnet trimmed with sprigs of hydrangea, Lucie entered the apartments with a hasty knock.

"Have you come to empty the bath?" Sophia asked.

"Yes, milady, but . . . they sent Ernest across the way wiv' a message. Sir Ross wants ye, an' 'e's asking for ye to come to 'is office."

The request was unusual, for Ross rarely sent for her in the middle of the day. "Yes, of course," Sophia said calmly, though she was conscious of an inner throb of uneasiness. "The carriage is most likely waiting at the front. Will you tell the driver that I will be delayed for a few minutes?"

"Yes, milady." Lucie bobbed deferentially and left.

Ernest was waiting downstairs to accompany her to No. 3.

"Ernest," Sophia asked as they walked out the back and crossed the courtyard, "have you any idea why Sir Ross has asked for me?"

"No, milady . . . except . . . there's been some grand to-do this morning. Mr. Sayer 'as come an' gone twice already, an' I 'eard tell that Sir Grant 'as sent for the militia to go to Newgate, an' dragoons to come 'ere!"

"They're expecting riots for some reason," Sophia murmured, while cold suspicion gathered in her chest.

The boy fairly wriggled with excitement. " 'Twould seem so, milady!"

An unusual number of constables and patrols were being summoned to No. 3. Groups of uniformed men nodded respectfully and removed their hats as Sophia passed by. Distractedly she bade them good morning and continued with Ernest until they reached Ross's office. Leaving the boy to stand in the hallway, Sophia pushed through the half-open door and saw Ross standing over his desk. Sir Grant Morgan stood staring out the window, an austere expression on his face. They both turned at her entrance, and Ross's gaze locked with hers. For one breathtaking moment the intimacy of the previous night flashed between them, and Sophia felt her pulse quicken.

Ross approached her and took her hand in a brief, hard clasp. "Good morning," he said quietly.

She forced herself to smile. "I assume you are going to explain why there is so much activity at the public office this morning."

He nodded and answered bluntly. "I want you to leave London and go to Silverhill. Just for a few days, until I decide it is safe for you to return."

She gazed into his face with dread. "You are expecting some kind of trouble, I gather."

"Nick Gentry has been arrested and charged with receiving and selling stolen goods. A witness has come forward with solid evidence. I've bound Gentry over to the King's Bench and enjoined the Chief Justice to give him a fair trial. However, if the proceedings last too long, the masses will erupt in a way that will make the Gordon riots seem like a May Day festival. I don't want you anywhere near London until the matter is concluded." Although Nick's arrest was a goal Ross had long worked for, there was no triumph in his tone.

Sophia felt as if she had received a blow to the stomach. Nauseated and out of breath, she wondered why her brother had to be such a notorious criminal. If he were just a bit less successful, he could have prospered in relative anonymity. But no, he had to court fame and become a lightning rod for controversy, dividing the public and thumbing his nose in the faces of legally sanctioned police. Nick had made it virtually impossible for anyone to help him.

Blindly she groped for the chair behind her. Seeing her unsteadiness, Ross lowered her to the seat. He half crouched before her, staring into her ashen face with sudden anxiety. "What is it?" he asked, taking her cold hands in his. The warmth of his fingers did nothing to thaw her prickling skin. "Do you feel ill? Is it the baby—"

"No." She looked away from him, trying to force her wildly scattering thoughts into some coherent pattern. Her bones seemed to have turned into ice, coldness radiating from the inside out, making her skin hurt. Even the familiar, gentle touch of Ross's hands hurt. She considered telling him the truth about Nick, because the price she would have to pay for her continued silence was too much to bear. And yet the truth was likely to be just as costly. No matter what choice she made, her life would never be the same.

Tears forced their way into her eyes until Ross's beloved face was a fluid blur.

"What is it?" Ross repeated, his voice urgent. "Sophia, are you well? Do you need a doctor?"

She shook her head and took a ragged breath. "I'm fine."

"Then why—"

"Is there nothing you can do to help him?" she asked desperately.

"Help Gentry? Why in God's name would you ask that?"

"There is something I haven't told you." Using her sleeve, she blotted her eyes until he came back into focus. "Something I learned just before our wedding."

Ross was silent, remaining on his haunches, his hands coming to grip the arms of her chair. "Go on," he said quietly.

Out of the corner of her eye Sophia saw Sir Grant move toward the door, tactfully leaving the two of them alone. "Wait," she told him, and he paused at the threshold. "Please stay, Sir Grant. I think you should know as well, in light of your position at Bow Street."

Morgan slid a questioning glance at Ross and cautiously resumed his place by the window, though he clearly did not wish to be part of the scene.

Sophia stared down at the strong, hair-dusted hands that rested on either side of her. "Do you remember when you told me that Mr. Gentry was the one who had given me the diamond necklace?"

Ross nodded.

"I already knew it," she said dully. "Earlier that day, I encountered Mr. Gentry near Lannigan's. He . . . took me into his carriage. And we talked." Pausing, she watched her husband's tanned hands grip the arms of the chair until his knuckles and the tips of his fingers were white. The office was as silent as a graveyard, except for the sound of Ross's controlled breathing. The only way Sophia could continue was to keep her tone flat and emotionless. "Gentry said that in his youth he had been on the same prison hulk that my brother had been sent to. He told me what it had been like for John, the things he had suffered . . . and then he told me—" She stopped, then spoke with a break in her voice. "He told me that John did not die. He took the name of another boy on the ship so that he could gain an early—"

"Sophia," Ross cut in softly, as if believing she had gone mad, "your brother is dead."

She put her hands over his hard, corded ones and looked right at him. "No," she said urgently. "Nick Gentry is my brother. He and John are one and the same. I knew it was true the moment he told me. He could not deceive me, Ross . . . we were children together, he knows everything I know about our past, and . . . just look at him, and you'll see the resemblance. We have the same eyes. The same features. The same—"

Ross flung off her hands and strode away from her as if he had been scalded. His chest moved with his labored breaths. "My God," she heard him say through his teeth.

Sophia sagged in her chair, certain that she had lost him now. He would never forgive her for hiding something that she should have told him before they were married. Numbly she went on to describe the rest of the conversation with her brother, as well as the information he had asked her to obtain from the records room. Ross kept his back to her, his hands clenched tightly. "I am sorry," Sophia finished stiffly. "I wish I could do it all over again. I should have told you about Nick as soon as I learned that he was my brother."

"Why tell me now?" Ross asked hoarsely.

There was nothing left to lose. She focused on a distant spot on the floor as she answered. "I hoped you could save him somehow."

A caustic laugh escaped him. "If I could, it wouldn't matter. Before long Gentry would do something else, and I'd be forced to arrest him again. And we would probably be in this same situation a month from now."

"I don't care about next month. All I care about is today." Ross would never know what it cost her to say next, but she forced the words out. "Don't let them hang him," she begged. "I can't lose John again. Do something."

"Do *what?*" he snarled.

"I don't know," came her frantic reply. "Just find some way to keep him alive. I will talk to him, convince him that he must change, and perhaps he—"

"He'll never change."

"Save my brother just this once," she persisted. "One time. I will never ask again, no matter what happens from now on."

He did not move or speak, his shoulders bunched tightly beneath his shirt.

"Lady Sophia," Morgan interjected gently. "I should not speak, but I must point out what is at risk for Sir Ross. All eyes are on Bow Street. Keen attention is being paid to how we handle this matter. If it is discovered that Sir Ross has interfered in the process of law, his reputation and everything he has worked for will be ruined. Furthermore, questions will be asked, and when it comes to light that Gentry is Sir Ross's brother-in-law, the entire Cannon family will suffer the consequences."

"I understand," Sophia said. Painful pressure built behind her eyes, and she dug her nails into her palms to keep from crying. She stared at her husband; he still refused to face her.

There seemed to be nothing left to say. She departed the office silently, knowing that she had asked the impossible of him. Moreover, she had wounded him beyond his ability to forgive.

The two men remained alone. A long time passed before Morgan spoke. "Ross . . ." In all the years they had known each other, he had never called him by his first name. "Do you think there is a chance she is telling the truth?"

"Of course it's true," Ross replied bitterly. "It's so damned appalling that it *has* to be the truth."

* * *

After Sophia left Bow Street No. 3, she was not certain what to do. She was suddenly exhausted, as if she had gone for days without sleeping. Desolately she tried to think of what Ross would do with her. With his extensive political connections and influence, it would probably be fairly easy for him to obtain a divorce. Or perhaps he would simply install her somewhere in the country, out of sight and out of mind. Whatever he decided, Sophia would not blame him. And yet she could not conceive that he would reject her absolutely. Perhaps there was some remnant of his feelings that remained, some fragile foundation on which they could rebuild their relationship. Even if it turned out to be a flawed imitation of what they'd once had.

Dazedly she went into the bedroom they shared and changed into a light robe. It was only midday, but her weariness was overwhelming. She lay down on the wide bed and closed her eyes, welcoming the dark oblivion that rolled over her.

Much later she was awakened by the sound of someone entering the room. Groggily she realized that she had slept all afternoon. The room was much cooler, and beyond the partially drawn curtains she could see the sun yielding to the slow encroachment of evening. She sat up, watching as her husband crossed the threshold and closed the door in a decisive motion.

They regarded each other like two gladiators who had been released into the ring but were reluctant to battle.

She was the first to speak. "I'm certain that you . . . you must be furious with me."

A long silence passed. Assuming that they were going to have a civilized discussion, Sophia was startled when he sprang at her in two swift strides and seized her in a rough grip. His hand tangled in her hair and he tugged her head back, crushing his mouth over hers. The bruising kiss was not meant to give pleasure but to punish. Gasping, Sophia yielded completely, opening her mouth to the aggressive thrust of his tongue, answering his angry passion with utter surrender. She told him with her lips and body that whatever he wanted of her, she would give without reserve. Eventually her lack of resistance seemed to soothe him, and he softened the kiss, still probing deeply, both of his hands cupping around her skull.

However, the embrace was short-lived. Ross let go of her as abruptly as he had seized her and put a few yards of distance between them. He sent her a baffled glare, his eyes light and piercing in his flushed face.

And then Sophia understood, as clearly as if his thoughts and feelings were her own. She had lied to him, kept secrets from him, abused his trust. Yet he still wanted her. He would forgive her anything, even murder. He loved her more than honor, even more than his pride. For a man who had always been so completely self-possessed, the realization was a unpleasant shock.

Desperately she wished for a way to reassure him that from now on, she would be worthy of his trust.

"Please let me explain," she said in a raw voice. "I

wanted to tell you about Nick, but I couldn't. I was so afraid that once you knew—"

"You thought I would turn you away."

She nodded, her eyes stinging.

"How many times do I have to prove myself to you?" His face twisted with fury. "Have I ever blamed you for your past mistakes? Have I ever been unfair to you?"

"No."

"Then when are you going to trust me?"

"I *do* trust you," she said hoarsely. "But the fear of losing you was more than I could bear."

"The only way you could lose me is by lying to me again."

She blinked, and her heart drummed furiously in her chest. Something in his words implied . . . "Is it too late?" she managed to ask. "Have I already lost you?"

Ross looked grim, his mouth twisting. "I'm here," he pointed out sardonically.

Her lips shook until she could hardly form words. "If you still want me, I-I promise never to lie to you again."

"That would be a pleasant change," he told her curtly.

"And . . . I will keep no secrets from you."

"Also a good idea."

Wild hope flooded her as she realized that he was willing to give her another chance. Furious, but willing. And there could only be one reason that he would put himself at such risk.

Carefully she approached her husband, the room

darkening as the buildings and spires of London fractured the falling sunlight. She put her hands on his
chest, gently covering the violent thud of his heart. He
stiffened but did not pull away. "Thank you, Ross," she
whispered.

"For what?" he returned, stone-faced.

"For loving me." She felt his heart lurch at the
words, and she realized that until this moment, Ross
had not acknowledged his feelings for her, even to
himself. He had not wanted to put a name to the emotion. Holding his stare, she saw the blaze of resentment
in his eyes . . . and the smoldering need he could not
conceal.

She could think of only one way to dispel his anger,
to reassure him and soothe his aggravated pride.

Sophia's sapphire eyes were grave as she reached up to
Ross's neck, her fingers working at the knot of his cravat. She concentrated on the task as if it were of momentous importance. The knot loosened, and she drew
the length of dark, warm silk from his throat. Ross's
body was as rigid as carved marble, his thoughts in a
welter. Surely she did not think that a romp in bed
would solve anything. But the deliberateness of her actions indicated that she was trying to demonstrate
something.

She undressed him slowly, removing his coat, waistcoat, and shirt, then kneeling to unbuckle his shoes.
"Sophia," he said tersely.

"Let me," she whispered. Standing, she brushed her fingertips over the matted curls on his chest. Her fingers delved lightly into the black hair, sifted through it, stroked the hot skin beneath. Her thumbs found his nipples, circled delicately, bringing them to hard points. Leaning closer, she flicked her tongue over the dark circle until the nipple was slick and sensitive. He could not restrain a primitive grunt as her hand slid to the stiff bulge of his erection, tracing it slowly.

She glanced at his face then. "Are you sorry for loving me?" she whispered.

"No," he said gruffly. Somehow he managed to hold still as her slim fingers dipped inside the waist of his trousers.

"I want you to know something," Sophia said. The first button popped free, revealing the swollen head of his sex. Her fingers stole to the next button. "I am more in your power, Ross, than you could ever be in mine. I love you." A quiver ran through him at the words. "I love you," she repeated deliberately, plucking at the fourth button.

She continued down the row until his trousers were wide open and his erection was unhindered. Grasping him carefully in both hands, she stroked up and down the hard shaft. She wet her finger in her mouth, then stroked a moist circle around the taut purple crown. The muscles of his thighs stiffened, and he breathed in harsh pants as passion ignited and roared through his body. Sophia's head lowered until it hovered just above the rearing length of him. "Enough," Ross choked. "Christ, I can't—"

"Tell me what to do," she said, the words blowing against him.

Whatever sanity Ross had left promptly burned to cinders. He gasped out instructions, his hands trembling as he clasped her head. "Use your tongue on the tip . . . *yes* . . . now take as much as you can in your . . . oh, God . . ."

Sophia's fervor more than made up for her lack of experience. She did things that Eleanor would never have tried, tugging at his aching flesh, her velvety tongue swirling and lapping. Ross sank to his knees and pulled at her clothes, tearing them, and she gave a breathless laugh at his roughness. His mouth caught greedily at hers, while she wriggled to help him strip the shredded gown down her legs.

A primal sound of satisfaction escaped him when Sophia's naked body was finally revealed. He lifted her to the bed, pausing only to remove his trousers before he joined her. Eagerly she slid between his legs and took his sex into her mouth once more, resisting his efforts to bring her face up to his. Groaning repeatedly, he surrendered to her ministrations, his fingers tangling in the long locks of her hair. However, he was not satisfied for long—he wanted more, he craved the taste of her. Impatiently he seized her hips, maneuvering her until she was positioned at his mouth. He buried his face amid the intimate curls, his hands gripping her thighs as she jerked with surprise.

He searched her with his tongue, licking deeply into the seam of moist folds. Avidly he hunted for the tiny engorged peak where her pleasure was concentrated. Finding it, he nibbled, stroked, darted his tongue at it, as he felt her stiffen in approaching climax. He backed off, gentling, while she moaned pleadingly around his cock. Twice more he brought her to the edge, making her suffer, tormenting until she responded with desperate tugs of her mouth.

Each time Sophia drew on him, Ross sank his tongue deep inside her, matching his rhythm to hers, until she shuddered hard as her pleasure finally reached its zenith. She cried out against his groin, her mouth still clamped around him. His own culmination approached rapidly, and he moved his hands to her head. But she resisted his attempts to dislodge her, and the silky strokes of her tongue became too much to bear. The climax broke over him, and he arched and gasped as he was consumed in an explosion of pure white fire.

Eventually Sophia turned and climbed over him, resting her head on the center of his chest. Ross held her tightly. His lips moved against her throbbing temple as he spoke. "I don't care who your brother is. He could be the devil incarnate, and I would still want you. I love everything about you. I never expected to find such happiness. I love you so much that I can't bear the thought of anything coming between us."

Sophia's slim, damp body flexed against his. "There is nothing between us now," she said throatily.

Ross parted his legs to allow her to settle between

them, his cock stirring briefly against her stomach. Sighing in relaxation, he clasped his hands behind his head and contemplated her thoughtfully. "Sophia," he murmured, "I don't think there is any way I can save Gentry from the hangman. Nor am I particularly disposed to try. I can't overlook his crimes, even though he is your brother. The fact is, Gentry is beyond redemption. He has proved that on many occasions."

She shook her head in disagreement. "My brother's life has been very difficult—"

"I know," he interrupted as gently as possible. It was apparent that any arguments concerning Nick Gentry would result in nothing but frustration for both of them. Sophia would never stop hoping that her brother's ruined soul could be salvaged. He smiled slightly, stroking the fragile sweep of her jaw. "Only you would continue to love a brother who blackmailed you."

"No one has ever given him an opportunity to change," she said. "If he had just one chance at a different life . . . think of the kind of man he could become."

"I'm afraid my imagination fails me," came Ross's sardonic reply. Rolling over, he pinned her beneath him, his muscular thighs straddling hers. "Enough about Gentry. He has occupied my thoughts enough for one day."

"All right," Sophia agreed, although it was obvious that she wanted to discuss him further. "How shall we pass the rest of the evening?"

"I'm hungry," Ross murmured, bending over her naked breasts, "I want supper . . . and then more of you." His mouth covered one swollen nipple, his teeth catching at it gently. "Does that sound agreeable?"

Thanks to Ross's preparations, there had so far been no violent demonstrations from agitators on behalf of Nick Gentry. The following day, however, he expected a few public skirmishes. Therefore Bow Street had been blocked off with troops and militia, and a party of three runners and a dozen constables was busy clearing away onlookers who tried to gather at Newgate. Families of magistrates had been given notice to barricade their homes, while employees at banks, distilleries, and other businesses were given guns to help defend against possible looting. Sophia had vehemently refused Ross's attempts to send her to the country until the situation was resolved. She did not want to be bustled off to Silverhill Park to sit helplessly with Catherine, Iona, and Ross's grandfather while her brother's fate was being determined.

As the day progressed, Sophia sat in the private parlor in Bow Street No. 4, frantically considering what might be done for her brother. Her head ached and throbbed. Ross did not take luncheon, only sent repeatedly for jugs of coffee while a stream of visitors came to the magisterial office. Gradually evening approached, and the city swarmed with armed foot patrols that kept a lid on the simmering rookeries and flash-houses. On his way to deliver a message to a justice in Finsbury Square, Ernest stopped at No. 4 to give Sophia a brief report of the situation. "I 'eard Sir Ross and Sir Grant talk as 'ow they're surprised the public 'as taken Gentry's arrest so quiet-like. Sir Ross says it's a sign that many opinions 'as swung against Gentry." Ernest shook his head at the masses' disloyalty. "Poor Black Dog," he murmured. "Bloody ingrates, all o' 'em."

Were Sophia not so miserable, she would have smiled at the lad's ready defense of his tarnished hero. "Thank you, Ernest," she said. "Be careful when you go out. I would not like for you to be hurt."

He blushed and grinned at her concern. "Oh, no one'll lay a finger on me, milady!"

He dashed off, and Sophia was left to brood alone once more. The sun set, leaving London covered in hot, black night. The air was pungent with coal and the stench of a foul east wind. Just as Sophia considered changing into her nightgown in preparation for bed, Ross strode into their private apartments. He stripped off his sweat-dampened shirt as he crossed the threshold.

"Is there any news?" Sophia demanded, following him into the bedroom. "How is my brother? Are there any reports? Has there been agitation near the prison? I'm going mad from the lack of news!"

"Everything is relatively calm," Ross said, pouring water into a washbasin. The long muscles of his back flexed as he sluiced water over his face, chest, and beneath his arms. "Fetch me a clean shirt, will you?"

She hurried to comply. "Where are you going? You must eat something first. At least a sandwich—"

"No time," Ross muttered, donning the fresh linen

shirt and tucking it into his trousers. Deftly he positioned the collar and tied a cravat around his neck. "An idea occurred to me just a few minutes ago. I'm going to Newgate—I expect to return soon. Don't stay up on my account. If I have news of any significance, I'll wake you."

"You're going to see my brother?" Quickly Sophia pulled a patterned gray waistcoat from the wardrobe and held it up for him to slide his arms through. "Why? What is this idea? I want to go with you!"

"Not to Newgate."

"I'll wait outside in the carriage," she insisted desperately. "You can give the footman a brace of pistols, and the driver as well. And there are patrols all around the prison, aren't there? I'll be as safe there as I am here. Oh, Ross, I'll go mad if I have to wait here any longer! You must take me with you. Please. He's *my* brother, isn't he?"

Pelted by the flurry of anxious words, Ross gave her a hard stare, a small muscle jumping in his cheek. Sophia knew that he wanted to refuse her. However, he also understood her anguished concern for her brother.

"You swear that you will stay in the carriage," he demanded.

"Yes!"

His gaze held hers, and he muttered a curse. "Get your cloak."

Afraid that he might change his mind, she obeyed with alacrity. "What is your idea?" she asked.

Ross shook his head, unwilling to explain. "I am still

considering it. And I don't want to raise your hopes, for it will probably come to naught."

As a temporary lodging for those awaiting trial or execution, Newgate was often called the stone jug. Anyone who had ever visited or been incarcerated in the place swore that hell itself could not be more wretched. The ancient walls echoed with the constant howls and jeers of prisoners chained like animals in their cells. No furniture or comforts of any kind were allowed in the open wards or solitary cells. The gaolers, who were supposed to maintain order, were often corrupt, cruel, mentally imbalanced, or some combination of the three. Once, after depositing a condemned man in Newgate, Eddie Sayer had returned to Bow Street with the comment that the gaolers alarmed him more than the prisoners.

Although the prisoners suffered mightily in the bitter cold of winter, it was nothing compared to the unholy stench that accumulated in the hot summer days. Armies of cockroaches scurried across the floor as Ross bade the head gaoler to take him to Nick Gentry's cell. It was located in the heart of the prison and nicknamed the "devil's closet," from which there was no escape.

As they proceeded through one of the twisted mazes, lice crackled underfoot and squeaking rats fled from the approach of heavy boots. Distant cries of misery rose from the cells on the lower floors. It unnerved Ross to think that he had allowed his wife to wait in a carriage just outside, and he sorely regretted his decision to bring her here. He comforted himself with the knowledge that she was in the company of an armed footman, a driver, and two runners bearing cutlasses and pistols.

"That Gentry, 'e's a quiet one," Eldridge, the head gaoler, commented. An enormous, stocky individual with bulbous features, he reeked almost as badly as those who were incarcerated. The top of his head was bald, but long, greasy strands trailed from the sides of his scalp and fluttered down his back. Eldridge was one of the rare prison-keepers who appeared to enjoy his job. Perhaps that was because he made a nice profit each week by selling his accounts of prisoners' experiences within Newgate, including the final confessions of the condemned, to London newspapers. No doubt he would make a pretty penny with his tales of the infamous Nick Gentry.

"Nary a peep from 'im all day," Eldridge grumbled. "I ask ye, what kind o' story can I sell if 'e keeps 'is gob shut?"

"Inconsiderate of him," Ross agreed sardonically.

Apparently gratified by Ross's concurrence, the gaol-keeper led him to the entrance of the devil's closet. A six-inch-wide window had been cut in the heavy oak-and-iron door to allow the prisoner to speak to visitors. "Gentry!" Eldridge grunted through the hole. "Visitor!"

There was no reply.

Ross frowned. "Where is the guard?"

Eldridge's oily face turned toward him. "There is no guard, Sir Ross. 'Twasn't needed."

"I specifically ordered a guard to be placed at this door at all times," Ross said curtly. "Not only to prevent escape attempts, but also for Gentry's own protection."

A deep laugh rose from Eldridge's pendulous gut. "*Escape?*" he scoffed. "No one can escape the devil's closet. 'Sides, Gentry's been handcuffed, an' irons fitted on his legs, an' 'e's weighted with three hundred pounds o' chains. 'E can't move to pick 'is nose! No man alive could get in or out o' that cell, wivout *this*." He brandished a key and worked to unlock the door.

The thick slab of oak and iron groaned in angry protest as it was pushed open. "There," Eldridge said with satisfaction, the lamp in his hand jangling as he walked into the cell. "Ye see? Gentry is—" His huge frame jiggled from a start of surprise. "Bloody 'ell!"

Ross shook his head slightly when he saw that the devil's closet was empty. "My God," he muttered, filled with a combination of admiration and fury at his brother-in-law's resourcefulness. A bent iron nail gleamed beside the massive pile of chains on the floor. Gentry had managed to pick the locks on his handcuffs and leg irons—in the dark, no less. A bar was missing from the inner window on the other side of the room. It was inconceivable that Gentry could have loosened that bar and squeezed his large frame through such a narrow space, but he had done it. There was every likelihood that he'd had to dislocate a shoulder to accomplish it.

"When was the last time someone saw him here?" Ross barked to the dazed-looking gaol-keeper.

"An hour ago, I think," Eldridge mumbled, his eyes bulging from his sweat-drenched face.

Staring through the inner window, Ross saw that

Gentry had broken through the moldy wall of the next cell, probably using the window bar. He strove to recall the details of the Newgate layout that was tacked to the wall of his office.

He shot a murderous glance at the gaol-keeper. "Does that key work for all the cells on this floor?"

"I-I think so—"

"Give it to me. Now get your fat arse to the ground level, and tell the runners at my carriage that Gentry is escaping. They'll know what to do."

"Yes, Sir Ross!" Eldridge fled with surprising speed for someone of his girth, taking the lamp with him and leaving Ross in darkness.

Gripping the key, Ross left the devil's closet and unlocked the adjoining room. Swearing profusely, he climbed through the hole in the wall, following his brother-in-law's tracks. "Damn you, Gentry," he muttered as rustles and squeaks of unsettled vermin greeted his intrusion. "When I catch you, I'll hang you myself for putting me through this."

Breathing hard from exertion, Nick Gentry pushed a swath of damp hair from his eyes and emerged onto the roof of Newgate. Cautiously he placed a foot on an outside wall that connected to a neighboring building. The wall was about eight inches thick, and so old that it was crumbling along the top. However, it was the only route to freedom. Once he made it to the other side, he would enter the building, find his way to the street, and then be unstoppable. He knew London as no one else did—every alley, every corner, every hole and crevice. No one could find him if he did not wish to be found.

Slowly Nick proceeded along the wall like a cat, heedless of the possible fall that would see him crushed on the ground. He squinted fiercely, the dense sky relieved by a mere glimmer of moonlight. One foot after another; he tried to keep his mind clear. But a thought broke his concentration—Sophia. Once he left London, he would never be able to see her again. Nick did not identify his feelings for her as love, because he knew himself to be incapable of that emotion. But he was conscious of a rip in his soul, a sense that to leave her for good would mean the loss of the fragment of decency he still possessed. She was the only person on earth who still cared for him, who would continue to care, no matter what he did.

One step, another, right foot, left . . . Nick shoved the thoughts of his sister away and considered where he would go when he was free. He could make a new start somewhere, take a new name, a new life. The idea should have been cheering, but instead it sank him into gloominess. He was tired of the balancing act that never allowed him to relax for a minute. He was weary, as weary as if he had lived a hundred years instead of twenty-five. The thought of starting again revolted him. It was his only choice, however. And he had never been one to wring his hands over what he couldn't change.

Part of the wall crumbled beneath his right foot, sending chunks of mortar and showers of dust to the ground. Silently Nick fought for balance, his arms out-spread, his breath hissing between his teeth. Regaining equilibrium, he continued more cautiously, using in-stinct more than vision to cross the wall in the dark. There was little movement from the ground below, only a few foot patrols crossing back and forth. The groups of demonstrators who tried to gather were quickly ushered away. It was a mere fraction of the crowd that Nick had expected to protest on his behalf. He grinned in ironic appreciation of the obvious wane in his popularity. "Thankless bastards," he muttered.

Fortunately, no one noticed the figure poised high above on the prison wall. By some miracle of God—or whim of the devil—Nick finally reached the neighbor-ing building. Although he could not quite get to the nearest window, he found a carved lion's head jutting from the stonework. Settling a hand on the ornamenta-tion, he deduced that it was not real stone but Coade stone, an artificial material that was used for quoining and sculpture when using real stone was too expensive. Nick had no idea if the thing would hold him. Grimac-ing, he grabbed at a tattered blanket he had draped over one shoulder and tied it around the lion's head. Jerking hard to tighten the knot, he focused on the window, three feet down. Good, he thought, it was open, and he didn't care much for the prospect of breaking through glass.

Holding his breath, Nick gripped the blanket, hesi-tated for one reluctant moment, then jumped from the wall in a decisive plunge. He swung through the open window with an ease that stunned him, as he had bargained for a bit more difficulty. Although he landed on his feet, the momentum brought him forward until he fell with a pained grunt. Swearing, he rose and shook himself off. The room appeared to be an office of some sort, the window left open by some careless clerk. "Almost there," Nick murmured, striding through the office and hunting for the stairs that would lead him to the ground.

Two minutes later, Nick eased through a door he had found at the side of the building, which had turned out to be a furniture factory. Armed with a turning-blade and a heavy stick of wood, he kept to the shadows as he moved forward.

He froze when he heard the click of a pistol being cocked.

"Stay there," came a woman's quiet voice.

His breath hitched in astonishment. "Sophia?"

His sister stood there alone, the gleam of a pistol in her hand, her steady gaze pinned on him. "Don't run," she warned, her face tense.

"How the hell did you get here?" he asked incredulously. "It's dangerous, and— For God's sake, put that away or you'll hurt yourself."

She did not move. "I can't. If I do, you'll run."

"You wouldn't shoot me."

Her reply was very soft. "There's only one way to find out, isn't there?"

Nick braced himself against a rush of utter despair.

"Have you no care for me, Sophia?" he asked hoarsely.

"Of course I do. That is why I had to stop you. My husband has come to help you."

"Like hell he has. Don't be a fool! Let me go, damn you!"

"We are going to wait for Sir Ross," she said stubbornly.

Out of the corner of his eye Nick saw patrols and a pair of runners coming toward them. It was too late now. His sister had ruined any chance of escape. With fatalistic acceptance, Nick forced himself to relax and drop his makeshift weapons. All right. He would wait for Cannon. And Sophia would learn that her precious husband had lied to her. It would almost be worth it, to expose Cannon for what he was, rather than have Sophia worship him. "Fine," he said evenly. "We'll let your husband help me—right to the gallows."

Chapter 18

*R*oss was covered in filth by the time he followed Gentry's trail up to the prison roof. Feeling as if he would never be clean again, he climbed into the open air, which was indescribably sweet after the stench inside. Walking along the edge of the roof, he found a prison wall that connected to a neighboring building. At first there was no sign of Gentry, but then Ross saw the flutter of the dark blanket dangling from the stonework. He growled in frustration. There was no telling how far the man had gotten by now.

Leaning over the wall, he tested it with his foot, discovering that it was as unstable as shifting sand. At this point, following Gentry's path to freedom was no longer an option. Ross would be damned if he would try a feat that even a circus performer would have rejected. Before he could draw back, however, he heard a woman calling from the ground.

"Ross?"

His heart stopped as he saw the tiny figure of his wife from his vantage point four stories above her.

"Sophia," he thundered, "if that is you, I'm going to beat you senseless."

"Gentry is waiting with me," came her voice again. "Don't try to cross that wall!"

"I wasn't planning to," he retorted, struggling to contain his fury as he realized that she had disobeyed his request to stay safe. "Stay there."

It seemed to take forever to make his way back through the prison. Ross moved in contained panic, running when possible, ignoring the screams and epithets that filled the air as he passed floor after floor. Finally he went out through the entrance and headed around the building in a full-tilt run. He saw a small crowd of onlookers, horse and foot patrols, and Sayer and Gee, all waiting at a respectful distance from his wife and her captive.

"Sir Ross," Sayer said anxiously, "she got to him before any of us saw him—she told us to stay back here or—"

"Keep everyone away while I deal with this," Ross snapped.

Obediently the runners steered the crowd back several more yards as Ross strode to his wife. Sophia's face relaxed when she saw him, and she yielded the pistol to him without a murmur.

"Where did you get this?" he asked mildly, his voice strained with the effort to keep from bellowing.

"I took it from the footman," Sophia said apologetically. "It wasn't his fault, Ross. I'm sorry, but I heard the gaol-keeper tell Mr. Sayer that Gentry had escaped . . .

and then they left, and I was looking through the carriage window, and I happened to see my brother on the rooftop—"

"Later," Ross interrupted, yearning to apply his hand to her posterior until she howled. Instead he focused on solving the problem at hand.

He glanced at Gentry, who observed them with a sneer. "So this is how you take care of my sister?" Gentry demanded. "Well, she's in good hands, isn't she? Traipsing around Newgate at night with a pistol!"

"John," Sophia protested. "He didn't—"

Ross silenced her by placing a firm hand on the back of her neck. "You are fortunate that she stopped you," he informed Gentry coldly.

"Oh, I'm a lucky bastard indeed," Gentry muttered.

Ross stared at him speculatively, wondering if he was about to make a grave mistake, and knowing that he probably was. He had conceived of a plan that might save his brother-in-law's neck and even benefit Bow Street, but it was an obvious gamble. There was an explosive mixture of elements in Gentry's character—the brave thief-taker, the sinister underworld lord, the hero, the devil. Curiously, Gentry seemed caught in the middle, unable to decide what he was going to be. But if placed in the right hands, and molded by a will stronger than his own . . .

No one has ever given him an opportunity to change, Sophia had said. *If he had just one chance at a different life . . . think of the kind of man he could become.*

Ross was going to give him that chance, for Sophia's

sake. If he did not try to help her brother, it would be a permanent wedge between them. "I am going to make you an offer," he told Gentry. "I advise you to consider it carefully."

A cynical smile crossed the young man's face. "This should be interesting."

"You're aware of the evidence against you. If I choose, I can make it disappear."

Gentry stared at him with sudden alert interest, as he was entirely familiar with the process of deal-making. "What of the witness who is ready to testify?"

"I can also manage that."

"How?"

"How I handle it is none of your business." Ross did not glance at Sophia when he heard her sharply indrawn breath. He sensed her astonishment that he would be willing to compromise his principles for her brother's sake. In almost a dozen years in the judiciary, he had never done anything that could be considered corrupt. Manipulation of evidence and witnesses went completely against his nature. However, he swallowed down his scruples and continued grimly. "In return for my efforts, I want something from you."

"Of course," Gentry said sardonically. "That's not hard to guess. You want me to leave the country and disappear."

"No. I want you to become a runner."

"*What?*" Gentry demanded.

"Ross?" Sophia asked at the same time.

Were Ross not so doggedly intent, he would have

been amused by the blank looks in the identical pairs of blue eyes before him.

"Don't play with me, Cannon," Gentry said in annoyance. "Tell me what you want, and I'll—"

"You call yourself a thief-taker," Ross said. "Let's see if you are man enough to do it by the rules. Without brutality or lies or false evidence."

Gentry seemed aghast at the notion of becoming a public servant. "How in God's name did you come up with such an insane idea?"

"I thought of something Morgan says . . . a runner and the criminal he catches are two sides of the same coin."

"And you think Morgan is going to trust me?"

"Not at first. You'll have to earn his trust day by day."

"I'll be damned if I scrape and bow to a bunch of Robin Redbreasts," Gentry sneered, using the nickname inspired by the runners' dress uniforms.

"You'll hang if you don't," Ross told him. "I'm going to keep possession of the evidence against you, and I will use it at the first sign that you are not performing your job to Morgan's satisfaction."

"How do you know I won't bolt?"

"Because if you do, I will personally track you down and kill you. Your sister's life, not to mention my own, would be far more pleasant without you in it."

The atmosphere was alive with hostility. Ross could see that Gentry almost believed the threat. He waited patiently, letting him mull over his options.

The young man sent him a baleful stare. "You're going to use me," he muttered. "I'll be some kind of damned feather in your cap, and you'll use any public favor I've got left to further your own plans for Bow Street. The newspapers will hail you for converting Nick Gentry into a Bow Street runner. You'll make me betray everyone I know, and give evidence against all my accomplices. And after ensuring that I'm despised by every man, woman, and child from Dead Man's yard to Gin Lane, you'll send me to catch thieves and murderers in the places where I'm most hated. On top of all that, the salary you give me won't be worth a damn."

Ross considered the accusation thoughtfully. "Yes," he said, "that sums it up fairly well."

"Jaysus." Gentry let out a mirthless laugh. "Go swive yourself, Cannon!"

One of Ross's black brows arched. "Shall I take that as a yes?"

Gentry responded with a curt nod. "I'm going to regret this," he said sourly. "At least the hangman would have snuffed me quickly."

"Now that we've come to an agreement, I'll take you back to your cell," Ross said pleasantly. "You'll be released tomorrow morning. In the meanwhile, I have some arrangements to make."

"Ross," Sophia said anxiously, "must John go back in there tonight?"

"Yes." His gaze dared her to protest.

Prudently she kept her mouth closed, although it was clear that she longed to plead for her brother's sake.

"It's all right, Sophia," Gentry murmured. "I've

stayed in worse places than this." He slanted a baleful glance at Ross as he added, "Courtesy of your husband."

Over the course of a ten-year relationship, Ross had never managed to shock Sir Grant Morgan as he did now. Returning to Bow Street No. 3, he went directly to Morgan's office and described the agreement he had reached with Gentry.

Morgan stared at him with complete incomprehension. "What did you say? Nick Gentry can't be a runner."

"Why not?"

"Because he's Nick Gentry, that's why!"

"*You* can make him into a runner."

"Oh, no," Morgan said vehemently, shaking his head. "God, no. I haven't complained about the extra work you've heaped on me, or all the trials-by-fire you've put me through. And if the appointment goes through, I'll do my best to fill your shoes. But I'll be damned if you're going to retire and leave me with the task of training Nick Gentry! If you think he can be a runner, train him yourself!"

"You are better equipped than I to manage him. You were a runner—you came from the streets just as he did. And remember, he's only twenty-five—still young enough to be influenced."

"He's a hardened case, and only a fool would believe otherwise!"

"In time," Ross continued, ignoring the protest, "Gentry might be the best man you've got. He'll do the worst and most dangerous jobs without flinching. I am giving you a weapon, Grant—one that could be used very effectively."

"Or blow up in my face," Morgan muttered. Leaning back in his chair, he stared up at the ceiling with a surly grunt. Clearly, he was envisioning the prospect of training Nick Gentry. Suddenly he let out a sardonic laugh. "It might be worth it, though. After all the trouble that little bastard has caused us, I would enjoy running him through the wringer."

Ross smiled, reflecting on Nick Gentry's strapping form and thinking that only someone of Morgan's stature could refer to him as "little." "You'll give it some consideration, then."

"Are you giving me a choice?"

Ross gave a brief shake of his head.

"I didn't think so," Morgan muttered. "Damnation. I hope you retire soon, Cannon."

Sophia was in bed by the time Ross entered the darkened room, and she remained still and quiet, hoping he would think she was asleep. He had refrained from venting his displeasure with her during the carriage ride from Newgate, and she knew that he intended to wait until they were in the privacy of their apartments. Now, however, was the time of reckoning. She reasoned that if she could delay him until the morning, his wrath might cool.

Unfortunately, it seemed that Ross was not inclined to wait. He lit the lamp and turned it up until it emitted a relentless glow.

Slowly Sophia sat up and gave him a placating smile. "What did Sir Grant say when you told him—"

"We'll discuss that later," he said tersely, refusing to be distracted. Sitting on the edge of the bed, he placed his large hands on either side of her, pinning her in place beneath the covers. "Right now, I want to discuss your actions this evening. And you're going to explain how you could have taken such a risk when you know how I feel about your safety!"

Sophia shrank backward against the pillows as he proceeded to deliver a blistering lecture that would have caused anyone else to wither. However, she knew that his ire was born of his love for her, and so she received every word with humble agreement. When he was finished—or perhaps he was merely taking a breath before resuming—she broke in remorsefully.

"You are absolutely right," she said. "If I were in your position, I would feel the same way. I should have stayed in the carriage as you asked."

"That's right," Ross muttered, his wrath seeming to ease when it became clear that she was not going to argue with him.

"With your experience, you know best in these situations. And not only did I put myself in danger, but I jeopardized the baby's welfare, and I am *very* sorry about that."

"As well you should be."

Leaning forward, Sophia rested her cheek against his shoulder. "I would never intentionally cause you a moment of worry."

"I know that," he said gruffly. "But dammit, Sophia, I refuse to be known as a man who can't control his own wife."

Sophia smiled against his shoulder. "No one would dare think such a thing." Slowly she eased onto his lap. "Ross . . . what you did for my brother was so wonderful . . ."

"I didn't do it for him. I did it for you."

"I know. And I adore you for that." Gently she plucked at the knot of his cravat, loosening the dark silk.

"Only for that?" he asked, his arms tightening around her slender body.

"For a thousand different reasons." Deliberately she rubbed her breasts against his chest. "Let me show you how much I love you. How I need you in every way."

Abandoning the lecture, Ross pulled his shirt over his head and threw it to the floor. When he turned back to Sophia, she was smiling, amusement and arousal mingling deliciously inside her.

"What is so funny?" he asked, jerking the hem of her nightgown up to her waist.

"I just thought of how the Cockney phrase for wife is 'trouble and strife,' " she said, gasping a little as his hand settled on her bare stomach. "In my case, it has turned out to be accurate, hasn't it?"

Ross's eyes glinted with an answering smile, and he bent to capture her mouth with his. "Never too much trouble for me to handle," he assured her, and spent the rest of the night proving it.

Epilogue

*A*fter the birth of their daughter, Dr. Linley commented that it was the first delivery at which he had feared more for the father's well-being than the mother's. Ross had remained in a corner of the bedroom despite everyone's efforts to make him wait outside. He sat in a straight-backed chair and gripped the edges until the satinwood threatened to splinter in his fingers. Although his expression was blank, Sophia understood his fear. She tried to reassure him in the intervals between contractions that she was all right, that the pain was horrid but manageable, but eventually the effort of giving birth required all her attention, and she almost forgot his presence in the room.

"You're being awfully quiet," Linley said, regarding her with an encouraging smile. "Give a shout when the pains come, if it helps. At this point in labor, I've had women cursing me and my entire ancestry."

Sophia giggled weakly and shook her head. "My husband might faint if I scream."

"He'll survive," Linley said dryly.

Toward the end, when the pain finally overwhelmed her, she did let out a cry of distress, and Linley supported her neck with his arm and held a damp white handkerchief before her face. "Breathe through this," he murmured.

Obeying, she inhaled a sweet, dizzying fume that soothed the pain and gave her a surprising moment of euphoria. "Oh, thank you," she said gratefully as he lowered the handkerchief. "What is that?"

At the same time, Ross appeared at the bedside, looking suspicious. "Is that safe?" he asked.

"Nitous oxide," Linley replied calmly. "It is used at 'inhalation frolics,' at which people entertain themselves by taking whiffs. But a colleague of mine, Henry Hill Hickman, proposed using it to relieve pain during dentistry. There has been little interest shown by the medical community so far. However, I've used it a few times to relieve women in labor, and it seems both harmless and effective."

"I don't like the idea of your experimenting with my wife—" Ross began.

Sophia interrupted as another wave of intense pain gripped her. She seized Linley's wrist. "Don't listen to him," she gasped. "Where is that handkerchief?"

With another breath of nitous oxide, and a few hard pushes, Amelia Elizabeth Cannon was born.

The next day, as Sophia sat with the tiny black-haired infant nursing at her breast, she glanced at Ross with a vaguely apologetic smile. Although she was privately thrilled with her newborn daughter, it was usually considered a failure for a woman to give her husband a girl instead of a boy as his firstborn. Predictably, he was too much of a gentleman to express disappointment, but Sophia knew that most of the Cannons, especially Ross's grandfather, had hoped for a male to continue the family line.

As Ross's long fingers traced gently over the silky dark hair that covered his daughter's miniature skull, Sophia spoke softly. "I am certain that we'll have a son the next time."

He looked up from the baby with a puzzled glance. "Another daughter would be equally welcome."

Sophia smiled doubtfully. "You are very kind to say so, but everyone knows that—"

"Amelia is exactly what I wanted," he said firmly. "The most beautiful, perfect baby I've ever seen. Give me a houseful of daughters just like this, and I'll be a happy man indeed."

Sophia caught at his hand and brought it to her mouth. "I love you," she said fervently, pressing kisses to the backs of his long fingers. "I'm so glad you didn't marry someone else before you met me."

Ross leaned closer and slid his arm behind her back. His mouth moved over hers in a long, caressing kiss that made her shiver with pleasure. "That would have been impossible," he said, drawing back to smile into her eyes.

"Why?" Sophia leaned back against the support of his arm while the baby continued to nurse at her breast.

"Because, my love . . . I was waiting for you."

...er of Romance

LISA KLEYPAS

...VER ME
...8.99 Can

...RMS
...9.99 Can

MIDNIGHT ANGEL
0-380-77353-8/$6.99 US/$9.99 Can

DREAMING OF YOU
0-380-77352-X/$6.99 US/$9.99 Can

BECAUSE YOU'RE MINE
0-380-78144-1/$6.99 US/$9.99 Can

ONLY IN YOUR ARMS
0-380-76150-5/$5.99 US/$7.99 Can

ONLY WITH YOUR LOVE
0-380-76151-3/$6.50 US/$8.50 Can

THEN CAME YOU
0-380-77013-X/$6.99 US/$9.99 Can

PRINCE OF DREAMS
0-380-77355-4/$5.99 US/$7.99 Can

SOMEWHERE I'LL FIND YOU
0-380-78143-3/$6.99 US/$9.99 Can

WHERE DREAMS BEGIN
0-380-80231-7/$6.99 US/$9.99 Can

SUDDENLY YOU
0-380-80232-5/$6.99 US/$9.99 Can

LADY SOPHIA'S LOVER
0-380-81106-5/$7.50 US/$9.99 Can

....

Available wherever books are sold or please call 1-800-331-3761
to order.

LK 0302